SOUL
CATCHER

ALSO BY MICHAEL WHITE

The Garden of Martyrs
A Dream of Wolves
Marked Men
The Blind Side of the Heart
A Brother's Blood

SOUL CATCHER

MICHAEL WHITE

Quercus

First published in Great Britain in 2007 by

Quercus
21 Bloomsbury Square
London
WC1A 2NS

A CIP catalogue reference for this book is available
from the British Library

ISBN (HB) 1 84724 158 1
ISBN-13 978 1 84724 158 0
ISBN (TPB) 1 84724 159 X
ISBN-13 978 1 84724 159 7

10 9 8 7 6 5 4 3 2 1

Printed and bound in Great Britain by Clays Ltd, St Ives plc.

For Diane

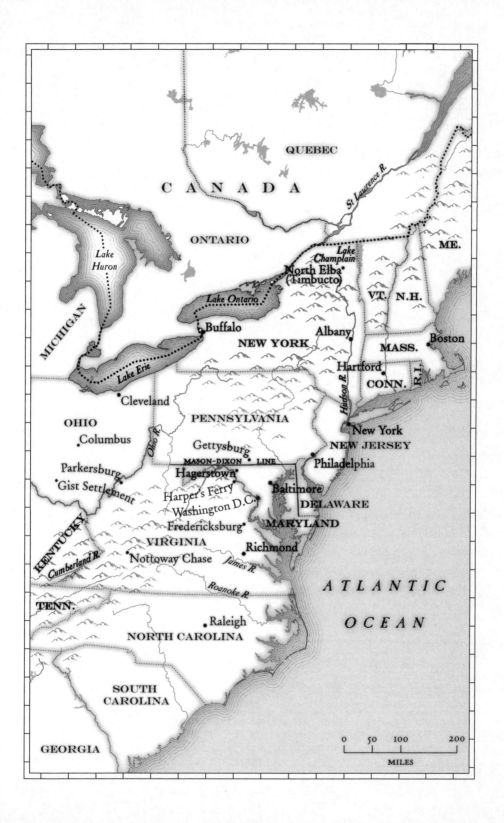

QUEBEC

C A N A D A

ONTARIO

St. Lawrence R.

Lake Huron

MICHIGAN

Lake Ontario

Lake Champlain

North Elba (Timbucto)

ME.

VT. N.H.

Buffalo

Lake Erie

NEW YORK

Albany

MASS.

Boston

Hartford

CONN.

R.I.

Hudson R.

Cleveland

OHIO

Columbus

PENNSYLVANIA

Gettysburg

MASON-DIXON LINE

Ohio R.

Hagerstown

New York

NEW JERSEY

Philadelphia

Parkersburg

Gist Settlement

Harper's Ferry

Baltimore

DELAWARE

Washington D.C.

Fredericksburg

MARYLAND

KENTUCKY

Cumberland R.

VIRGINIA

Nottoway Chase

James R.

Richmond

Roanoke R.

A T L A N T I C

TENN.

Raleigh

O C E A N

NORTH CAROLINA

SOUTH CAROLINA

GEORGIA

0   50   100   200

MILES

PART ONE

I have just received your line by Mr. Deny and commit to his and your care and to all wise Providence
the precious Charge that has been for a few short
days sheltered beneath my humble roof, from the
foul soul catcher of our detestable South. Oh may
the God of the oppressed speed this interesting refu-
gee from our southern prison-house to a land where
slavery is not known.

LETTER FROM WILLIAM M. CLARKE TO
GERRIT SMITH, OCTOBER 25, 1839

I, John Brown, am now quite certain that the crimes
of this guilty land will never be purged away but
with blood.

JOHN BROWN,
ON THE WAY TO HIS EXECUTION

1

Cain had been awakened by the frenzied whinnying of a horse below his window in the street. Still half asleep, his head throbbing and barley soaked, he recalled the dream he'd had of the place called Buena Vista. The brave, foolish Mexicans throwing wave upon wave against the left flank of the American line, the slaughter coming so easily it made him sick at heart. Later, when the sheer size of Santa Anna's charge had overrun the American position and captured the wounded left behind, Cain, his leg shattered, lay helplessly among them. He remembered the cries of his comrades as the enemy had gone from soldier to soldier with a bayonet, silencing them with "*Recuerde Agua Nueva.*" After that, as night crept in over the high desert and the stars flashed like sparks from a grindstone, there was the stillness of what he felt had to be the approach of death. And finally, opening his eyes upon the mestiza girl hovering over him, her dark head aglow in morning sunlight, his first thought was that she was some otherworldly creature come to usher him to Hades. Now in bed, staring up at the stained ceiling of his room, the thought of that girl, the silken feel of her skin, the playful glint of her black eyes, caused an ache such as he had not felt for years to rise up in his chest like a wave of seawater slamming into him. He sat up, barely able to catch his breath. *Cain*, he heard her whisper to him. *Cain*.

It was then that a loud knock erupted against his door.

"Go away," he called. He figured it was Antoinette, the elderly madam of the house, coming to inform him he'd have to vacate the room for paying customers.

The knock came again, more insistent this time, the side of a large fist hammering the wood in anger.

"The devil take you," Cain called out, looking for something to heave at the noise. "If you don't—"

But suddenly the door flew open and two men burst in. They were both armed, and Cain's thoughts ran immediately to the possibility that he was about to be robbed. One of the two intruders was of considerable size, tall and heavy limbed, thick through the belly, with a bushy beard and small iron-colored eyes like a pig's. He wore farmer's clothing, a floppy brimmed hat and muddied boots, and he brought with him into the room the acrid smell of the barnyard. He carried a Shaffer single-barrel shotgun in one big paw, and while he didn't actually aim the thing at Cain, he kept it at the ready. The other intruder was older and slight of build, a dignified-looking man of the southern planter class, not tall so much as a man whose erect bearing and good breeding gave the impression of size. He was well dressed in a brown riding coat, knee-length boots burnished to a high shine, and black leather gloves. He had the sharp features of a red-tailed hawk and cold, blue-gray eyes that fixed Cain where he lay with an imperious gaze. On his hip, he carried a sidearm, a pearl-handled, small-caliber pocket revolver, a pretty weapon of the sort that riverboat gamblers kept in their coat pockets and women carried in their purses. The two made an unlikely pair of robbers, but you could never tell in this part of the city. Cain glanced around, searching for his own weapon. It lay across the room on the bureau, above which hung a cracked mirror. *Damn*, he thought.

"What in the hell you think you're doing?" Cain cried.

It was the old man who spoke up. "I've come for money," he said.

Cain laughed at that. "If you've a notion to rob me, mister, you're up a creek without a paddle."

The well-dressed man offered a patronizing smile to this comment. There was, Cain felt, something familiar about that gesture, about his mouth and the haughty way he looked at Cain, though he couldn't place him. Certainly, he'd seen his ilk before.

"I've come only for what you owe me." When Cain furrowed his brow in bewilderment, the man added, "You don't remember me, do you?"

"Should I?"

"Last Saturday night," the man explained, removing his gloves one finger at a time. When his gloves were off, he unconsciously rubbed the palm of his left hand, where a knotted scar snaked across it from little finger to thumb. It was the sort of wound that would have been made had he grabbed hold of a knife blade in self-defense. "At the Morgan Brothers."

Cain still drew a blank. There had been so many such evenings of gambling and drinking of late, that like the others, this one formed a grayish blank in his mind, as if burned away with a branding iron.

"My aces beat your queens," the man offered.

Only then did it come back to Cain how he knew the man. He never forgot a hand, especially a losing one. It had been in one of the back rooms of the Morgan Brothers, a well-known gambling establishment in Richmond. He fumbled around in his thoughts and then the name appeared with the aces: Eberly. A wealthy tobacco planter with a reputation for losing a thousand dollars on a single hand, as if it were so much paper. The card game, attended by mostly wealthy merchants and plantation owners, should have been much too rich for Cain's blood. But he'd been drinking heavily and he felt he could part them from some of their money, and when he'd seen the three ladies turn up in his hand like a rainbow after a string of bad weather, he'd felt lucky, and he wasn't going to let such an opportunity slip through his fingers. So he'd cast reason to the wind and stayed in the hand much longer than sense should have allowed or means should have permitted. All the while, he recalled this Eberly sitting back staring over his cards at him with that cool, hard glare and that smile that stuck in his craw like bad corn liquor. *The son of a bitch's just bluffing*, Cain kept telling himself. He felt he knew when someone wasn't holding anything. It was only after he'd seen the three aces spread out over the table and glanced up to that smile of Eberly's that he realized just how wrong he'd been.

"Yes, I recall it now," he said, getting up. He was wearing only a pair of drawers. Grabbing what clothes he could find strewn on the floor and tangled among the sheets, he quickly dressed. He didn't want to be in the vulnerable position of negotiating without his pants on, for now he figured he must have owed the man some money, and they would have to arrive at some reasonable schedule and terms for the repayment of the debt. But, of course, the old man would have to get in line behind the others to whom he owed money. He pulled on his trousers and his shirt, which smelled of stale whiskey and even staler sex. He wondered if there had been a woman last night and how much money Antoinette had fleeced him for her services. But try as he might, he couldn't remember, which he took as a blessing. Nor could he remember where he'd left his boots. They were an old but still serviceable pair, purchased during better times from McElheny and Sons, one of the best booteries in the city.

"I am presently, sir, somewhat short on readily available funds," he told the man as he searched the room for his boots. "But I soon expect to be in a position to make good on whatever debts I've incurred to you. Plus a fair rate of interest. You have my word as a gentleman."

"A gentleman?" Eberly scoffed, offering up that smile of his.

"Yes. As one gentleman to another," Cain shot back, annoyed at his tone.

Cain was, in fact, already in debt to half a dozen others because of his gambling. What he could now count among his worldly possessions were those few things in the room with him, some eleven dollars plus loose change on the dresser, his clothes, his gun and holster, a silver flask. There were a few more items at his room in the boardinghouse but nothing of real value. Not counting his saddle and saddlebags, and, of course, his horse, which he had stabled at Fogg's Livery over on Franklin, he was penniless.

Where are my damn boots, he cursed to himself, glancing around the room. He squatted down to look under the bed, his head throbbing, his right leg, the bad one, bellowing with pain. There, he came across a large pair of women's lacy underdrawers, an unemptied bedpan oozing a sour stench, and a bottle of Moody's Pain Elixir, a patented laudanum medicine. He picked up the bottle, hoping at least a sip remained, but sadly discovered it to be bone-dry. He also found one boot hidden behind the bedpan. Where its twin could be, he hadn't the faintest notion. He grabbed the boot and hobbled over to a cane-back chair near the window to pull it on. Fortunately, it was the boot for his left leg, the good one, so perhaps his luck hadn't completely abandoned him after all. If he had to kick someone, at least it would be with his booted good leg. Cain's gambler mind was already working the options, doing the best with the hand he was dealt, jumping ahead to the possibilities of the situation he found himself in.

"How much is it that I owe you?" Cain asked. He figured it might be fifty. Perhaps, if he had been really cornered and had thrown caution completely to the wind, a hundred. Even drunk, he never went in the hole for more than that. It was one of his rules.

"I hold an IOU, with your signature, for three hundred dollars," said Eberly.

Three hundred! Cain thought. *Good God!*

"It is now past due," the old man said, "and I am here to collect."

Cain couldn't recall signing anything like that, though he didn't doubt the possibility that he had. He knew that, when in a certain state of inebriation and in the midst of a card game, it was quite likely that he'd signed an IOU, especially when he was holding a hand he felt he couldn't lose with or if he'd sensed that his fortunes were about to take a turn for the better. He'd made such a mistake before, in fact, many times. Just never for so much.

"As I have already mentioned," he explained to this Eberly, "you've caught me at a bad time, sir. But I will be more than happy to honor my debt fully in short order. We can shake on it if you'd like," Cain said, offering his hand as collateral to his word. Eberly just stared at the proffered hand, and Cain, after an awkward moment, let it drop to his side.

The son of a bitch, Cain thought angrily to himself.

Right then the whinnying noise out in the street commenced again, and Cain turned and glanced out the window. A man seated in a wagon filled with coal was flogging an old roan nag with a rawhide whip. The road was muddy and the wagon's wheels embedded in the muck, and it was obvious the load was far too much for the animal. The horse's back was flayed almost raw, yet the man continued to strike the poor creature. Cain couldn't stand to witness such treatment of a horse. He was fond of horses, felt they had more common sense and loyalty than most people he knew, and under different circumstances he would have called down to the man to desist, might even have rushed out into the street and confronted him. But he had his own concerns right now.

Antoinette's was in Shockoe Bottom, down near the waterfront, a rough, squalid section of Richmond composed of cheap doggeries and gaming houses, cockfighting pits and faro banks, and brothels like the one he was in. It being springtime, the roads were muddy and deeply rutted. Street vendors and fishwives were pushing carts and calling out their wares. The dead-fish-and-sewage stench of the river floated on the air of this fine, bright morning. Dowling's, a boardinghouse where he had lived on and off for the past two years, was just two streets over. Ships were anchored at the wharves, and small boats plied the James. To the west, past the canal, he saw a train crossing the Richmond and Dunville Railroad Bridge. Beyond that were the smokestacks of the Tredegar Iron Works, and farther out, in the middle of the river, Belle Isle. In front of Antoinette's, he spied a young Negro boy holding two horses.

"I have made it a rule not to conduct business on credit," Eberly said.

"I am only asking that you give me some time."

"I've already given you a week."

"But I am good for it, sir. Ask anyone in Richmond. They'll vouchsafe Augustus Cain's word."

"I have," the man said cynically. "That's why I am demanding payment now."

Cain, who had something of a temper, had struck men for much less, especially if his sense of honor was at stake. He knew his frailties and faults as well as any man did his own shortcomings, but he held firmly to the conviction, even now in his present humble circumstances, that he was at his core an honorable man, despite any and all evidence to the contrary. When he was twelve he'd gotten into a fight with a much older boy when the other had made a reference about Cain's father having a mistress in town. Though Cain knew the accusation to be true, he went at the boy savagely, with fists and boots and teeth, whereupon the larger boy thrashed him soundly, bloodying his nose and blackening both his eyes. It wasn't out of love certainly that he defended his father, perhaps not even out of begrudging respect for the man. Rather it was out of some quaint notion of family honor, of respecting his name and, too, the memory of his beloved mother. Later, when he was a man, in a card game a Yankee businessman had once made the mistake of accusing him of cheating. Cain had reached across the table and grabbed the man by the throat and started to throttle him. When the Yank tried to draw a piddling little vest-pocket derringer on him, Cain had slapped it out of his hand and placed his own gun against the man's skull. He told him he'd either have an apology or the man's brains on the spot. The man promptly apologized. But Cain was also a realist. He was outnumbered now, they were armed and he wasn't, and he was still feeling the immobilizing effects of a sour-mash-and-laudanum hangover. Besides, he was wearing only one boot. He was more than a fair street fighter, but he didn't like to engage in fisticuffs without his boots on, which limited his capabilities.

"You won't get blood from a stone," he replied.

"I am prepared to squeeze as hard as it takes," Eberly countered. "I have friends in high places in Richmond. And I am well aware of your other creditors."

"That's my damn business," Cain shouted. It seemed that this Eberly knew quite a bit about him.

"Passing IOUs you have no intention of making good on could land you in prison."

"Go ahead and try it," Cain bluffed. Still, he didn't relish the notion of jail. He wasn't the sort of man that could abide being locked up, told when to eat, when to shit, when to sleep. He'd been to jail twice, once in the war, and then two years earlier he'd spent six months in the county jail for assaulting a man who turned out to be a judge, and so he knew a little about such accommodations. He already disliked this Eberly. He knew his sort. The wealthy planter who treated the rest of the world as if they were his slaves, the kind of man who thought he could buy anything he wanted.

"You think you can scare me?" Cain said.

"I'll have satisfaction, one way or the other," replied Eberly, throwing a sideways glance at his burly companion.

Cain wondered now if the big man's presence was intended to bully him into settling accounts. He'd known of men who brought along such characters as this to exact payment of debts. Enforcers. Shoulder hitters.

"Who do you think you're dealing with?" Cain scoffed.

With a glance from Eberly, the big man stepped forward. "I reckon you'll want to square up with Mr. Eberly now, you know what's good for you."

"Is that so?" Cain replied.

"Yes sir," the man said, resting the shotgun against the door and pushing back the sleeves of his coat.

Cain hadn't paid much attention to the man before this, but now he sized him up as a possible adversary. He was big, about Cain's own height, but powerfully built, must have outweighed him by sixty pounds. His fists were broad and gnarled, his forearms knotted with muscle like those of a smithy. Cain suspected that on his best day he'd have more than he could handle with this man, but hungover as he was now and missing a boot, he wouldn't give three-to-one odds on himself. He quickly glanced over at his revolver again. He guessed that by the time he got to it, pulled it from the holster, and cocked it, they'd have had ample opportunity to use their own weapons. He felt in the back pocket of his pants for his blackjack but was hardly surprised not to find it there. Not the way his luck was going today. So Cain stood, fists clenched at his sides, his one booted foot prepared for a kick to the man's groin should it come to that.

But the old man suddenly intervened. "Wait, Strofe," he said, with a hand to the other's shoulder. "I have an offer to make you, Cain."

"An offer?"

"I've been told that you are quite skilled at catching slaves."

"Who told you that?"

"A Palmer Whitcomb, from down Petersburg way."

He remembered Whitcomb, all right, as well as the runaway he'd hired Cain to catch. Eben. A tall, striking-looking buck with a brand on his right cheek, punishment for an earlier escape attempt. Whitcomb had been willing to pay Cain two hundred dollars for the slave's return, a quite sizable sum for an unskilled field hand, especially given that the usual reward for the capture of a slave was fifty dollars if caught within the state, double that if he'd crossed over into a free state. He had tracked Eben for several weeks, catching him finally in Baltimore, where he had kin. There was something else, too, that Cain recalled about this particular runaway. Whitcomb had a young daughter who'd secretly taken a fancy to Eben. When it came to light that her virtue had been compromised and that she was in a family way, and that the father was none other than Eben himself, Whitcomb had wanted him back in the worst way. Of course, that wasn't any of Cain's business. Why an owner was willing to pay good money for a slave's return and what he did with him once he got him back, well, that wasn't any of his concern.

"Palmer spoke quite highly of your skill as a slave catcher," Eberly offered. "I am prepared to make you an offer."

"What sort of offer?"

"I have two runaways. A buck and a young wench. I am willing to write off your debt, if you bring them back for me."

"Not interested."

"Hear me out, Cain. I am even prepared to pay you a modest reward for their capture and return."

"Like I said, I'm not interested."

Cain hadn't gone after a runaway in months. He'd grown tired of working for men like Eberly, wealthy planters who treated him like the dirt beneath their boots, men who thought their money made him their nigger. Tired of having to grease the palms of corrupt jailers or being honeyfuggled by thieving auction agents trying to cheat him out of his reward. Tired of being shot at by abolitionists, chased by vigilance committees, pelted by stones and rotten fruit thrown by antislavery crowds up north, spat upon by uppity Yankees who looked down their goddamned noses at someone like him, just trying to make a living. Tired, too, of fighting with fugitives, of fending off blows, of having knives or razor blades pulled on him (snaking down over his chest was a jagged pink scar from where a runaway had cut him with a razor, this after he'd been decent enough to take the irons off the black bastard so he could eat). He was tired of sleeping on the ground, eating jerked beef and not bathing for weeks. Tired of freezing his tail off waiting in the night outside some cheap doggery, hoping to catch a drunken runaway come staggering out. In short, he'd had his bellyful of the whole stinking business. For a long time now, he'd been hoping to make a change, just waiting for his luck to pick up some wind, to make a big killing at the card table or faro banks, and using his winnings to head out west and try his hand at something new. Something that wouldn't put him at the beck and call of men like this Eberly.

"You're hardly in a position to refuse me, Cain."

Cain stared at him and snorted. "Go to hell. Find yourself some other bootlick, Eberly."

The old man nodded condescendingly. "You own a chestnut stallion?"

"It's not for sale."

Eberly then removed a piece of paper from the pocket of his waistcoat and strode across the room, his boot heels clicking loudly on the wooden floor. He waved it in front of Cain.

"What's that?" he asked.

"A bill of sale," Eberly explained.

"For what?"

"For your horse."

"What? How in hell did you come by that?" Cain cursed. He tried to snatch the paper from the man, but Eberly pulled it back with surprising speed and returned it to his pocket.

"I guess you were drunker than you recollected. You put the animal up as surety against the promissory note. I am here to collect what I am owed."

Son of a whore, Cain cursed to himself. He'd wager most things he owned—his last two bits, his gun, his boots, even the flask his father had given him—but he'd *never* put up Hermes. No matter how drunk, no matter how good a hand he held, no matter how much he was losing, his horse was off limits. He'd had him for almost eight years. Had purchased him shortly after he'd returned from the war in Mexico, when he'd first gotten in the slave-catching business and often had to travel long distances. Fifteen hands, a chestnut Arabian stallion with a blaze, Hermes was the finest piece of horseflesh he'd ever seen: fast and sleek as a white-tailed deer, sure-footed as a catamount, the horse never spooked, could go forty miles a day on the trail of a runaway and keep it up for days on end, hardly breaking a sweat, and like his desert forebears could do without water or food or slowing down in the least. But he was more than an investment, more than merely a tool of his trade. Hermes was a boon traveling companion for the long days and nights on the hunt, a friend and ally, sometimes, he felt, his only one. He couldn't count the times the animal had brought him home when he was too snapped to sit straight in the saddle, or when, pursued by vigilance committees, the horse had outraced them back to the safety of the South. Besides, Hermes was patient enough to put up with most of Cain's eccentricities. Why, he'd rather sell his soul than part with his horse. And yet, here the man was holding the bill of sale for him.

Eberly then turned to the big man and said, "Strofe, wait downstairs for me."

"You sure, Mr. Eberly?" he said, shooting his pig-eyed look at Cain.

"Go," Eberly commanded. "Here," he said, taking a coin from his waistcoat pocket and tossing it to the man before he went out the door. "Pay the boy for watching the horses."

After he was gone, Eberly walked over to the bureau and gazed into the cracked mirror above it. He ran a hand through his graying hair, and he turned his head ever so slightly this way and that, inspecting himself. He was the sort of man, Cain saw, who, even in his declining years, took an inordinate pride in his appearance. His reflection was distorted because of the crack and he appeared almost to be two separate men, his face split down the middle. He caught Cain's gaze in the mirror.

"As I said, I have two runaways," he explained, turning to look at him. "The buck is of only passing interest to me. But he went off with another slave, a wench, and I believe if you find him you will find her. She's the one I want back."

Cain had a good mind to tell him to go to hell, but he had to be careful. He didn't want to chance losing Hermes.

"There are plenty of men who can catch your runaways for you."

"But I need someone I can trust." He glanced over Cain's shoulder, off toward the river in the background. "I am willing to write off your debt. Even to pay you a modest reward, if you'll find her and bring her back."

"As I told you, I'm not interested."

"Goddamn it, man!" Eberly cursed. He turned back toward the mirror and swept his hand over the bureau, throwing Cain's holster and gun as well as the ceramic washbasin crashing to the floor. Water had splashed over Eberly and spilled out over the floor in a dark, spreading stain, like blood leaching out of a wound. Cain's gun lay at his feet, and as he made a move to pick it up, the old man said, "I wouldn't do that if I were you."

Cain glanced up to see that Eberly had already placed his hand on his revolver, ready to draw it.

"I'm prepared to go to the sheriff right now and have him seize your horse as part of what you owe me."

"You can't do that."

"Just watch me," the man hissed. "And I'll have you arrested." He calmly took out a lace-edged handkerchief and wiped his face where the water had splashed on it. He had a large ring on the finger of one pale, veiny hand. For a moment he stared at the ring, seeming to forget about Cain. Then, having regained his composure, he said, with restraint, "I am in a position to make things very hard for you, Cain. I have you by the balls and I'm going to squeeze until you cry uncle."

"Is that so?" Cain said, but he realized he had already lost. At least when he was sober, he knew when to fold, cut his losses, and wait for the next hand. "Let's just say for a moment that I was interested. My debt will be completely canceled?"

"Yes."

"And the bill of sale for my horse?" Cain asked.

"I'll give it back to you once they are returned."

"I'll need a horse to travel."

"I can provide you with a horse."

"No. I want *my* horse. Or I won't go."

"Very well," Eberly said offhandedly, the victor enjoying his magnanimity. He glanced down at the floor, and with the toe of his boot he nudged a jagged piece of ceramic. He moved it cautiously, the way someone might move a chess piece. Then he squatted and picked up Cain's holster and gun.

"I suppose you'll need this, too," he said, handing it to Cain.

"How much of a reward?" Cain asked, figuring now to make the most of the situation.

"I am offering one hundred dollars for the boy and four hundred for the girl."

Four hundred! Cain thought, catching himself from raising an eyebrow. It was, he knew, an extremely generous sum all by itself. But with the cancellation of the three hundred that he owed Eberly, it was a staggering amount for the capture and return of a slave. Seven hundred for a woman! In his experience, owners would pay such a sum to get a female back for one of two reasons. She could have been a very capable house servant, perhaps a valuable cook or seamstress or wet nurse, someone who was worth a good deal because of her skills. Or she could have meant something beyond dollars and cents to her owner. On more than one occasion Cain had been called upon to hunt down a female runaway whose owner had had a more personal reason for wanting her back.

"Five hundred and you have a deal," Cain said, sensing his advantage and pressing the issue.

"Very well. Five hundred."

With the ease with which Eberly conceded, Cain kicked himself that he hadn't bargained for more.

"And I'll need some money for expenses."

Eberly reached into his inside coat pocket and brought out a billfold. He removed several bills and tossed them indifferently on the unmade bed. It was as if he didn't want to come into physical contact with Cain.

Then Cain asked the usual questions, things he would need to know to track down and capture a runaway: How long had the slave been gone? Did he leave behind any clues, such as comments made to other slaves, about where he seemed to be headed? What was he wearing at the time of his flight? How much food and extra clothing and money did he have? Had he any weapons in his possession? Could he read and write, and perhaps therefore forge a pass he could show to patrollers? Had anyone heard from him since? What was his marital status? Did he have kin up north he could flee to? Had he run away before, and if so, which way had he gone? And especially if it was a woman runaway, did she have any children she was trying to be reunited with?

"Did your nigger wench have any young'uns?" Cain asked.

"No," Eberly replied.

"Are you sure?"

"Yes, I'm sure."

"I see. How long did you say they've been gone?"

"They ran off January seventh," Eberly explained to him. "Recently, a letter came into my possession. It was written by the runaway boy, Henry, to his mother on a neighboring plantation. The overseer intercepted it and brought it to me. It was written from a place called Timbucto, in North Elba, New York. Have you heard of it?"

Cain nodded. It was, he recalled, a place for freed and runaway slaves.

"Here," said the old man, handing him the letter. "It is my belief that they are there together."

"Are the two involved?" Cain asked.

"What?" said Eberly.

"Is the buck fucking the girl?"

"Hell, no," he said. "If that nigger so much as laid a finger on her I will personally cowhide his black ass."

"What does the woman look like?" Cain asked.

Eberly paused for a moment.

"A high yellow octoroon. Tall, perhaps five nine. Her features are refined for those of a Negro."

"Any distinguishing marks on her? Scars. Brands. Birthmarks?"

The old man shook his head.

"She been flogged? " asked Cain.

"No," Eberly said. Then, as if it had just occurred to him, he added, "She has blue eyes."

"Blue eyes?" Cain said. "Those shouldn't be hard to follow."

Eberly then told him he'd be working with three other men.

"I work alone," Cain said.

"Since I'm paying your fees, you will work with the devil himself if I so decide. Is that clear, Cain?"

He stared at the man and shrugged. "It's your show."

"You will be responsible for her welfare. For seeing that nothing happens to her. My overseer, Strofe," Eberly said, indicating with his thumb the man below in the street, "and his brother will accompany you. Strofe will be in charge of the other two men. He knows what both runaways look like. Their habits. The Strofes are not very bright but they are dependable in their way. The third is a man called Preacher."

"Does he have any experience tracking?"

"I'm not sure. He has worked for me before, though. He is good, shall we say, at disciplining slaves."

Cain knew the type of man that Eberly was talking about, the kind that made a living dishing out torture, scaring slaves to keep them from running. "I don't want that sort around."

"*I* want him there," Eberly said sternly. Cain suspected even then, and his suspicions would only later be confirmed, that this Preacher's role wouldn't so much be in tracking slaves as in making sure that Cain did what he had been paid to do. The three hundred dollars that the horse represented was a lot of money. Normally a slave catcher wasn't paid until he brought back the goods. This fellow was Eberly's insurance that Cain would return with his investment.

"Then their payment comes out of your pocket, not mine," Cain said.

The man nodded. "You let me worry about them."

"When do you wish me to start?"

"Immediately. The others are waiting for you over at Spivey's Saloon. Do you know of the place?"

"Yes," Cain said. "Were you so certain I would agree?"

Eberly reached into his waistcoat pocket again and pulled out a gold eagle and flicked it dismissively toward Cain, who snatched it out of the air the way a man might an annoying fly. "Get yourself a new pair of boots," he said, a final indignity.

"She must be valuable property," Cain said.

"That's not your business. I will pay you what we agreed when the job is done."

"You didn't tell me her name?"

"Rosetta. And mind you, Cain, I don't want so much as a hair on her head to be harmed. Do I make myself clear?"

"Yes."

"One more thing, Cain."

"What's that?"

"Do I have your word?" Eberly said, extending his hand. It was an odd gesture for a man used to making commands, not entreaties.

Cain hesitated, then said, "You have my word."

Eberly's grip was surprisingly strong, and as he shook his hand he searched Cain's face for another moment, as if trying to read there whether or not he was the sort of man he could depend upon. Then he turned and headed briskly for the door. He opened it and was about to step out, but he stopped and turned.

"Bring her back," he said. For a moment Eberly's hawklike features softened ever so slightly, his frozen bluish gray eyes warmed by something. Anger, fear, desperation? Cain couldn't say.

"I gave you my word," he offered.

Eberly paused for a moment, then said, "Cross me, Cain, and you'll wish you'd never been born."

Then he turned and strode out of the room.

Cain stood there on one boot, canted to his right, the gold coin warming in his hand, listening as Eberly's footsteps receded down the hall. He told himself he would make this one last hunt. But that was it. Never again. He was shut of this business. And then, though it wasn't as if he had much choice, he wondered if he'd come to regret it.

2

They started out that same day, having first provisioned themselves at Valentine's dry goods for the long journey north. They brought with them foodstuffs and medical supplies, ammo and knives and hatchets, extra clothing and blankets, oilcloth and needles and thread, boxes of locofoco and cans of coal oil for the lanterns, liquor and quids of tobacco, as well as various other supplies, including, of course, the shackles and rope that Cain always brought with him when hunting runaways. As soon as they left Richmond, the order of their riding seemed to fall naturally into a pattern which, once established, remained most days. Cain, the best tracker and the most experienced, usually rode lead on Hermes. He was followed by Strofe's brother, whom they referred to as Little Strofe because he was both younger and smaller, on a bad-tempered, one-eyed mule who had a tendency to nip, especially when approached on his blind side, and he was followed by the pack mule, which carried their supplies. Little Strofe's pair of hunting dogs, Louella and Skunk, ran alongside, occasionally flushing up a rabbit or squirrel and bolting into the woods after it. Next came Strofe on a hulking but skittish Percheron, a clumsy beast who gingerly picked its way across streams with the trepidation of a nearsighted old lady. Bringing up the rear was the one named Preacher, who sat astride a Cracker horse, a silver-blue roan with a single-footed gait Cain had heard the mountain folks refer to as a coon rack.

They passed first through lowlands and salt marsh, bog and tidal flats. Occasionally, they spied in the distance harbors filled with ships, their holds being loaded with tobacco and corn and wheat bound for northern or European ports. They rode by unplowed spring fields and pasturelands with cattle and horses grazing, and through small towns and villages, sometimes stopping at an inn or general store to reprovision, though they skirted the larger cities like Washington and Baltimore and Philadelphia because of the problems such places posed with their abolitionists and vigilance committees. They crossed spring-swollen rivers by bridge and ferry and flat-bottomed boats, occasionally having to ford them, dismounting and holding on to the horse's mane as the animal carried them across the surging waters.

Cain found out that the older Strofe, whose full name was William Lee, had been in the employ of Eberly since he was a boy, first cutting lumber for him, then running his tannery, and now as overseer. He learned this from his garrulous brother, as Strofe himself was a taciturn man who used words as if they cost hard cash. He was wamble-cropped in the bowels, complaining of stomach pains and cramps, followed by bouts of uncontrollable diarrhea. He often had to stop and jump off his horse and dash frantically into the woods, where he was barely able to pull down his trousers before a brown stream erupted from his backside.

"Got him a case of the flux," the one named Preacher said. "My pappy had a bad case a that. Near died from it."

Little Strofe wore a floppy farmer's hat and a wool coat patched so many times with multiple colors that he resembled a harlequin. His face was soft and fleshy, the no-color of lard, with small eyes like his brother's shoved into it like nails. Not actually feebleminded, he nonetheless looked upon the world with a child's eye, and usually had a dull half smile pasted on his face. Short but stocky, he was a smaller version of his brother. Though unlike his brother he was friendly and gregarious, especially to Cain. He had taken to prefacing Cain's name with a "mister" and Cain responded in kind, saying things like, "Mr. Strofe, the rabbit stew you made tonight was especially good." The

Strofe boys, when they called each other anything other than "hey" or "you," usually just referred to the other as "Brother." "Brother, don't eat all them beans." The two often argued, scrapping like a pair of tomcats whose tails had been tied together.

The younger brother had a bad stutter, which was made worse when he was nervous. He was here primarily because of his skills as a cook as well as on account of the dogs. They minded no one but him, and even then they were headstrong. When they'd take off after a scent, Little Strofe would call them and sooner or later they'd come slinking back, tails tucked between their legs, though sometimes he'd let them "have theirselves a little fun," as he put it. Louella was docile and normally obedient, but Skunk had his own mind and would take off for long periods, sometimes all day. Now and then Little Strofe would have to discipline him. "You c-come when I c-call you, y'hear," he'd yell, grabbing him by the loose flesh beneath his jaw and roughly shaking him. But it was obvious that he loved his dogs. He would pet them and fawn over them, talking to them as if they were people, sharing his meal with them, even sleeping with them at night.

While the brothers were employed full-time on Eberly's plantation, Preacher, Cain learned, hired out his services as a kind of independent contractor. From the first he'd laid eyes on him back in the saloon in Richmond, Cain had taken an immediate and strong dislike to the man—and when it came to people, he had an intuition as unerring as a dog's. And during the long journey north, his instincts hadn't proved wrong either. Cain had seen his share of churlish miscreants in the slave-catching vocation, one which drew them like maggots to a festering wound, but this Preacher was one of the most cross-grained, ill-favored, cantankerous fellows he'd ever had the displeasure of meeting. A rough-edged haw-buck from up in the western hills of Virginia, Preacher was coarse and foul-mouthed, illiterate as a stump, with a smell to him like a bitch dog in heat. He had a pallid complexion, long, greasy blond hair that fell in his face, a space between his front teeth, and eyes black and deep-set under pale brows, a look in them as spiteful as those of a stepped-on cottonmouth. Preacher could not lay claim to an ounce of fat or softness anywhere on his person; his narrow face was fashioned by sharp angles and held together by skin and gristle and pure malice. Cain could not even approximate his age. He looked old and boyish at once, as if his face couldn't decide what it wanted to be, and when he smiled his malignant gat-toothed smile it almost looked as if something inside him had been grievously wounded by the mere doing of it.

The other thing of note about him: along the side of his jaw and neck ran a port wine stain in the shape of a hand, which gave one to believe it was the bloody print of some demon midwife who'd assisted in pulling him into a world he was reluctant to enter and which was equally reluctant to claim him. When he grew agitated, the birthmark seemed to glow, as if on fire. They called him Preacher, though there was nothing preacherly about him, and Cain could only surmise it was owing to the fact that he dressed all in black, with a flat-topped riding hat and a long black duster that came down to his ankles. Besides the bowie knife strapped to his leg, which he referred to as his Arkansas toothpick, he carried in his belt an ancient North flintlock .69 caliber pistol, a formidable thing that would put a hole in a person the size of a young girl's fist.

The feeling Cain harbored for Preacher appeared to be mutual. From the start, the man seemed dead set against him. He was always second-guessing Cain's decisions. If Cain said they should stop for the night, Preacher would insist they had a good half hour of light left in which to ride. On the other hand, if Cain said they should push on, Preacher would grumble that they were flat-out tired and he was riding them too damn hard. If Cain suggested they take one road, Preacher, who'd never been out of Virginia in his life, would advocate another. "That way looks a might untraveled," he would say. If Cain suggested avoiding a certain city where there were known to be abolitionists or vigilance committees, Preacher would say Cain was just being finicky. At night, when Cain preferred his own company and would be reading his Milton, Preacher would glare at him with his snake eyes. More than once Cain had overheard him say he considered it "a thang womanish for a growed man to be readin' po'tree." And when Cain tried to ignore him, the other would purposely make noises, talk loud or fart or make fun of something Little Strofe had said, all with the aim of trying to distract Cain, or draw his attention—Cain could never tell which. The two had had words on several occasions, nearly coming to blows once over who had drunk the last of the coffee. Cain knew—just as surely as he knew it would rain when his bad leg ached—that there would be trouble with Preacher before this was all over.

When they crossed the Mason-Dixon line not far from a small town called Gettysburg, Cain halted, waiting for the others to catch up.

"We're in the North now, boys," he explained to them.

"So?" Preacher replied.

"We'll need to be careful. In this line of work, if you're not careful you could wind up dead real quick."

"Maybe you're a'scart of these yellow-bellied Yankees, Cain. But I ain't," the blond-haired man continued.

"It's not a bloody matter of being scared," he snapped at the other. "I'm just saying we need to watch our step."

"We got the law on our side," Preacher said. "Got us a warrant for them two darkies."

"Law makes no difference. Up here, they don't give a rat's ass about what the law says on runaways. From now on there'll be people that won't look kindly on our being here."

"If'n they want trouble, they'll get a bellyful of it," he said, touching his pistol.

"I won't risk my neck because you're a damn fool."

"Who you callin' a fool?"

"You heard me," Cain said.

Preacher stared coolly at him. Then he let out a laugh. "They can kiss my corn cracker ass for all I care," he taunted as he spurred his horse on and pushed past Cain into the North.

In eastern Pennsylvania, they came across the scarred, hump-backed hills where they saw huge mounds of coal and entire mountainsides clear-cut and oozing a black sludge. As they rode past a group of filthy miners trudging back after a day's work in the mines, Preacher called out, "Hell, they's blacker'n niggers."

Several of the men stopped. They carried shovels and picks.

"Who you calling niggers?" said one with a heavy German accent.

"Let's go, Preacher," Strofe said.

The farther north they went, the more they found themselves climbing mountains whose summits were still covered with snow, as the temperature dropped and the vegetation changed. So, too, did the accents of the people they ran into, from the soft Maryland twang to the formal lilt of the Quakers to the impatient and brutal tongue of those New Jerseyites, and again to the clipped and nasally dialect of those Yankees north of the city of New York, pale, flinty-souled folk scored by icy winds and snow, who had the surly aspect of one woken up from sleep in the middle of the night. They entered finally the frigid far north woods where, it being early spring, the lakes and ponds were mostly still frozen over with ice the strange blue hue of a robin's egg. As they passed by one frozen mountain tarn in the Catskills, Little Strofe called to the others. "Looky there," he said, pointing at the ice. Perfectly intact and locked just below the surface was some sort of furry creature—dog or wolf or fox, they could not tell—eyes still open, its bared fangs inches from the surface seemingly about to yap, its forefeet seeming to scratch at the underside of the ice, as if still entertaining the notion of escape. Cain, a native Virginian, had been this far north only once in his life. When he was a boy he had accompanied his father on a steamship to Portland, Maine, to look at a new breed of cattle newly arrived from Scotland. But that was nothing like this ice-locked and frigid landscape.

"Them Yankees can have this cold," Preacher complained one time, blowing on his hands. "Freeze they damn balls off."

Little Strofe, who happened to be riding next to Cain, asked, "Y'ever see you such c-cold weather in springtime, Mr. Cain?"

"No, indeed, Mr. Strofe," he replied. Cain had developed a fondness for the stuttering, simple man.

"Why, up in the hills it weren't never like this, even in the hardest winter. 'M-member back in forty-two, Brother." He turned and called over his shoulder to Strofe. "That was some cold spell."

"Hit were forty we had the bad winter," Strofe replied.

"I reckon you're mistaken on that."

"How the hell would you know?" Strofe said. "You were still shittin' in your drawers."

Even Preacher laughed at this.

Each evening, after the long day's ride, after the horses were hobbled and brushed and fed, after supper was made and eaten, after all the pans and cups were cleaned, the fire banked for the night, the bedrolls laid out—after all this they'd sit around the campfire for a while before sleep finally overtook them. Bats would come out, flittering and gliding in the twilight sky like a child's mobile. A screech owl's quavering cry might erupt nearby or a catamount's snarl echo down through the mountains. They'd sit there, four men whose only connection was the hunting of human prey, each occupied by his own devices. Drinking from a bottle of applejack, the hulking Strofe would get out his maps and by the lantern's light plan how far they'd get the next day. Some nights Preacher would remove his deck of cards and play solitaire, or talk Strofe or his brother into a game of poker, for which they played for coppers or quids of tobacco. On those occasions that he was drunk, Preacher might jabber on about some tight-fisted farmer he used to work for back in Botetourt County or relate a story about how he'd cut up somebody bad in a tavern fight. But most nights he would sit there silently sharpening his big knife with a whetstone and then take to whittling a piece of wood with such single-minded concentration it almost seemed he'd fallen into a fugue state. Yet when he'd eventually come back from wherever it was he'd gone, and look up and catch Cain staring at him, he'd wink and offer a smile whose meaning Cain could no more fathom than he could the expression of the man in the moon.

Some nights Little Strofe would take out his Jew's harp and play something, a jig or reel, some tune from the hills. Sometimes he'd sing with a lilting voice "The Pretty Plowboy" or "The Girl I Left Behind Me" or "Lilly Dale," usually some sad lament of too-early death and the loss of a lover. When he sang, his stammer seemed almost to vanish and his voice turned fluid and smooth, as if greased by whale oil. It slipped out of his homely face like the sun breaking through a gray and overcast day. Cain, reading his copy of Milton by firelight and sipping from his flask filled with laudanum, would be distracted for a moment as Little Strofe conjured up visions of doomed love. Sometimes he'd even ask Little Strofe if he knew a particular tune, like "Bury Me Beneath the Willows." If the man wasn't familiar with the song—after all, he couldn't read a lick—Cain would usually just have to repeat a few verses or hum a little of it, and Little Strofe would pick it up right quick. Even Preacher seemed not immune to the beauty of the man's voice; he'd sit there, whittling a piece of wood or sharpening his knife, and his snake eyes would momentarily soften and take on a slightly confused, wistful look. If Cain didn't know better, he'd have said the words almost wounded him, made him long for something he had lost but couldn't remember what it was.

Bury me beneath the willows
Under the weeping willow tree
When she hears that I am sleeping
Maybe then she'll think of me.

At such moments, Cain would remove the spectacles from his nose and look up from his reading, letting himself be carried away by the words and rhythms of the song. Sometimes his mind would drift back to the war and the Indian girl he had loved. He pictured her, the playful gleam of her feral eyes as she came to him in the night, the earthy musk of her, the way his name slipped like honey from her mouth: *Cain*, she would say, seemingly fascinated by the sound, like a child with a new plaything. He remembered the beguiling warmth of her as she lay next to him on the ground of the shed, high among the desert mountains. Even naked, she was as natural and innocent as some wild untamed creature. He could still see her smooth, brown belly, her hard, sinewy arms, the small breasts rising and falling in the early-morning sunlight that came slanting through the mud-chinked holes in the wall. Her dark eyes searching his, her lips forming words that never materialized. Yet the two didn't need words; they spoke their own language, one of touch and taste and hearts, her skin scorching against his, the tang of her in his mouth salty and sweet at once. At times, he felt she'd been nothing more than a phantasm, a teasing mirage conjured up out of the heat and distance of that long-ago time and place, or perhaps, a mere by-product of his laudanum-clouded mind. But then he'd touch his shattered leg, feel the knotted scars along his shin and the permanent ache imbedded there and know that, like the old wound itself, she *had* been something real, something that had happened. Something he'd had and then lost. At such times he would feel the familiar ache rise up in his chest and seem to squeeze the very life out of him like an iron fist.

One night they had camped along a ridge overlooking a frozen lake. The night was cold and clear, with a sharp wind howling down from the north and raking the flesh like nettles, and in the dark the lake seemed almost to glow, to give off its own eerie illumination. Cain was reading, and he kept having to switch hands, keeping the free one warm in his pocket.

"What you reading there, Mr. Cain?" asked Little Strofe, who sat close by, huddled beneath a blanket.

Cain always brought along something to read wherever he went, packed away in his saddlebags for an evening's diversion. This book, his favorite, a dog-eared, broken-spined edition of Milton he'd received as a present from his schoolmaster, the ancient Mr. Beauregard, who'd studied classics at Harvard and had fought with Old Hickory at the battle of New Orleans. Milton was Beauregard's favorite poet, and he'd fostered in Cain a similar appreciation. Cain had found the character of Satan endlessly fascinating. Sometimes when he hunted alone, Satan's was the only voice Cain would hear for days. He reminded Cain of a southerner: both honorable and petty, vainglorious and doomed from the start, yet too proud and foolish to know when he was beaten. He put Cain in mind of the stubborn, proud men at the Alamo, those heroes every southern boy had read about and dreamed one day of emulating—Bowie and Travis and Crockett.

"It's a long poem by a blind fellow," Cain explained.

"How'd he writ it if'n he was b-blind?" Little Strofe asked.

"He had somebody take down the words."

Little Strofe chewed on this notion for a moment. "I ain't n-never learned me to read a lick. What's he say in there?"

"It's a story about Satan's rebellion against God."

"Do tell? And who won the thing?" the man asked straight-faced.

Cain smiled, though not with condescension. "I guess the outcome is still in doubt."

"C-could I hear a smidgin?"

Cain read a few lines, the part where Satan addresses the synod of hell:

Long is the way
And hard, that out of Hell leads up to Light;
Our prison strong, this huge convex of Fire,
Outrageous to devour, immures us round.

"What'all do them fancy words mean?" Little Strofe asked.

"They're plotting revenge on God. They're going to use Man to get back at him."

"You mean like with the s-serpent and all a that?"

"That's right."

Little Strofe rubbed his chin in thought. He was both a religious and a superstitious man, often mixing the two together into a compost of cautionary wisdom. When he wasn't praying, he was worrying about bad omens and ill-favored signs. If they passed a red-haired woman in the road first thing in the morning, it meant they were certain to have bad luck later that day. Or if a man was plowing in a field, they were not to come within his shadow lest a horse come up lame, or if they heard a cat sneeze thrice, which they had once in front of a feed store, it meant that someone was to get the ague (while no one came down with the ague, his brother's bowel problems did indeed worsen).

"The evil one been using us to d-do mischief ever since the Garden, Mr. Cain."

"That's when we're not doing it all by ourselves."

"They's some truth to that way of thinking, too. Good night, Mr. Cain."

"Good night, Mr. Strofe."

The man mumbled some prayers, then curled up between his dogs, as he did most nights, and pulled his blanket over the three of them. In a moment he was sound asleep, snoring along with his dogs. Cain envied the man's stonelike simplicity, his dreams probably no more complex than those of Skunk and Louella. Cain's bad leg ached, as it always did from the cold. From an inside pocket of his coat he took out his silver flask, opened it, and had a pull at the sweet-tasting laudanum. The liquid did its magic, fanning out through his frozen limbs like a warm summer breeze. The flask had been an odd present from his father on his twenty-first birthday. Mr. Cain, a stern and disciplined man, had sharply disapproved of his eldest son's debauched and shiftless life, but equally he held that all southern boys should know how to hold their liquor as a matter of honor and a sign of manhood. Dented from a fragment of grapeshot in the war, it had etched along its side the words *Augustus Claudius Cain, This 14th of May, Eighteen Hundred and Forty-two.*

His father, a farmer of only modest means by Virginia plantation standards, had raised tobacco and corn, horses and cattle and hogs. At any one time he owned only about a dozen slaves. All were field hands except for Lila, and a man named Handy Joe, who chopped wood, toted supplies back from town, and occasionally got Mr. Cain's horse or wagon ready for him. If success was measured by the number of acres and slaves a man owned—and in the South it most decidedly was—Mr. Cain, though he'd worked doggedly all his life, had managed only a partial attainment of his goals. He didn't have a large enough farm to have need of an overseer, so he supervised his slaves directly, often working in the fields shoulder to shoulder with them as well as his two sons. This permitted him to know his slaves in ways that most other planters didn't. He never asked them to do anything that he himself wouldn't; he was a reasonable and fair master, progressive even in his thinking, though he could be firm when the situation called for it, believing that, with Negroes as with children, sparing the rod would spoil the child. In farmers' magazines such as the *Southern Cultivator* and *De Bow's Review*, which he perused religiously, Mr. Cain read articles on "The Judicious Management of Negroes," or "Developing Labor through Effective Breeding Techniques," or "Reducing Runaways through the Reasonable Application of Punishments and Rewards." In his reading, he came across, and fully subscribed to, such terms as *drapetomania*, which

explained why otherwise contented slaves would suddenly up and run
without the least cause, or *dysaesthesia aethiopica*, which accounted for
why the African race was prone to rascality and any number of other
mental deficiencies beyond their control. Everyone in Nottoway
Chase said that Mr. Cain was a model of slave ownership.

And he'd instilled in his sons, Cain and his younger brother TJ,
four guiding principles regarding the nature of the South's "peculiar
institution," as well as the nature of being a southerner. These
principles were, his father had insisted, part of an irrefutable natural
order of things, one that had to be obeyed unstintingly if there was not
to be general chaos. The first principle derived from the simple fact
that one should always respect one's property: that it was necessary to
care for and protect it, to never misuse it, as it will someday be called
upon to care for and protect you. Whether it was greasing a wagon's
axle before going on a trip, or cleaning and oiling a gun after using
it, or feeding a valuable draft horse nothing but the best alfalfa and
oats, and never pushing it beyond its God-given capacity, respecting
one's property was a fundamental truth.

Once when Cain was a boy, he'd ridden a roan gelding hard
through the hills and woods behind their farm and put the horse
away when it was still blowing and sweaty; his father gave him a
severe whipping with a leather strop to make an impression on the
young boy—it did, and Cain never abused a horse that way again.
The same was true with one's slaves. Mr. Cain treated his Negroes
with the same respect and the same reasoned self-interest—with care
and good sense, with a utilitarian eye toward the benefits derived
from them, and with the full knowledge of what each had cost him
on the auction block, how much he had invested in each in terms of
food and clothing, doctoring and training.

The second principle was that a Negro was in many ways like
a child, and a willful child at that, and it was the moral duty of the
white man not only to reap the benefits of his labor but also to look
after and guide him, to amend his wayward tendencies with a firm
hand, as one would a stubborn hunting dog or a horse that tended to
nip, or even a son that was headstrong and badly behaved. Mr. Cain
fed his slaves a full five pounds of rice or potatoes a week and two

pounds of bacon, when most planters only provided four and one of each, respectively. Moreover, he clothed them and took care of all their needs with a liberality that was almost unheard of; he provided extra food and clothing at Christmas and allowed them to attend church on Sunday or to marry and have families, which, with one exception, he never broke up; he treated them with the consideration and benevolence due their station in life. In return he asked of them only their hard work, their loyalty, their unquestioned obedience. No more, no less, than he'd ask of a mule or, for that matter, a son.

The third principle his father had taught Cain about slavery, which derived naturally from the first two and which every slave owner taught his child, was that he, Cain, was born white, and was, therefore, fundamentally different from the Negro, that his very whiteness not only set him apart from and above them—morally, intellectually, physically—but that it also linked him in a blood bond with every other white man, especially every other southern white man. Whites and Negroes, Mr. Cain believed, were created by the Almighty to be separate, and that was what made miscegenation such a crime against nature. Cain had grown up not so much *believing* in slavery, as he did *accepting* its existence, as one would accept the sun's rising in the east or women giving birth to babies or a dog chasing a rabbit. It was all part, as his father often said, of "the natural order of things." He didn't believe, as the hypocritical abolitionists put it, in amalgamation, the mixing of the races, which he considered an abomination of that natural order God had intended. Cain accepted, too, that the Negro was fundamentally different from himself. He looked different. He smelled different. He certainly behaved differently. He thought in ways that were as fundamentally different from those of the white man, as a hunting dog's mind worked differently from that of, say, a squirrel or a deer. It was, to him, an abundantly clear fact of life.

Although Cain had decided early on that he wasn't cut out for the life of a farmer and thus would have no personal need for slaves himself, he agreed with those who felt that no Yankee, no court up north, no politician or abolitionist or amalgamationist, was going to tell a southerner how to live his life or what to do with his property. Like nearly all his fellow Virginians, he looked upon their peculiar institution as one would a troublesome relative; it was his by virtue of blood and birth, tradition and natural bonds, and, like the fact or not, if anyone attacked kin, you came to their rescue. Though he himself had never owned a slave and never would, if it ever came to a question of taking up arms to protect their right to it—as many had said it eventually would—he knew full well what side he would be fighting for.

And that led, of course, as all things did, to what Mr. Cain preached was the most important principle of all, the one that every child below the Mason-Dixon line was raised to accept and revere, that became part of their very fiber, that grew into their religion—the southern notion of honor. It was with Cain's father, as with many such men, a thing distorted and self-serving, molded around their own needs and failings and views of how the world should be governed. For instance, to his father, having a mistress had nothing whatsoever to do with the question of honor or the notion of white womanhood, a thing sacred and to be protected. Despite his shortcomings, his father believed in honor and taught Cain that it was to a southerner what cold, hard cash was to a Yankee. They would defend it at all costs, including laying down their lives if it called for that.

They rode through rain and snow and hail, through fog banks so thick they couldn't see ten feet in front of them, through forests that grew more tangled and desolate and intractable with each passing mile north. They slogged through spring thaws and slipped on icy trails. Sometimes the path they were on just seemed to end in the middle of the woods or in an ascent too steep for the horses, and then they'd have to double back and try another route. During it all, Little Strofe kept up a constant banter. Now and then his brother might say, "Would you just shut the deuce up and ride, Brother?" There was game aplenty for the taking, deer and turkey, pheasant and grouse, rabbit and squirrel and possum, and the streams were filled with trout and salmon. Sometimes Strofe would take his shotgun and shoot them some quail or partridge. On one occasion as they were fording a river, they spotted an odd creature feeding in the shallows near the far bank; it was enormous, taller than a horse, big snouted, with antlers as wide across as a man's outstretched arms.

"The hell's that, Mr. Cain?" Little Strofe cried. "Ain't never seen such a sizable deer."

"That's a moose," Cain explained to him.

"Is it a thing to be et?"

"I suppose it's edible," Cain told him.

So with that, Little Strofe dismounted his mule. From the buckskin scabbard, he removed his Boyer over-and-under flintlock rifle and took careful aim. That night they had fresh meat for dinner. Little Strofe, who handled most of the cooking duties, fashioned the moose meat into a stew with dumplings on top. It was a welcome change from the usual fare of fried corn pone and dried beef and salted herring. He wasn't a half-bad cook, and he had a nose for finding delectable things that popped up along the trail, like wild carrots and leeks and basil, fiddleheads and thyme. Once he located a nest of partridge eggs, another time a rabbit he'd snared in a leg trap. He made mint and sassafras tea, and on one occasion he sneaked into a farmer's field and pilfered a handful of potatoes left over from the previous year's harvest, and that night he made potato pancakes. On another occasion, Cain got out some string and a hook he kept in his saddlebags, and they caught themselves a mess of brook trout, which Little Strofe fried up in lard that night. Now and then they had a treat of venison or wild turkey roasted over a spit on the fire, but mostly it was the monotonous diet of soldiers, corn pone and dried fish, salt pork and jerked beef.

Save for the growing tension between Cain and Preacher, the journey north had been fairly uneventful. Each evening around the fire, Strofe would get out his maps and he and Cain would look them over, deciding on the best route. For the most part they steered clear of the cities and only ventured into a town when it was absolutely necessary. Negroes in general, and runaways in particular, Cain knew, had a sixth sense when it came to spotting a slave catcher. It was as if they carried a peculiar and strong scent about them that only Negroes could detect. Cain had experienced that before. Despite such precautions, they'd nearly run into trouble in Albany, New York.

Strofe's horse had thrown a shoe and they'd had to stop at a livery in the town. While waiting for the horse to be shod, they'd headed over to a tavern to get something to eat. Someone must have spotted them and passed the word, for when they returned a small but vocal crowd of Negroes as well as some whites had gathered in the street outside the livery. Some of them carried pitchforks and cudgels, a few even had fowling pieces. They started to call things out.

"We don't want your kind around here," someone yelled.

"G'yon and git, soul catchers," cried a Negro man. *Soul catcher*. That's what blacks called men like them. Cain had heard the term many times before. It was as if to them, as bad as it was to have their bodies brought back to bondage, it was a thing far worse that their very souls were being snatched from them.

"We'd b-bess skedaddle," Little Strofe said to the others.

"They got the wrong sow by the ear," Preacher said, starting to reach for his big pistol. "They's so all fired up for a fight, I say we give it to 'em."

"Don't," Cain warned, putting his hand on Preacher's forearm.

Besides being outnumbered, if things escalated to violence now, they might as well turn around and head home. Word would spread faster than a wildfire about slave catchers being on the hunt, and every Negro from New York City to the Canadian border would be on the lookout. Still, as they made their way through the crowd to their horses, Cain clutched the blackjack he kept in his back pocket. He'd made it himself, a sheaf of heavy leather filled with buckshot. It struck against anything solid such as bone to devastating effect, and it had often come in handy while fighting a frenzied runaway. The four quickly saddled their mounts and rode out of town without incident. Cain led them south for a while, trying to mask their real intent, but then doubled back and circled around the town and continued north.

3

After several more days' ride they finally reached Keene, New York, a small village in a notch between two high mountains, not forty miles from the Canadian border. There they stopped at an inn, the first time Cain wouldn't be sleeping on open ground in the nearly three weeks they'd been traveling. The innkeeper was a frail, scaly-headed man with yellow cat eyes.

"Have you heard of a place called Timbucto?" Cain asked the man.

"You mean, the nigger town? Half day's ride west," he said. "You folks hunting a runaway?"

Cain ignored him, asking instead, "How much for a room?"

"Two dollars a night. What's your business there?"

"Our business ain't none of yours," Strofe informed the man.

"I got no quarrel with that."

"Much obliged for the information," Cain said.

While the others stayed in the public room drinking, Cain headed up to his room, where he indulged liberally from his flask and lay reading by candlelight. When he was a boy, his mother used to read to him and his brother TJ, a novel of the Scottish moors, or some slender volume of Burns or Gray, or something from the Bible. She was partial to Proverbs, fond of saying things like "But the path of the just is as the shining light." Or "Even a child is known by his doings."

From her, Cain had acquired his fondness for reading, as well as his dreamy gray eyes, a taste for laudanum, and a certain melancholia, which made even the brightest of days look as if a partial eclipse were taking place.

An image of her came unbidden to him now. She had been a woman of ungainly comeliness: too tall and angular to be considered a beauty by traditional southern standards, her doelike eyes excessive for her narrow, bony face, a mouth too small to contain its pleasure, so she was given to presenting an awkward, toothy grin to the world. Still, as a boy Cain thought her the most beautiful woman alive. There was about her a delicate, almost ethereal loveliness, made all the more exquisite by her illness. Pale, with dark circles beneath those pretty gray eyes, eyes that always seemed to have an otherworldly gleam to them, a look that had its source both in the illness that sapped her body and in the laudanum that she consumed in ever-increasing quantities. And when she'd lean down to kiss Cain good night, she smelled of honeysuckle and burnt sugar, the sweet aura that floated around her from the medicine. Cain loved his mother with all the tenderness and affection and precocious sadness of a child whose parent has already died, for in his heart he knew that she would soon be gone. She was a woman oddly matched to her husband's stern and pragmatic temperament: she filled with the gossamer essence of poetry, he with the hard red dirt of a Virginia planter. When she was alive his father had been neither mean nor cruel to her, if one didn't count his long-standing dalliance with a woman in town, but he was with her, as he had been with everyone else, distant, removed in ways beyond physical proximity.

During her final illness Cain's father had been even more remote, as if preparing himself for her absence and not wanting to be hurt more than he had to. He'd moved out of their room and slept mostly in his study, where he spent long nights poring over his account books or reading Roman history. And so it fell to Cain to keep her company for hours on end, listening to her talk of her parents who had grown up on the rocky coast of the Hebrides, reading to her from Shakespeare's sonnets, bringing her a cup of tea laced with horehound that the house slave Lila had made for her weak lungs. He'd fetch her a glass into which she'd pour herself a drink from the bottle she kept hidden under the bed: Dr. Wilmer's cough cure, which was supposed to be, the bottle claimed, a restorative for "catarrh, inflammations of the lung, dyspepsia, and low back pain," but which was really only alcohol laced with a tincture of opium. Sometimes she would let him have a drink of it, too. It burned and tasted sweet at the same time, like a jagged piece of ice going down his throat, and afterward it would make him feel warm, his head floating, barely tethered to his neck. "Our secret, Augustus," she would say to him, and smile her toothy smile. He would sit by her bedside holding her thin hand as she coughed bloody sputum into a lace handkerchief. Occasionally she would ask that he get her scrimshaw brush and brush her hair. She had beautiful auburn hair, long and dark and glistening, and Cain loved brushing it (in her coffin, it was her hair that Cain had kept his eyes fastened on, for it seemed the one thing of her still alive and because of it she was not yet irrevocably lost to him). Sometimes, though, she would turn and stare at him. Whether feverish with her illness or under the effects of the laudanum, now and then she'd get a look in her pale eyes that scared the young boy. They shone fiercely, as if she were not so much seeing him but something beyond this world—angels or demons, he couldn't tell.

She would hug Augustus to her frail body and call him "My sweet boy." Once, he recalled her touching the middle of his chest. "I will always be right here. Will you remember that for me?"

He would. Always.

Her too-early death would stunt something in the boy that would never fully recover, his heart like an apple deformed and gnarled by a late frost. For his part, Cain's father refused even to utter his wife's name. The boy was never sure whether it was out of a dearth of love on his father's part, or rather, a surfeit of it, that her loss had caused him such pain that bringing up her memory only overwhelmed him with grief, even years later. He wouldn't display a single portrait or memento or keepsake of hers around the house. If either Cain or his brother TJ would bring their mother's name up in conversation, Mr. Cain would set his jaw as if he'd received a wood sliver in his flesh, and then get up and leave the room. The young Cain had once crept

into his father's study and from his desk taken a small locket he knew
was kept there. Inside was a miniature likeness of his mother, staring
out at him with those dreamy gray eyes of hers.

T he next day Cain woke lethargic from the laudanum, his head
pounding the way it did after he'd had too much. They saddled
up and rode out, arriving at the outskirts of Timbucto around midday.
Though it was April now, a cold rain with bits of snow and ice fell all
day, and low gray clouds hung just above the treetops, making it seem
as if a huge piece of sky had broken off and fallen on them. They waited
in the woods outside the village, hidden in a dense thicket of laurel.
The cleared area of the Negro village was a half mile away, set on a
high table of rocky land ringed by steep blue-gray mountains whose
peaks were shrouded in clouds and snow. It wasn't really a village so
much as just some shanties thrown haphazardly together in a futile
attempt to fend off the weather. The fields they worked seemed to
be some distance removed, while their houses were huddled cheek by
jowl as a kind of defense, presumably against would-be attackers. Yet
the place appeared to have neither rhyme nor reason behind its design;
it seemed fashioned by a blind madman who didn't know which end of
a hammer to use. The houses were not built level or plumb; the roofs
pitched at arbitrary angles, some with snow on them still, and none
faced in a southerly direction. Dark plumes of green-wood smoke
wafted upward from rusty stovepipes. A couple of hastily assembled
outbuildings leaned precariously in the wind. Pigs and chickens and
guineas rooted around, while feral-looking dogs wandered freely about.
The squalor was heightened by the fact that a number of dung piles
had been placed right next to some of the front doors. The whole place
looked inhospitable, cold and gray and foreboding, with its disheveled
huts, and the gray skies and the dark mountains looming ominously
in the distance. In the middle of the village, a bark-covered limb stuck
out of the muddy ground at an angle, with a tattered red rag at the top
flapping in the breeze. Cain supposed it was some sort of pennant to
remind the former slaves of their freed status, but it seemed more a
sign of bloody surrender than anything else.

"My pappy, may he rest in hell," Preacher offered, "said a darkie ain't got the sense of your average dog. Leastways a dog knows not to shit where it eats."

"It do look like hard land to farm," Little Strofe added.

"Fact is, without somebody behind him with a whip, your nigger's just plain lazy as a hog," said Preacher, spitting tobacco juice on the ground.

Like the Gist Settlement out in Ohio and Fort Mose down in Florida, Timbucto was a settlement where freed and runaway slaves were welcomed to come and live. A wealthy abolitionist named Gerrit Smith had provided the land to any Negro who wished to work it. The man had conceived of it as a place where they could make their own way, separate from whites but still here in America, unlike those that advocated a forced return to Liberia for all freed blacks. It was, Cain felt, a pathetic and wrongheaded attempt by white northerners who didn't know the first thing about the Negro temperament, an endeavor doomed to failure. He had to agree with Preacher on this point. Everyone knew your Negro was no more capable of living independently than, say, a four-year-old child. And he wondered why any black would choose this sort of life over that of being on an orderly, well-tended farm down south. It didn't make sense to him. Then again, if slaves were rational he'd be out of a job.

From his saddlebags, Cain took out his brass spyglass and scoped the village. With the steady rain he saw little activity there save for the occasional trip to an outhouse or to a barn for milking their few scrawny cows or to the henhouse to collect eggs. He didn't see any sign of the runaways. The four men waited and watched all day. When it grew dark, they rode deeper into the woods to make camp that night beneath an outcropping of rock that offered them some feeble respite from the savage rain. They lit a fire and cooked their supper. Nearby ran a stream from which they watered their horses.

"I don't m-much fancy this place," Little Strofe said as he ate.

"What you w-worried about?" Preacher taunted, making fun of his stammer. "You think them n-niggers is gonna come and get you?"

"Brother here always been skeersome of darkies," Strofe said.

"That's a lie."

"Hit's true. They usta be this nigger work for Mr. Jacobs, the undertaker man in town. Brother wouldn't even cross in front of his place. And if he heard the cock crow in the middle of the night, he wouldn't go out and do his business on account he was 'scart some darky would snatch him up."

"*Woo,*" said Preacher, making his eyes wide and furling out his lips. He ambled like an ape toward Little Strofe. "Them darkies gonna git you tonight."

"I ain't a'scart a no niggers," Little Strofe said, embarrassed. "I'm just s-sayin' I be glad when we git what we come for and can leave." He looked over at Cain. "You like this place, Mr. Cain?"

"Not particularly," he offered, looking up from his plate of corn pone and dried beef.

"See. He don't c-care none for it neither."

Preacher glanced at Little Strofe and said, "Never seen such a pair a old biddies in all my born days. You with your d-damn singin' and him with his readin'." Cain glanced over at Preacher.

"Least I *can* read," he said.

"I can read just fine," Preacher scoffed. "What I needs to. Not some damn pomes. Hell, Cain, you're like some dried-up old schoolmarm with your nose always in a book. And when it ain't in a book, you're picklin' your brain with what'all's in that flask a your'n."

"You just mind your own damn business, Preacher."

"Hell, I don't even see why Eberly needed to hire you on in the first place. We coulda found them niggers our ownselves."

Cain told himself not to pay him any mind. The man was an ignorant fool and just itching for a fight. Wait till they were done. If he still wanted one, then he'd give it to him.

The next morning, the rain had stopped, though the sky had remained overcast and gray as a pair of old socks. They rode back to the village, and from the cover of the laurel, Cain watched as the men and a few of the women headed out of the village, carrying hoes and picks and spades, one of them driving a wagon pulled by a pair of swaybacked mules. Cain took note of two men toting guns, a couple of old fowling pieces. Whether for hunting game or for protection, he couldn't rightly say, but the fact spoke to the need to be careful. Freed Negroes, or ones who had been on the run for a while, were much more dangerous. They'd had a taste of freedom and usually wouldn't give it up without putting up a fight, nor would they permit their fugitive comrades to be peacefully taken back either. Cain always tried to err on the side of caution, not to underestimate the desire in a Negro for this thing called freedom. He made it a point not to rush in, but to plan out carefully when and where he'd capture a fugitive slave.

The one time he'd had to kill a runaway was when he'd overlooked this principle. He was hunting for a runaway named Benjamin, who'd worked as a puddler for the Tredegar Iron Works in Richmond. Cain had finally located him in Pittsburgh. He was staying with a Negro family, in a neighborhood predominately made up of freedmen. He worked in a foundry, and Cain would watch him going back and forth to work, waiting to catch him when he was alone, in a place where the odds would be with Cain. Usually the Negro was with half a dozen fellow black ironworkers, big, burly men who would have put up a good fight.

Finally, though, Cain could wait no longer. He was running out of funds and he needed to capture the runaway and bring him back to Virginia to collect the reward. So he broke one of his own rules. He jumped the runaway coming out of a doggery with another Negro. Cain pulled his gun and informed Benjamin he had a warrant for his arrest as a fugitive slave. The other Negro started to yell at the top of his lungs, "Soul catcher! Help! Soul catcher!" Soon Negroes came running out from the tavern and surrounding dwellings, and the next thing Cain knew, there were a couple of dozen black faces surrounding him. Emboldened by their presence, Benjamin pulled a knife on Cain. "Get yo white buckra ass outa here." But Cain, for all his cautious nature, needed the money the Negro represented. Besides which, he didn't like leaving business unfinished, liked completing what he'd set out to do, nor did he like the image of being chased off by a Negro. So he told the runaway he was bringing him back one way or the other. That's when Benjamin rushed at him with the knife. Taken by surprise, Cain had little choice but to defend himself. He'd hoped only to wound him, because a dead runaway wasn't worth a plug nickel. But the bullet caught the Negro in the throat, and he dropped like a sack of wet grain.

With that, the others fell on Cain. Wildly swinging his blackjack with one hand and his Colt with the other, he fought his way out of the crowd and made for his horse, tied at the end of the alley. He managed to mount and ride away as they threw stones and curses at him. After that, he was always careful to pick the safest place and circumstances for a capture. Patience was something a slave catcher needed as much as shackles or a gun.

All that morning they watched the village, but they didn't spot the runaway named Henry among the men heading out to work the fields, nor the girl among the women who stayed behind and washed clothes and tended to the chickens.

"Think they're hidin' her?" Strofe asked Cain.

He shrugged as he scoped the village with his spyglass. He thought perhaps one of the Negroes coming through Keene two nights before might have spotted them and brought word back that a group of soul catchers was approaching, and they'd had time to hide both of them in the woods. Maybe that was why the men carried guns.

Around noon, they saw a young Negro boy leaving Timbucto, heading for the nearby village of North Elba with a basket of eggs to sell.

"Wager he'll know where they're at," said Strofe.

"Let's git him and make him talk," Preacher added, mounting his roan.

"We ought to wait," Cain cautioned. He felt, sooner or later, if they were there, one or the other would show himself. If, on the other hand, the four slave catchers exposed themselves too soon and the entire village learned of their presence, it would make things all the more difficult.

"You're 'scart a them niggers, too, Cain?" Preacher taunted. "Why, I'm surprised, big war hero like yourself."

Cain stared up at him seated on his horse. Nothing would have pleased him as much as pulling the man from his saddle and throttling him. He didn't know how the man had come by the knowledge that he'd been in the war, that he'd received a medal. Maybe Eberly, who seemed to know everything about him, had told him. In any case, he wouldn't let the man see that the comment prickled him.

"I'm not fool enough to get into a scrap if I don't have to," he replied coldly.

"But a famous nigger hunter like yourself, I figured you to go marchin' right in here and pluck them runaways easy as pie," Preacher said sarcastically. He looked down at Cain and smiled his gat-toothed smile. "Then again, maybe all them drams you're asippin' has made you lily-livered."

Cain gave him a stone-hard glare. "Whenever you're a mind to test me, Preacher, you go right ahead."

"Think I'm scared a you, Cain?"

"Would you two stop your damn squabblin'?" Strofe said. "I say we catch the boy and make him tell us where they're at."

After several weeks in the saddle and the past two days of waiting and watching in the cold and rain, they'd grown anxious; they wanted to finish their business and leave this place behind. Even Cain. Finally, he conceded and they decided to follow the boy until he was safely away from the village. Strofe muzzled the dogs and put them on ropes to keep them from running off after the Negro. Then they mounted up and cautiously rode through the woods, keeping the boy in sight but maintaining their distance so as not to scare him into flight. At last, when they figured he was far enough away from the settlement, they split into two groups, one circling ahead of the boy and approaching him from the front, the other coming at him from the rear. Warily, the boy watched them approach, four white men on horses and a pair of hounds. He was wearing a wool coat, homespun trousers, and a pair of brogans much too big for his feet. When they reached the boy, Strofe asked about the two runaways.

"One goes by Henry," he explained. "He's a right stout nigger. Missing an ear. The other's a high yeller gal name of Rosetta."

The Negro stared up at him mutely, as if English was not his own language. He eyed their guns.

"We know they're here," Strofe said. "So you might's well tell us and save yourself a whole heap a grief."

Frowning, the Negro glanced down at his basket of eggs. Then he did an odd thing. He looked up and silently held the basket out to Strofe, as a kind of offering. Funny how when a man is offered something, no matter what it is, he tends to take it, and Strofe instinctively leaned down from his saddle and reached for the basket. Before he could take hold of it, though, the boy suddenly dropped it, spun around, and took to his heels, dashing between the horsemen before anyone could grab him. For a short distance, he ran along the muddy road leading back to the village. He was surprisingly fleet of foot, a natural runner, but it quickly must have dawned on him he was no match for men on horses, and so he angled into the dense woods, breaking through thickets of mountain laurel and briars too close packed for the horses to travel with ease. They pulled up, and Little Strofe jumped down and released the dogs.

"Steboy," he said, urging them after the Negro.

The pair went off baying and yapping, slashing through the dense woods as sleek as fish in water. A quarter mile into the forest, the four men came upon the boy, halfway up a crab apple tree, the dogs below barking up a storm. He put up a good fight when Preacher and Little Strofe climbed up to get him down, kicking and flailing away, even biting Little Strofe on the wrist. But finally Preacher clubbed him with the barrel of his pistol and the boy fell leadenly to the ground. Preacher let out with a whoop like somebody who'd won something at a fair. They tied him up, put a gag in his mouth, and then headed back to their camp in the woods, where Preacher tied him to a sycamore tree.

It had started to rain again, a fine gray mist that fell out of the low sky like sifted flour. Little Strofe built a fire and began cooking supper.

Preacher removed the gag from their captive's mouth and asked him again about the two runaways.

"Where they at, boy?"

The Negro just stared at him. Cain guessed him to be about thirteen years old, a lean but muscular lad, broad shouldered, with coal black skin that had never been diluted by a single drop of white blood. At first he didn't say a word, just stared blankly at them as he was asked questions, and Cain wondered for a moment if they'd captured themselves a deaf mute. But then Preacher took out his knife and waved it in front of him. With that, the boy finally broke his silence.

"I'm free. I gots my papers," he said defiantly, staring at the knife.

"Would you listen to the cheeky nigger?" Preacher scoffed. He removed a whetstone from his pocket and calmly ran it up and down the blade of the knife, the way you would if it were hog-butchering season and you were fixing to gut one.

"I don't gots to tell you nothin'," the boy cried.

"Is that so?"

"Yessum. I'm a free man. I gots rights just like you."

Preacher smiled. "You'll do what we goddamn tell you to, boy," he said, striking him on the side of the head with the flat of the knife blade. "You hear me?"

"White bastard," the boy cursed, for which he received a second and harder blow.

This time the boy just gritted his teeth and stared hatefully back at the white man in front of him.

Preacher then tried to grab the Negro's ear, but the boy shook his head wildly, sensing what was coming. So the blond man turned to Little Strofe, who was squatting a few feet away, frying the eggs the boy had been carrying. "C'mere."

"Me?" asked Little Strofe.

"Yeah, you. C'mere and grab hold a this here nigger's head."

Little Strofe didn't move at first.

"Y'hear me?" Preacher cried. "Get your ass over here."

Little Strofe glanced at his brother, who sat there sipping from a bottle of applejack. Finally, he stood and walked over to Preacher.

"Hold him still," Preacher commanded.

Reluctantly, Little Strofe grabbed the boy's head with two hands.

Preacher took the boy's right earlobe and stretched it away from his head until the boy cried out.

"You know where they at, you'd better talk."

The boy's face was contorted in pain and in fear, but he didn't say anything. Then in one cat-quick motion, Preacher swung the bowie knife and severed the earlobe. Blood spurted out and the boy winced from the pain but somehow managed to remain silent. Preacher held the bloody piece of flesh up in front of the boy.

"See that, nigger. That there is only the first part of what you're gonna lose if'n you don't start talkin'."

The boy stared at him. There was fear in his eyes but something else, too. Something that Cain had had a glimpse of now and then in certain blacks, say, after an overseer's flogging, or when a man was humbled by a master in front of his woman: hatred certainly, but nothing quite so simple and unadulterated as that. Something commingled with fear and humiliation, given shape by bitterness and rage and desperation yet tempered by patience, and above all, held in check by a kind of stubborn, rocklike pride, this cool burning in the eyes like a fire enclosed in ice, waiting, biding its time, always ready to flare up and consume the thing it viewed. And he saw its complementary half in the eyes of whites, a thing that, when it surfaced, was hidden beneath a show of violence or a swaggering bluster or a contemptuous laugh, but was, at its very core, Cain suspected, a kind of fear. A fear that the docile, fawning slave would one day slough off his subservience and become a threat, something of unimaginable terror. He felt it in the impassioned voice of the minister back in his hometown of Nottoway Chase, Virginia, a Reverend Sammons, whose sermons spoke of the natural order God had intended, with whites in charge and slaves serving the role the Almighty had intended. He saw it in the disdainful spit of tobacco juice of the old men in Treacher's General Store in town, when they recollected the names of Gabriel Prosser or Denmark Vesey, rebellious slaves before Cain's time, or the slave Cain himself was alive to remember, the feared and detested Nat Turner, who'd led his uprising over in the eastern part of the state—those crazy niggers who'd had the audacity to turn that quiet anger outward into actual violence. He saw it sometimes even in his father's eyes when he'd flog a willful slave named Darius for running off yet again, a momentary hesitation—because of something he saw in the icy-hot glare of the slave.

With some Negroes, Cain knew, punishment or its threat would make them obedient, servile and malleable to the will of the master. With others it broke their spirit and reduced them to sniveling, worthless creatures, like a dog kicked too often. But with some, like this boy, violence had the opposite effect; it would embolden them, harden and strengthen their resolve, like a piece of iron tempered in a smithy's forge. They were the Negroes not cowed by all the chastisements, by the beatings and floggings their masters or overseers could serve up, who'd witnessed ears or noses cut off, brands burned onto living flesh, who'd seen slaves chained by the neck to a post for weeks, who'd seen others lynched from a tree, their carcasses left to rot in the August sun as a reminder to the rest, who'd had their wives or sisters, daughters or mothers, raped in front of them, or sold downriver—they were the ones impervious to violence, for whom it had not only *not* broken them but made them all the more resilient and stubborn, all the more convinced of the unwavering legitimacy of their hatred, a thing that burned brightly in them and sustained them like air. Cain had seen it in the eyes of slaves he had captured and was returning. In the evening while sitting chained to a tree, they might look out at him from behind the silent mask of black skin. He sometimes wondered what it was they were thinking—was it the fantasy of getting their hands on him while he slept, killing the buckra, the term they used among themselves for a white devil? He could remember Darius, his father's slave who, when he was being flogged, would cry out, as slaves often did during their punishment, "Do, massa. Do it hard, massa." It was almost as if he welcomed the pain, accepted it, brought it deep into his dark and inscrutable soul, cradled it there like some precious thing, which, of course, it was.

Cain didn't have the stomach for this business. He never resorted to torture to get information about a fugitive slave, preferring instead to use his cunning or his tracking ability. He prided himself that the profession hadn't turned him into a sadist, as it did to so many. He could kill a man if the situation required it, and had on several occasions, both black and white. He could bring a Negro back in irons to a harsh master and sleep soundly that night, because he'd only done his job. But cruelty for cruelty's sake was another thing altogether and he could not abide it. Some men relished it. Like this Preacher fellow. Still, this wasn't his concern. Let Strofe keep Preacher in line. That wasn't what Cain was being paid to do. His job was to bring back the girl.

The bloody hell with it, he thought. He stood up on his creaky leg and went over to his horse, untied him from the tree, and led him down to the stream. He reached into his coat pocket and gave Hermes a piece of sugar. The horse sucked it off his palm with his clever lips and set about masticating it with a wonderful intensity of pleasure, one dark eye locking conspiratorially on Cain, as if to say, *We are not a part of all that, you and I.* He gave him another piece and then stroked the thick, muscular neck, running his hand down the silky blaze. The horse's agile lips pulled at his pockets in search of more. "Last one, boy," Cain said, handing him another piece. He reflected on how much he cared for the animal, more perhaps than was naturally right, and how he was here, in some measure, precisely on account of his attachment to the horse. Another man might have let the thing go, gotten another mount. There were, he supposed, other horses to be had, even ones as fine as Hermes, though he had not laid eyes on one. Then again, another man would not have wagered him to begin with. *You can't blame him for your own drunken foolishness*, Cain told himself.

From the pommel he got the canteen. At the water's edge, he squatted with difficulty, his bad leg creaking with the effort. He filled his canteen, then took a long drink of the water. It was cold and sweet, tasting of autumn leaves and rotting wood and the deep stony secrets of the earth. The stream had slowed here to form a small pool perhaps twenty feet across. The fine rain barely wrinkled the water's skin. Looking down into it, he saw reflected the thick forms of trees, the tangle of naked branches overhead not yet budding out with the liberality of spring, and beyond, the gray vault of sky like a vast coffin lid. Angling his head a bit over the water, he caught sight of his own muted reflection. He had taken to avoiding looking into mirrors, as a man might who had long since stopped appreciating what he saw there. Beneath the broad-brimmed leather hat, he noted the wind-and-sun-scarred features, the angular jaw, which in others would have suggested strength of character but in Cain merely denoted a certain mulishness, the jagged scar over the brow where he'd been struck by a whiskey bottle during a fight, the full mouth turned sullenly downward at the corners. A still good-looking face taken all in all, but one which now had been aged well beyond its thirty-six years, with deep fault lines around the eyes that gave a certain tentativeness to his otherwise self-assured expression. And though he couldn't make them out in the dark mirror of water, the eyes were, he knew, the wistful, gray ones of his mother.

As he was musing on these things, Cain found himself staring down into the water at something that lay on the bottom a few feet away. A stick, dark along one side, with colorful markings along the other. One end was flattened and broad, a handle of sorts. It almost looked like a fancy walking stick that a person had fashioned from a piece of ironwood and then painted. He thought how he hadn't used a cane to get around, not since the old mestiza woman had made him that one from a piece of piñon. So he rolled back his coat sleeve and began reaching his hand into the frigid water to take hold of it. That's when the stick moved. He jerked his hand away just as the thing came suddenly to life and went slithering rapidly toward the far bank. He felt a silken movement in his chest and then a sudden emptiness, as if his soul had been yanked out of him by the snake and carried off.

W hen Cain returned to the camp, Preacher was still at it. Now, though, the gag was back in the boy's mouth and held in place by a piece of rope that circled his head and affixed him to the tree behind him. It was tied so tight that his mouth was drawn back into a frightful grimace.

"You gonna tell us where she at, or you want I should cut the whole gawddang thing off, boy?" Preacher threatened.

Squatting on his haunches like some demented gargoyle, Preacher looked back over his shoulder at Cain and grinned mischievously. His smile was thin and cruel, drawing the skin of his skeletal face hard over the sharp hill features. Preacher held what remained of the bloody ear in his left hand, pulling it tautly away from the Negro's skull so when he did finally draw the razor-sharp knife across it with his right hand, it would come neatly away in one stroke, as if he were filleting a trout. In the time Cain had known him, he had come to learn that Preacher was the sort of man who not only had an aptitude but a passion for inflicting pain. He often bragged about how wealthy planters back where he came from in Botetourt County would pay him two dollars to whip a disobedient slave or to part an ear from the head of a runaway, though he said he'd just as soon do it for nought. ("Ever see a no-earred nigger?" he'd offered as proof that cutting one ear off curbed their desire to run a second time.) Around the campfire once, he'd even related the story of how they'd lynched a nigger for not giving way on the sidewalk to a lady. "Shoulda seed how that darkie danced when he was aswangin' from that tree," he'd bragged.

In Cain's profession, he saw a good deal of this sort of cruelty. Saw it with certain masters or overseers, agents or traders, patty rollers or slave catchers. A kind of sadism born out of wielding power over another living thing, to do cruelty simply because you could, like a boy casually pulling the wings off a fly. It wasn't violence so much he objected to. Cain was on fairly intimate terms with it. He'd been called upon to kill men—four in peacetime and only God knows how many in the war—and often he'd had to hurt people or cause suffering, but on every single occasion it had been a necessity, something he'd no choice but to do. Not something he had taken pleasure in.

The boy's coat front was covered in blood, though Preacher had as yet cut only the lobe off one ear. In the light of the campfire, the blood shone dark, the color of claret wine. Nearby, the two dogs that belonged to Little Strofe lay tethered to a spindly birch. They were some mixed breed of hound, lean and long of ear, with tapered muzzles and coats a dappled brown. Wet and shivering against the cold mountain rain, the two looked on the scene with some odd expectancy in their glossy eyes, almost as if at any moment they'd be released and the boy would, too, and he'd run and they'd be called upon to hunt him down again. The excitement of the chase, a wonderful game of hide-and-seek—that's all this was to their canine brains.

Cain glanced over at Strofe, who sat on a log, eating eggs and corn pone. He wondered when the big man was going to put a stop to this, rein in Preacher's craziness. But Strofe didn't seem concerned. Since they'd started out, he'd been more or less in charge of the other two: directing them to water the horses or start a fire or shoot some game. Generally speaking, Preacher followed his orders, though with a surly, ill-tempered acquiescence, as if the notion were actually his own idea and he hadn't to obey anyone he didn't want to. Even as big as Strofe was and despite the fact that he was Eberly's overseer, and thus Preacher's boss, he sometimes appeared wary of confronting Preacher directly and giving him a command. If he had to tell the skinny blond man to do something or to stop doing something, he would tell him without making eye contact. Maybe say that Mr. Eberly wouldn't look favorably on such and such a thing.

"You save me some a them eggs, Strofe," Preacher called over. "I'm workin' up a considerable appetite."

Cain headed back to his horse and removed his rifle scabbard and then from his saddlebags got a section of oilcloth as well as the wooden case containing his gun supplies. He went over and sat near the sputtering balsam-wood fire, trying to coax some of its frail heat into his chilled bones. He draped the oilcloth over himself and his lap so as to keep out the rain while he worked. He methodically cleaned and oiled his Sharp's rifle, then put it back in the leather scabbard. Next, he set about reloading his pistol, concerned the powder might have gotten wet in the damp weather; he didn't like to take the chance of its not firing if called upon to do so. The Walker Colt was a large, heavy gun, .44 caliber with a nine-inch barrel and ornate engraving along the side. Designed for Captain Walker by Sam Colt himself for the war in Mexico. Cain had had it since '46 when he'd joined the fray. It was a good and dependable gun, one that shot true and didn't jam, and it had seen him through some close calls both in the war and after. He first melted lead in a frying pan over the fire and then poured the molten metal into his bullet mold. When the lead had hardened sufficiently, he clipped off the bullet's sprue and polished the round with a cloth. After that, he cleaned and dried the gun, then poured fresh powder into the chambers and rammed home the six large-caliber balls and topped off each chamber with lard to prevent flashover. After that, he placed the percussion caps in place, all except for the sixth chamber, which he kept open. He'd seen men accidentally shoot themselves in the foot because of such an oversight. For all that his life was a thing of wild disorder and impending mayhem, when it came to the tools of his trade, his gun and horse and saddle, Cain was a precise and careful man. Cautious. Even fastidious. Someone who didn't know him well—and few did— might have said he was timorous of heart or that he set too high a value upon his own neck. He wasn't and didn't. The truth was he simply took pleasure in his small rituals, in doing a thing the right way, just for its own sake. *Do it right the first time and it would stay done*, his father had taught him. One of the few tidbits of wisdom that his father had given him that he held on to. Finished, he wiped the gun lightly with a greased rag and slid it into the holster on his hip and covered it beneath his greatcoat.

Then he reached into an inside pocket, grabbed hold of the flask, and took a long draft of laudanum, hoping to quiet the throbbing ache in his bad leg. He thought of his father again. He had not seen him, had not so much as exchanged a written word, since that night he'd run off to join the fight down in Mexico. Cain could still recall the moment vividly. His father had been in his study perusing ledger books. The man's life had been governed by such things, shackled by lists of expenses and profits, penned in by crop and livestock prices, feed and grain costs, the purchase and upkeep of his slaves. He had his head down in concentration and didn't see his son standing out in the hallway trying to work up the gumption to tell him something of importance. Cain, who was to be married in less than three days' time, had wanted to talk to his father. He'd wanted to tell him . . . what? That it was a mistake, that he didn't love the woman he was about to tie his future to? That the life his father had, more or less, chosen *for* him was not the one *he* himself wanted? That he'd envisioned another sort of life, one that he could not even shape into words, let alone words his father would understand? That he was planning on going off and fighting in a war that had nothing to do with him in the least? Of course, he couldn't have told him any of that. His father would have understood that about as readily as if he'd told him he was going down to the slave quarters and telling them they all had the next day off from working in the fields. So, instead, he'd turned and walked away. Just walked away. Left everything he'd known or cared for—home and family, a soon-to-be bride, an inheritance, a way of life. That night he'd packed a few things, borrowed fifty dollars from the cash box in his father's study, saddled his dependable roan gelding, and lit out for the Texas border. Since then, Cain had ceased to exist for his father, might well have died there on that battlefield of Buena Vista for all the man cared.

Glancing up from his reverie, Cain saw above the fire that the boy was staring at him. The flames seemed to consume his coat, flaring up with the blood on it as if it were turpentine.

"C-c'mon, Preacher," said Little Strofe. "Reckon he's had enough."

Preacher turned savagely on Little Strofe. "*I'll* damn well say when he's had enough and not before."

"I j-j-j—" Little Strofe stammered.

"You j-j-j what?" Preacher mimicked. He was always mocking Little Strofe, teasing him about his stutter. "What in the Sam Hill you j-j-jabbering about?"

"I'm only s-sayin' he m-might come 'round now." Little Strofe turned solicitously to the boy. "You ready to t-talk, ain't you, boy?" The Negro's eyes angled sharply to his right, staring at Preacher's knife, which glistened in the firelight.

"He right, nigger?" Preacher said. "You fixin' to tell us where they at?" The boy looked at Preacher, and slowly moved his head in such a way it might be interpreted in the affirmative.

Preacher started to untie the rope holding the gag in place.

"Now I'ma ask you only one more time, boy," Preacher said. "I'm done foolin' with you."

As soon as the gag was out of his mouth, a remarkable change came over the boy. His expression altered, the fear seemed suddenly to leach out of his eyes and the other thing in them, the one Cain had noticed earlier, took over completely. The boy stared at Preacher, his gaze honed to an edge that would cut. Cain hated this. The whole bloody thing. Hated Preacher for his mindless cruelty. Hated the cold nights, the long days in the saddle, the rain which made his leg ache. Hated these dark, gloomy mountains. Hated the boy for his race and for being stubborn and not giving in to the simple logic of pain. This was why he liked to work alone. He didn't have these problems when he was by himself. He preferred using his wits rather than violence or force to get the job done whenever possible. But in any case, this would be the last of it, he reminded himself again. After this, he would be finished with his foul profession. Of course, he'd said that before, many times, in fact, and then reneged as soon as he had need of money, as soon as his gambling debts or the drinking or womanizing placed him at the mercy of others and his will was no longer his own. But this time he meant it. He would find some other more suitable employment. He might head out west and have done with this gray, dismal land once and for all.

The boy coughed once, hawking phlegm into his mouth. Cain thought, *No, he won't. A stone would have more sense than that.* And yet, Cain was already mulling over the consequences of what the boy was about to do, parsing out what Preacher would do and what his own response would be. A split second before Cain could cry out *Don't*, the boy spit what he had in his mouth at Preacher, hitting him squarely in his narrow snake-face.

"Why you black devil!" he cursed, punching the boy viciously several times in the face. Then Preacher grabbed him by his ears and started to slam his head against the tree. "I'll learn you to spit on me, nigger." The boy was calling out something, something distorted by his head being whacked against the bark. But they were more than a mile away from the boy's village, and well out of hearing range of anything but gunshot. As his head struck the tree trunk, his eyes rolled back into their sockets so only the whites could be seen.

Cain glanced at Strofe, who was sipping on his applejack. "You going to stop him before he kills the boy?"

Reluctantly, Strofe called to him, "That'll be enough, Preacher."

"But the dang nigger spit on me." Preacher cursed, continuing to slam his head against the tree.

"You kill him, we won't get nothin' outa him."

"I won't kill him. Leastways not before he talks," Preacher said. He shoved the gag back into the Negro's mouth and tied it there with the rope.

The boy, his face now a bloody, swollen mess, looked at his tormentor, then angled his gaze toward Cain once more. Cain held the boy's gaze for a moment, then released it and glanced away. He told himself he had nothing to do with this. With Preacher and the others. They were Eberly's concern. Not his. His job was to find the girl and bring her back. He took out his flask again, and had another pull at the laudanum. This time, as always, the effect was far less dramatic. Like an itch that had been scratched too often and no longer brought relief, it was just its own form of pain now.

Instead of stopping, though, Preacher ripped open the boy's shirt and began to cut on him. He'd make these little slashes in the boy's flesh, like designs someone might carve in a piece of wood. Each time he was cut, the boy would jerk and strain violently against the ropes that held him fast. He cried out but only a muffled noise emerged from his mouth.

After a while, Cain couldn't ignore it anymore.

"All right, that'll be enough," Cain called over to Preacher. When he didn't even acknowledge him, Cain hobbled stiffly over to him and aimed a kick at the man's leg, not hard enough to do any real damage but enough to get Preacher's attention.

"The hell you doin'!" the man cried, jumping up and confronting Cain like a bantam rooster in a cockfight. As Cain was well over six feet tall and with Preacher barely five eight, the top of the smaller man's hat reached only to Cain's chin; Preacher had to angle his head back to stare up at him. The blond man was so close that Cain could smell his scent, a hard, metallic odor like the musk of a gutted buck. In his hand he still clutched the bloody knife, and Cain knew if he made a move for his gun, the last image he'd have on this earth would be Preacher's black serpent eyes smiling at him as he shoved the blade into his guts.

"I told you to stop," Cain advised him.

"I don't give a good gawddang what you told me. I ain't some cur to be kicked by the likes of you."

"Then don't act like one."

"I won't abide any man layin' a hand on me."

"I didn't lay a hand on you," Cain said, pointing out the distinction. "And if I had, you wouldn't be in a position to talk about it now."

Preacher glanced down at his own right hand, the one holding the bowie knife, then back up at Cain. He smiled arrogantly, the way a man does who knows he can kill another with impunity. Cain had seen the same sort of expression on men in battle, a kind of boyish glee as they sighted down their barrels just before pulling the trigger.

"If'n you've a mind, go for that fancy gun a yourn," Preacher said, staring up at him. "I'd be happy to oblige you, *Mister* Cain."

Cain didn't say anything, just continued to stare levelly at him. Like a dog discomforted by a man's stare, Preacher finally wavered and looked away.

"Aw, to hell with you," he cursed at last. Then he turned and marched over to where Strofe was sitting. He snatched the bottle of applejack from the other and took a long, angry drink.

"Uppity sum'bitch," he mumbled under his breath.

Cain knelt down in front of the boy.

"You thirsty?" he asked.

The boy just stared at him. Cain released the rope that held the gag, then he reached into his pocket and took out his flask. He unscrewed the top and put it to the boy's lips, which were swollen and bloody from Preacher's blows. He swallowed a little, then began coughing.

"Easy," Cain said. "It's strong."

He held the flask to his lips again, and the boy took another sip.

"What's your name?" He hesitated, so Cain added, "Don't worry, we not after you."

Finally, the boy mumbled, "Joseph." It was one of those biblical names fugitives took on after running north, trying to put their slave identities behind them. How many runaway Josephs and Jameses and Thomases had he come across?

"How long have you lived here, Joseph?" The boy looked over at Preacher, who sat near the fire, slugging down the applejack.

"Five year," the boy replied.

"Where did you live before that?"

"Kentucky. But I haves my papers. I'm a free man now."

"We're not after you. Do you have kin in the village?"

Fearing that he might be endangering them if he said anything, he remained silent.

"Never mind. We're looking for a pair of runaways. You tell us where they are and we'll be on our way."

The boy eyed him warily. "I don't have to tell you nothin'."

"Yes, you do. Have you ever heard of something called the Fugitive Slave Law? Well, it says that anybody, black or white, free or slave, is required by law to help in the apprehension of a runaway. That means you *have* to help, too. That's the law. Somebody's property was illegally removed from its rightful owner and we're here to see to it that it's returned to him."

"Like you done stole my eggs?"

Cain couldn't help but smile at both the logic and the pluck of such a comment.

"See what a cheeky nigger he is," Preacher called over.

"Just tell us where they are and nothing will happen to you or to your people. I promise."

He looked at Cain, searching his eyes to see if he could trust him. "We gots no runaways here. They's all freemen."

"But we know they're here," Cain insisted. "The boy wrote a letter saying he was living at the settlement called Timbucto. You have nothing to be ashamed of. You're a brave lad. We're going to find them one way or another, so why don't you save yourself a lot of trouble and just tell me the truth."

"I *am* tellin' da trufe. We gots no runaways," the boy said.

"Lyin' gawddang nigger," Preacher cussed. "If'n you'd kept your nose out of it, Cain, I'da had him singin' like a songbird by now."

Cain leaned into the boy and whispered, "I mean you no harm, Joseph. I promise. But if you don't tell me where they are, that man over there is going to hurt you some more. I don't want that. And I know you sure as hell don't want that either. So just tell me where they are."

The Negro looked from Cain to Preacher and back to Cain again.

Finally he said softly, so softly only Cain could hear him, "Don't know nothin' 'bout no girl. The boy he been here. But he gone now."

"Where did he go?"

"He be workin' for Captain Brown."

"Brown? John Brown?"

"Yessum, that be him," the boy replied.

Cain had, of course, heard of the infamous Brown. Kansas Brown and his boys. Osawatomie Brown. Captain Brown of the famous battle of Black Jack, pitting his Free-Soilers against the Border Ruffians. A monster to those of the South, a man capable of taking innocent men out of their homes in the middle of the night and butchering them with machetes and broad-axes before the horrified eyes of their families. With that business out west the year before, the entire country knew him, or at least knew *of* him. Most reasonable people knew that the fight over the soul of Kansas was a prelude to the much larger contest over the nation's soul. That the bloodshed out there was just a taste of what it would be like if war was to come, or rather, *when* it came. You couldn't go into a saloon or gambling establishment or livery in all of Richmond without hearing the name John Brown bantered about. For the southerner, he epitomized the meddling, hypocritical, immoral North, a place that lacked any sort of honor or code of decency. If there was going to be trouble between the South and the North, it would come because of someone like this Brown. Cain then asked the boy where Brown lived, and the boy explained that his farm was in North Elba.

"Just a ways over that mountain," replied the boy, pointing toward the north.

Turning, Cain called to the others, "All right. Let's saddle up, boys."

"Why?" Strofe asked.

"They're not here."

"That what he tell you?" said Strofe.

"Hell, you ain't puttin' stock in what some lyin' nigger tells you?" Preacher said.

"The boy was here but now he's working on a farm nearby. And the girl can't be far off. We find him, we find her."

They started to break camp.

"What do we do with him?" Strofe asked, pointing toward the Negro boy.

"I say we take him with us," Preacher offered. "Big strong buck like that, he has to fetch five hundred or better on the block."

"We're not taking him," Cain said, saddling his horse. "We don't have a warrant for him. Besides, you heard him, he's a freeman."

At this, Preacher laughed a high-pitched cackle, his blond hair falling into his angular face. "Shee-it," he cried. "Like papers makes a rat's turd of a different. Them traders down in Richmond ain't gonna worry about no damn bill of sale or a warrant."

"I'm not some blackbirder," Cain said.

"Well, la-de-da for you," Preacher scoffed. "Slave catcher, blackbirder. They's all the same in my book. We're all of us catchin' niggers."

"No, we're not all the same. I'm carrying out the law."

"You think it makes a nevermind to that boy who brings him back?" Preacher said.

"What you're talking about is common thievery. I'll have none of it."

"Don't get all high-and-mighty on me, Cain. My folks never owned no slaves."

He stared at Cain with a gaze full of insinuation, as if somehow he'd known that Cain's father had owned slaves. Preacher was still smarting from being struck earlier and looking to pay Cain back.

"I'll have no part of it," Cain said again.

"Suit yourself," Preacher scoffed as he stood up. "More split three ways than four."

"I said no," Cain repeated. But Preacher disregarded him. He got up and walked over to the pack mule and started to take the shackles out of the saddlebags. When he turned around he walked straight into the muzzle of Cain's drawn revolver.

"I *said* we're not taking him. Now put those back."

Preacher didn't make a move to turn around. He stared past the barrel at Cain.

"You best be willin' to use that thing, Cain," Preacher said.

"I assure you, I am."

Cain felt a hot, bitter rage well up in him at the man, felt this hammering commence in his temples.

Preacher smiled that loony, gat-toothed smile of his. "Ain't so good at cipherin', are you, Cain. They's three of us and only one of you. What do you say, boys?" he said to the Strofe brothers. "We could split the money 'twixt us."

Cain didn't avert his gaze, kept it trained on Preacher, the way you wouldn't look away from a rattler that was coiled and about to strike. The other's eyes were glossy and black, and looking into them was like looking into a well whose bottom you couldn't estimate.

"Hell, you ain't man enough," Preacher scoffed, taunting him. The two stood locked like this for another moment, before Preacher said, "See. I knowed you was just talk." He pushed the gun from his face and brushed by Cain, moving toward the boy. That's when Cain felt something crackle in his skull just behind his brows, as if a stiff birch rod had been snapped in two by a pair of strong hands. He wheeled and struck Preacher with the gun barrel across the back of head, knocking him to the ground. Then he pounced on him, shoving the gun into Preacher's face.

"I should kill you," Cain hissed at him. "Do you hear me, you son of a bitch?"

The Strofe brothers were up then, calling to him, but their voices reached him as if from a great distance. Or perhaps it was that he had left, gone off someplace. The only thing he was aware of was that crackling in his head.

"Mr. Cain." It was Little Strofe's voice that finally reached him. "Mr. Cain."

He glanced up and saw Little Strofe standing there.

"You all right, Mr. Cain?"

Cain slowly released the hammer, holstered his gun, and stood.

Preacher scrambled to his feet. "When this is all over, Cain, me and you's a score to settle. Remember that." He headed back over to his horse and mounted up.

"Let me deal with him from now on, all right?" Strofe said to Cain.

"Fine by me. Just make sure you do."

"What do we do with him?" he asked, nodding at the Negro.

Cain walked over to the boy and squatted down. He took out his pocketknife and sawed the rope holding him halfway through.

"It will take you some while to work the rest of your way through that," he told the boy. "By then we'll be long gone. Don't concern yourself with this. It's not your affair." Then he took out a silver dollar and shoved it into the boy's coat pocket. "For the eggs."

4

They rode hard toward North Elba, trying to make the village before word got there ahead of them. But the road was little better than a deer path that meandered through the thick forest of birch and ash, tamarack and mountain laurel. Emerging finally from the woods, they came upon a clearing with a small cabin in the middle of it, and they decided to stop there and inquire the way to Brown's place. Before they could even dismount, an old man came shuffling crablike from around the side of the cabin.

"Don't get down," he commanded. He was carrying an ancient fowling piece, and he appeared equally old, wizened and bent-backed. From his sunken, toothless maw tobacco juice dribbled out and down his chin. When Cain mentioned Brown's name, the old man eyed them suspiciously.

"That fellow John Brown, you mean?" he asked, moving the business end of his gun ever so slightly upward.

"The same," Cain replied. He wasn't sure if the old man was sympathetic to Brown's cause or not. You never could tell with these Yankees. For all he knew, he was a personal friend of his and about to let fly with a barrelful of bird shot. Cain cautiously slid back the flap of his greatcoat so his holster was clear, then he removed the leather loop that held down the Colt's hammer. This wasn't lost on the old man, though; he cocked the shotgun, marshaled his sunken lips into a smile aimed at Cain, and spat disdainfully on the ground.

"If you're more of his nigger-loving rabble come to stir up trouble, you can just keep on riding."

Behind him, Preacher snorted. "You watch what you're doin' with that thing, old man," he said. "'Fore somebody gets hisself hurt."

"We're not part of all that," Cain explained to the man.

"You ain't one of his ab'litionists?"

"Hell, no," Preacher piped up. "We're after us a coupla runaway niggers."

Cain glanced over his shoulder at Preacher, who touched the brim of his cap and smiled at him.

"We're looking for property that was stolen from a Mr. Eberly of Henrico County, Virginia," Cain explained. "We have reason to believe he's hiding out at Brown's farm."

The old man stared at them for a long time, then spat on the ground again. Finally, he raised a bony finger and pointed toward the northwest.

"Take the road through the pass. On the far side follow the Ausable till it bends east. Then you want to cross it and head north half a mile. That's his place. Has some fine Devon cattle. If he stuck to that he might be a passable farmer."

Cain thanked the man and they turned to leave.

"He don't speak for all of us," the man called after them. "For all I give a damn, you can have every last darkie back."

They had to cross a high, narrow pass that cut between two looming mountains whose summits were hidden in the clouds. Lower down, the road was muddy from spring rains and thaws, yet as they began the ascent it soon hardened and turned frozen. Much of the higher ground was covered in ice or snow. The horses lost their footing, and for the last couple of miles up the pass, the riders had to dismount and walk them. The dogs ran along beside them, playing in the snow and yapping loudly. The mountain to their right was covered with birch and spruce and tamarack, while the entire south face of the opposite one was a sheer rock cliff. Waterfalls plunged hundreds of feet, before crashing with a deafening roar into a fast-moving river that churned below the road. With his spyglass, Cain saw, up amid the crags, aeries with eagles nesting in them. The day was one of oddly indeterminate nature. While it had remained cold and raw, one minute it would be raining, the next snowing so hard they could barely see, and the one after that the sun would break through the clouds and they would feel themselves sweating as they ascended the pass. By late afternoon, shafts of bold sunlight had torn through the ragged cloud cover and swept over the earth like God's own hand claiming possession.

Cain noticed that Little Strofe was limping as he walked his mule up the snowy pass.

"How are you holding up?" he asked the man.

"My f-feets are near 'bouts f-froze solid, Mr. Cain," Little Strofe replied.

Cain had him mount Hermes, who was extremely sure-footed, and they continued on up the pass. In a small grove of tamaracks near the summit, they stopped and built a fire so Little Strofe could warm his feet. Cain removed from his saddlebags a pair of clean, dry socks and tossed them to Little Strofe.

"Much obliged, Mr. Cain," the man said.

They only stayed long enough to fill their bellies a little and warm themselves. It was getting on toward dark and Cain didn't want to get stuck on the mountain during the night. If it snowed up here they'd be in trouble, he knew. They had no experience in this sort of weather. So they pushed hard with what little light remained, and by dusk they had made it off the mountain and down into a wide, rolling valley. On the banks of the river, they decided to make camp for the night. They lit a lantern and Little Strofe began fixing supper, fried corn pone and dried beef and a pot of strong coffee. They ate in a stony silence, the dispute between Cain and Preacher from earlier that day still lingering in the air like a bad smell. Preacher took his plate and went off by himself to eat. Now and then he'd glare at Cain. Cain knew he would have to be careful from now on. If push came to shove, he couldn't count on the Strofe boys. They might not side with Preacher, but he also knew their loyalties were with Eberly, not him. He doubted Preacher would try anything until after they got the girl. But who knows? One thing was for certain: he'd have to watch his back.

After eating, Strofe got out his bottle of applejack, took a sip, offered it to Cain, who declined. Then Strofe tossed it over to Preacher, who took a long drink and wiped his mouth on the back of his sleeve.

"This nigger gal," Preacher called to Strofe. "She must be somethin' real special."

Strofe shrugged. His stomach was bothering him again, and he sat there rubbing it, occasionally belching and farting.

"Heard tell she's a blue-eyed nigger," Preacher said. "Saw me a albino nigger once in a traveling show."

"That right?" Strofe commented.

"Yes, indeedy. All white. Even his hair. And his eyelashes was pink, like a hog's." He took another long drink, then a short one on top of that, as if to wash the first one down. "You 'spect Eberly's ridin' her?" he said to Strofe.

"If he be, tain't none of your concern," Strofe said.

"Just figurin' the old man's having him some dark meat on the side," Preacher joked. "Why else he putting up all this money to get one nigger gal back?"

"And what's it to you?"

"No skin off my ass," Preacher said with a shrug of his thin shoulders. "Just saying this one must be somethin' extry special is all."

"All's you got to fret about, Preacher, is catching 'em. That's if you want to get paid."

"If she's as fine as y'all make out, maybe I'll take me some in trade."

"Mr. Eberly don't want a hand laid on her," Strofe proclaimed sternly. "You hear me, Preacher?"

"Yeah, I hear you."

At that Strofe cursed suddenly, stood up, and rushed off into the woods to relieve himself. They could hear him making groaning sounds.

"Hell, the way I see it," Preacher continued, speaking to no one in particular, "what the old man don't know won't hurt him. Besides, if I was to put a young'un in the oven, he'd be gettin' back two loaves for the price of one."

He laughed at his own joke. Glancing over at Little Strofe, he said, "What about you? Wouldn't you be wantin' to g-get yourself a little dark p-pussy?"

Little Strofe blushed at this sort of talk. A religious fellow, he didn't like swearing or cussing of any kind, and talk of women like this turned his pale complexion pink and set him to a flurry of stammering.

"Hell, I bet you ain't never had you any pussy a'tall," Preacher teased. "Black, white, or yeller."

Instead, Little Strofe got up and went to see about his dogs.

"Why don't you leave him be?" Cain said to Preacher.

"Just funnin' with him is all. And besides, I don't got to answer to the likes of you."

Later, Little Strofe came over and sat down near Cain. He offered Cain a fid of tobacco. Cain, who didn't chew, took a bite anyway just to be friendly.

"That P-preacher's a mean'un," Little Strofe said.

Cain nodded in agreement.

They were silent for a time. Then Little Strofe said in an undertone, "She run before."

"Who? The Negress?"

"A-huh."

"When?"

"It was some time back. And we had to g-go chase after her. But it weren't nothing like this. She didn't even m-make it out of the county that time." He paused for a moment, then added, "That the time she cut him."

"Cut who?"

"Why, Mr. Eberly. Cut him p-purty good, too. She knows her way around a knife, that gal. Headstrong, she is. Hit's almost like she don't know she's a nigger."

"Where'd she cut him?"

"Got him in the hand. Near 'bout took off his thumb."

Cain remembered suddenly Eberly rubbing his palm, the raised scar he'd noticed. Then he recalled something the old man had told him—that she'd never been under the lash. "What did she receive as punishment?"

The man wagged his head. "Nothin'."

"She knifed her master and he didn't punish her?"

Glancing over his shoulder to see if anyone was listening, he explained, "She got Mr. Eberly wrapped around her little bitty finger."

"Why did she cut him?" Cain asked.

Little Strofe shrugged nervously. "'Tain't none of my business. I w-work for Mr. Eberly and he can do whate'er he wants. I'm gonna turn in, Mr. Cain. G-good night."

When he'd finished praying, he lay between his dogs. He stroked them and whispered to them, and in a moment he was snoring loudly, as oblivious to the world as his hounds.

Cain had no such luck with sleep. He took several sips from his flask to no avail. The leg continued to throb and he cursed the damned appendage and wondered if it would have been better had he lost it completely. At least then it wouldn't ache, though, of course, he'd known men from the war who'd lost legs and still felt pain in them. Ghost pain, they called it.

He put his spectacles on and from his saddlebags got out his tattered copy of Milton and tried reading. He took pleasure in the act and would usually read well into the night, whether he was back in his boardinghouse in Richmond or on the trail of a runaway. Where some, like his father, could be lulled to sleep by reviewing ledgers and account books, or others took comfort in perusing the Bible before bed, Cain had his Milton—or in a pinch, Dante or Homer or Shakespeare. He liked reading about men of grand visions, of bold imagination, even though he knew he was not one himself. The Bible had men of grand visions, it was true, but he didn't care for it particularly. Cain thought the book, especially the Old Testament, just so much empty bluster, less about God and morals and right ways of living, and more about vengeance and the killing of one's fellow man over the flimsiest of excuses.

D espite his mother's influence and his love of Milton, Cain was not a religious man, although as a boy he'd attended service every Sunday. Even after his mother's death his father made him and TJ go. Mr. Cain thought such customary duties good for a young boy's development, especially for one without the benefit of the softening effects of maternal influence. After all, they would someday be called upon to take themselves a wife and become responsible fathers and respected members of their communities, and such regular and dutiful patterns of behavior would be expected of them. Mr. Cain, a hardworking, driven man, was someone who extolled the virtues of order and routine and hard work. So rain or shine, he would hitch up the wagon to his best team of Morgans (he was not averse to parading what material success he had attained), and he'd instruct Lila, their Negro housekeeper, to get the boys looking presentable as the sons of a modestly successful Virginia planter ought to be when going to church. Lila would scrub their faces until they shone and see to it that their good clothes were clean, their coats brushed, their hair combed. "Ain't gone to church lookin' like a coupla ragamuffins," she'd tell them. Then the three of them would get in the wagon and ride the five miles to the Methodist Church in Nottoway Chase, a small town in the western piedmont of Virginia, within sight of the Blue Ridge Mountains.

On their way, they rode in silence past the cemetery where Cain's mother and younger brother who'd died in infancy were buried, never once stopping there. If the subject of their mother's grave chanced to come up, Mr. Cain would turn inward, grim-faced, his eyes filled with a fierce gleam Cain could never tell was sadness or anger. He'd pass on to church without a word. Yet his father never seemed a particularly religious man to Cain's way of thinking. Church was just something he did, the way he might walk his fields of an evening, surveying the progress of his crops or overseeing the hog-butchering, or the way he might attend the meeting of the International Union of Tobacco Growers in town. Or the way he'd taken a wife or fathered sons—something that was part of the business of life.

Besides, the weekly ride into town served a highly pragmatic function as well, for his father was, above all else, a pragmatic man who kept his eye on the main chance. While there, he would use the time profitably to buy feed or supplies or a new bridle, perhaps get the Richmond paper to see what prime-quality burley was expected to fetch in the fall, or pick up the new farming supply catalog he'd ordered from MacKenzie and Sons, direct from Glasgow, Scotland. Or once a month, with the same grim pragmatism, Cain's father would visit a certain buxom, blond woman who lived in Cowart's boardinghouse down near the railroad tracks. Cain had spied her once in the second-story window of Cowart's as they rode out of town. Their father would give Cain and his brother two bits each and tell them he'd meet them at a specified time over at the general store. Such an impulse of their father's for this woman was, Cain suspected, of the same species of emotion as that of a bull mounting a heifer, something to be acknowledged and rectified, so that he was then able to move on with the more important affairs of business.

Cain could remember his mother saying grace before meals and teaching him to offer up his prayers at bedtime or reading to him from the Bible. His father, though, had always considered "Sabbath" duties more than adequate religion, that saying prayers and grace and all that nonsense throughout the week was an excessive show, almost as bad as the damn Baptists. He thought their mother would make his boys soft with her continual praying and her reading of books. If his boys wanted to read anything at bedtime, he would give them a book on animal husbandry, which was, after all, their destined future.

Cain was the elder of two boys. His brother, Tiberius Julius, a name mercifully shortened to TJ, was two years his junior. There had been a third brother, Claudius Nero, who'd been carried off by a fever at six months, and his passing seemed the last nail in his mother's coffin. His father, whose only reading besides ledger books and husbandry journals was Roman history, had named his three boys after emperors, as if tempting the hand of fate toward greatness but perhaps merely bestowing on them greater prospects for failure. Mr. Cain was a taciturn and distant man, of narrow but certain vision and erect bearing, not hard-hearted so much as hardened by facts, someone who felt that emotions, at least the visible sort, were manifest signs of weakness in a man. A widower, he'd assumed as his job the sober one of dragging unwilling boys into the thorny realm of manhood, turning them into good farmers, loyal Virginians and southerners, fair masters, stolid husbands, and eventually, strict fathers themselves—more or less in that order. Cain being the eldest, it was naturally assumed he'd take over the farm when the time came. Yet it was TJ who was always more at home with the tools, not to mention the mind-set, of agrarian matters—more adept than Cain with plowshares and hayracks and scythes, more interested in talk of planting moons and the chance of rain, with the price of seed and tobacco and slaves. Even as a boy Cain had found all of that exceedingly tedious. On Sunday afternoons, when he was momentarily set free from chores, he especially loved to ride up to the top of a hill some miles behind his house, and there he'd sit under a big poplar tree and read a book he'd brought along, or just stare out over the hazy Blue Ridge to the west, wondering what lay beyond them. He'd always had a wanderlust in him, a sense of adventure that could hardly be bounded by the circumspect and mundane existence of a farmer.

It wasn't that he didn't love the South, for he did, with all his heart and soul; he loved its hills and mountains and woods, its slow-moving muddy rivers and tangled swamps, its deep swales and lush green lowlands, the vibrant insect ticking that filled a summer's night with life. He loved the land of the South as both home and country, and, too, as a way of thinking and being. He just never took to the notion of farming, of being tied down to a certain plot of earth, bound by dirt and growing seasons. He much preferred to fish and hunt, to scour the fields and woods behind their land, to ride a good horse across into the mountains to the west of their farm. He'd started hunting when he was eight, when his father gave him his grandfather's old Kentucky musket, the one he'd used in the Revolution. He could hardly raise the cumbersome thing then, but he soon learned to shoot it, to become an excellent marksman, to track game through the deepest hollows and thickest woods, to hunt deer and bear, wild boar and catamount, turkey and coon and possum. He was also a superb horseman, several times having won races at the county fair.

Cain and his brother had received a passable education. In addition to their mother's having read to them every night when she was alive, their country schoolmaster, the white-haired Mr. Tyler Beauregard, taught them enough Latin to read Cicero and Virgil, enough Shakespeare and Milton to smooth the rough edges of their rustic upbringing, enough Johnson and Dryden and Pope to have developed a critical ear for their native language. Before bed, Cain would read Scott's tales of medieval knights, Defoe's *Robinson Crusoe*, the adventures of Cooper's Natty Bumppo. He imagined a life filled with daring, one that was open to vast possibilities. After reading the accounts of Nelson at Trafalgar or the brave stand of those at the Alamo, he and his brother would act out scenes of heroism in the hayloft, falling finally amid a hail of imagined bullets and equally imagined glory. Cain could not have told you precisely what that other life would look like, except that it would be filled with gallant and noble deeds and that it would not follow the dull routine of a farmer.

When Cain and his brother were older, they'd sometimes accompany their father the sixty miles to the big city of Richmond, to sell cattle or tobacco or to buy supplies or to purchase another field hand as the Cain farm grew and prospered. After the tedious business of life had been conducted, Mr. Cain would permit, albeit reluctantly, his sons to taste some of the city's entertainment and culture. They'd be allowed to go to the theater or a museum or to the lecture hall to hear someone speak on the subject of efficient slave management. But Cain much preferred to visit Hoynby's, a bookseller on Grace Street near the Capitol. There he'd spend a pleasant hour or two walking up and down the aisles, touching the musty-smelling books, reading passages of *Tom Jones* or a young author named Dickens, debating whether to spend his meager savings on a copy of Chapman's Homer or the collected works of Coleridge. Once when Cain visited the city, he attended a production of *Macbeth* with Edwin Booth playing the title role; another time he had gone to the Exchange Hotel, to hear a Mr. Edgar Allan Poe lecture on "The Poetic Principle."

As the brothers got older and traveled to the city by themselves, in addition to the culture, Cain took in the more illicit attractions the city had to offer: the horse races and gambling houses, the faro banks and cockfighting pits, the taverns and houses of ill-repute down near the James River. His brother TJ, sober and hardworking, took after their father and was disinclined to engage in such activities. Cain loved his brother, but as they grew older he had less and less in common with him. TJ, though, remained loyal, never telling their father about his brother's escapades, sometimes even lying to cover for Cain's mistakes. When Cain was sixteen he became enamored of an Irish whore named Eileen McDuffy, a lovely girl with flaming red hair and sparkling green eyes. Beneath all the debauched behavior, Cain had an uncorrupted romantic spirit; the fact that Eileen McDuffy had made a living by selling her body to men only made him love her all the more intensely. He wanted to save her, to carry her away. He'd write her letters, grand, youthfully hyperbolic missives, in which he quoted Byron and Shelley, and to which, of course, she never responded. He ached for her so much that one night, he got on his horse and rode all the way to Richmond and demanded that she see him. When he was told that she was busy with another client, he left and tried to comfort his broken heart in the tavern. Drunk and wielding a pistol, he returned to the brothel and went among the rooms, searching for Eileen McDuffy, yelling out that he loved her. A couple of men who worked there finally grabbed the young Cain and tossed him out into the muddy street on his ear.

For a time his father cast a blind eye on such practices by his son, figuring it was merely a necessary part of growing up, of his worldly education, something all young men needed to get out of their system before they settled down to the serious matter of family and farm and responsibilities. But as this sort of behavior continued, the senior Cain worried that Augustus was habitually inclined to a life of debauchery and dissipation. When he came across a draft of a love letter to this Eileen McDuffy, he realized the time had come to lay down the law. He forbade Cain to see her again and wouldn't let his son go to Richmond anymore; he tried to stanch the flow of money into his hands, feeling that without funds he couldn't enjoy such amusements as gambling and faro banks and whoring; and he tried to occupy every minute of his waking day with work. By working him to the bone he felt he'd be too dog-tired for the other business.

At the same time, he also tried to give him more responsibilities on the farm and to get him used to seeing that this was his rightful vocation and his legitimate future. In short, his fate. He would seek his counsel before purchasing a new stud bull or ask whether they should clear and put under plow ten more acres of woodland down near the river.

He also began to press for the match, which had until then been implicit, between Augustus and the pretty daughter of his next-door neighbor, a wealthy plantation owner named Throgmorton. Sometimes of an evening, his father would pour young Cain a bourbon and they would sit on the back porch, which looked west out toward the more impressive plantation of their neighbor. James Throgmorton was said to be the wealthiest man in five counties; his farm was some two thousand acres of the richest land in all the Piedmont, requiring over a hundred slaves to work it. It was no secret that Mr. Cain had long held out the hope that his elder son would someday marry Alexandra Throgmorton and that their two properties might be merged into an estate that would be of truly impressive proportions. His father might lift his glass toward the west and say to Cain, "Someday, Augustus, if you play your cards right, this will all be yours." Yet these were not the sort of cards that Cain wished to play, not the hand he would want to be dealt. Instead of rejoicing, Cain looked upon such a prospect as a man sentenced to life imprisonment would look upon his cell. He shuddered at the thought that his life would become just like his father's, parceled out into growing seasons and ledger books. When he told his father that while he was fond of Alexandra he did not love her, Mr. Cain said that fondness was a start, that love would follow.

"But I won't ever love her, Father," he said to Mr. Cain.

"Son, this world isn't guided by love," he said. "Besides, you can always run off to Richmond and have some fun with that whore of yours anytime you've a mind to."

Though he wanted to tell Mr. Cain that all of it—Alexandra and her father's estate, his future here running a farm—wasn't what he wanted, he could only manage in defense, "She wouldn't make me happy."

"What you need to understand, Augustus, is you don't get to pick the life you want. Life picks you," his father advised. "Besides, Throgmorton owns over a hundred slaves."

Cain wanted to tell him that he didn't need a single slave for the life he had imagined for himself, but, of course, he didn't. His father wouldn't understand. To Mr. Cain, owning slaves was something both highly desirable and equally honorable. He used to bring his boys to the auctions in Richmond. Cain was seven or eight when he'd seen his first auction. His father would inspect the Negroes on the block, feeling their arms and legs, estimating the amount of work each could perform, forcing their mouths open to inspect their teeth the way one would a horse—all of this as much intended for the education of his sons as for the appraisal of the slave's value. "That one's lame in the knee," he'd whisper to the boys. Or, "They got that buck all fattened up but he'd got scrofula." One morning they went to Odd Fellows Hall, where they held auctions. A sign out front read:

Yardly & Scruggs
Auctioneers for Sale of Fine Negroes
Auction today at 10 in the morning
Porters Always Available

Just then, they saw a line of Negroes being led into the hall. They were bound hand and foot by chains, and connected by a length of rope tied to a metal collar around their necks. The slave trader conveying them from the holding pens on Lumpkin's Alley to the auction block in Odd Fellows was screaming at them. He whipped them savagely with a short cat-o'-nine-tails because they'd been moving too slowly. One old woolly-headed Negro who shuffled with a bad limp seemed to bring out an especial hostility in the slave trader. He flogged the old man mercilessly, calling him every foul name he could think of, this despite the fact that women and children were passing by within earshot.

"That fellow ought to be taken out and horsewhipped himself," Mr. Cain said to his sons. It wasn't so much that his father was averse to using corporal punishment with slaves as it was that he thought it should be used sparingly, and then only when necessary, the way you might use a corrective to purge something bad from your system or a hard bit in the mouth of an overly rambunctious horse. His father showed the same outrage when he heard stories of a slave owner having relations with a slave woman or siring a mulatto child. Cain's father considered it the lowest form of indecency, an affront and violation not so much to the Negro race as it was to the white race, which debased itself by such an act. His own visits to the woman at the boardinghouse were, he obviously felt, of a completely different order, she being white and—at least for a price—willing. But to coerce a woman supposedly under your care and guardianship to such a thing was, to Mr. Cain's view, a corruption of everything decent and noble in the southern character.

His father owned one slave named Darius, an incorrigible buck who ran off many times. This slave seemed out to prove all of Mr. Cain's theories about Negroes' need for guidance and a strong hand. Each time he ran, Cain, a good tracker and horseman, would hunt him down, with Darius sometimes getting as far as the Blue Ridge Mountains, a day's hard ride to the west. They didn't need to hire slave catchers or the patty rollers who patrolled the county roads on horseback, looking for runaways, not when the young Cain himself could do a better job and for no cost. Besides, he secretly looked forward to the boy's running, for it broke up the monotony of farm life. He got a reprieve from the tedium of looking at the backside of a mule, and he considered hunting Darius an "adventure," more sport than anything else. He didn't even use hunting dogs, or the specially bred Cuban "Negro" dogs that some, like Mr. Pugh, the farmer down the road, raised to hunt human prey. Cain thought dogs an unfair advantage, sort of like shooting fish in a barrel. He could follow a trail in a blinding rainstorm, through swamp and bottomland, into thickets of rhododendron and laurel so dense and tangled you couldn't ride a horse but had to crawl on hands and knees. He knew each swamp and swale, holler and ridge, cave and corner of the county that Darius would try to hide in. Sometimes the Negro would make the Blue Ridge, and Cain would track him there, occasionally not finding him for weeks. Eventually, though, he always did. When

Darius was apprehended, he gave up without incident, smiling and fawning, wagging his head as if it were indeed just a game to him as well, and he rode peacefully back to Nottoway Chase behind Cain on the horse, without need of shackles or rope, and without the least coercion.

"When the hell you going to learn, Darius?" Cain had said to him, though privately he wished he wouldn't stop.

"Reckon when I's too old ta run, massa," replied the Negro, who was twice Cain's age.

Of course, for Darius his attempts at freedom had their more serious repercussions. Once returned, he would be lectured by Cain's father in front of the dozen other slaves, and maybe be given ten or twenty good ones with a silk cracker. Mr. Cain didn't administer punishment out of vengeance or spite or anger as some masters might, but calmly, even attentively, as a means of his edification, the way a schoolmaster might cane one of his students. He would say to his son, "He that knoweth his master's will and doeth it not, shall be beaten with many stripes." Cain looked upon Darius's attempts at fleeing his father's farm in two more or less contradictory ways. On the one hand, he agreed with his father, seeing Darius's behavior as a childish willfulness, a stubborn, self-destructive force he could not understand, a mental aberration in the Negro character that needed to be curbed with firm resolve. Why would someone want to run away from a place where all his needs were taken care of, where he only had to do what he was told and life would unfold agreeably for him.

But on the other, he could secretly identify with Darius's desire to strike out on some new path, as Cain himself longed to do. Cain could not imagine wasting his life hoeing a furrow in a field, picking cotton or tobacco, whether it was his own or someone else's. Of course, the fundamental difference was that Cain was white and Darius black, that the former had the innate capacity to make decisions for himself, and thus had been given free will, and the latter didn't. It was all as simple, as clear-cut, as that.

He became so adept at hunting down his father's runaway slave, so skilled at tracking and knowing his ways, that other slave owners and farmers and planters in and around Nottoway Chase would call upon Cain to help them find their runaways, too. He soon realized he was good at it, had an aptitude for the trade, a nose for his prey. As with hunting deer or bear, he found that he could think like the thing he was hunting, know where he'd go, where he would try to hide, how he would act if cornered. Soon he acquired something of a reputation: Augustus Cain, slave catcher. He was proud of his so-called notoriety, delighted in the fact that wealthy planters or respected townspeople would come to him, a mere youth, for his advice, his expertise, his knowledge. They treated him with respect, and he felt important, something he'd never felt working on his father's farm.

Mostly he worked for them as a matter of courtesy, though when he refused their money they would usually offer him an expensive gun or a fine saddle horse, which he accepted as a courtesy of one gentleman to another. Sometimes over cigars and whiskey, there would even be the not-so-veiled allusion to the proffered hand of some daughter in marriage. Cain was, after all, considered one of the most eligible bachelors in Nottoway Chase. Tall and raw-boned, perhaps a little too long of face, yet with his curly brown hair and those sad gray eyes, he was the object of much speculation among the females of town. Often, wearing a broad-brimmed felt hat sporting an ostrich plume and set at a jaunty angle on his head, Cain cut a dashing figure as he galloped wildly down Main Street astride an impressive roan gelding, scattering chickens and pedestrians alike. At the county fair he'd usually win the horse race or the turkey shoot, or be asked to judge a pie contest. When he passed by, the heart of every marriageable woman, and, for that matter, many a married woman, too, would go all aflutter at the sight of the young Augustus Cain.

The name, though, that was most often mentioned in the same breath with his was that of Alexandra Throgmorton, the daughter of Cain's neighbor. He had known her all his life. As a child she was called Lexi, a tomboy with blond hair and hard, bronzed arms and the lithe body of a boy. She used to fish and ride horses with Cain and his brother TJ. When the Cains were invited to the Throgmorton residence for dinner, the three adolescents would mount up and ride down to the creek that divided the imposing Throgmorton estate from the much smaller Cain farm. Sometimes the three of them would go fishing or swimming in its cool dark waters. Lexi handled herself well on a horse, rode as skillfully as TJ, and almost as well as Cain himself. She and Cain would race back to the house, she on a fast bay named Princess, her long blond hair flying backward as she rode.

Perhaps because it was her fate, she grew into one of those delicate creatures of southern womanhood, demure and charming with a reserve that seemed almost instinctual. Hardly unattractive in a pale, genteel sort of fashion, she had no shortage of suitors, especially those with an eye to the main chance, because of her father's wealth. Yet Cain would have had to be blind not to notice the coy looks and meaningful smiles she began to throw his way. Once, the Throgmortons had held a grand affair at their house, inviting nearly half the county. Alexandra—as she was known now—quickly found her dance card full, but near the end of the night had managed to find Cain and ask him to dance. He had felt the stiffness of her stays pressing into him and he breathed in the heady fragrance of her hair and perfume, the appealing aura of her newly found womanness. Later, under the pretense of getting a breath of air, she suggested they take a walk in the moonlight, which they did. Stopping under a tulip poplar, she had looked up at him, smiling expectantly. She was lovely, he thought, and, feeling she expected him to kiss her, he did so. He'd always been fond of Lexi, held her in high regard as a friend, and he had no doubt she'd make a wonderful wife—for some man. He understood, too, that both families expected *him* to be that man. Perhaps he even expected it of himself. Somewhere down the line, he supposed it was a thing destined, inevitable that he marry her, just as it was inevitable that he would take over his father's farm. The word *love* never entered his thoughts. At least not the sort that existed between a husband and a wife. Not even the sort he'd felt for Eileen McDuffy, the whore.

Alexandra, too, assumed they would be married. After a while she began to treat him as if he were already her husband. She rebuked him when she'd heard of his having gotten so slewed in Richmond that his brother had to lay him out in the back of a wagon and cart him home. Or when they'd ride out into the fields together, sometimes she'd bring up the subject of where they'd eventually build their own house. When Cain remained mute on the topic, Alexandra would say, "You *do* want our own place someday, Augustus? After all, we wouldn't want to live with my parents forever." And Cain, not wanting to hurt her feelings, would finally say, "Of course."

One time a valuable slave of Mr. Throgmorton's named Gabriel had run off and the man had called upon Cain's services. Cain hunted him for nearly a week before apprehending him finally in Charlottesville, where he'd hidden out with a freed aunt. Out of gratitude, Mr. Throgmorton invited him over to his place. In his study lined with vellum-covered books the man had never opened, he plied Cain with Cuban cigars and well-aged Kentucky bourbon. Cain was twenty-five, and Mr. Throgmorton talked not only of Cain's future but also of that of his beloved daughter, too. Like Cain's father, it seemed that Mr. Throgmorton had had designs on uniting their two properties. Nevertheless, Cain didn't cotton to the notion of putting himself in the other man's debt, or of shackling himself to a piece of ground by virtue of marriage. He told Mr. Throgmorton that he liked his daughter very much, to which the man gave him a fatherly pat on the back and poured him another drink. However, somewhere along about Cain's sixth or seventh whiskey that night, Mr. Throgmorton must have made a formal proposal of his daughter's hand, to which Cain must have acceded, or at least hadn't had the heart to refuse, and things were set in motion. The next morning he woke to a splitting headache and to the hearty congratulations of his father on the news that he and Alexandra were finally to be wed. His father thought that his wayward son was at last going to settle down. More than that, his father's dream of uniting the two properties would finally be realized.

B ut that was all a long, long time ago, almost another life. He'd been slave catching for the last ten years or so, ever since he returned, wounded, from the war. He wasn't ashamed of his profession, which was fully sanctioned both by two hundred years of precedent and by the Congress of the United States through the Fugitive Slave Law of 1850. What Cain *had* always found objectionable was the sort of person the slave-catching business attracted, drawn to it like flies to a dead possum. The riffraff and scoundrels, the no 'counts and rogues, the illiterate fools and men of no honor— the human flotsam that became slave catchers and slave traders, blackbirders and agents, auctioneers and jailers. Even the owners. *Especially* the owners. Men like this Eberly. Men who thought they could buy you, heart and soul, to do their bidding, so that you were little better than a nigger yourself. But he couldn't deny the seductive attraction of the money it offered. He could make more in a week's time bringing a slave back than he could doing just about anything else in a year. Besides, when he'd gotten back from the war, hobbling with his bum leg, there wasn't much open to someone like himself. He couldn't go back to Nottoway Chase. From TJ, with whom he maintained an infrequent correspondence, he'd heard that his father had left his brother the farm, and TJ, ever the dutiful son, had gone ahead and done the dutiful thing and married Lexi. Cain hadn't even been surprised when he read that. He even wished them well.

Cain had made a go of a few jobs—as a puddler in the Tredegar Iron Works, a teamster driving horses, even a sheriff's deputy. None of it suited him. All seemed to ask of him what he didn't have to give. Down on his luck, not a rock in his pocket, he chanced to see a wanted ad in the Richmond newspaper:

$100 REWARD!

Ranaway slave. Negro buck named Samuel eloped from my farm in Chesterfield County, 28th inst. Said Negro is about 24 years of age. Dark brown or gingerbread complexion. Has scar over his right eyebrow, about five feet ten inches, bulky made. Clear marks from previous lashings. Has an agreeable personality. Last seen wearing striped pantaloons, a blue frock coat and vest. Samuel has been used to housework. Reads and writes some. May attempt to flee to Cincinnati, Ohio, where he has kin. Will pay anyone for bringing runaway to county jail. Contact Pierce Butler of Miss Lucy plantation.

So he answered the advertisement, got more information about the runaway, and hunted him down. It took him a week, but he caught the man just before he crossed over the Ohio River, and he brought him back and claimed his reward. Not counting gambling, it was just about the easiest money he'd ever made. So he answered another reward notice for a runaway. Then another. And just like back in Nottoway Chase, he quickly gained something of a reputation first in Richmond, then in all of Virginia, for his prowess as a slave catcher. Wealthy planters and factory owners and businessmen from all over soon started to seek him out, looking to have him return a valuable piece of property. Men who knew he could be depended upon, knew he could be discreet. Northerners who resided above the Mason-Dixon line but who secretly owned slaves in the South and didn't want anyone to know about it back home. Or like the big-shot senator from South Carolina, whose son had, as the father put it, "fallen under the spell of a nigger witch" and helped her escape to the North. They trusted him, knew he would not only get their slave back but also keep his mouth shut to boot. Besides, in the past seven years since the Fugitive Slave Act, Cain had seen the need for men in his profession grow, as more slaves took off for the North and the prices that slave owners were willing to pay doubled or even tripled.

The problem was that slave catching was not a vocation Cain had ever seen himself doing, or certainly not for very long. He'd viewed it as something he'd do until something better came along. Problem was, nothing ever did. He told himself that as soon as he had saved up enough he'd pursue another calling. And when he was flush with cash in his pocket, having just brought back a valuable runaway or from his winnings at cards or the faro banks, he would set his mind on that something else, perhaps traveling to Europe or sailing the seven seas. Or his favorite pastime, especially when he was drunk or his head floating in a laudanum haze—heading out to California. He'd always been taken with that possibility. Ever since '49 he'd toyed with the possibility of striking out for the West, seeking his fortune there, as so many others had tried. In all the years he'd been hunting down runaways, he always thought he'd do it for just a bit longer,

one more slave, just *one* more, just until he could get a little ahead.
But then he'd gamble or drink away what little he'd managed to save,
or lavish it on some woman he'd become infatuated with. A while
back, when his luck was running high, he'd won almost a thousand
dollars at a faro bank; he'd decided, once and for all, he *would* quit the
slave-catching profession and with the money he'd finally head out
to California, throwing in his lot with those other forty-niners, those
dreamers and malcontents, searching for a new life out there. He'd
like to see San Francisco. With all the gold out there, he figured he
could make a killing at the card table or faro bank. But once more,
he had managed to squander that away, too, on women and drinking,
and on the laudanum, which had started to get out of hand, as it often
did with Cain.

He took another long drink from his flask. He no longer felt the
ache in his leg, or rather, he no longer cared about it. His head
felt both pinched and loose, the way it got when he'd taken too much
of the laudanum. He heard the lone howl of a wolf somewhere up in
the mountains. It was a sound high pitched and mournful, filled with a
vague sadness made all the more so by the cold wind and the shadowy
mountains, and, too, by Cain's own melancholic bent. He tried to
picture the wolf, to imagine him up on some remote outcropping of
stone, his head angled heavenward. In his imagination the creature
had red, demonlike eyes that seemed to stare right at Cain. He then
gazed off into the darkness surrounding and seeming to creep in on
him. Just at the edge of light from the campfire, his eye chanced to
fall on an image on the trunk of a gnarled hickory tree. A strange
confluence of bark and limb and shadow, and given shape by Cain's
own weary imagination and the conjuring properties of the laudanum.
As he looked upon it, the figure slowly seemed to coalesce, to become
something definite and not merely a figment of his imagination. After
a while he could make out a nose, a mouth, even eyes aflame with a
wolflike red gleam. "Get away," Cain called. Yet it seemed to inch
closer, its mouth gaping wide and in its glare the accusation of some
unstated crime. He picked up a stone and heaved it, but the thing

grew nearer. Finally, Cain reached for his holster lying on the ground beside him, drew his revolver, and fired.

In a moment there was a chaotic scrambling about him. The others appeared suddenly, weapons drawn.

"The hell you shooting at?" Strofe said.

Quickly regaining his senses, Cain mumbled, "I saw something. A wolf, I think."

"Which way, Mr. Cain?" asked Little Strofe, angling his big musket toward the dark.

"Awh, hell," Preacher scoffed. "Ain't no wolf come this close to camp."

"I saw something," Cain insisted. "I tell you I did."

Preacher smiled at him. "He just stewed is all."

5

The predawn morning found Cain awash in a dream of the mestiza girl. A sharp, sweet pain started just behind his breastbone and worked its way up into his mouth and pulsated there like a toothache. It was, though, a pain he was loath to relinquish. In the chilled darkness before sunrise, he lay on the ground, trying to hold on to the dream, clinging to it the way a freezing man might cling to a memory of fire. In it he wasn't wounded nor was she dead, yet at the periphery of his consciousness he sensed both facts as things irrevocable, lurking beyond the frail boundaries of the dream; in fact, such knowledge colored and deepened what he felt, made it all the more poignant, for he sensed the image was ephemeral and would not last. And so, for several moments he remained still, fighting to stay in her warm embrace. But even in the dream, he soon felt the pull of duty, the weight of worldly concerns. *I have to go*, he told her. *Cain*, she cried, pleading in her strange tongue, trying to dissuade him with kisses and the sweet lure of her body. In the next moment, he heard someone come clomping into camp, curse when he stubbed his foot in the semidarkness, and the dream of the girl slipped out of his mind and vanished like smoke on a windy day.

Cain got up and stumbled down to the river, relieved himself, then headed back up to get his straight razor. He washed his face in the dagger-cold water. With his razor he began to hack away at his beard, the first time in nearly three weeks. When his face was clean-shaven, he felt better for it, nearly human.

"See any more a them wolves, Cain?" Preacher taunted when he returned to camp.

After they ate breakfast, they saddled up and rode toward John Brown's farm. The day continued cold, but at least the skies were clear, the sun offering a faint warmth. For the first time they could see the tops of the mountains, which looked to them like arrows of ice piercing the heavens. They reached the place just as the sun was coming over a peak to the east shaped like the head of an elephant. As they had outside the Negro village, they took up a position in the woods where they could watch unseen. Cain took out his spyglass and scanned the place.

"Is that it?" Strofe asked Cain.

"I reckon."

Cain was surprised by Brown's farm, modest, even spartan—a small two-story main house with a barn and several smaller outbuildings, hog pen, chicken coop, corncrib. The other thing he noticed was that the place didn't look as if it had been tended to with more than a cursory hand. The barn roof was badly in need of being reshingled, and a couple of fence posts holding in the cattle were down. One of the hay fields hadn't been cut the previous season and it was rife with ragweed. And the pastureland was strewn with rocks and sapling trees and thistle, which could cut the bag of a milk cow. In front of the main house, some twenty yards away lay a huge boulder, something that looked altogether alien there, as if a part of the moon had broken off and fallen to Earth. Beside it rested a single weathered headstone, whose inscription Cain couldn't make out from this distance. He wondered what his own father would think of a man who ran such a shoddy enterprise. Then again, he supposed that someone hell-bent on a race war wouldn't have much time to concern himself with such mundane things.

For a while nobody stirred out of the house, and save for the frail line of smoke weaving its way from the top of the chimney, the place looked almost abandoned. Finally, though, a young, lanky, red-haired man emerged from the front door and went out to the barn, carrying a milk pail. He was clean-shaven, of medium build, and he walked hunched over, not with the plodding strides of a farmer but with the sullen, distracted steps of a jilted lover. He returned after finishing the milking and entered the house. For a long time after that, they saw no more movement.

"Dang, them Yankees k-keep banker's hours," Little Strofe kidded.

Finally, the door opened again and three men came shuffling out. They stood talking in the dirt path in front of the house, their breaths smoky in the cold air. With his spyglass, Cain inspected them more closely. Two were younger, one the red-haired man they'd seen earlier, the second a tall youth, broad shouldered, with a full beard and dark hair that came to his collar. Both were well made, handsome in an obdurate, uncompromising sort of way, and had enough similarity of feature to suggest they were siblings. They looked to the third as small schoolchildren might view a stern master from whom they expected either enlightenment or severe punishment at any moment. Though facing him, they kept their eyes downcast and waited upon his word. This man was older, in his fifties, of average height, stiff and erect as a gravestone, with a wild bush of gray beard that spilled down his frock coat. He was dressed all in black—hat, vest, coat, homespun wool trousers, though his clothing appeared well worn and a bit on the shabby side. In his hand he held a paper of some sort, which he tapped impatiently against his leg. His face was weathered as a cedar fence post, his deep-set eyes, even at this distance Cain could tell, sharp and forceful. He remained silent for a prolonged time, looking out over his property, as if lost in thought.

Brown's gaze was at once very much that of a man of this world, vigilant and cautious, filled with a crusty shrewdness, like a farmer surveying the lay of his land, taking note of the weather, weighing the chance for success of his crops, whether he should put more land under plow or use it for grazing. At the same time, there was in his stare a muted fierceness, something distant and hard and intractable, otherworldly, even demonic. Cain thought it the look of one who'd seen either paradise or hell, or perhaps both, and could not pry the competing visions from his thoughts. The image seemed seared on his countenance. It put Cain in mind of Satan's words to Beelzebub after their failed rebellion—*But O how fall'n! how chang'd.* That's what Brown seemed like, a man who'd gone through some sweeping alteration. Perhaps, Cain thought, it was what Moses must have looked like when he'd returned from Mount Sinai.

"That him?" Strofe asked.

"I would say so," Cain replied. So here was the infamous abolitionist, the cold-blooded murderer of entire families out in Kansas. Cain had seen a single sketch of Brown in the Richmond paper after the massacres out in Kansas. It bore, he supposed, some slight resemblance to this man, but the sketch was more an artist's caricature, for in it he had appeared like some terrible beast, an animal gone berserk—a rifle in one hand, a bloody machete in the other, his fevered eyes burning with his fanatical mission. At his feet were the bloodied carcasses of women and children, whole families he'd slaughtered in his attempt to keep Kansas free. Just a newspaperman's hyperbole intended to sell papers. Still, Cain had seen such men in his travels north, dangerous men, fanatical abolitionists who would not stop at murder to free the Negro, who would sacrifice anything, all their material possessions, their very lives and those of their children, even the country, to set the black man free. He believed what others had said about Brown, how he was ready, even eager, to die for his ideals. Cain would rather fight ten men who preferred living for what they believed in rather than one like Brown, who didn't give a fig for his own neck. He knew him to be the most dangerous sort of adversary, as his own life was but a pawn in the service of his grand vision.

"Those his boys?" asked Strofe.

Cain shrugged.

From the scabbard on Little Strofe's horse, Preacher had taken out the Boyer and was now aiming it at the man, aligning him along the peep sight.

"What you d-doing with my gun?" Little Strofe asked.

"Could take the bastard out right now."

"Put that away," Strofe said.

"Deserves it for what he done."

"We don't want no truck with him," replied Strofe.

"He's the one brought trouble on his own self. Weren't for his kind, our niggers wouldn't get all these quare notions about running off."

"Let the devil take him," Strofe said. "Mr. Eberly's not paying for his hide."

But Preacher continued to aim the gun at Brown.

"You heard him," Cain said. "Put that damn thing away before it goes off."

Preacher turned so the barrel of the big gun was angled in Cain's direction. "Ain't nothin' gone go off till I wants it to," he said, and smiled. Nonetheless, he got up and went over and put the gun back in the scabbard.

After a few minutes, the three men they were watching stopped talking and headed into the barn. When they emerged finally, Brown's sons were astride a roan and a bay, while Brown himself was seated in a wagon hitched to a large dappled white draft horse. Before they pulled out, Brown called something back toward the barn, and a young Negro came sauntering out. He stood talking to Brown in the wagon.

"Well, I'll be," Strofe replied with a little laugh.

"That him?" Cain asked.

"That's Henry, all right."

"So the girl can't be far off," Cain added.

Brown pointed off toward a field to the south and seemed to be giving the Negro instructions of some kind. The black man nodded. Then Brown did an odd thing. He paused, turned, and looked beyond the Negro, toward the woods where Cain and the others waited. It appeared as if he were looking at them. Through the spyglass, Cain watched the man up close. His eyes were dark, a slate gray like winter rain, but, too, with a bright gleam to them of one who has been or should be in a lunatic asylum. For just a moment, Cain felt as if he'd spotted him, as if the man were looking eye to eye with him. But then he turned away and gave the reins a sharp crack, and the white draft horse started off along the road.

The Negro went back into the barn and came out leading a mule. He hitched the mule to a cart and then brought it around to the side of the barn, where he started to load the back of the cart with dung from a large pile. The four men in the woods watched him. When he was finished, he got in the seat of the cart and rode it out into the field some quarter mile distant from the main house. Cain told them to mount up, and they followed him, careful to stick to the cover of the woods. They watched as Henry swatted the mule with a switch, and the animal began plodding mechanically along the field; the Negro followed on foot with a pitchfork, spreading the manure. Cain and the others waited until he came close to the edge of the woods, and when he turned and started going the other way, they charged out of their hiding place on their horses. The Negro tried to run as did the boy they'd captured earlier, but this one was heavier and slow of foot, and the field was easy to ride over with the horses. They caught up with him before he'd gone twenty paces and pounced on him. Unlike the other one, this one offered little resistance. They shoved a rag in his mouth and threw a canvas hood over his head, then placed the shackles on his wrists. They draped him over the pommel of Little Strofe's mule and they all rode hard off into the woods, just in case anyone from up at the house had seen them.

They stopped finally in a clearing that had been ravaged by fire in the recent past. All of the tree trunks in the area were scorched and naked, sticking up out of the ground like blackened fingers. Half-burnt logs lay fallen at angles this way and that. They threw the Negro on the ground and yanked off his hood. He held his shackled hands over his eyes against the sunlight. Squinting, he stared up at Strofe as if he were viewing a specter.

"How'do, Henry," said the man, who squatted beside him.

"Mr. Strofe, dat you?"

The big man laughed. "Didn't figure to lay eyes on me again, did you? Not this side of hell anyway."

"No suh. I sholy didn't," he said, tittering nervously.

"When you gonna learn to stay where you belong? Instead of making me chase after you all over creation."

"I didn't mean you no trouble, Mr. Strofe. I swear I didn't."

"But you did. You caused me a whole heap a trouble. When you get back, Mr. Eberly's gonna have you whupped but good, Henry."

"Oh, please no," the Negro pleaded, folding his manacled hands together in supplication. "I won't run no more. I promise."

"Bet you get a hunnerd this time. Enough so you get the flyblows."

Cain had heard the expression before. It was when a slave was flogged so hard that the flesh on his back started to rot and draw flies.

"Lordy, Mr. Strofe. You knows I bleeds real easy."

"Should a thought of that before you up and run again."

"You put in a good word for me, won't ya, Mr. Strofe. Tell massa I didn't put up no fuss comin' back with y'all."

"Too late for that, Henry. How did you manage to escape the dogs?"

This brought a smile of pride to the Negro's lips. "I found me a new grave in the cemetery and took some a dat dead folks dirt and put it in my shoes."

Curious, Cain asked, "What good would that do you?"

"Why, ever'body know dogs can't set on no trail if'n they's grave dirt on the feets."

Cain guessed him to be in his early twenties. He was stout, tending to softness, with a pudgy face and a round plump body. He didn't look much like a field hand, didn't have that lean, muscular frame of one used to working hard. Cain did notice, however, the stained fingernails and palms, and he guessed he'd worked in the tannery. And then, of course, there was the missing right ear, a sign that he'd run before. Cain stood by his horse and glanced out over the burnt section of forest. Not far away he saw on the ground the white skull of some animal. It was long and narrow, broad between the empty eye sockets. Deer, he thought. He wondered if the animal had been dead before the fire started. Or if it had been trapped here and waited in a panic as the fire came surging through.

"What were you doing for Brown?" Cain asked.

"Workin' fo' him."

"Stupid darkie. Run all this way to be somebody else's nigger," Preacher tossed in with a laugh.

"No suh. Massa Brown he doan b'lieve in slavery. He pays me freeman's wages."

"Then he'll just have to get hisself another, won't he now?" Preacher said.

"So where is she, Henry?" Strofe asked.

"Who?"

"Don't play dumb with me. Rosetta."

"Oh, her."

"Yeah, her. Mr. Eberly's mighty interested in her whereabouts."

"I don't know where she at, Mr. Strofe. I truly don't."

"We know you two ran off together."

"Didn't do no such a thing."

"You saying Rosetta didn't run with you?"

"No suh. We run off at the same time. But not together."

"You 'spect me to believe that?" said Strofe as he struck the Negro with the back of his hand. Though the blow couldn't have hurt that much, Henry nonetheless cried out as if in mortal pain.

"Hit's true, massa," cried the Negro. "I swear. I come acrost her out in the woods. She jumped me and near 'bouts cut my throat, she did. She said, 'Whatchu you doin' followin' me, nigger?' Told her I wasn't followin' nobody. Jess runnin' off by my lonesome. You know how Miss Rosetta can be. Plain ornery. But after a while she quiet down and said we could throw in together for a spell."

"You'd better not be lying, Henry," Strofe said, wagging a thick finger in the Negro's face.

"Ain't lying, massa."

"You touch her?"

"Me? No suh. I ain't crazy."

"For your sake, I hope not. Mr. Eberly's already considerable mad at you," the big man repeated. "So where is she, Henry?"

"I done tole you, I don't know."

"You lie to me, it's just gonna make things worse for you."

"Ain't lyin'. Me and Rosetta we split up."

"Where?"

The Negro paused, frowning. "Be a while back. Don't rec'lect too clearly."

Strofe struck the boy again, this time with a fist to the side of his head.

"Where?" the big man repeated.

When the Negro continued to deny knowing where the girl was, Strofe hit him again, harder, this time in the mouth, which brought a trickle of blood.

"Please, Mr. Strofe," he said, holding his hands up in front of his face. "Don't know where she at."

Strofe then instructed his brother and Preacher to come over and give him a hand holding him down.

"This feller here," explained Strofe, indicating Preacher with a nod of his head, "he gets paid two dollars an ear for runaways. So if'n you don't want to part with the other one, you'd best start talking."

Preacher grabbed hold of the remaining ear and yanked it hard so that Henry hollered out.

"Stop your damn caterwauling, nigger," Preacher cried. He then removed his knife from the sheath he kept tied to his leg and brought it up in front of the Negro, twirling it this way and that, for the Negro to have a good look at it. Preacher smiled then, like a child with a new toy. He glanced over at Cain and winked.

"Last chance, Henry," Strofe said. "Where is she?"

"I told you, Mr. Strofe, I don't know."

He nodded to Preacher. But before Preacher had a chance to slice the ear off, the Negro cried, "All right, all right. Back in New York we done split up."

"Where did she go?"

"I don't know 'zactly."

Strofe looked to Preacher again.

"No, wait!" Henry pleaded. "Heard tell she gone to Boston."

"Now why would she go to Boston? You're lying, Henry."

"Ain't lyin', massa."

"Was she fixin' to meet somebody there?"

"Yessum. Some of dem ab'litionist folks, I think."

"What was their name?"

"I don't rightly know."

"Their name, Henry?" demanded Strofe. "Tell us their name, or you're goin' to lose that damn ear."

He lifted his shoulders, and Preacher yanked hard on his ear. The Negro howled again. "Wait, wait. It comin' back to me now."

"I thought it would."

"Name Miss Rosetta said was Howard."

"Howard? You sure?"

"Bes' I can rec'lect."

"Was that the first or last name?" Cain asked.

"Doan know. All's I know she said she gone meet some feller name of Howard."

Strofe glanced over at Cain. "You believe him?" he asked.

Cain looked down at the Negro. "Boston is at least a five-day ride. If we go all the way there and it turns out you're lying, we won't take it kindly, Henry. In fact, we will be downright angry. This Rosetta is going to be there?"

"She say she gone meet up with some folks in Boston. Dat's all I know."

"You're speaking the truth?"

"Yessum, massa, I swear."

"So what do we do now?" Strofe said to Cain. "We could split up. Two of us could bring Henry back while the other two continued on to Boston for the girl."

"But if he's lying, we ought to have him there," Cain said. "Besides, there's Brown to consider."

"What do you mean?" Strofe asked.

"When he finds out the boy's missing, he'll come after him. We oughtn't be split up."

"The hell you talkin' about. Brown don't even own him," Preacher said. "What's in it for him to come after this here nigger?"

"He come after me," Henry piped up. "You watch."

"You just shut your yap, nigger," Strofe cautioned.

Cain looked down at the Negro, then over at the blond-haired man. "He's right. Brown will come after us."

"How the hell do you know what he'll do?" countered Preacher.

"When he finds the boy missing, he'll come looking for him."

"What's he gonna risk his neck for some damn runaway that's nothin' to him?"

"I know the cut of man he is," Cain said. "He sees himself as God's scourge and he won't stop until he finds him. And us."

Several times in his years of slave catching, Cain had found himself the hunted instead of the hunter. Abolitionists or kin of the fugitive or sometimes even the law would form a posse and come after him. All of the skills that had made him good at finding a runaway would then be called upon to keep him from being found. One time he'd tracked a fugitive all the way to Chicago, before catching him and heading back to Kentucky, from where he'd escaped. But some men from the vigilance committee there gathered a posse and chased him as far as the Ohio River before giving up and heading home.

Strofe picked at his beard. "I agree with Cain. We stay together."

"Well, we'd better pull foot then," Cain said.

They mounted up and rode off at a gallop. The runaway, hands manacled, sat on the pack mule behind Little Strofe, who held the reins. They headed back up the long mountain pass they'd crossed two days earlier, and made Keene by noon. Cain purposely stopped at the inn and talked to the nosey innkeeper and let it be known that they were heading due south, for Virginia. He knew that Brown would stop there and inquire if they'd passed through. They left the village and rode south along the valley for a mile, then doubled back before cutting across the river and striking a course for the east.

"What in the Sam Hill we doing, Cain?" Strofe asked.

"Brown will figure we're headed south. At least until he loses our trail."

6

The next morning, Cain opened his eyes as something hit his face. Then another. And another after that.

"You fixin' to sleep all day, Cain?" a voice came to him. Squinting at the light, Cain opened his eyes to see Preacher squatting a few feet away. He was picking up pebbles and tossing them one at a time at Cain. He threw another, but Cain caught it.

"We s'posed to set on our asses and wait for your majesty? Maybe you'd like me to fetch you some tea and biscuits."

Cain threw off his blanket and sat up. He shivered in the damp cold of morning, stretched. His head wobbled like a worn wagon wheel.

"You w-want I should fix you something to eat, Mr. Cain?" Little Strofe asked.

"Just coffee, please, Mr. Strofe."

He bolted down the cup of coffee, and they quickly saddled up and continued on their way.

Mornings mostly went like that. Each day broke gray and cold over the mountains, with a damp rawness in the air seeping into the men as they slept and tainting their dreams and turning them surly and short-tempered as they went about the business of making fires and cooking breakfast and feeding and saddling the horses. Strofe, who continued to have bowel problems, would rush off into the woods, where they could hear him grunting and groaning as he relieved himself. As they rode along, the runaway, Henry, chatted almost as incessantly as Little Strofe, and it seemed at times as if he wasn't a prisoner so much as one among them out for a pleasant ride. By midday, it usually turned sunny and mild, and the riding became something almost agreeable in its mindlessness. Cain liked the afternoons best, the warm sun lulling on the back of his neck, the sweet smell of pine and horse leather and new earth coming awake after the long sleep of winter, the pleasing palette of colors of birch and tamarack and spruce, the quavering call of mourning doves and the sharp bleat of jays. The two hounds catching scent of something and commencing to howl as they took off after it. An eagle gliding a foot over the river, one talon poised to grab a fish. A fox forming a splash of red as it slipped through the green forest. A moose loping awkwardly across a clearing. Such times as these released his head from the lock of the past, freed him from the ache in his leg, and it felt good to be in the saddle, riding a fine horse, good to be alive and breathing and moving about over the earth instead of silent and still and rotting beneath it. The farther they got from North Elba without any sign of Brown, the more Cain relaxed and felt that perhaps he'd been wrong about the man after all.

Little Strofe would keep up a constant prattle with anyone who was game. He'd often get into friendly arguments with the runaway, as he was usually the only one who'd listen to him. For a long stretch they debated what was the better eating, possum or rabbit, and which was the preferred method of cooking each, with Little Strofe coming down on the side of fried possum while Henry favored rabbit that was done in a stew. Henry, it was obvious from his physique, was fond of almost any sort of food, and he wolfed down whatever was put in front of him without complaint.

"What do you favor, Mr. Cain?" Little Strofe asked him.

"I'd have to say I'm partial to rabbit, Mr. Strofe," he replied. "With some greasy-back beans."

"Oh, I d-do declare, I love them g-greasy-back beans."

Cain could remember their Negro housekeeper, Lila, cooking green beans in pork fat and bacon. Her Sunday ham with okra.

Grits and gravy. Collard greens. Sweet potato pie. She was a good cook. After his mother passed away, Lila became the sole maternal influence of his young boyhood. Without her, his child's world would have collapsed in a lonely heap. It was she who tucked his brother and him in most nights. Who bandaged a cut hand. Who made little treats for them. Who mended a ripped pant leg. Who spanked their bottoms when they cussed and chastised them if they sassed their father behind his back. "I won't be hearin' no talk about Massa Cain," she would tell them. It was Lila who sang the old plantation song when she was doing their wash down at the creek:

> *Oh the stars in the elements is falling,*
> *And the moon drips away in the blood.*

And yet, he took her for granted, as children usually take a loving parent. He knew, too, had always known, that she had her own boys who lived down in the slave cabins, just past the tobacco sheds and the hog pen. Cain saw them walking past the house on their way to work in the fields each day. Not much older than he. Her sons, her own flesh and blood. Despite this, she'd treated Cain and his brother as if they had come from her own womb. A part of him had always wondered about this, struck even his child's mind as odd, the way the intricate workings of the adult world often do to a child—the roundness of the earth, the illogic of death, how babies are made. But growing up often meant accepting what didn't make sense, including the maternal instincts of slaves for the children of their masters. One hot summer day, for instance, he and TJ had been out riding in the fields, and had come into the kitchen where Lila was fixing supper. She poured them some of her sweet mint tea and set out for them some molasses cookies she'd just made. Outside, her boys happened to be trudging past the house after their day in the fields. She scooped up a mess of the cookies and hurried out the back door to give some to her own children. When she returned, Cain could remember his brother expressing surprise that they liked cookies, too.

"Why, 'course they do," she had said. "They boys just like y'all."

Despite not seeing any signs of their being trailed, Cain kept a watchful eye to their rear. Several times he'd have the others ride on ahead while he stayed behind, on the lookout for Brown and his boys. Once, he even saw some half dozen riders advancing hard on them. From the scabbard on his saddle he removed his Sharp's, loaded it with the .52 caliber paper cartridge, adjusted the rear sight, and took careful aim at the leader. But as they drew near, none of them turned out to be the Brown clan. Nonetheless, Cain continued to keep a cautious eye over his shoulder.

As they entered the valley of the Hudson River, the land gradually flattened into broad, green, rolling pastureland. It was milder here, spring already having commenced. They came upon small dairy farms with black-and-white Holsteins and pretty Guernseys grazing in fields. Passing a field of cattle late one evening, Little Strofe suddenly jumped down off his mule and, holding a metal pot, climbed a stone wall and made his way over to a cow. "Ain't gone hurt you, bos," he said to the animal as he cautiously approached it. Then he started to sing to the animal, some song he made up off the top of his head. "You're my own true love, my darlin' big-breasted girl." Instead of bolting, the cow seemed mesmerized by the sound of his voice. When he got close, he stroked her tawny flank and talked soothingly to her the way he did to his dogs. After she'd accepted him, he squatted behind her legs and calmly proceeded to milk her into the pot. He used it that night to make flapjacks, and they drank the sweet buttermilk. Cain hadn't tasted anything so good in a long time.

After they'd eaten, Little Strofe headed down to the stream where he began to wash the pots and pans. Cain followed him.

"Those were good flapjacks, Mr. Strofe," he said.

"Thanks."

"May I ask you something?" Little Strofe stopped what he was doing, glanced up at Cain. "The other day when I asked why this runaway girl stabbed Eberly, you seemed to know more than you were letting on."

"Like I said, it w-weren't none a my business."

"I can appreciate that. But you see, if I'm going to catch this girl, I'll need to know everything I can about her. Why she ran and where she might be headed. You'd actually be doing Mr. Eberly a service if you told me."

Little Strofe scratched his beard, then glanced over toward his brother and Preacher, seated around the campfire. "It was on account of what he done with her young'un."

"She had a child?"

Cain thought back to his meeting with Eberly. How he'd asked him if the runaway had had a child she might be running toward, and how the old man had denied it.

Little Strofe nodded, went back to scouring the pots.

"What did he do with her child?"

"Sold it."

"Why?"

The squatting man jerked his shoulders upward. "I s'pose on account of her running off. To teach her a lesson."

"Is Eberly married?"

"Was. The missus she died a long time back. Afore I come to work for him."

Cain nodded. "Was the child Eberly's?"

Little Strofe stopped and looked up at Cain. "Wouldn't know nothing 'bout that, Mr. Cain. Like I said, it weren't none of my bidness. I do my work and keep my mouth shut."

"That's a good philosophy, Mr. Strofe."

He knew the man was lying but decided to leave it there for now. He wondered why Eberly had bothered to lie about her having a child. Unless, of course, it *was* his. It didn't matter to Cain a whit if, as Preacher had joked, the old man was having his way with the Negro girl. He'd seen plenty of that in his job. Hell, every mulatto, quadroon, or octoroon was the product of some lecherous master or overseer or slave trader. It wasn't anything new under the sun. Still, he wondered why the old man had lied to him. Perhaps it was just his sense of pride. There were those, Cain knew, who didn't like to be thought of as miscegenators.

They had to take a side-paddle ferry across Lake Champlain, which was still partially frozen over. Though it was clear and sunny out, a strong wind kicked up once they got out into the middle of the big lake, churning the water into violent whitecaps that forced the boat to pitch from side to side. The large paddle wheels made an infernal racket as they pummeled the water, tossing up a spray of frigid mist. As they crossed, they had to make their way past huge ice floes that lay submerged in the water like enormous whales. Now and then the ferry captain would have to turn the craft to avoid hitting one, and another man stood in the bow with a long pole to try to push them off. Cain noticed that the runaway Henry, who was manacled to one of the metal railings near the engine house, had turned gray from the rough crossing. He was leaning over vomiting into the gunwales. Cain grabbed the canteen from the pommel of his saddle and went over to check on him.

"Here," he said to Henry, handing him the canteen.

"'Preciate it, massa." The Negro had to tilt his head at an angle to drink. He drank for a while, took a breath, and drank some more, the water running down his neck and into his shirt. The swelling around his mouth where Strofe had struck him two days earlier had nearly gone away. During the ride east he hadn't put up any fuss, had proven to be docile and obedient, if somewhat too talkative for Cain's liking. Cain hadn't paid him much mind really. He figured the boy was the others' responsibility, his being the girl when they found her. Besides, he usually made it a point not to get involved with his prisoners, not to become chatty and friendly, not to learn their stories, why they had run or what it was like under a particular master or what they might face once back home. Sure he might talk with a slave, casual banter that passed the time on the often long journey home, but he would never ask him much about his life, and he certainly wouldn't offer anything about his own. He was never mean nor cruel to his charges, simply professionally distant in his dealings with them. In fact, he liked to think that he was both fair and reasonable in pursuing his job. As he viewed it, his obligation was to find his man as quickly and economically as he could, and return him without damaging the property and without getting hurt in the bargain.

"Are you all right?" Cain asked the Negro.

"Ain't never took to water much," Henry replied, glancing fearfully out at the churning lake.

"We'll be across shortly."

Henry nodded, unconvinced. "We get back, you put in a good word for me with the massa."

"He's not interested in you."

"Still, he gone be awful mad. Miss Rosetta taking off like that and me with her."

"I'll see what I can do." He looked out toward the Vermont side. In the air, a red-tailed hawk was being attacked by a pair of smaller dark birds that looked like swallows. The hawk was trying to get away and the two birds kept swooping down on him, throwing themselves at their larger opponent. Cain turned back to Henry. "Eberly seems like a reasonable man." Cain threw this last statement like a fly to a trout, not because he believed it as much as because he wanted to see what Henry would do with it.

The Negro shrugged his shoulders loosely.

"I don't really know him," Cain said. "That was just my impression."

This time Henry let out with a mouthful of sour air.

"Is he a hard master to serve?"

Henry looked up at him the way a Negro looked at a white man who was asking him to speak honestly about another white man: there was wariness in his eyes, the caution that you didn't talk about one white man to another because you could never trust them.

"Massa all right. Mostly. Got him a temper 'casionally."

"He ever whip you?"

"He has Strofe to do that."

"How about the girl?"

"Not that I knows of. He treat her like a jewel."

"A jewel?"

Henry nodded.

"You were pretty certain this Brown fellow will come after you?"

The Negro paused for a moment, then, almost working up to a smile, he said, "Oh, Massa Brown come after me all right. He come after the bof'a us."

Cain stared into the slave's eyes but knew he wouldn't get more than that. Then he headed back over to where his horse was tied. He fed Hermes some oats and then got out his copy of Milton and sat on the deck and turned his collar up against the strong wind. He put his glasses on and began to read.

> *for how*
> *Can hearts, not free, be tri'd whether they serve*
> *Willing or no, who will but what they must*
> *By Destinie, and can no other choose?*

Occasionally, Cain would look up from his reading. Some of the other passengers stared openly at the Virginians and their prisoner. In particular, they were curious about the one-eared, manacled Negro in their custody. Two well-dressed men in frock coats and tall beaver hats seemed to take a special interest in Henry. One was younger and gaunt, with a long scrofulous neck, the other older with a thick paunch and a wispy gray beard that hung from his face like Spanish moss. His eyes floated loosely in their sockets. The two men whispered between themselves, the younger one gesticulating and explaining something to his companion. Finally they walked over to Cain, the older one clutching the arm of the younger to steady himself on the pitching deck.

"I don't mean to interrupt your reading, sir," the bearded one began. Up close, Cain could see that something was wrong with his eyes. They had a light bluish-gray film coating them, like the glaze that forms over the eyes of a fresh-killed deer. "May I ask you a question?"

Cain stood and, glancing at the man's companion, said, "Of course."

"Is that man a fugitive?" the older man inquired, indicating with a flick of his woolly head the general direction of the Negro, as if he could actually see him.

"He is," Cain replied.

"And you, sir, are a slave catcher?" the blind man asked.

"I catch runaways as mandated by the law. If that's what you mean."

"That is man's law, not God's. Slavery is an abomination in the eyes of the Lord."

Cain smiled at the man. "Is that so?"

"We are your friends," the man said.

"My friends?"

"Yes. And we come to warn you that your soul is in immortal danger."

"I don't reckon you know much about my soul, mister," he replied.

"No, I don't. But the Almighty does," the blind man said. He gathered his beard together in one hand and stroked it the way one might a cat as his cloudy eyes drifted upward toward the heavens. "He knows every last thing about your soul. Every act you've ever done. Every thought you've ever had."

Cain raised his hands, as if in surrender to someone whose defect made him an opponent he couldn't challenge. He then glanced at the younger man, as if he might translate this gesture for his friend and call him off. "I reckon the Almighty has more important things to fret over than my soul," he said, trying to make light of it. "Have a good day, mister."

He started to turn, but the blind man said, "But that's where you are wrong, sir. He is as concerned about your immortal soul as he is that of the poor wretch over there. And he would not have you tainting it by selling a man into slavery."

"I'm not a slave trader," Cain said curtly. "I don't own slaves. Never bought or sold one. I am merely returning stolen property to its rightful owner."

"This poor man isn't chattel to be bandied about like so many goods."

"I don't make the law, mister. I just enforce it."

"Slavery is unjust," the blind man continued. "All laws regarding its promulgation are equally unjust."

"There's always been slavery," Cain said. "Even in the Bible. In Leviticus doesn't it say something about buying bondsmen and women from the heathen?"

"I see you know your Bible, sir. Yet in Deuteronomy it is written, 'Thou shalt not deliver onto his master the servant which is escaped from his master onto thee.' And in Galatians, Paul says, 'There is no longer Jew or Greek, there is no longer slave or free, there is no longer male and female; for all of you are one in Christ Jesus.'"

Cain chuckled. "I won't get into chapter and verse with you. I can see that's a losing proposition. But I've heard all this abolitionist talk before. You Yankees would have us set the black man free. Then what?"

"Then he could assume his rightful place at the table with his brethren. The one that the Almighty intended."

"And how would the three million slaves survive? Like the Irish working in your stinking factories? Or in your cities where young girls sell their bodies or children beg on the streets for a handout. You call that freedom? Emancipate the Negro and you will invite chaos into the land."

As Cain said this he heard his father's voice behind it.

"It is already here," the skinny man said, the first time he'd spoken up. "Chaos."

The blind man leveled his gaze at Cain, almost as if he could actually see through the gauzy film that covered his eyes and make out his features. And yet Cain could perceive only a gray nothingness, an opaque emptiness like looking into a snowstorm.

"You, sir, strike me as a man who has lived much," the blind man said.

"Like I said, you don't know me from Adam," he replied.

"Blindness may have robbed me of sight. But God has given me another and grander gift than physical sight."

"A gift?"

"Yes. I can see by an inner sight."

Cain smiled. "Ah," he scoffed. "A modern-day Tiresias."

"You don't believe me. Most people don't." He turned toward his younger colleague, as if to have him vouch for him.

"It's true," said the skinny man, who looked deferentially upon the older man, as an acolyte might look upon his master. "Mr. Willowby has a gift. He can see a man's future. He has lectured all over the States."

"Is that so?"

The skinny man was about to go on when his blind colleague stopped him with a touch of his hand.

To Cain he said, "I can tell that you are a man both of learning and of rectitude."

"Rectitude?" Cain repeated.

"It means—"

"I know what the hell it means."

"Well, it's my duty to warn you to give up this immoral path you're on."

"What path is that?" Cain asked.

"Satan's. Surely you can appreciate the nature of the wrong you commit in bringing this poor Israelite back to bondage in Egypt."

"I am only doing my job," Cain replied. A second time he made as if to turn away, but the old man grasped his arm. His grip startled Cain.

"A moment, sir. Please," the man begged.

Cain pulled his arm free but turned to face him again.

"Your job is working as Satan's lieutenant," the blind man said. "Renounce it! Before it is too late. If thine eye offend thee, pluck it out." Then the man did an odd thing. He reached out and touched Cain's chest with his right hand. His hand moved slowly upward over his coat until it came in contact with the skin of his neck; his light, feathery touch moved delicately over his neck to his chin, then his nose and cheeks, finally touching his eyes one by one so that Cain had to close them. Cain didn't know whether to laugh or be offended at the fellow's audacity. He'd never let another man lay a hand on him before, at least not with impunity. He felt like slapping the hand away, but for some reason he allowed it to remain there. The blind man's eyes fluttered rapidly as his fingers spread out over the left side of Cain's face, touching it gently.

"I see two souls."

"What?" Cain said.

"Two souls shall be entrusted to your care."

Cain wondered how he knew there was another runaway. He figured it was just some sort of illusionist's sleight of hand. A clever trick. Still, his interest was piqued.

"That's good," Cain said. "But if you really do have a gift, you would know where the other fellow we're after is."

The man smiled. "Do you really think I would tell you if I knew?"

"See, you're just talking bunkum. You don't know anything."

The blind man paused for a moment, one hand still touching Cain's face. His sightless eyes fluttered again, and it was now his turn to smile. "You shall have to find her without my help," he said.

Her, Cain thought. He was good, this Willowby. A skillful con man. Then he moved his hand over Cain's forehead. The blind man's eyes narrowed, as if sighting something at a great distance.

"You will have a choice to make."

"What choice is that?"

"You shall have to find that out for yourself. But I can tell you this. If you make the wrong one, I see hard times ahead for you. Make the right one, though, and you shall be freed."

"I am not some slave."

"You are wrong there, sir. Like it or not, slavery binds us all. Master and slave alike. And God has in store for us a terrible day of reckoning. When the country will have to pay for its sins and brother shall slay brother. When rivers will run red with blood and fire shall consume the land." The blind man leaned in close so that Cain could smell his sour breath, like a whiff of a charnel house. "Choose wisely, my friend. Choose wisely."

When they reached the Vermont side, they headed southeast along a toll road. At the first tollhouse, they had to pay a bald, sleepy-eyed man five cents for each man to pass and two more for each horse, mule, and dog. There was no charge for the Negro. It being April, back in Virginia farmers would already have been plowing their fields, but this far north the fields remained untended and muddy, some, especially those in the shadow of a mountain, still covered with snow. For half a day, the road followed a surging river as it coursed through low, hump-backed mountains. Several times the road traversed the river by way of a covered bridge. As they passed through one, Little Strofe said, "This is a waste of a good barn," his voice reverberating through the tunnel-like structure.

The road they were on was broader and more well traveled than what they'd ridden on back in New York. Here they passed other travelers, some on horseback or foot, others driving wagons filled with goods or sitting in a stagecoach with other people. They saw small villages clustered around whitewashed churches and brick courthouses, not so very different from what Cain had been used to growing up in the rolling hills of western Virginia. They saw large factories built on rivers, their smokestacks belching black soot. Just outside of White River Junction, a mill town at the confluence of two rivers, they made camp in the woods down near the water. They were almost out of certain supplies—cornmeal, bacon, smoked fish, boxes of locofoco, as well as coffee and plugs of tobacco and whiskey—so they decided to go into town. However, recalling the trouble they'd had back in Albany, they felt it prudent that only two should head in so as to not draw attention to themselves. It was decided that Cain and Strofe would go, while the other two would remain behind with the runaway at their camp.

Preacher, though, objected to this arrangement. "How come you two git to go into town," he complained.

"We're just pickin' up some supplies is all," Strofe said.

"Oh, I reckon that's all it'll be," Preacher replied sarcastically. "And how come he gets to go?" He nodded over at Cain, who was cinching the belt of his saddle.

"He's got to wire Mr. Eberly where we're at."

"Why couldn't I do that?"

"'Cause you cain't write a lick, Preacher," Strofe said with a laugh.

"Well, next time it's gonna be my turn," Preacher said. As they rode off toward town, Preacher called after them, "Make sure you bring back some liquor."

The streets were muddy from the spring thaw and rutted with wagon tracks. Women walked along holding up the hems of their skirts, and everyone was pale and had the pinched look of someone with constipation. Along the main thoroughfare were a courthouse and town hall building, three white steepled churches within spitting distance of one another—Congregational, Methodist, and Unitarian—a lending library, a blacksmith and livery, two saloons, an inn, various shops and business concerns, and a long brick mill whose sign out front said NEW ENGLAND TEXTILE MFG. When they reached a general store, Cain said to Strofe, "I'll look for a telegraph office. Meet you back at camp."

He stopped a small boy in the street and asked where the telegraph office was. The boy, brown haired, with pretty features, was lugging two heavy pails of milk on a yoke balanced over his thin shoulders; he told him it was just past McCreavy's Saloon, at the other end of town. Cain tossed him a penny and continued on his way. He first went over to the livery and had a loose shoe on Hermes attended to—the last dozen miles the horse had been favoring the foot. Cain also bought a sack of oats. Finished there, he then rode down the street and stopped in front of a trough so Hermes could drink. He dismounted and wrapped the reins around a hitching post. He spotted a mangy-looking dog sauntering out of an alley. It was an emaciated thing, a brindled color, with patches of fur missing, its narrow head low to the ground, its bony shoulder blades jutting almost through the splotchy coat. The thing was growling at nothing, it seemed, other than the general state of affairs. Cain kept his eye on the creature to make sure it would not lunge at him, then he turned and headed toward the telegraph office across the street.

"That your dog, mister?" the operator asked him as he came through the door. The man was standing at the window looking out. He had orange-red hair and big scablike freckles all over his face, and the dull, satiated grin of someone either feebleminded or just having eaten too much.

"No."

"Ought not to let that dog just walk around like that," the man persisted.

"I'd like to send a telegraph," Cain said.

"Where to?"

"Richmond, Virginia."

"You're a long way from home, mister."

When Cain didn't offer any explanation, the man walked over and sat at a high stool behind the counter. He gave Cain some paper, a quill pen, an inkwell. Cain wrote out a message for Eberly, disguising it in case the telegraph operator was an abolitionist sympathizer:

Have bagged the buck. Presently on trail of the doe. Should return within a fortnight. Cain.

The operator looked at him curiously before he sent it, but whatever he was thinking, he didn't let on.

Cain paid the man. Before he left, though, he took another piece of paper, dipped his pen in the inkwell, and gave some consideration to composing a letter.

"You got something else for me to send?" the man asked.

"Maybe."

"I'm going home for lunch soon."

"I won't be but a moment."

"I shut down from noon to one. My wife don't like my lunch getting cold."

Cain ignored him. The operator raised his eyebrows and got up and came around from behind his counter, and walked back over to the window. Looking out, he removed a handkerchief from his back pocket and blew his nose, his whole body convulsing with the effort, as if he were trying to hurt himself.

"Don't like the looks of that animal," he said.

Not bothering to respond, Cain dipped his pen in the ink.

"Folks shouldn't let their dogs just wander around like that."

Cain started to get that feeling he did right before he needed a drink. His leg ached and a kind of tightness coalesced in his chest, followed by a small rapping in the back of his head, as if a shoemaker's hammer were driving tiny nails into his skull. If he'd been back in Richmond, he'd have gone over to Spivey's Saloon and bought himself a bottle and gotten himself good and corned. Then he'd have gone over to Antoinette's and bought somebody for the night so he wouldn't have to wake up alone the next morning.

He thought of writing to his brother, asking how the old man was doing. The last letter he'd received from TJ, over two years ago, had mentioned that their father's health had been in decline. His brother had pleaded with him to come home, said it was time he and their father put aside their differences. For all Cain knew, the old man could've died by now, though he figured TJ would have informed him if he had.

"Somebody ought to take and shoot that thing," the red-haired man said.

Cain glanced out the window. He saw the dog staggering as it moved down the street. The animal was panting heavily, his scrawny ribs moving in and out like a ripped bellows, while around his mouth a white foam had gathered. He heard a noise somewhere outside, the shriek of a woman's voice.

Cain turned his attention back to the piece of paper in front of him. He remembered a time when he was eleven. Their father had taken them to church in the wagon. On the ride home they were passing the cemetery where their mother was buried, and Cain had asked if they could stop and visit her grave. Other people he knew went to the graves of loved ones. Their mother, in fact, used to visit that of his own dead brother, sometimes bringing him and TJ along with her. Because her husband refused to go, she would have Handy Joe or even Cain hitch up the wagon and he'd drive her there. She'd kneel in the grass and say a few prayers, her eyes turning misty as morning fog. To his knowledge, his father had never gone, not to visit his son's grave nor his wife's either. Each time they passed the cemetery, Cain imagined going there with some flowers he'd picked and kneeling by his mother's grave and saying something to her.

"No," Mr. Cain had said to him, his face turning ashen, in his dark eyes anger and sadness warring for supremacy. For a moment,

Cain thought that he'd strike him, that he would take off his belt as he sometimes did when he'd done something wrong, cursed or lied or broke a piece of farm equipment, and "put the strap to him," as he called it. But instead, he pulled the wagon to a stop, set the brake, got down from the seat.

"Go on home, son," he told him, handing the reins to Cain.

"Did I do something wrong, sir?" Cain asked.

"No. Just do as I say. Make sure you unhitch the horses and brush them real good. Have Lila go ahead and start dinner without me." That was all he said, all he'd ever said about their mother's death. Cain never brought the subject up again, nor had he ever gone to see his mother's grave even when he was old enough to go by himself. Now when he thought about returning home, it wasn't so much to see his father, for whom he didn't feel much of anything, as it was to visit his mother's grave.

The small hammering sound in his head had increased to a dull pounding.

"If I had a gun, I'd do it myself," the red-haired man said.

Cain turned around. "What?"

"That dog. He's fixing to bite some child. Could I borrow your gun?"

Cain never let anyone borrow his gun. Instead, he got up and walked over to the window. The dog was emitting a low growl. It was crouched, its brown shoulders hunched and the muscles in its hindquarters knotted as if it was about to lunge. Standing not ten feet in front of it was the object of its interest—the boy who'd been carrying the milk pails. The animal had pinned him against the wall of a building. The boy was frozen in his tracks, leaning back into the wood, afraid to cut and run with the heavy yoke over his neck. Some of the milk had already sloshed over the lip of the pail, staining the packed dirt of the street. Several people had stopped and were viewing the scene with trepidation. One woman was crying out. "Help! Somebody help!" she kept saying.

Cain stepped out into the street. The harsh sunlight exploded into his field of vision, his head pounding harder now. It glinted off the tin roof of the saloon across the way, off the bright fear in the boy's ashen face. He could see the surface of the milk in the pails quivering, as if keeping time to the boy's heartbeat. The dog had gathered what remained of its strength and was crouched low, its legs tense, about to rush the boy. That's when Cain called out.

"Hey," he cried, whistling. "Over here."

The dog half turned on Cain and let out a low, deep-bellied growl, baring its yellow fangs. Its eyes were glazed and empty, lost things, already seeing objects from a world other than this one. Cain pulled back the flap of his greatcoat and removed the leather loop holding the hammer of his gun down. In one smooth, unbroken motion he drew, cocked, and aimed his Colt, all without the dog's moving. He would have dispatched the animal on the spot, but the boy happened to be directly in line with the dog, and he worried about a bullet ricocheting off bone or gristle or even passing through soft tissue and causing problems on the other end. Cain hoped the dog would come toward him a little more before he fired. Which is exactly what he did, the animal turning slowly and taking a step in his direction.

"Atta, boy," he called to the thing. "Come on." Cain also took two sideways steps so that the dog was no longer in line with the boy. He laid the dog's skinny chest on the rear notch of the hammer and took a breath, held it as he prepared to put the animal out of its misery.

But it was at that moment that the boy decided to make a break for it. He took several steps, stumbled and fell, the milk splashing over the ground and himself, too. Immediately the dog turned its attention back to the boy and rushed for him, his opened jaws level with the boy's face. Cain didn't have much of a chance to be pretty about his gunplay. He jerked his first shot and the .44 caliber ball slammed into the dog's hindquarters, spinning the animal around and taking its back legs out from under it. For a moment, the dog just sat there, momentarily dazed, its head turned toward its hindquarters, almost as if he were going to scratch himself, but then he seemed to remember the boy again. The bullet must not have hit bone, for the animal stood and started to hobble toward him. Cain took a little more time with the second shot and caught the dog in the back just behind the shoulder blades. This time the thing went down, straight down, its legs splayed out to either side, a high-pitched yelp shivering the air. The second bullet had shattered its spine, for the animal lay there in the dirt, motionless save for its jaws, which snapped savagely at something only the dog saw, the froth at its mouth now turning a bright pink and dribbling down onto the muddy road. After a while, it stopped, stiffened, and finally lay still. Cain went over and nudged the thing with his boot just to be certain.

Then he walked over and squatted down near the boy, who lay on the ground too afraid to cry or to move.

"You all right, son?" he asked.

The boy nodded. Cain helped him up and the boy stood, looking from the dog to the empty milk pails.

"My father's going to tan my hide," he said, looking at the spilled milk on the ground.

Cain thought how that was something his own father might do.

B efore he left town, he stopped at the apothecary and bought another bottle of laudanum. Then he rode over to the saloon. One, he thought. Maybe two. He sat at the bar and bought a whiskey. The barkeep was a heavyset man with bushy side-whiskers and a labored breathing, as if he had just come running up a flight of stairs. The man poured him a frugal shot, and Cain threw it back in one draft and asked for a second, this one with some liberality to it. The barkeep seemed to take some offense at this, but this time he gave Cain a bigger glass and filled it up three fingers' worth. Cain took out the bottle of laudanum and poured some in his glass. He drank this one a bit more slowly, savoring it. He felt the tightness in his chest loosen a little, felt the pounding in his skull not leave so much as move off to a comfortable distance. Even his leg didn't hurt as much.

Down the bar a little ways sat a man about his own age wearing a felt bowler and a tailcoat well worn and threadbare. The left coat sleeve, Cain noticed, was empty and pinned at the shoulder.

"That was some pretty fair shooting, mister," the man said to him.

Cain looked at him, nodded, then went back to his drink. He didn't feel like talking. He wanted to invite the whiskey and laudanum to enter him, to shush the noise in him, to lull him the way a roaring fire did on a frigid winter day. He wanted to have a couple of drinks and be alone for a while, without the Strofes and Preacher. He recalled with unease the blind man. How he'd touched his face, the warning he'd given him. How he'd have to make a choice. And if he made the wrong one, how things would go hard for him. What the hell did that mean? He didn't usually set much store on such things, signs and omens and prophecies. Just a bunch of superstitious nonsense. People made their own destinies, he felt. But as he sat there he couldn't get the blind man out of his thoughts. How did he know there was a second runaway? And that it was a woman? He finished his second drink, hoping to forget all this business, and had the barkeep refill his glass again. He went to pay for it, but the barkeep said the fellow in the bowler hat had already taken care of it.

Cain turned toward him again and saluted with his glass.

"Where'd you learn to shoot like that?" the man asked.

"Here and there."

The man looked down at Cain's gun. "That there looks like a Walker Colt."

Cain nodded.

"Ain't seen one of them in a goodly while. Here's to Captain Walker."

The man raised what he was drinking and made a toast. Cain smiled at the man, raised his own glass, and repeated, "To Captain Walker." Then he went back to sipping his drink.

"Used to have one myself," the one-armed man said. "Not the big one. A thirty-six caliber. Damn nice gun. Sold it a few years back when I was in need to whet my whistle and was short on funds," he said, chuckling. "You fight down in *Mejico*?" he asked, pronouncing it in Spanish.

"Yeah."

"Me, too."

Cain looked back over at him. "That where you lose it?" he asked, touching his own arm.

"What, this?" the man said, wiggling his empty coat sleeve like a magic trick. "Hell, no. Lost this damn thing over at the mill. I was three sheets to the wind and got'er caught in a roller. When I come to, this is the way I found myself. Hell of a thing. Where'd you see action?"

"Resaca de la Palma. Monterrey. Buena Vista. You?"

"Was with old man Scott when he took Mexico City. Hotter'n a whore's twat, that place, and twice as stinkin'," he said with a laugh. "Them señoritas was something, though. What regiment you with?"

"I got there late and they put me in the Second Indiana. Under General Lane. Fought with Captain O'Brien and later Colonel Jeff Davis's Mississippi Rifles at Buena Vista."

"I heard that was something," the man said, making an empty whistling sound.

Cain shrugged. "We lost some good men."

"That where you pick up the limp? I noticed it when you come in."

"Yeah."

"Well, here's to a couple of dumb sons-a-bitches," the man said, holding up his glass. "What business I ever had going off and fighting in that damn place, I'll never know. Wasn't none of my affair."

"Mine neither," replied Cain.

That seemed enough of an invitation for the man to take his drink and move down and pull up a seat. As it turned out, he wasn't a bad sort, and he got better with the drinking. They talked and drank and ate pickled eggs, and then talked and drank some more, each of them buying the other drinks, though at some point it was Cain doing all the buying with the other fellow saying he was a little short. They lost track of the time as they reminisced about battles and commanders, the heat and dust and swamps, the mosquitoes and flies and bad water, the fevers and dysentery. The ineptness of most of the Mexican generals and some of the American ones, too. The superiority of the U.S. weaponry, including the gun that Cain now carried on his waist (he even took it out of the holster to let the man hold it, wield it about until the heavyset barkeep threatened to kick them out unless he put the thing away). They both agreed on the sheer doggedness of the Mexican soldier, how he'd keep attacking under that crazy and ruthless Santa Anna no matter how many of them fell.

"They died by the hundreds," the man said. "After we kicked ole Santa Anna's ass, we shoulda took that fellow out and shot the bastard, the way he led those poor devils to slaughter."

"You're right there, fellow," Cain agreed.

"Joshua Strong," he said, extending his hand.

"Cain."

"Where you from, Cain?"

"Virginia."

"You're a long ways from home. What brings you way up this way?"

"Business" was all Cain said, and the man didn't push.

It was late when Cain staggered out to his horse. A gaudy silver moon hung over the street like a great eyeball, white and ragged, staring down at him, with little gray veins etching its surface. He was so slewed he didn't even remember which way north was, and as he unbuttoned his fly to piss there in the street, he hoped to hell Hermes would remember and just take him where he needed to go, as he had many times in the past. The horse nudged him, looking for his piece of sugar. It took Cain two tries to get his foot in the stirrup and mount the horse. "Take me home, boy," he said to Hermes when he was finally in the saddle. As he rode along in the moonlit night, he started to sing the lyrics to "Barbara Allen":

Twas in the merry month of May
When Flowers were a-bloomin'
Sweet Willie on his deathbed lay
For the love of Barbara Allen.

Into his disordered thoughts, winging itself wildly like an evening bat, came the memory of Buena Vista and the men who died there. And the young Indian girl who'd saved his life.

7

Cain had gone to war for the same hackneyed, mule-stupid reasons that young men had been going and dying ever since the Trojan War—out of vanity or arrogance, out of a sense of adventure, or out of the mistaken belief that glory was not only attainable but a thing to be sought and cherished, to be won at all costs, even if it meant dying like Bowie and Travis and Crockett. He went, as others had before him, to escape a life he felt trapped in, to leave it before the jailer forever locked his cell and threw away the key. And most important, Cain went out of fear—the fear of what would happen to him if he didn't go, of what his life would look like if he were foolish enough to be left behind. He thought war was a way of getting out of Nottoway Chase and not having to marry Alexandra Throgmorton. He felt that going off to war would be a way of, if not actually avoiding, at least delaying, settling into a life of ledger books and feed costs and tobacco prices, a life of watching the skies for rain and seeing the years drain, year by miserable year, into the red Virginia soil. The war, he felt, might even change his perspective. He told himself that, upon his return (it didn't occur to him that some men going to war *didn't* return), he might even settle down and *want* to marry Lexi. The distance and time, he'd convinced himself, might actually make his heart grow fonder of her; the purifying light of war might return him with a fuller appreciation for the peace and quiet of agrarian life.

So he'd taken the horse and the money, packed a few clothes and some of Lila's biscuits and a slab of bacon, and left in the middle of the night, exactly three days before he was to have been married. He left a note on his father's desk, one that put the shiniest gloss on his motivations:

Dearest Father,
Have gone off to do my duty for country and for the great state of Virginia. I hope to make you proud. Give my heart-felt apologies to Lexi. Tell her I shall return, at which time, if she will still have me, we may then be joined in matrimony.

With affection I remain,
Your son,
Augustus

Like many young men, Cain rode off to Texas to fight against Mexico with hardly a notion of what the war was about, except that the Mexicans had, a decade earlier, slaughtered the valiant men of the Alamo, and that now they were once again trying to make war on the state, this time a part of these United States. So he headed off to sign up with old Zack Taylor. On the road heading away from Nottoway Chase, he'd had a heady sense of freedom and adventure and limitless possibilities, feelings he'd never had before. As he fell in with other young men riding south, talking around the campfires and sleeping under the stars, a notion was kindled in him that he was now embarked on a grand and sacred mission, one whose particulars he couldn't quite fathom but whose general outline he never doubted for a moment. No longer would he be sucking dirt behind a plow or smelling the shit-encrusted rumps of cattle that he drove toward a stock pen. Cain pictured himself a sort of modern-day Achilles, off to Troy to do glorious battle.

"Where you from, Cain?" a bucktoothed boy from Tennessee asked him one night as he passed around a jug of homemade white lightning.

"Virginia," he replied.

"Y'ever kill nobody?"

Cain shook his head. "You?"

"Hell, yeah. This y'here feller come at me with a knife. I give 'im a barrel of number eight shot right 'twixt the eyes. Pshaw. He was dead 'fore he hit the ground. But you get used to it. After the first one it ain't so bad." The boy, seventeen or so, didn't even have fuzz on his cheek to shave. Yet he acted as if he was an old hand at killing, as if he and death were old friends.

"We're gone learn them Mexican niggers who they're afoolin with," the boy said. Later, in the bloody street fighting at Monterrey, Cain would see the boy take a bullet in the gut, and die calling out for his mama.

And as with most young men, for Cain, the reality of war quickly extinguished any notion of glory or truth or moral certitude that he had harbored when he enlisted. Since he was good with horses, they made him a driver of a wagon that brought the wounded from the battlefield to the hospital. The abstractions quickly fell away before the sight of men hit by grapeshot and cannonballs, the screams and curses of the wounded, the stench of rotting flesh, the fear that caused men to soil their pants. He witnessed the brutality of war close-up. He helped the doctors hold men down while they sawed off their limbs and picked out pieces of shrapnel. He listened to the final words of men about to die. Sometimes he had to pick up a rifle and fight alongside the other soldiers. He grew to understand the secret knowledge of killing, to know how easy a thing it was, how dirt cheap a human life was. He also saw the atrocities that were committed on both sides. He saw the scorn the Americans heaped on the "half a nigger" Mexicans, as they were called, and their peculiar religion. There was the Massacre of the Cave near Agua Nueva, where, in an act of supposed retribution for the killing of captured Americans, Arkansas volunteers rounded up some thirty Mexican civilians and slaughtered them, then proceeded to scalp them and place the bloody scalps on the altar of a Catholic chapel. There was the harsh treatment of the Irish in the ranks, who were ridiculed for their accent and their Catholic religion, so much so that one group finally defected to the Mexican side and became known as the San Patricios brigade—after St. Patrick—only to be hanged after the war as traitors.

He came to realize that the life of a soldier was mostly filled not with glory and adventure, but with boredom and routine, with tedium and repetition, with pointless tasks and grinding monotony all aimed, it seemed, at whittling a fellow down to an unthinking draft animal who simply plodded onward until told to do something else. It was an existence worse even than that he'd experienced back on his father's farm. Still, Cain proved himself a good soldier. He marched when he was ordered, slept and ate when he was told, didn't complain much, and, when commanded, he fought and fought well. He drove his wagon fearlessly through musket and cannon fire, sometimes right into the thick of battle to pick up the wounded. In fact, for his actions at the battle of Resaca de la Palma, he received a special commendation for bravery. If he no longer understood the cause for which he fought, at least he admired the men with whom he fought. That, he learned, was the real reason men continued to fight and give their lives in war. When he put his life in danger, it wasn't for some abstract notion like glory or country or freedom, or even nobility of cause; it was simply because of his comrades who died fighting beside him, their blood draining away onto the sands of some stinking desert. If he died, it would be in helping them, defending them. Around the campfire at night sometimes, a man would get out a fiddle and play something, about war or home or some lost love. The other men would be smoking pipes or writing letters to sweethearts, and he would sit there looking up into the desert sky, at the stars, so cold and remote, and yet so perfectly clear and purposeful. It almost made him want to believe in a god; at least it made him believe he had a reason for his life now. He had no one to write to, at least no one he wanted to write to. But he didn't feel alone. He told himself his family, his life, were here, among his comrades, and like all soldiers he had to convince himself of this truth. Otherwise he couldn't fight.

Then came Buena Vista, where Santa Anna had amassed an army of twenty thousand to attack the much smaller American force defending a hacienda in a mountain valley just outside the town of Saltillo. The riflemen of the Second Indiana were stationed on the left flank along the side of a ridge below a steep mountain range. It was here that Santa Anna threw the bulk of his force, hoping to outflank and overrun the American position. The fighting was fierce, with the Mexicans laying down a murderous crossfire of canister and grape and musket fire. The Second Indiana held their ground for a long while but finally were overwhelmed by the superior numbers of the enemy. While most of the line retreated, running wildly down the ridge toward the American rear, Captain O'Brien's and Captain Washington's artillery companies remained behind and fought. Cain had been there to help gather up the wounded.

As the Mexicans began to breach their lines, he grabbed a rifle and returned fire. He picked off the advancing Mexican lancers in their bright blue uniforms, hitting them as easily as shooting bottles on a fence post. It was so easy, in fact, so much death for the taking, it almost made him sick to his stomach. Still, he continued killing, and, as if by some unspoken agreement, the brave, stupid Mexicans continued dying. They kept advancing, getting closer and closer. Finally, he had to pull his Colt revolver and fire at point-blank range. They were close enough now that he could see the color of the eyes of the men he shot, looked right into them, saw that one was missing a tooth, another had a scar on his cheek. One man got so close that Cain could see the hint of a smile on his face, as if he thought the whole thing a bloody joke somehow. *Damn fool*, Cain thought before he shot him in the face. The man fell down at Cain's feet.

Then grapeshot struck Cain's position, and he was thrown into the air and everything turned to a buzzing gray, as if he had fallen headfirst into a beehive.

When he came to he felt a dull ache in his chest just below his left shoulder, but it was his leg that howled with pain. It felt as if it had been placed in a fire, and a blacksmith was pounding it with a hammer, with the intent of reshaping it into something other than a leg. Trying to rise up, he felt his leg give way and buckle beneath him. He saw that the bone was fractured, his pant leg shredded and bloody. He found his Colt nearby and took it up, checked how many rounds he had left.

Around him he could hear the cries and screams of the wounded and the dying, the neighing of the horses lying on their sides, interspersed with other voices speaking a strange tongue. Pretending to be dead, he closed his eyes and listened as the Mexicans went from one wounded soldier to the next. Before they stuck a bayonet into a chest or slashed a throat with a saber, they'd cry out, *"Recuerde Agua Nueva."* Remember Agua Nueva—where the Massacre of the Cave had taken place. Cain heard them getting closer, and he cocked the hammer of his gun, prepared to kill as many of the bastards as he could before they got him.

He tried, too, to ready himself for death, for surely this was the end. He tried to remember some prayers, a proverb perhaps, something his mother had taught him long ago, something to make his passing easier, but nothing came to him. He remembered her, though, her toothy smile and those gray eyes, and her sweet honeysuckle smell when she'd lean down to kiss him good night. And thinking of her like that, he reckoned then he was as ready to die as he'd ever likely be. The pain in his leg was excruciating, and he'd do almost anything to be shed of it; and what, after all, would he miss from his life? He had no one special waiting for him. He wondered if Alexandra, when she heard, would even shed a tear, or would she think he got only what he deserved for the way he'd abandoned her?

But in war as in life, luck is often the final arbiter of one's fate. The Mexicans happened to take a siesta from their killing spree (that was the thing about his enemy, he'd learned, they didn't do anything, including killing, with the dispassionate intensity of the Americans). With this reprieve, a sudden change of heart came over Cain, and he found himself desperately wanting to live. Despite the pain in his leg, he crawled and pulled and willed himself into a narrow arroyo where he hid behind some rocks. He lay there for the rest of the scorching day, his mouth parched and cracked, his tongue swollen, dreaming of water the way some men dreamed of wealth, others of women. Circling overhead, he saw a few scraggly buzzards, harbingers of death. From his hiding place, he listened to the crying and pleading of his wounded comrades. "For the love of God, no," one voice would exclaim, and then fall silent. Another: "Please don't. I got me a—" before a bayonet silenced it, as well.

He felt an extraordinary sense of guilt. He told himself he should try to get up and fight, should die with his comrades, but for some reason he remained hidden. That wasn't quite true; he knew the reason. He was afraid of dying. It was as simple, as undeniable as that. After a while, the cries stopped altogether. Soon the Mexicans moved off, and night slowly settled in over the mountains like a black shimmery cape. Cain lay there, looking up at the flickering desert stars; he shivered in the cold night air, growing weaker, feeling the life ebbing slowly out of him. He fought to keep his eyes open. He thought if he closed them he would die. He recalled Mr. Beauregard reading from the *Iliad*, Patroclus's death by Hector—*and his eyes were closed in death*. But at last he couldn't fight it anymore, and he gave in to the pressure and let himself drift downward into what he was sure was the cool, sour-smelling embrace of death.

When he opened his eyes in the morning—some morning, maybe days, weeks later, he couldn't say—he was certain he *was* dead, for he was looking up into the sweet face of an angel. Albeit, a brown one, with broad cheekbones and coal black hair pulled into a single thick braid that snaked down her back. Eyes to match her hair, almond shaped, solemn. Light freckles over the bridge of her nose and cheeks. Smallpox scars. A young Indian girl, sixteen, seventeen, though at times she would seem as old and as much lived-in-the-world as the grandmother she stayed with. Much later, through signs and a crude sort of pantomime, for neither could speak the other's language, he would learn how he'd come to be there. How the girl had found him behind the rock, as she and her grandmother had searched the bodies of the dead on both sides, looking for valuables. As the girl rifled through Cain's tunic, besides finding the big Colt revolver and the silver flask with the strange writing on it that she could not read, she'd found something else—a spark of life in the dead soldier.

She'd stared down at Cain, peering at his handsome face, pulling up the lids of his eyes to see if his soul was still a resident there. It was she who'd suggested they bring him back and try to nurse him to health, while the grandmother argued that he would only bring trouble to them, that they should simply leave him as food for the buzzards. The girl, clever beyond her years and willful, said perhaps he was a rich American and that his family might be willing to pay money to have him back alive. The grandmother didn't like the idea of bringing a dead man back with them and threw her hands in the air in disgust. But she knew her headstrong granddaughter would do what she wanted. She always did. On her own, the girl fashioned a travois out of a horse blanket and some cottonwood branches she managed to find and hack into poles; she attached it behind their donkey and dragged the tall American back to their hut high in the desert mountains.

But all of this, he would learn later. In the meantime, he struggled for his life, a man swimming upward as if from the ocean's depths. For several days he was in and out of consciousness, crossing back and forth between the bright realms of the living and the shaded realm of the dead, almost like a courier carrying messages between the two. He had the odd dreams of one suspended between worlds. Some were filled with cool, green water cascading over him, others with a harsh light that blistered the skin like fire. In one he saw his mother. She was at some distance from him, standing by herself in a barren field that had been harvested of its crops. He made for her, but as he drew near she put up her hand and called, "Go back, Augustus. Go back." In another, he lay helpless on the ground as soldiers went among the wounded, administering the coup de grâce with a bright silver blade. He finally regained consciousness, and that's when he saw the girl looking down at him, wiping his face with a wet rag. Her hands smelled earthy, of clay and of onions, and when she breathed on him, her breath was warm and sweet, like that of a nursing puppy.

"Where am I?" he asked hoarsely, glancing around.

She said something in a tongue he didn't understand. He then used the only word he'd picked up of Spanish in the year he'd been in Mexico, a word taught to him by the war itself. "*Muerta?*"

She looked down at him and smiled, showing small, white teeth.

"*Non muerta*," she said. And to prove it she took hold of the flap of skin between his thumb and forefinger and pinched it so hard he cried out in pain. So he knew he was alive because of the pain.

From behind her, an old woman muttered something to the girl and gave her a cup with a bitter liquid for him to drink. She was an ancient crone, bent backed and toothless, her face as parched and furrowed as the arroyos that surrounded her. She wore a brightly colored serape and a floppy panza de burro hat tied under her chin. From her sunken mouth protruded a corncob pipe that she puffed on. The girl's grandmother. He'd come to learn that while the girl had brought him back, it was the old woman who had kept him alive. She knew about herbs and poultices and Indian remedies. When he looked around, he saw he was in some sort of shed that held animals. There were chickens and goats, a pig snorting nearby, in the corner eating from a pile of hay, a donkey who occasionally looked at Cain and brayed noisily, as if he'd taken his spot.

He tried to get up but found he was too weak. Whenever he breathed deeply, his chest burned from the wound there, and every time he moved his leg the least little bit, it would begin throbbing with a pain so bad he almost passed out. So he tried to lie very still on the pile of straw that was his bed. At night he could hear the whisperlike scurrying of tiny feet—mice or scorpions or snakes? He was too sick to care. He didn't sleep well. He kept thinking about his comrades being slaughtered by the Mexicans. He could hear their screams, their pleading, the hollow sound of a blade entering a chest, the mud-sucking *slllppp* as it was withdrawn. Even then he felt the guilt of having lived, and yet he savored his life as never before. Though he had no appetite to speak of, the young girl insisted he eat. She brought him food every morning and evening, a watery mush made of ground cornmeal and flour and milk; with one hand she held his head up and with the fingers of the other shoved food into his mouth, as one might feed a persnickety baby. When he tried to spit it out, she would push it back in until he swallowed it. He was too weak to fight her. Too weak even to get up to go to the bathroom, so he'd do his business in a clay pot that they brought him. A few times the old woman would come to him in the shed, kneel by his side, and pray, sometimes holding a set of rosary beads in her withered old hands, other times a hawk's feather. She would tend to his wounds, too, brusquely, jabbing his flesh so he cried out, putting foul-smelling poultices on them, making him drink something that tasted sour like vinegar.

But slowly the cures began to work. By the second week he was out of danger of dying; by the third he was sitting up and starting to get his appetite back; and by the fourth, with the girl's help, he was standing and hobbling the few paces across the shed. He leaned his full weight on her, and though she was slight and small-boned as a cat, she had a surprising strength. He could feel the corded muscles in her thin back, the heat of her breath against his naked chest as she urged him on. At first, only a few steps exhausted him and he collapsed onto his straw pallet again.

"What's . . . your name?" he asked, out of breath.

"*Yo no entiendo.*"

She knelt beside him, stared uncomprehendingly with those dark, solemn eyes of hers. Around her slender neck hung a silver cross.

Tapping his chest with his fingers, he tried again. "*Cain.* I'm *Cain.*" Then he reached up and touched her shoulder. "What's your . . . name?"

She frowned, then her expression cleared and she said, "*Pecosa.*"

"Your name is *Pecosa*?" he said.

"*Sí.*" She smiled at him and ran her fingers over the freckles across her checks. "*Pecosa. Mi nombre es Pecosa.*"

"Freckles?" he said. "That's your name?"

"*Sí,*" she nodded. "*Pecosa.*"

About the time he was finally able to stand on his own and move about a little, the old woman fashioned him a crutch from a weathered piece of piñon, and he used that to get around. He thought he'd been lucky not to lose the leg, that is, until he saw it. His knee and shin had been shattered. The bone, broken in several places, hadn't healed correctly, and one leg was shorter now than the other by a goodly amount. In addition, a fist-size chunk of flesh had been ripped away from the calf muscle, as if a bite had been taken out of it by a grizzly bear. The pain in his leg didn't go away either, would never completely go away, and from then on he would have a decided limp. He tried to do what little he could to help out around the place, to show his appreciation, but also to prove to himself that he wasn't a cripple. He'd scatter feed to the chickens, split firewood with one hand, tote water on the donkey from the watering hole.

The girl and her grandmother lived twenty paces away in a small mud hut on a high mesa overlooking the valley of Buena Vista. They were mestizas. Half-breeds. Cain had learned about such people during his year in Mexico. Like the Indians back in the States, they were scorned and ridiculed, made outcasts by the "whites" and their government. The mestizos didn't care about the war, it didn't concern them. Whoever was running things—Santa Anna or President Herrera or General Paredes—it was all the same to them. Not that they sided with the invading "gringos" either. They were just more white invaders to them, here to steal what they could. The two women lived north of Buena Vista, a half day's journey from the town of Saltillo. They scratched out a living raising a few chickens, some feral-looking pigs, and a couple of goats for milk, and they grew a small garden of corn and beans and squash. The old woman made clay pots, which they took to Saltillo to sell. They gathered firewood from among the ravines and arroyos and, on the donkey, toted two large clay jugs of brackish, salty-tasting water from a spring at the base of the mountain. Once a month, on a Sunday, the two would pack up the donkey and they'd go into the village to barter eggs and goat cheese and chickens for some flour and sugar and salt, and for the tobacco that the old woman smoked in her pipe. While there they would go to mass at the small Catholic chapel. The old woman was very religious. Every day she would light a candle and pray before a small clay Madonna that stood in the corner of their hut.

When he was well enough, the old woman permitted him to come into the hut where a fire burned in a small hearth made of stones. The desert nights were cold, and the three would sit cross-legged on the hard-packed dirt floor before the blazing fire, Cain and the girl opposite each other, the old woman between them, smoking her pipe and watching them watch each other. During the day, as they worked together, feeding the animals or gathering firewood or milking the goat, Cain and the girl would exchange furtive glances or the faintest trace of a smile. If she caught them, the old woman would frown and nudge the girl back to the business at hand. When he'd return from getting water with the donkey, the girl would come running up to him, as if he'd been gone for years, and say something to him in Spanish, the only word of which he recognized was *Cain*. Once, they were gathering wood along a high ridge, and he tripped and pitched headlong down an incline. He lay there on the dusty earth for a moment with his eyes closed, pretending to be seriously injured. The girl rushed to his side, grabbed his hand, and put it to her mouth.

"Cain!" she cried, worry clouding her features.

He lay there, still for a moment, enjoying the attention.

"Señor *Cain*!" she said, petting his head.

At last he looked up at her and smiled.

She pretended to pout for a moment, then finally gave in to a smile.

Another time he was helping her pluck a chicken whose neck she'd just wrung. They were so close he could smell her bronze skin warming in the afternoon sun. When they happened to brush arms, Cain felt himself shiver, felt a stirring in his chest and belly, down in his loins. She looked at him and he knew she felt it, too. If the old woman caught them flirting, she might say something to her granddaughter in a tone of obvious reprimand. The girl, strong-willed, would argue with her grandmother, their voices growing heated, though finally she would lower her eyes and appear contrite. At least for a few seconds. As soon as the old woman left, she'd turn to Cain and smile again.

At night he shivered under a thin blanket, trying to keep warm in the chill desert air. He'd hear the donkey farting or a mouse scratching in the hay. Through the open window of the hut he could see a square of night sky, framed like a painting—blue-black and shot through with more stars than he'd ever seen before. The war already seemed a distant thing, something he'd read about in a book as a child. On the few occasions when he'd think of home, of his father and brother, of Alexandra, they, too, seemed to him parts of another life, a life that had died in him out on the battlefield. He would think of the girl's warm arm brushing his and how her skin smelled and the silken way it felt beneath his hand, and the way she looked at him with those dark, serious eyes, gleaming like a cat's before a fire. Then one night he had a dream in which the girl appeared to him as he slept. When he awoke, though, he was startled to realize that it was no dream. She put her hand over his mouth as she crawled beneath the blanket. She shed her clothes, and her body felt warm and liquid in his arms. "Cain," she whispered hotly into his ear. By the way she moved and understood a man's body, what to do and when, he sensed that he was not the first man she'd been with. Still, it didn't matter. She had her own sort of innocence, the unblemished virtue of some wild, untamed thing. He loved her supple body moving against his, loved her dark eyes, loved the way she murmured deep in her throat as he entered her. *Cain*.

Sometimes when they were together, he felt as if he *had* died out on the battlefield and gone to heaven. This was his heaven, the only one he'd ever know. And he never wanted to leave it. When they were finished, she pulled on her clothes and kissed him once more and whispered, "Cain," before quietly slipping back to the hut. From then on, she came to him each night. After they were finished, she would dress and slip cautiously back to sleep with her grandmother. In the morning when he woke up, it would seem like a fantastic dream. But then she'd look at him in the daylight as they fed the chickens or hoed the garden, and her expression would tell him it had happened.

He sometimes wondered if his family had heard that he was missing and had presumed him dead. He felt sorry for them. What of Alexandra? How would she take the news of his death? Perhaps she wouldn't even care after his betrayal. Then again, even this pseudodeath brought to him a certain freedom. He would never have to go back to that other life. Sometimes, however, the call of duty would stir in him; he would tell himself he should try to get back to his company. He didn't even know how the battle had turned out or even how the war was going. It was as if he had stepped out of time, and everything had passed him by. Were they looking for him? Or had they assumed he'd died with the others? Each day as he got better, stronger, a part of him thought he should make some sort of attempt at contacting them, maybe ask to borrow the donkey and ride down out of the mountains to see what he could find out. He had, after all, signed up to fight. He wasn't a coward. His own notion of honor was at stake. Of course, going back was not without danger. What if the Mexicans still controlled this territory? Might they not kill him as they had the others? And even if he managed to make it to the American lines, wherever they were, what then? Did he really want to go back to the war? To all that dying and killing and bloodshed.

So, for days which flowed seamlessly into weeks and then into months, he did nothing. He stayed there with the Indian girl and her grandmother, keeping out of sight, helping with the chores, making love at night. Unlike back home, here he couldn't tell the passing of the seasons. The days arrived bright and hot and dry, the nights grew frigid and stark. Occasionally, when he was off gathering firewood or toting water, he'd see a rider in the distance, and, fearing it was a Mexican, he'd duck and hide behind a rock or a tree. One time, a Mexican on a horse actually appeared at the home of the two women. Luckily, Cain was in the shed milking one of the goats at the time, so he wasn't seen. He watched as the man spoke to the old woman. Though Cain couldn't understand what was being said, it was obvious that the man was angry. He waved his arms about and pointed and yelled at the old woman in Spanish. The old woman yelled back at him, and with her hand waved him away. Cain cocked his revolver, ready, if need be, to use it. But soon the man turned and rode off. Cain tried to find out what the matter was from the girl Pecosa, but she merely shook her head, made it seem as if it were nothing to worry about. And once when he had gone for water, he saw in the distance a company of American cavalry crossing the battlefield of Buena Vista. He tried to tell himself that it wasn't his war, that it had *never* been his war. That he'd been running from a life he felt trapped in and the war was just a way to escape it. Why couldn't he stay here forever? Why couldn't he spend the rest of his life with this girl? He was, for the first time in his life, happy, content, in love.

Yet he couldn't stop feeling that he was a deserter, that he had dishonored himself. Here there were men, good and brave men, fighting and dying, and what was he doing? Hiding with a girl and an old woman. Doing the sort of farmwork that he'd always thought tedious. He kept remembering that day at Buena Vista where the Mexicans had killed his comrades. He felt guilty. He believed he should have died with them, instead of hiding like a cowardly cur. Yes, he needed to go back. He needed to do his duty. The girl and what he felt for her, though immediate and palpable, were not, he had managed to convince himself, as strong as the pull of obligation, of duty and honor.

"I have to go back," he told her finally.

She sensed what his words meant and she clutched him, wrapping her arms around his neck, as if she could keep him from returning to the madness of war. He tried to make her understand that he would be back, that as soon as the war was over, he'd return to her, that he was only going away for a while. But she cried and held him harder, so that finally he had to pry her away from him. "I love you," he said. "I'll be back." He kissed her, and as the old woman held her, Cain turned and walked down from the mountains.

After journeying for several days, with his leg howling in pain, he ran into a company of Texas Rangers. The war, he learned, was in fact just about over. The American forces under Winfield Scott had captured Mexico City, and it was only a matter of time before Mexico surrendered. For several months he was placed, with other deserters, in the brig of a man-o'-war off the coast of Veracruz. There was even talk about court-martialing him for desertion. The pain in his leg continued, was at times so unbearable that the prison doctor finally gave him opium, as he did all the wounded soldiers. That's where his craving for the substance began. Cain would lie on his bunk, chewing opium until the pain's edge was blunted if not obliterated, and think about the Indian girl. All the months he remained in his cell, he thought of her. He came to realize two things: that he loved her more than anything in the world, and that his leaving had been a foolish mistake. His one thought now was to make his way back to her.

As soon as the war ended, his commanding officers spoke of his good service, his bravery, his wounds, and in one of the many ironies of war, they not only didn't press charges against him but they also awarded him a medal for his bravery at Buena Vista. Once released, with what little money he had, he bought a swaybacked nag, a frayed saddle, and enough food and water and ammo to last him until he reached Buena Vista. As he rode north, he found himself thinking about the girl, about the life they'd have together. He knew what he was doing was crazy, crazier even than the time he'd fallen in love with Eileen McDuffy. But he also knew it was the most sane thing he'd ever done.

He rode high up into the desert mountains. As he got closer, he could feel his heart beating faster in anticipation of seeing his beloved. Yet as he approached, hanging in the air was the distinctive foulness of postbattle, the stench of fire and ash, of burned and rotting flesh. At last, he reached the meager parcel of ground where the girl and her grandmother lived. What he saw choked the breath from his lungs. All that remained of the hut and shed was charred rubble. The old woman's pots were broken and scattered, and the putrifying carcasses of the animals lay covered under bluebottle flies and maggots. *No!* he cried. *No!* He frantically searched through the ashes, looking for their bodies, but didn't find them. He kept thinking, *What happened? Who did this?* He made out the hoofprints of a dozen riders. Saw in the forehead of the donkey a hole made by a musket ball. Then he recalled the Mexican who had argued with the old woman. Cain fell to his knees and began to cry.

Though he already knew in his heart that they were dead, he searched the mountains for them for several days, trying to convince himself that somehow they'd managed to flee before the riders came, that they were still there hiding out, waiting. But he saw no sign of them, no tracks, nothing. Finally, he rode north into the village of Saltillo, searching for answers. There he asked about the Indian girl and the old woman. Few spoke English, and those who did said they knew nothing about the two. Yet the more he asked around, the more he felt something wasn't right. Other women, he learned, were missing, too, sisters, daughters, mothers. Finally, Cain was in the livery having his horse reshod. The man who ran it spoke some English.

"Señor, you are the one looking for the Indian girl, *sí*?" the man said to him as he worked on the horse.

"Yes. She was called Pecosa. Do you know her?" Cain asked.

"A little."

"What happened to her?"

Looking cautiously out into the street, he said to Cain in an undertone, "*Vaya al sacerdote.* He knows."

"He knows what?" Cain asked.

"What they did to them."

The old man went on to tell him how, after the war, the priest had wanted revenge for what the Americans had done, the slaughter of those in the chapel near Agua Nueva. He'd incited the men of the village to round up women who'd befriended Americans, like those of the brothel who'd slept with the soldiers, others who'd simply sold them a drink or danced with them in the cantina. They called them "gringo whores." The priest, a certain Padre Juan, the old man told Cain, had worked the men of the village into a frenzy of vengeance.

"What did they do to them?" Cain asked once more, fear and anger boiling in him.

"*Ellos los mataron*," he said. "Kill them."

Cain's heart turned to a piece of jagged iron in his chest. "How?"

"*La colgaron*," he explained, pretending a rope pulled his neck at a sharp angle. Then the man made the sign of the cross.

Cain felt two emotions at once. He felt a burning guilt for having involved her, and for having left her. He told himself that if he had stayed she would still be alive. That somehow he could've prevented it, protected her, or, at least, died trying. The other emotion he felt was a terrible thirst for vengeance; he wanted to kill whoever was responsible for her death.

That night, Cain waited in an alley across from the small chapel. He saw Padre Juan, a stocky, bearded man with the ruddy complexion of a peasant, come out and welcome people to mass. The man seemed kindly, a caring minister of his flock—which only made Cain the more incensed. As Cain watched, he would remove from his pocket the medicine the army doctor had handed out in prison. He had begun to take it even when he felt no pain in his leg. Its absence now was a form of pain. When the last communicant left, Cain slipped in the chapel. Inside, it was dark except for the flickering light of candles up near the front. He found the priest kneeling before a statue of the Virgin, praying. He wore a long hooded cassock and his florid face was hidden in shadow. Cain crept up on him, stood listening for a moment. He recognized only a little of the Latin: *requiem, aeternam, Domine*. Then he moved quickly up behind the priest, took his head in his left hand and pulled it back against his own chest so the neck was drawn taut and exposed. He brought his knife around and in one movement slit the priest's throat from ear to ear. The dark blood spurted over Cain's sleeve and down onto the floor. The priest struggled for just a moment in Cain's arms, then he relaxed and accepted his death as a man must. Cain lay the priest gently down in front of the Virgin and left the chapel.

He got on his horse and rode hard through the night, heading for the border. Killing the priest left him feeling neither good nor bad. It was just something he'd had to do and he'd done it, just as he'd killed men in the war. Another form of duty. Though he was headed in the direction of home, he knew he would never go there again. He knew that his former life was over, that it had died for him on the battlefield that day in Buena Vista, but that the one he was leaving now was over, too. He had no idea what his life would look like from then on, and right then he didn't particularly care. He was a man suddenly cut off from all the things that normally attached a person to his world. He felt weightless, but not in a good way, not in the way he had once wanted to be free. He felt almost as if he could float right up into the night, higher and higher into the black firmament, rising up until he was lost among the stars.

When he ran out of the medicine he had by then come to depend on, he would stop at an apothecary's or a physician's house and buy a bottle of laudanum. As he put the bottle to his mouth, he recalled the way his mother smelled when she drank it, a thickly sweet odor. One night, as he rode along a lonely stretch of South Texas highway, he had taken so much that he started to see demons coming at him. They swooped and dove at him from the night sky. They cut his skin with their razor-sharp claws. They were joined by those other men he'd killed during the war and by the priest, too, Padre Juan, whose throat flapped open like the bloody gills of a fish out of water. Cain drew his Colt and fired on them, fired until the gun was empty, but still they came on. He found a hollowed-out tree and crawled into it. Before the night was over, he had actually considered taking his own life, of putting the gun in his mouth and joining the priest in hell or wherever he was. But he didn't.

As he rode along the next morning, he thought of the girl, her smell and her touch and the way she smiled when she called him Cain. He knew in the cool light of day that it was somehow for the best that he had loved her, despite the terrible emptiness he felt with her loss.

PART
TWO

For by this cunning arrangement, the slaveholder, in cases not a few, sustains to his slaves the double relation of master and father.

FREDERICK DOUGLASS, *NARRATIVE*

8

They reached the outskirts of Boston just after sunset. From a small rise of land south of the city, they looked out across a bay filled with more ships than they'd ever seen before—sloops and schooners, steamships and ketches, clipper ships and whalers. Even at this hour, ships were coming and going, being unloaded or loaded. In fact, the entire city buzzed with activity. Elegant coaches and cabriolets wound about its streets, wagons pulled by plodding draft horses carted goods to and from the wharves, and along the many bridges leading from the city people were taking an evening stroll. The city's lights were just coming on, gaslights shimmering like the small fires of an army the night before a battle. On a hill in the center of town, the golden dome of the statehouse dominated the skyline, glittering like a diamond.

"Looky there," Little Strofe said, whistling. "Ain't n-never seen nothing so big."

"And from what I hear tell, ever dang one a them's a ab'litionist, too," Preacher offered.

Cain dismounted and removed from his pocket a piece of sugar and fed it to Hermes, who chewed on it noisily. When it was done, he nuzzled Cain's pockets for more, shoving him forcibly backward.

"We have to worry about the vigilance committee," he explained to the others.

"Vigilance what?" Strofe asked.

"A group that hides fugitive slaves," Cain explained, adjusting the bit in the horse's mouth. "Every city up north of any size has one. They hear that a runaway has been taken into custody, they'll be out in force. Sic their lawyers on them. Get all the Negroes in town stirred up. And then you've kicked up a hornet's nest. They take one look at us and they'll know right quick what our business is."

"I swear, you worry just like an old lady, Cain," Preacher said.

Cain glanced over at the blond-haired man.

"You ever heard of the Shadrach case, you ignorant son of a bitch."

"Cain't say as I have."

"It was in all the papers. Then again, that's assuming one can read," Cain said patronizingly. "You heard of Dred Scott, haven't you?"

"Yeah, I heard a that nigger, all right."

"Well, the Shadrach case was just about the biggest fugitive case before Scott. It happened right here in Boston," Cain explained. "A few years back, an owner's agent tracked a fugitive by the name of Shadrach Minkins to Boston. He had a warrant for the Negro and used a federal marshal to have him brought before a commissioner. They ordered him remanded to the custody of the owner's legal agent. But then the vigilance committee got wind of it and turned out a mob. They stormed the courthouse and surrounded him with a crowd of freed Negroes. Took him right out of the hands of the marshals and led him away to Canada. They never did get him back."

"Any nigger fucks with me," Preacher said, looking over at Henry, who was seated on the mule to his right, "that'll be the last person he fucks with, yessirree."

Cain loosened the cinch and removed the saddle. Hermes had developed a galling sore low on the withers where the saddle had been chafing, and he didn't want it to get infected.

"We headin' into town tonight?" Strofe asked Cain.

"I figure we'll make camp here and then ride in in the morning. One, maybe two of us."

Preacher let out a derisive laugh. "And I reckon one a them'd be you, right, Cain?"

"You heard a thing I just said? We go riding in there, all of us, they're going to know what we're up to, and we'll have hell to pay."

"Well, maybe y'all ought to stay back and I'll head in. How do that suit you?"

"He knows what he's doing, Preacher," said Strofe. "You don't."

"Huh! He ain't proved it by me. Not by a long shot."

"You're working for me, and you'll do what I say," Strofe warned.

Preacher stared at Strofe for a moment. "Not tonight, boss man," Preacher said. "Tonight I don't work for nobody. See y'all later."

"Where you off to?" Strofe asked.

"Gone have me some fun."

"Well, don't get in any trouble," Strofe warned.

"Don't you worry about me. I can take care of myself."

"And don't go shooting your mouth off to nobody. You heard what Cain said."

"What I got in mind don't call for talkin'. Fixin' to get me some of that Yankee pussy," he said, laughing.

He glanced at Cain, spat a greenish brown clump of tobacco juice at his feet, and wheeled his silvery roan sharply around. He took off down the hill at a wild gallop toward the city.

"Ain't been nothing but trouble that one," Strofe lamented.

While Little Strofe began a fire and set about making supper, Cain brought Hermes down to a small stream to drink. There he hobbled him, and while he was grazing on some grass, he curried him until his coat shone. Then he got some liniment from his saddlebags and rubbed it into the sore on his back.

He didn't like having to go into Boston to search for the girl. He'd been here back in '50, right after the new Fugitive Slave Law had gone into effect. Part of the Great Compromise aimed at averting the approaching storm, the bloodbath everyone, except perhaps old Clay and Webster themselves, knew even then was inevitable. Cain had been after two runaway slaves that time, brothers who'd fled from Newport News, where they'd worked as caulkers in a shipyard. He'd tracked them here and found them easily enough, living down near the docks of the North End. But just before he had a chance to grab them, the Shadrach case happened. Every Negro in the city suddenly became jumpy, arming themselves with guns or knives, and looking over their shoulders for the hand of a slave catcher to snatch them back into bondage. And the vigilance committee was keeping a sharp eye out for suspicious southerners, putting up posters and ads in the newspapers aimed at warning escaped Negroes of the presence of southern agents in the city.

It took him several weeks of spying on the two, biding his time, waiting for the right moment to act. Every time he was about to jump them and take them into custody, something would happen. The two would run into a group of acquaintances or they'd split up and go separate ways, or they'd turn into a busy thoroughfare and he'd have to give it up. During his stay in Boston, he lodged at the fashionable Tremont Hotel on Beacon, though he could hardly afford it on the three dollars a day he received for expenses. But he was able to supplement his income, as he often did, by gambling. Each night they had a friendly game of poker in a back room for some of the hotel's more wealthy clientele, and he talked himself into it. He acted the part of a well-to-do southern importer of silks from the Far East; he laughed congenially and talked knowingly about places like Peking and Siam as if he'd been there many times, all the while relieving the others of their money. Cain found several of the men to be dough-faced northerners, Yankees who sympathized with the South's position on slavery. One gray-bearded old man, a Captain Beardsley, would have supper with him in the hotel's dining room. He confessed to Cain that he'd captained an illegal slaver.

"Ran slaves out of Cuba," he explained, puffing on a large Havana cigar. He gave Cain a box of them. "Right under the nose of the patrols. Had to grease a few hands, of course. What the hypocrites up here won't admit is that without cotton, the North wouldn't survive. And without slaves there wouldn't be cotton."

Cain bided his time, watching the two fugitives. Then one night he followed the brothers home from a grog shop. He waited till they were in a narrow back alley in the North End, and then approached them speaking with a French accent. "*Pardonnez-moi, messieurs,*" he exclaimed. They were wary at first of a white man, until he told them he'd just arrived in America from France and was lost; he said he would be most appreciative if they could help him find his way back to the Tremont Hotel, where he was staying. He even offered them each a cigar. The brothers began to relax as they gave him directions. It was then that he pulled a gun on them and said he had a warrant for their arrest, that if they tried anything he would shoot them dead. Before they knew it they found themselves in irons and headed south. Having learned his lesson from the Shadrach case, Cain bypassed the legal niceties of the new slave law and spirited them out of Boston under cover of darkness.

Cain brought a plate of food over to Henry, who sat shackled to a birch tree near the horses. The spring night was cool and clear, salt scented, the sky laden heavily with stars. From where they sat atop the hill, they could see in the distance the ocean, whose sound came to them muffled, like the breath of an old man sleeping. A lighthouse shone a few miles out in the harbor, every now and then casting its light toward the shore.

"I'm going to take these off," Cain said, indicating the shackles. "Don't try anything."

"I sho'nuf won't," the Negro said.

Cain removed the key from his vest pocket—he kept one key on his person at all times, a second remained in the saddlebags with the other shackles. He unlocked the shackles and sat near him while Henry ate the cornmeal with his fingers and dipped his fried corn pone into it.

"You said this girl Rosetta went to stay with a family named Howard."

"Das right," he said, hungrily shoveling the food into his mouth.

"You're telling me the truth, right, Henry?"

"I swear to God."

Cain looked over his shoulder at the two Strofes seated around the campfire, some thirty feet away.

"Here, Henry," he said, handing him his flask." The Negro took it and drank from it eagerly, winced at the taste, then wiped the mouth of the flask off on his sleeve and handed it back.

"That sho warms a belly. Thank ye kindly, massa."

In an undertone, Cain asked, "May I ask you something, Henry? And I want you to tell me the truth."

The Negro nodded.

"How well did you know the girl?"

"Told you, didn't lay no hand on her."

"I believe you. I just want to know how well you knew her back on Eberly's plantation?"

"Knew her some. Saw her about, here and there. I works in the tannery making shoes and such. She be up in the massa house. Didn't have much truck wid her."

"She have an easy life?"

"What you mean easy?"

"I mean up there in the house, did she have certain privileges the rest of you didn't?"

"I reckon so. House niggers always does. Mr. Eberly he treat her right fine. Dress her up in fancy clothes. Treat her like a white woman."

"Sounds like she had it pretty good. Then why did she run?"

Henry paused in his eating for a moment and looked over at Cain.

"Ever' slave gits him a notion to run now and then. 'Sides, Miss Rosetta she ain't like reg'lar slaves."

"How so?"

"She uppity," he said with a laugh. "Think herself better'n ever'body else. You ax any slave on massa's plantation, they tell you about her."

"Did the other slaves resent her?"

"I reckon some did. Like I said, she got a high opinion of herself."

"Did she steal something, Henry?"

"Steal something?"

"Something of value from Eberly."

The Negro shook his head. "I don't rightly know. If she done so, she didn't tell me nothin'."

"What happened to her child?"

"Chile?" he said, knitting his brows.

"I know she had a child. Eberly told me," Cain lied. He wasn't even sure why he wanted to know all this. He told himself that by knowing more about her it would help him catch her. But then again, it was probably just his own curiosity. "What happened to it, Henry?"

Before answering, he looked uneasily over Cain's shoulder at the Strofes.

"Massa Eberly done sold him off," Henry said.

"Why?"

"I guess 'cause she run off."

"I heard it was on account of how she'd knifed him."

"Maybe so."

"Was it his? Eberly's child?"

Another look toward Strofe.

"I doan rightly know."

"I know there's talk among the slaves. What did they say?"

"Some say it was massa's."

"What else did they say?"

"Nuthin'."

Cain offered the flask again. Henry took another drink.

"Why did he sell her child, then?"

"Like I said, to learn her a lesson. Fo' runnin' off like dat."

"And for knifing him?"

"Fo' both, I reckon."

"Did you know what the child's name was?"

Henry considered that for a moment, screwing up his mouth. Finally he said, "Israel."

"Israel?"

"Yessum."

The next morning Strofe had his brother stay behind to watch Henry while he and Cain mounted up and rode into Boston. They followed The Neck, the strip of land that had once been a thin umbilical cord linking the city to the mainland but which now, due to all the dredging, was over a mile across and covered with roads and buildings. To the east, the sky over the water was overcast and leaden, the sun behind the clouds singeing the edges, turning them a fiery pink. A clipper ship was slowly being towed out of the harbor by a steam tugboat.

As chance would have it, they ran into Preacher on the roan coming the other way. Half asleep in the saddle, he had a raw-looking gash under his left eye that continued to ooze blood down his gaunt cheek. From ten feet, he stank of axle grease and rotgut whiskey. Cain thought there was something else different about him, though he couldn't at first put his finger on it.

"The hell happened to you?" Strofe asked.

"The fuckin' whore," he said, his speech still thick from drink. "She wouldn't take three dollars, though I done told her it was all I had. So I took me three dollars' worth, which was two more'n she was worth. But the bitch sicced her fancy man after me."

"Looks like you came out on the short end of the horn," Strofe said with a laugh.

"He knowed he was in a scrape," he said, with a crooked smile. "And I fixed that bitch's wagon but good."

"Where's your hat, Preacher?"

Preacher reached up and touched his bare head, as if he'd just noticed it was gone. So that was it, Cain thought. In all the weeks they'd been together, he'd not seen him without it. Hatless, his blond head looked small and unformed, vulnerable as the head of a baby bird.

"Damned if I know," Preacher said, spurring the horse and taking off. As he rode away, he teetered unsteadily in the saddle, as if he might fall out of it.

The city was filled with crowds of disheveled, scarecrow-looking people wandering aimlessly about. As Cain and Strofe rode along, they were approached several times by grimy urchins with dirty, outstretched hands. "Sir, could ye spare a penny," a child would say in a frail, lilting accent. Cain was amazed at how much things had changed since he'd last been here. Back in '50, the Irish had just started to spill out of their plague-infested famine ships, fleeing the holocaust of their homeland. He remembered Eileen McDuffy telling him about the terrible hardships that she'd left back in Ireland, and that was well before the famine. She would hold his head against her soft, white breasts and sing to him sad songs of home.

"Who the hell are all these no-account Jonathans?" Strofe asked.

"Irish," Cain replied.

"What're they doing here?"

"They've had a great famine back in their own country."

They were everywhere, sleeping in doorways, standing on street corners and in alleyways, pushing carts loaded with coal or fish. The worst of them were the children. Dressed in rags, their faces besmirched, gaunt and sallow skinned. Some hawked apples or roasted chestnuts, while many just stood there with their bony hands extended, waiting for a penny. Cain threw a coin to one or two, and rode on.

At the City Hall on School Street, he told Strofe to watch the horses while he went inside. He spoke to a tall, thin man with muttonchops and told him he was looking for someone but didn't know where he lived. The man led him to a stuffy, windowless room and got out a large ledger book that said *Boston Directory* on the cover.

"Anybody registered as living in Boston should be listed in there," the man told him. "Has occupations and addresses."

Cain turned to the *H*s, found five Howards listed, and wrote down their addresses. He suspected it wouldn't be this simple, though sometimes it turned out to be, and so he started there.

They spent the better part of the morning looking up the first two on the list. The first was named Samuel Howard, a bookseller whose store was in Cambridge across from the city jail. Before they went in, Cain asked Strofe if the runaway knew what he looked like.

"'Course she knows what I look like."

"Then whyn't you wait around back in the alley. If she's here, I don't want to spook her. I won't be long."

Cain went in and spent an hour leisurely looking up and down the shelves at all the books. He hadn't had the opportunity to do this in some time, so he enjoyed himself thoroughly. When he was a boy and his father would take him to Richmond, he used to love perusing musty old volumes in Hoynby's booksellers.

After a while Strofe came lumbering up to him.

"What are you doing in here?" Cain said to him.

"She here or not?" he whispered to him.

"I didn't inquire yet."

He watched as Cain turned back to a slender volume he held in his hands. "What in the Sam Hill you doin', Cain?"

"Do you know what this is?"

"A book."

"Not just a book. A first edition of *Rasselas*."

"We ain't come all this way to waste our time looking at a dang book."

"I'll be right out," he told him.

Strofe stared at him in disbelief.

"Mr. Eberly's gone hear about this," he said as he sulked out of the store.

When Cain went to purchase the book, he engaged Mr. Howard, an old man with long white hair, in a discussion about Johnson. During the course of the conversation, Cain drew the man out. He learned that Mr. Howard and his invalid wife lived above their store, and it was obvious from things he said that they didn't have the time or the inclination to be harboring an escaped slave. Cain bought the book anyway, thanked the man, and left.

The next Howard, an Edward, turned out to live in Fort Hill, a poor section in the southeast part of the city. Cain went up to the door and was greeted by a pale, dark-haired young woman with a Scottish brogue. He asked if he might speak to Mr. Howard on a matter of urgent business. The woman's eyes turned unfocused suddenly, and then she started to cry. Cain gave her a handkerchief while she explained to him that recently her husband, while sailing back to Scotland to visit his aging father, had contracted ship fever and died, leaving her a widow with four young children. Cain offered her his condolences and left.

The third on the list appeared more promising. This Howard, a lawyer, lived in a grand house in the Back Bay. When Cain had made inquiries about Elias Howard in a nearby pub, he learned that he indeed had abolitionist sympathies and, on at least one occasion, had defended a runaway slave in court. Cain and Strofe took up positions on either end of the street, which was lined with linden trees.

"Pull your hat down low and try not to look too obvious," Cain advised him.

They watched the residence for two days. While waiting in an alley, Cain bought a newspaper from a passing boy and spent some time perusing it. He read an article about several new cases of cholera breaking out among the immigrant ships in the harbor and another about the Panic and how a number of banks had closed on account of it. He read about the recently inaugurated President Buchanan sending more troops to Kansas to quell the continued fighting out there. Mention was also made of a certain Mr. Thoreau, who had given a lecture at the Concord town hall just the week before. In it he had praised John Brown's work on behalf of "our Negro brethren" and he'd asked for financial support so that the good captain might continue to carry on his noble mission. Cain wondered whether or not they'd seen the last of Brown. At the bottom of one page was the obituary of a young woman named Maria Howells, nineteen, who had drowned in a boating accident off a place called Nahant. Her betrothed had written an elegy to occasion the woman's death.

> The flowerlets of Summer were blooming,
> The pine Groves were thrilling with Song,
> And gay Birds on golden Wings mounting,
> Like Sunbeams were flitting along,
> While Clouds o'er the blue azure sailing,
> Like spirits of Beauty and more,
> And seemed, on the rapt Vision beaming
> Let down from the region of Love!

Cain knew the verse to be doggerel, but the poem made him think of his Indian girl. He wished he'd done something like that, written a poem to her memory.

On page two he came across an article about a murder. It said the body of a woman had been found down near the docks on Atlantic Avenue. She had been viciously beaten and her throat cut. The article said that she was well known among the police as Singapore Sally, a lady of the evening. Authorities were requesting that anyone having information about the crime contact the police. Cain thought of Preacher, of how he'd had a run-in with the whore he'd been with, how he said he'd fixed her wagon.

When they hadn't seen any sign of the runaway by the end of the first day, they got a room at a boardinghouse down near the Charles to save them the trouble of riding all the way out into the countryside. It was a squalid place, a haunt of tars and strumpets and men of questionable character. They had to share a bed. Strofe's stomach problems continued. He alternated between groaning and farting, and getting up and rushing to the outhouse in back. When he finally did fall asleep he snored so loudly he woke Cain up. Cain would elbow him in the side, and he'd turn over, only to fall to snoring again shortly.

The next morning they returned to spying on Elias Howard's residence. Mr. Howard was a short, stout, ruddy-faced man who wore a tall stovepipe hat. Each morning he went off to work and returned late in the evening appearing shorter and more ruddy-faced; his wife, willowy and delicate, usually left the house midmorning accompanied by a servant, a young Negro girl. They'd return with the servant straining under her purchases. They had two other Negroes who worked for them, a heavy, middle-aged female cook who lived with them and a gray-haired old man who showed up to drive their cabriolet or lug coal into the house. But they saw no sign of the runaway they were after. Cain finally concluded they were wasting their time here. They quit for the evening and decided to head back to the boardinghouse. On the way, they stopped at a public house and ordered supper.

"I'll break that nigger's neck he lied to us," Strofe said, sipping on a hot rum.

"We still have two more names on the list," offered Cain.

"Mr. Eberly's gonna be madder'n a wet hen we don't find her."

"If she's here, we'll find her."

"And what if she ain't?" Strofe picked something from his beard, inspected it closely, then put it in his mouth and chewed. "How come you do this, Cain?"

"Do what?"

"Hunt down runaways."

Cain shrugged. "The money is good."

"I wouldn't figure you for something like this."

"No?" Cain said. "What would you figure me for?"

"I don't know. Not this."

That night, as Strofe lay in bed snoring loudly away, Cain had trouble sleeping. Finally, he got up and went over to the window, staring out at the darkened city. He thought about his conversation with Strofe earlier. About why he did this. He couldn't say really, no more than any man could say why he'd chosen this path or that. A combination of luck and fate. Being injured in the war. Seeing that ad in the newspaper. He supposed money did have a good bit to do with it, as it always did in the affairs of men. But in any event, this would be his last hunt. He would get out of this filthy business once and for all. He would do something else with his life. Even if he did feel old, he was still a young man, with a young man's dreams. Maybe he would head out west. Men were still finding gold out there. Perhaps with the money he got for bringing back the runaway, he could head out there and use it as a grubstake to set him up. Maybe his luck would be better in California.

The following morning, they left early, heading for the next Howard on the list, a fellow named John who lived clear across the city in the North End. It was a bright spring day, sunny, with the dew already burning off and the pungent salt- and fish- and human-smell of the city already percolating. They were riding along Joy Street, a slovenly neighborhood made up of Negro freedmen and Irish immigrants. The street was crowded now with people heading off to work, carpenters and shipwrights, coopers and masons lugging the tools of their trade. Many emerged from dark, fetid alleyways in crowded, unkempt tenements. Raw sewage and horse manure and garbage littered the ground while, overhead, clothes dangled from lines strung between windows.

"Do you reckon—" Strofe began, but then stopped in mid-sentence.

Cain was riding ahead of him and he turned in the saddle. "Do I reckon what?"

But Strofe's attention was caught by something up ahead. "Son of a bitch," he said, pointing up the street. "There she be."

Cain looked where he was pointing. Walking up in front of them some thirty paces and on the opposite side of the street was a young Negro woman. She wore a blue dress of homespun, an apron over that, and on her head a red kerchief. She walked solidly in a man's sturdy dark brogans, and in the crook of an arm she carried an empty shopping basket, as if she were headed to market. She was tall and sinewy, long of neck and leg, with broad shoulders. He could tell she wasn't a field nigger by the way she carried herself, light and effortlessly, her bearing erect, someone not used to stooping to pick cotton or tobacco. Her stride was swift and agile, with the suppleness of a cat. Cain reined in Hermes, not wanting to get too close and tip off their presence to her.

"What we gonna do?" asked Strofe, leaning toward Cain.

"We wait."

"Hell, whyn't we just take her?"

"With all these people around, we'd have half the city down on us."

"So what's your plan?"

"We follow her for a while. See where she's headed."

They trailed her at a prudent distance. She kept her gaze down, not making eye contact, and she walked briskly toward Faneuil Market, which was on the east side of the city, toward the bay. She didn't acknowledge anyone she passed but moved anonymously through the crowd with the wariness of a deer that had caught the scent of the hunter, as if she sensed danger all around her, as if she felt at any moment a hand might light on her shoulder and draw her back into servitude. In Cain's experience, when most new runaways were among the free they still walked with the mentality of a slave, head down, trying not to catch the eye of someone who might recognize them. In fact, this very caution was often a dead giveaway as to their status. She turned into several side streets and narrow lanes, and each time she did Cain and Strofe held back, not wanting her to become aware of them. Yet, when she turned onto the busy Court Street, they'd followed a little too closely, afraid they might lose her. She stopped abruptly, and the two riders almost ran headlong into her. They weren't ten feet apart. Fortunately, the street was crowded at this hour with people going to and fro, with other riders and carriages, so they didn't stand out as much as they would have in some back lane.

She'd paused to gaze into a shop window at something. With the sun low and glinting off the glass, Cain couldn't see what it was. But it had obviously caught the girl's fancy. She stared dreamily, even wistfully into the shop window, her lips parted, her free hand absentmindedly playing with a loose tendril of hair. After a while she seemed to be staring at herself in the glass, for she pulled the strand of hair back behind her ear and she adjusted the kerchief on her head. Perhaps it was then that she noticed in the reflection the two men on horseback behind her. She turned and glanced over her shoulder in their direction. For a precarious moment, she seemed to look right at Cain, their eyes locking, as occasionally happens between the hunted and the hunter, right before the trigger is pulled. He was certain she recognized them for what they were, with that sixth sense runaways possessed to nose out a slave catcher even among a crowd. He was prepared, if she bolted, to run her down and take their chances with grabbing her in broad daylight. But two things worked in their favor. Luckily, Strofe had had the presence of mind to pull his hat down over his face and pretend to be occupied by a fit of coughing. And the lure of the article in the window proved too strong, for it drew her attention back into the window. She turned and continued staring at it, a vague smile slowly forming on her lips, a smile she fought to suppress but couldn't.

She was a light-skinned octoroon, her complexion the color of cured tobacco, with highlights of red in it suggesting some distant Indian blood. Her face was lean and angular, with high cheekbones and a nose somewhat long for a Negro, a mouth full yet held in check, almost against its own nature. And then there were the eyes, large and of a shade of blue Cain hadn't seen before, not even in a white person, and filled with a serious expression that was both defiant and yet restrained, a fearsome sort of energy barely contained by a sheer mastery of will. He'd seen that sort of look only in certain wild-spirited horses, ones who'd been saddle-broke but retained all of their mettle, who were always looking for the chance to throw a rider from its back and stomp him into the ground if the chance ever presented itself. She was, he thought, striking more than pretty, beautiful in a fierce, defiant sort of way, the way some forces of nature—a storm or lightning— could be considered beautiful. And she reminded him, vaguely but decidedly, of someone he'd once known. Some Negro perhaps who used to work on his father's farm. Or a runaway he'd once captured. Still, Cain suddenly knew why Eberly had set such store by her and was willing to go to such lengths to have her returned. She was not something an owner would want to lose. *Bring her back*, the old man had told him. Cain thought how vulnerable the arrogant Eberly had sounded, and now he could see why.

Then she turned and was in motion again, moving amid the morning crowd down Court Street. As they passed the shop she'd been gazing in, Cain cast a curious sideways glance. In the window hung an elegant woman's dress, long-sleeved, gathered at the waist with a bustle filling out the back, and delicate lace at the sleeves and around the high-necked collar. It was blue. The shiny material— was it silk or satin?—caught and reflected the light back into the street.

They trailed her into the teeming Faneuil Market place, which was dominated by a pair of large Georgian brick buildings. They tied their horses to a hitching post and followed her into Quincy Market on foot. Here farmers and artisans, bakers and fishmongers displayed their goods for sale. Rosetta went first to the produce section to buy onions, carrots, and potatoes. Then she headed over to where they sold eggs and poultry and bought a live hen and a half dozen eggs. As they watched her, an Irish boy with a basket full of apples approached them.

"Apples," said the shaver, a scrawny, red-haired lad of ten. "Nice and fresh. Two for a nickel, five for a dime."

Cain, who had forgotten to eat breakfast, bought two and tossed one to Strofe. As he tore into the apple he asked the boy, "What's your name, lad?"

"Michael O'Keefe, sir. That's a right nice-looking gun you got there. Have you kilt any Injuns with it?"

"Not a one," Cain replied with a smile.

"Do ye think I could see it?"

"I suppose so."

While he spoke, Cain didn't take his eye off Rosetta. He withdrew his gun from his holster and let the boy look at it.

"It's a big'un, for sure."

"Have you ever shot one, son?" Cain asked.

"Me? Never."

"Would you like to hold it?"

"Sure and I would."

Cain handed it to the boy. He could barely raise the big gun even with two hands.

"Careful now. It's loaded. Don't point it at anybody."

"I'm not daft."

While the boy was holding the gun and aiming it toward the rafters, Cain kept watching Rosetta. He knew what the law called for in order to have her returned to her rightful owner. The fancy legal niceties that the Fugitive Slave Law required, which tried to ignore the ugly realities that were at the heart of the division between North and South, between Free and Slave states, between the interests of property owners and those of abolitionists. He was officially supposed to find a federal marshal and present him with the warrant Cain carried, and it would be the marshal who would be empowered to take her into custody. However, if he did that, word might, in the meantime—especially here in the abolitionist capital of America—get out and the girl would either go into hiding or be whisked away to Canada. On the other hand, if they did try to apprehend her here and now in the crowded marketplace, there was a good chance that a scene would ensue, perhaps even violence, as had happened a few years before in the city when one man had been killed and many others hurt in the riots that followed the arrest of Anthony Burns. Then they would have to have her brought before a judge or commissioner for a hearing to prove that she was indeed escaped and that she was who the owner's agent—Cain, in this case—said she was. If a trial took place, especially a lengthy one, the girl would go to jail for an extended period of time to await trial. Eberly would be angry, and he might not pay the reward until she was back in his custody, and Cain would just have to wait for his money. And any number of bad things could happen, including the possibility of abolitionists breaking her out and secreting her away, as had happened in the Minkins case. Besides that, the poor girl herself would spend months in a dingy cell awaiting the decision of lawyers. Cain knew what was likely to happen to a fine-looking wench in a prison cell, the liberties that guards would take with her.

What was more, he thought about the defiant look he saw in the girl's eyes, and the stories Little Strofe and Henry had told him about her cutting Eberly with a knife when he'd sold her child downriver. He knew how violent she might be and how ugly things could turn if they tried to take her here and now by force. His way was usually to use surprise rather than force, if at all possible. And then an idea came to him; he thought of how any mother who was willing to fight her master like that would probably do just about anything to get her child back.

He took a pair of gold coins from his vest pocket and held them up in front of the boy. "How would you like to earn these, Michael?"

"Jaysus. Sure and I would, sir!" the boy exclaimed.

"See that girl over there," Cain said, pointing.

"The black nigger, y'mean?"

"Yes. I want you to bring a message to her."

"What sort of message?" the boy asked.

"I want you to tell her that some people have found her lost child."

The boy looked at him suspiciously. "How's that now?"

Cain glanced over at Strofe.

"I want you to tell her that her son is safe with an abolitionist family just outside of the city. That if she wants to see him again, to meet at the Cambridge Street Bridge tonight at midnight. Do you know the one I mean?"

"Aye, sir."

"Tell her that she will be met there and brought to see her son, Israel. Tell her, if she wants to see her child again, she must come at midnight. Can you remember all that?"

The boy nodded.

"What did I say her child's name was?"

"Israel, sir."

"You're a smart lad, Michael," said Cain, patting him on the head. "Make sure you say his name."

"I will. Who should I say sent me?"

"An old woman. She didn't give you her name. And don't look over this way. Do you understand my drift?"

"Aye, sir. Ye are a pair of slave catchers, ain't you?" the boy said, smiling at him.

Cain winked at the boy, then handed him one of the gold coins.

"Now go tell her what I said. When you come back its twin is yours."

The boy walked over to the runaway and began to talk to her. Cain watched as she stared down at the boy, first in disbelief, then, as she spoke to him and the incredible news slowly started to sink in, with a wild sort of joy mixed with terror and sadness and suspicion. Her hand flew to her mouth to cover a gasp.

"Who told you about her young'un?" Strofe asked Cain.

"Eberly," he lied. He didn't want to get Strofe's brother or Henry in trouble.

"She's a clever one, that nigger. Do you reckon she'll fall for that trap?"

"I'm willing to bet on it."

A smile broke over Strofe's meaty face. "For all your fancy ways, Cain, you're just as coldhearted as Preacher," the man said.

The boy returned after a while.

"Did you tell her everything?" Cain asked.

"Aye."

"Did she say she'd come?"

"She didn't say, sir. But I told her everything you wanted me to. Do I get me money now?"

Cain paid the boy the second coin, and the urchin took off, running with his prize clutched in his hand.

Just to be on the safe side, Cain and Strofe followed her when she left the market. They had to be more cautious now because she kept looking around as she walked, suspicious, wary. They trailed her to a stately house on Chestnut Street, where she went around back and entered by the servants' entrance. When Cain looked, he saw that the address was the next Howard on the list.

"So Henry was telling the truth," Strofe said.

"At least now we know where she works if she doesn't show up tonight."

L ate that evening, Cain and Strofe took up positions near the bridge. After hiding the horses down near the river, Cain concealed himself on one side of the street behind some bushes, while Strofe hid opposite him in an alley between a warehouse and a sail duck factory.

"Don't make a move until I do," Cain instructed him.

With the streetlamps lit, they had a good view of the road leading down to the bridge. At this hour it was pretty quiet, with few traveling in or out of the city. When it approached midnight and there was no sign of her, Cain began to have second thoughts that his plan would work. What was more, now her suspicions would be aroused and she might bolt on them. Maybe even flee to Canada.

Shortly after the bells of some church sounded midnight, they saw someone coming down the road. The figure wore a long skirt with a shawl pulled over her head, but other than her sex, little else could be determined about the person. At first, Cain didn't think it was the same woman he'd seen that morning because this one didn't walk with the same light tread. This person's shoulders were hunched, and she moved tentatively, like an aged woman whose bones hurt, glancing warily into the shadows on either side of the street. But as the figure drew near, she came beneath the illumination of a streetlamp and Cain got a glimpse of her face. It was the one they were after. Rosetta.

As she passed by, he also caught something else—the gleam of metal in her right hand. *She's got a knife*, he thought. And he remembered what she'd done to Eberly.

When she'd gotten a little ways beyond him, he slipped quietly from his hiding place and crept up behind her. His bad leg slowed him, but he still moved with all the stealth and cunning of a lifetime spent hunting. He was almost upon her when something—his scent? the sound of his boots on the gravel?—alerted her. Quick as a cat, she threw off her shawl and wheeled on him, slashing out with the knife, some sort of long-bladed, serrated thing. The first stroke barely missed Cain's face, but on the backward swing she snagged the cloth of his left sleeve and the blade entered hungrily, searching for flesh. He could feel the hot bite of metal sink into his upper arm. In a flash, she pulled it out and hacked at him again, several times, not wildly nor in fear, but coldly, calculatedly, aiming for the organs that would spell death—the eyes and neck, the chest, the stomach. And she held the knife with the blade toward the ground, slashing downward at him rather than upward, so her strokes had more force behind them.

During all this, except for grunting as she swung at him, hot, guttural exhalations of air he could feel on his face—they were *that* close—she didn't say a word. He sensed, as with a cornered and wounded animal, that some terrible force had been unleashed in her. She went at him with deadly intent, her knees bent in a crouch, circling him to his right, almost sensing it was making him pivot on his bad leg. Nor did she look at his eyes but kept her gaze on his hands and hips, watching them, waiting for a weakness, a flaw in his defense, a vulnerability she'd exploit, sort of the way a pugilist would size up an opponent's soft spots. But he managed to duck or block her attacks with his blackjack, which he used more as a means of protection than with any intent of hurting her, though several times he could have cracked her over the head. He didn't want to hurt her if possible, didn't like to hurt a woman, even a runaway. Besides, he knew Eberly was the sort of man who would deduct money if he brought her back damaged. Still, he didn't relish the notion of getting hurt himself, and that's exactly what she was hell-bent on doing. As she kept circling to his right, he thought, *Where in the hell is Strofe?*

"Look," he tried to reason with her, "it's no use. I have a warrant for your arrest. I have the legal right to return you to Mr. Eberly, of Henrico County, Virginia."

"You don't have no rights to nothin'," she cried, the first actual words from her mouth.

"Please. I don't want to hurt you. Put the knife down."

"You want me, soul catcher," she said, through clenched teeth, her eyes gleaming with anger, "you gonna have to kill me first."

She made a couple of short jabs at his belly, more a feint than anything, trying to draw him closer. For a while she was patient, waiting for him to make a wrong move. But then she made her first mistake— she lunged at him from too far away, aiming for his throat but falling just inches short. He was able to parry the blow with his blackjack, grab hold of the wrist wielding the blade, and bend her arm down sharply over his thigh, forcing her to cry out in pain. He easily wrested the knife from her hand, though she still wasn't ready to give up the fight. She tried to strike him with her free hand, tried to gouge his eyes, and she nearly missed kicking him in the groin. But he was able to twist her arm around behind her back, and get some measure of control over her.

"Stop, goddamn you," Cain cried. "It's over."

She continued to struggle, though, to squirm in his grasp. Finally, Strofe came up and wrapped her in his powerful embrace and squeezed her hard. Only then did she quiet down.

"Wondering when the hell you were of a mind to join in," Cain said.

"Thought you had it all under control," the big man said, laughing.

"You got her good?" Cain asked.

"I got her."

"That you, Strofe, you bastard?" the woman cursed.

"Yeah, it's me, Rosetta," he replied, dragging her down toward where the horses were tied near the water.

Yet as they headed down the slope, she managed to slip her mouth under Strofe's hand and sink her teeth into his thumb.

"Dang you, Rosetta!" he cried, pulling his hand back. She squirmed out of his grasp and started to scramble up toward the road, but Cain grabbed an ankle and pulled her down, then took hold of her hair and yanked it hard.

"Ahhhh!" she cried. "Buckra devil."

"Here," Cain commanded Strofe, "hold her." He went down to his horse and got some rope and a burlap bag from his saddlebags. He returned and began to tie her up.

"Get her shawl," Cain told Strofe.

About then they heard the pounding of hoofbeats on the bridge as two men on horseback approached from the east.

"What's going on down there?" one of them called, trying to see into the shadows below. He had a bay horse with one white stocking.

"Nothing," Strofe said, his hand covering the woman's mouth.

"Anything wrong?" the other asked.

"Everything's just fine," Cain said. "Thank you for your concern."

The two riders whispered among themselves for a moment. "Well, if you don't mind, we'll take a look for ourselves."

"I wouldn't do that, mister," Cain said.

"No. And why's that?" said the first as he started to dismount.

Cain pulled his gun and sent a round zipping just past the man's ear. The two wheeled their horses about and spurred them hard back across the bridge.

Cain finished tying her and then he pulled the burlap bag over her head and shoulders. He carried her to his horse and draped her across Hermes's back. Then he climbed into the saddle. They rode hard to the camp where Preacher and Little Strofe were sleeping. When they came riding in, the hounds took to barking and Preacher jumped up and pulled his big flintlock pistol on them.

"Wait. It's us," Strofe cried out.

"Hell's bells," Preacher said, "y'all nearly got your heads blowed off."

"We was startin' to get worried," Little Strofe said.

"We need to saddle up and get moving," Cain told them.

"Now?" Preacher whined.

"Yeah. Right now. We may have company soon."

"You done got her, huh?" Preacher said, walking over and slapping the squirming body on Cain's horse.

"Yeah, we got her," Cain said. "Now mount up."

Cain could feel a warm trickle down his arm where she'd cut him. He flexed his fingers, hoping she hadn't cut a nerve or an artery. Then he took out his handkerchief, balled it up, and slid it down his sleeve over the wound, trying to stanch the bleeding.

9

They rode hard until they couldn't see the lights of the city anymore and then they rode a little farther to be on the safe side. They saw no sign of anyone following them. They stopped finally beside a wide, slow-moving river and made camp for the night in a stand of alder trees and scrub growth. Little Strofe got a fire going while his brother manacled Henry to a tree and Preacher hobbled the horses. Cain had lifted the girl carefully down off Hermes—she was more solid than her lithe form would have suggested, her legs and back muscled and hard. He set her on the ground and removed the burlap bag, cautious as he would be with taking a rattlesnake out. He was prepared for her anger, but instead she lifted her manacled hands and rubbed her eyes like a child waking from a troubled sleep, and squinted at the people surrounding her. She didn't see Henry right away, and that was a good thing.

"Howdy, Rosetta," Little Strofe said.

She didn't reply. She sat silently, the ball of muscle in her jaw clenched, her gaze remaining at the level of their knees. The two hounds came up to her and started licking her face and she pushed them away, not meanly, just disinterestedly.

Preacher came up with the lantern to have a look. "So this here's what Eberly's got his pants up his crack about?" he said. His injured eye was black-and-blue, swollen nearly shut, the cut beneath it puffy and sore-looking.

"Ain't your bidness what Mr. Eberly does," Strofe said.

"I'm just talking is all."

"You're always talking."

"Hit's a free country," he said, bending down to inspect the captured runaway. He stared at her, then reached down and touched her bare leg. He stroked it the way one might a piece of wood for its smoothness and the quality of its grain.

"I told you," Strofe said, "Mr. Eberly don't want nobody layin' a hand on her."

"Just samplin' the merchandise," Preacher said with a smile. "I s'pose she'd do in a pinch. Now if'n it was me, I'd get one a them Creole whores they got down in New Orleans. I hear they're something special."

"You heard him," said Cain, squatting down in front of her. "Are you thirsty?" he asked her.

She cast those icy blue eyes of hers in his direction, then looked away. He could see that the ride had taken some of the fight out of her. But he guessed there was enough left that, given half a chance, she'd still have clawed his eyes out if she could.

"I have to . . . go," she said flatly.

"Oughta let the nigger bitch piss in her drawers, all the trouble she caused us," Preacher said.

Cain untied her feet and grabbed hold of the rope around her wrists and helped her to stand. He took the lantern and started to lead her farther into the trees where she'd have some privacy. Preacher made as if to follow them.

"Where do you think you're going?" Cain said to him.

"Ain't never seen a nigger piss before. Not a wench anyhow."

"Go feed the horses," Strofe told Preacher. "See they get an extra portion of oats."

When they got to an opening in the trees that looked out onto the river, he stopped and held the lantern up. "Before I untie you," he told her, "I'm going to have to search you. You understand."

She just stared at him flatly.

Early on in his slave-catching career, he'd made the mistake of not searching a captured runaway and nearly paid for it with his life. He was bringing back a slave with the improbable name of Jove Jones to a plantation in Columbia, South Carolina. While they were sleeping, the runaway had cut the ropes holding him, and Cain opened his eyes to the slave standing over him with a straight razor. The boy had hesitated, out of fear or some moral compunction about killing, Cain would never know. But it gave him enough time to draw his gun and tell the boy to drop it if he didn't want his head blown off.

He hung the lantern on a tree limb. As he ran his hands perfunctorily up and down her body, Cain happened to look into her face. Up close, her eyes were narrowed and hard as nail heads, and in the flickering lantern light, her skin shone a smooth ocher color, like hazelnuts. She stood immobile as he searched her, making herself go stiff. He could tell she was used to being touched without her consent. It was the way she seemed to retreat inside herself. When he was sure she wasn't hiding anything, he took hold of the rope binding her hands.

"I'm going to untie you. I want your word you won't try anything."

"My *word*?" she said, a sharp little laugh slipping from her mouth. "If I get me the chance, I'll slit your damn throat, white man. You can have my *word* on that."

"You nearly did already," he said, indicating the bloody hole in his sleeve.

"Next time I'll finish the job."

Though Cain took her at her word, he went ahead and untied her hands, then turned his back toward her.

"Go ahead," he said. "But don't try anything, I'm warning you."

As she squatted in the high grass, she asked, "Was it your idea?"

"My idea what?"

"About my baby? I figure it must a been, since them Strofes ain't smart enough to come in out of the rain. And that other fellow don't look none too bright neither."

"I didn't want anybody to get hurt."

"Not get hurt?" she said with a sarcastic snort.

"If I tried to take you into custody in public, somebody might have gotten hurt. Even yourself. It's been known to happen."

"You coulda left me alone is what you coulda done. I wasn't lookin' to do you no harm, mister. You the one come lookin' for me."

"I could have had you arrested and put in jail. Kept you there till they had a trial. Sometimes that takes months."

"So I should be thankful to some soul catcher?" she said, raising her eyebrows and snorting disdainfully.

"Don't you sass me, girl. I'm just saying that's what I could have done. I had every right."

"What right?"

"You're a runaway. You broke the law."

"Not my law."

"It's the law of these United States."

"I don't gotta follow no law that makes me out no better than a hog. What kind of law is that?"

"I didn't make it. I'm just following it."

"You made it, all right. You and every white buckra makes the laws."

When she was finished, she stood and lowered her shift and straightened out her dress. As he tied her hands again, she said to him, "I want to know something. What kind of man do what you did? Lie 'bout a woman's chile like that?"

"I told you, I didn't want things to go bad. Let's go," he said, pulling on the rope.

He led her back to camp and over to where Henry sat manacled to a tree.

"You!" she cried. "You low-down no'count nigger."

"Ain't had no choice, Rosetta," he replied. "I swear, they was gone cut my other ear off."

"I shoulda knowed it was you told 'em where I was."

She threw herself at Henry then, striking him as best she could with her hands tied. The others quickly grabbed her, pulled her off. They then manacled her to a tree a safe distance away.

"Gutless bastard," she cried, trying to spit at him, but he was too far away. "Wait till I get you, Henry. You bess sleep with one eye open from now on."

"Sorry, Rosetta. But what was I to do?"

"You coulda been a man for once. The other way around, I wouldn't a told on you."

Later, Cain was sitting near the fire, cleaning the wound to his arm with whiskey and a rag. She'd got him in the upper arm, just above the elbow. The blade had gone in sideways, leaving a jagged tear as it came out. It hurt like hell, but at least it hadn't struck any of the big arteries. He wrapped a clean rag around it, ripped the ends, and tied the dressing in place. He thought it might need stitches, but he would wait until the morrow, to look at it in the light of day. Then he got a new shirt from his saddlebags, as well as a fresh bottle of bourbon. When he glanced up, he happened to catch the woman staring at him.

"How's the arm, Mr. Cain?" asked Little Strofe. He was sitting nearby on the ground, picking burrs out of the coat of one of his dogs.

"It's all right," Cain replied, offering his bottle to Little Strofe.

"Thankee kindly," the other man said. He took a drink, wiped the bottle's mouth on his sleeve, and handed it back. "I w-warned you that Rosetta was a wild one."

"That you did."

He leaned toward Cain and said in an undertone, "Tell you the God's truth, I don't see why Mr. Eberly even k-keeps her around."

"Some men go through a lot of trouble over a woman."

"I reckon you're right on that score, Mr. Cain."

From his saddlebags he got out the copy of *Rasselas* he'd purchased back in Boston, and he put on his glasses and began to read. Yet he didn't read for long. He was bone tired, his leg aching, and the wound in his arm throbbing. Soon he put the book away and crawled under his blanket. He thought of what the runaway girl had said to him, that she would kill him if she got the chance. He knew she meant it, though the threat didn't worry him all that much. Fugitives often made threats. It was something they did. But what he thought about most was how she'd asked what sort of man he was, tricking her like that regarding her son. He told himself he had just done what anyone in his shoes might, what had saved them all a lot of trouble. Especially the girl. And if he'd had to do it over again, he'd have done the same thing. Besides, she was just some nigger runaway aiming to hurt him anyway she could for catching her. Still, her words didn't set well with him.

T he morning began cool and overcast, with a tattered fog drifting in off the river. Cain crawled out from his blanket, his face wet from dew and the wound in his arm pulsating. Little Strofe had already gotten a fire going and started breakfast.

"Some coffee, Mr. Cain?" he said, handing him a cup.

"Thank you, Mr. Strofe."

When breakfast was ready, Little Strofe brought plates of cornmeal and salted beef over to the runaways. As always, Henry dug in as best he could with his hands manacled and ate ravenously, but Rosetta just stared at the proffered plate.

"You got to eat, Rosetta," pleaded Little Strofe, squatting in front of her. "Mr. Eberly don't want you gettin' sick. Here," he said. As he went to put the plate on her lap, she slapped it away, knocking the food to the ground. "Now what you go and do that for?"

"You stay away from me," she threatened, pointing a finger at him.

He threw his hands in the air and walked over to Cain.

"She won't eat."

Cain shrugged. "Like they say, you can lead a horse to water but you can't make him drink. She gets hungry enough, she'll eat."

They saddled up and rode south, toward Rhode Island. They didn't have much choice, so they put Rosetta on the pack mule behind Henry. The two squabbled like children for a time, pushing and shoving for space on the mule's back, but they finally grew accustomed to the notion that it was this or one of them would have to get down and hoof it. It started to rain later in the morning and continued steady all day. The horses plodded along the muddy road.

The land on either side was flat and sandy and studded with rocks, with small farms tucked between rivers and stands of elm and chestnut trees, surrounded by lichen-covered stone walls. The people they passed on the highway were uniformly inhospitable, sober farmers in wagons filled with potatoes or turnips or chickens in crates, ministers and their stern-looking wives in buckboards, well-dressed gentlemen driving phaetons.

"Never see such sour pusses on folks," Strofe commented.

"These Yankees must not a took them a good shit in a long while," added Preacher.

They passed peddlers in horse-drawn caravans loaded with everything under the sun for sale: clanking pots and pans, articles of clothing, buggy whips and spurs, patent medicines and headache powders. The salesmen were a little more friendly, as salesmen always are. From a fat peddler with suspenders and a tweed coat, Preacher bought another hat, this one a gray felt bowler, which looked as absurd on him as it would have on one of Little Strofe's hounds. For one thing it was too large, came well down onto his head, pushing his ears out and almost covering his eyes.

"That looks quite fetching on you, sir," the fat man offered up, holding up a tortoiseshell mirror for Preacher to inspect himself. Preacher kept taking the hat off and putting it back on, turning this way and that to view himself.

"It's all the rage now in London," the man said.

"Yeah?"

"Yes, indeed. Why, Prince Albert himself wears one."

"How do it look on me?" he asked Little Strofe.

"Makes you look like a duke," he replied.

"No," his brother challenged, "what it makes him look like is one a them Pinkerton men."

"What's that?" Preacher asked, not knowing if he was being made fun of.

"Railroad detectives. They all wear hats like that."

Though, of course, he'd never seen a Pinkerton man, Preacher decided he was fond of the notion of being likened to a railroad detective. It sounded important. He strutted about like the cock of the walk. As they rode along, he could be seen turning the hat at various jaunty angles atop his narrow head and viewing his shadow as it rode along beside him. He'd also purchased from the peddler a bright blue neckerchief which he tied about his neck in a fashion he considered to be jaunty, and some hard candy and quids of tobacco.

Now and then, Preacher would ride up from his position in the rear so that he was parallel with the two Negroes on the mule. Cain could see him offer the girl a piece of hard candy or try to strike up a conversation with her. While Cain was too far away to make out what he said to her, Preacher even threw his head back and laughed out loud once. The hat seemed to bring out another side to him, though Cain was not altogether sure what that side was or if he didn't actually prefer the more ill-tempered aspect of the man to this. And one thing was for sure—he wasn't about to trust this change, whatever prompted it.

From a farmer's roadside stand they bought some eggs and potatoes and onions, and from a little boy fishing by a river they purchased several freshly caught trout, their flesh full and firm. They stopped for lunch at the fork of two roads, and Little Strofe made a fire and cleaned the fish and peeled the potatoes, and then fried it all in a pan with lard. When the meal was ready, he again tried to give Rosetta a plate of food and again she refused. He looked over at Cain and shrugged his shoulders. Then he brought the plate over to his dogs, and they devoured it in two shakes.

Cain, too, dug into his food, eating with the hearty appetite of a man who'd accomplished something of import and was treating himself. He felt better than he had in a while, light and buoyant. They had the girl in custody, and in a few weeks they'd be back in Richmond, and he'd get the bill of sale for his horse as well as the reward, square up with those whom he owed, and be on his way west. It would still be early enough in the year to make it through the western mountains before winter set in. If he made Denver by July, he could be through the passes before the snows. Be in San Francisco for the new year. He found himself filled with a feeling that was alien to him—hope.

After eating, he rolled up his sleeve and inspected the wound in his arm. It looked worse in the light of day, the edges ragged and oozing a pinkish fluid. Yes, he thought, it would need stitches. From his saddlebags he got the box with the few medical supplies he kept with him for emergencies—bandages, clean rags, a needle and some thread, a lancet for letting blood, some of Rush's purgative pills. After pouring a little whiskey on the wound, he set to work stitching it. He'd picked up a little doctoring back in the war, and over the past ten years he'd often found himself in need of the services of a doctor but was too far away, so he'd had to learn to patch himself up. One time he'd been shot in the leg by a crazy man in a card game around a campfire; another he was knifed by a strapping Negro he'd been hunting. There'd also been various cuts and broken bones, fevers and infections he'd had to tend to himself. When he was finished stitching the wound in his arm, he tied a clean rag around it and rolled down his sleeve. To ease the pain a might, he took a sip of laudanum.

He glanced over and saw that the girl was looking at him. He could not quite decipher the look in her eyes, though he guessed it was some form of rancor. He thought of her threat, how she'd slit his throat if she ever got the chance. It wasn't so unusual. Most Negroes, if you could get them to speak their minds truly instead of their normal fawning and lying, would like to do violence to a white man. Yet he wasn't going to dwell on what she might or might not be thinking. He didn't want to spoil the good mood he was in. In a few weeks' time he'd be back in Richmond, settling his affairs with Eberly. He tried picturing what the Pacific Ocean would look like. When he was a boy he'd seen an artist's rendering of Lewis and Clark's first view of the coast. Sunlight glinting off the water. Waves crashing onshore. A vastness filled with light and possibility. A place where a man could fashion for himself a new life, a new beginning. Against the throbbing in his arm, he took another sip of laudanum. *To hell with her*, he thought.

T he next day the rain had let up, though it was still overcast and gray. By noon they'd reached Providence. They rode past the

statehouse and the Seekonk River, which was crowded with boats of
every variety and size. Down at the wharf they saw a whaler unloading
its cargo of oil while out in the bay a clipper ship was sailing south.
Cain stopped at a telegraph office and sent Eberly a message:

Have taken doe into custody. Return in a fortnight. Cain.

They stopped to buy some fried dough from an old Dutch woman
tending a fire in a metal can. While they ate, a small crowd had gathered
nearby in a park to hear a hurdy-gurdy man in a tall stovepipe hat
play an organ grinder. On his shoulder sat a little monkey wearing a
jacket gilded with gold and fake gems and on his small gray head a fez
like a Mohammedan. The monkey was no bigger than a squirrel and
had large nervous eyes that darted about the crowd. When the man
was finished playing, the monkey jumped down and went among the
people, collecting coins with his hat. He seemed to take little relish
in his job.

"See them fingers of his," Little Strofe said, "works 'em better'n
a raccoon."

"That monkey's straight from Afrikay," Preacher offered
authoritatively. "That's where your folks is from," he said to Henry.

"My folks's from down Georgia way," the Negro replied.

"Like hell."

"Yessum. My grandpap come from a plantation down there."

"You ain't from Georgia anymore'n I am. I'm talkin' way back.
Ever' nigger come from Afrikay way back."

"We all comes from somewheres else way back."

"Don't you get smart with me, boy," Preacher said.

"Ain't gettin' nothing, massa. Just tellin' you where I's from."

Preacher looked at him to see if he was secretly making fun
of him; only when he was sure he wasn't did he spur his horse and
move on.

Late in the day they came to a river swollen by rain and spring
thaws. A section of the bridge they'd been planning to cross was
underwater, and so they had to ride south several miles before they
found a ferry. It was a small, flat-bottomed craft manned by a thin,
jug-headed fellow with a long pole. Hanging from the gunwale was a
bell, which the man rang to let people know he was about to launch.

"I'll have to make two trips to bring all of you over," the man informed them. Cain decided to stay behind with the girl while the other four crossed over first.

"I don't like the looks a dat," Henry said warily as they boarded.

"Look at it this way, Henry," Strofe kidded, "if you drown, you won't get cowhided when you get back."

As they waited, the girl squatted on her haunches, watching as the ferryman slowly poled the craft across. Cain considered removing the shackles until they made the other side, but he recalled her threat from the previous night and thought better of it. He liked to consider himself generous, but he was not a fool. He fed Hermes a piece of sugar and then extended another toward her. She had to be hungry by now. She looked at his hand but turned away without taking it. When the ferryman returned, Cain and the girl proceeded to board the raft. She stood in the bow, looking straight ahead. "It might get rough," he told her. "You'll want to sit." When she didn't, he said, "I'm not asking you. Now set yourself down." The brackish water crashed into the ferry and surged over the starboard side, spilling over the deck. Hermes, normally a horse of unflappable calm, became skittish, began to prance and wag his head nervously as they crossed the churning river. The thin ferryman had all he could do to keep the craft on course. Yet he was obviously skilled in his profession. Despite the fast-moving water, he was able to negotiate the currents and ferry the boat across. In fact, they'd almost reached the far side without incident when Cain heard a noise from behind them.

He turned to see a group of men on horseback congregated on the far side. They were calling out something, but the river's noise drowned out their actual words. From his saddlebag, he took out his spyglass and glassed the area along the bank. He instinctively sized up the situation, noting the wind and distance, the number of men and what they rode, the kind of weaponry that might be brought to bear against them. He counted ten men, all armed, some with Jennings repeating rifles, a few with Springfields or muskets, several already having removed their guns from scabbards and resting them across their laps, as if ready for business. One fellow on a roan saddle horse was even looking back at Cain through the scope of his rifle. At first, he thought perhaps it was just a posse from Boston and that they were here after the girl. He felt sure that they wouldn't fire on them, not with the woman there in plain view, and even if it did come to a scrape, he doubted they'd put up much of a fight, for they had little at stake. He'd seen abolitionist posses like this before. After a few shots to show they believed in their cause, they'd more than likely scatter like chickens.

But as he was scoping the shoreline to the north, he saw a man mounted on a large, dappled gray farm horse. He was back among the trees, partially hidden from view, but as Cain focused in on him, he recognized the long gray beard and grizzled face, the inimitable stare of one who saw the Infinite—John Brown. He had come, after all, just as Henry predicted and just as Cain knew he would.

While Cain was watching the men through the scope, he suddenly heard a gunshot crackle in the air behind him. The ferryman immediately dropped to the deck, and without someone steering the raft, it quickly started to veer off course. Cain squatted and glassed the far bank again. He could see no telltale black powder smoke there, no one having so much as raised a weapon. Instead they were scrambling up the bank for cover, heading back into a stand of willow and poplar trees. Then it occurred to Cain that they weren't the ones to have fired. He turned and looked toward the opposite side. There was Preacher in his new derby standing on the shore with Little Strofe's Boyer rifle, already having reloaded and taking aim again. The crack of another round abused the air. *The stupid bastard*, Cain thought.

With that, all hell broke loose. Brown's group returned a hail of bullets, which bit and tore and slammed into the trees and rocks around them. The Strofe brothers and Henry had taken cover, but Preacher stood right out on the bank, exposed, defiantly daring them to hit him. He remained fixed there, almost as if he were posing for a daguerreotype. He reloaded in plain sight and fired again. Then he waved his arms and thumbed his nose at them. "C'mon, you yellowbellied Yankee sons-a-bitches. I'm right here. You couldn't hit a barn if'n you was standing inside it." Right then a ball ripped through his sleeve, which for some reason struck him as funny, and he laughed maniacally and did a little jig, taunting the shooters. Another round tore through the ear of Little Strofe's mule. It set the poor creature to bellowing, "*Eeee-awwww, eeee-awwww*," and dashing off into the woods.

The ferryman remained hunkered down, his hands covering his large head as balls plunked into the water around them. One *pinged* off the bell hanging from the gunwale. Cain thought of getting his Sharp's from the scabbard on the horse, but the bullets were flying all around him, and the next best thing he could do was draw his handgun and begin to return fire, though at this distance it amounted to little more than name-calling. The ferry had, by now, been swept downstream some distance, putting him well out of pistol range, though not out of reach of their rifles. The men on the far side continued to pepper the raft as it drifted wildly downstream. Cain turned to see the girl standing and waving her manacled hands toward Brown's position. "Get down, for Christ's sake," he cried. When she continued standing there waving, he crawled over to her and yanked her forcibly to the deck.

"You fixing to get yourself killed?" he cried.

"They're here to save me," she said, trying to squirm out of his grasp, though he held the manacles tight.

"You're as likely as not to get hit."

The ferry happened to slam into something then, violently tossing the three passengers and the horse across the deck. The raft had run aground on a small sandy island and now was hung up as water rushed over the opposite side, tilting the craft at a precarious angle. Hermes began to whinny apprehensively and back awkwardly away from the edge.

Cain turned toward the ferryman and yelled, "Try to push us off."

The man didn't budge. So Cain yelled to him, "Move the damn boat, mister."

"But they're shooting at us," he cried.

"I'll shoot you if you don't. And I'm a better shot."

This had the desired effect, for the man jumped to his feet and grabbed hold of the pole. He went to the side of the raft, but before he attempted to free them from the shoal, he turned and flung himself into the river, and began dog-paddling for the far side.

Cain grabbed hold of the pole himself and tried to shove them free, but the raft hardly budged. It was wedged firmly on the muddy island. As he was occupied with this task, he heard another splash behind him. Turning, he saw the girl being carried downstream by the water. "Damn," he cursed.

He took Hermes's reins and led him to the edge of the ferry. "All right, boy," he assured the animal, whispering into its ear. "Here's your chance to show me you're worth all that sugar. Now gid-up."

The animal hesitated for just a moment, then plunged into the maelstrom, with Cain clutching his mane. He tried to steer the horse toward the girl, who was some fifty feet ahead of him and being carried downstream fast, but Hermes's natural instinct was to head for shore. Cain had to keep pulling him away, yanking on his bridle. The girl flailed ineffectually at the water with both manacled hands out in front of her, the chains obviously weighing her down. Now and then her red-kerchiefed head momentarily slipped below the surface and she came up gasping and coughing and shouting something. Cain wished he'd taken the shackles off. At one point, the current swallowed her completely, and for several anxious seconds he lost sight of her. But then she popped back up like a brightly colored bobber not twenty feet in front of him. This time she appeared spent and terrified, her arms thrashing feebly, as if she'd run out of the will to struggle. She looked toward him and called again.

"Help," she cried, before going under again, this time seemingly for good.

Cain made a last-ditch attempt to reach her. Guiding Hermes and stroking with his free hand, he made for where he'd last seen her. When he arrived at the spot, he saw a bright swirl of red floating just beneath the surface of the brownish river water. He reached for it and clutched it, his hand pulling out of the water nothing but the red kerchief she had worn. She was gone! Desperately, he looked around for her, searching to the right and left in the churning water. Finally, weary himself and feeling Hermes starting to panic, he was about to turn and head for shore when he spotted a head break the surface a short ways downstream.

"Help," she cried again. He swam toward her and when he was close enough he reached out and grabbed hold of whatever he could, grasping the collar of her dress and drawing her toward him. Holding her tight under his arm, he allowed Hermes to carry them to shore.

"Let's go, boy," he cried, urging the horse on.

At last having gained the far shore, he dragged her up onto the bank and, now out of range of Brown's party, collapsed in a heap. For a while, the girl lay as if dead, so he turned her on her stomach and struck her back several times, as he'd seen someone once do to a drowning victim. After a few seconds, she started coughing, spitting up all the water she'd swallowed.

"You all right?" he asked after she'd stopped coughing.

She nodded her head. He rolled her onto her back, then helped her to sit up. Her breathing was labored. Water dripped down her face. Her black hair, woven into long thick plaits, hung down over her face like bars. He tried brushing them back, but she pushed his hand away. She looked up at him, her eyes slate colored.

"Don't 'spect me to thank you," she said.

"I don't. Just looking out for my interests," he said.

"You think this makes you better than them others. Well, it don't. Not by a long shot."

He helped her to stand. "Let's go."

After getting out of the river, he met up with the others. They searched unsuccessfully for Little Strofe's mule for a while, but they had to put some distance between themselves and Brown's party, so they decided finally to put Henry behind Little Strofe on the pack mule, while the girl rode behind Cain. They headed south for some time before crossing a stream and then riding northwest to throw off their pursuers. They kept to the back roads and little-traveled cart paths, avoiding any sort of contact with their fellow man. When they'd see a rider or a wagon coming the other way, they'd slip off the path and into the woods until the other had passed by. Just before nightfall, they pitched camp in a gulley deep in the woods so their fire wouldn't be seen. Cain had finally had a chance to change his clothes, but the damp and cold had sunk into his bones, and he was chilled now. The good feeling he'd had just the day before had vanished completely, and he felt old and raggedy, his leg throbbing like a toothache. Even the laudanum didn't help.

Cain met with Strofe to broach the subject of having someone stand guard through the night—in case Brown found their trail. He suggested two-hour shifts, with Cain volunteering to take the first.

Later, Little Strofe came over and handed him a plate of biscuits and salt pork and beans, and a cup of steaming coffee.

"Thank you, Mr. Strofe."

"How's the arm?"

He'd almost forgotten about the wound. He touched his arm. It was sore, but it didn't hurt as much as the rest of him. "All right, I reckon."

"This is hers," Little Strofe said, setting down another plate beside him. "She wouldn't take it from me. Figured you might have b-better luck."

"I doubt it," Cain said.

"She don't eat she'll g-get sick."

"I can't make her eat. In fact, it seems like no one can make her do a goddamn thing she doesn't have a mind to."

"Told you she was headstrong," Little Strofe replied. "Mr. Eberly'll be right cross anything was to happen to her."

"Then that'll be just too damn bad, won't it?" Cain snapped at him. "He should have thought of that before she ran off."

Though he knew he wouldn't get a penny if he didn't bring her back in one piece and would more than likely lose his horse and get thrown in debtor's prison to boot, he was getting sick and tired of hearing about what Eberly would or wouldn't approve of. If he'd wanted her back so badly, why didn't he go after her himself? *To hell with him*, Cain thought. Here he'd been shot at and knifed and almost drowned, not to mention threatened by Preacher. He had a good mind to up and quit, to send a telegram to Eberly saying, You want her back, old man, then go and get her yourself. I'm done.

But when he'd had a chance to simmer down and reflect on things, of course, he had a change of heart. After all, they'd already done the hard part, and if things went smoothly they'd be back in Richmond in less than a fortnight. He thought of the five hundred dollars, and that went a good ways to improving his mood.

After he'd eaten his own supper, he picked up the other plate and hobbled over to where the girl sat chained to the tree, with Henry a few feet away. She sat with a blanket wrapped around her, except for her shoulders, which were bare. The night was chilly and he could see her lips trembling.

"Are you cold?" he asked.

She didn't respond.

"I have your supper here."

"I ain't hungry."

"You got to eat sooner or later."

"I don't *have* to do nothing," she hissed.

"She don't want it, massa," said Henry, "I'll take it."

"You fixing to starve yourself?" he asked her.

"You let me worry about that."

Cain squatted down so he was at eye level with her.

"Now here's the problem. I'm responsible for getting you back safe and sound. I don't do that, I don't get paid."

"So you saving my neck today was only on account I'm worth something to you. That what you're saying?"

"Pretty much. But whatever my reasons, you still need to eat."

"Name me one good reason why."

"You want to live, don't you?"

She let out a thin, sarcastic laugh.

"That's a good one, a white man telling a slave what she got to live for!"

"You gone eat that or not, Rosetta?" Henry interrupted again.

"Shut up, Henry," she said to him.

"Mr. Cain bein' nice to you. Why you gots to be so low-down mean all the time?"

"I'm warning you. Stay out of this." Then to Cain she said, "You know what I got to live for? Going back to my cage."

"Didn't sound like a cage to me. From what I heard, this Eberly treated you well."

"Huh!" she snorted. "You don't know nothin' 'bout him."

He put the plate of food next to her and stood. He told himself to drop it. That it wasn't his business. He'd tried at least. Whatever Eberly's reasons for wanting her back, whatever her reasons for running—they weren't his concern. Still, he had to admit to a certain curiosity about this woman. He'd never seen her like before, certainly not in a slave.

"When did he sell your child?"

"What difference it make to you?"

"I'm just asking."

For the first time she glanced up at him. In the light from the fire her eyes blazed with a silent rage, like those of a bear cornered by a pack of dogs.

"He sold him downriver when he was just a baby. I ain't seen him since."

"How long ago was that?"

"I reckon I was about fourteen then. Israel, he'd be eight come November."

Twenty-two, thought Cain. She looked older than that, especially her eyes. She had knowing, lived-in-the-world eyes.

They were both silent for a moment.

It slipped out before he knew it: "I'm sorry," he said. He'd never said such a thing before to a slave he was returning.

"Huh," she snorted.

He was going to say something else but decided he'd already said too much. Instead, he stood and started to walk away.

"You got young'uns, Cain?"

He was surprised to hear her refer to him that way. Runaways, if they called him anything at all, called him massa or Mr. Cain. He hesitated, then said, "I never had any children." He added with a smile, "'Least none I knew of."

"Then you don't know what it's like to lose 'em."

"I suppose you're right. I'll just leave the food right here," he said. "In case you change your mind."

He went over and sat down with his back against a pine tree. *Hell with her*, he thought. When she got good and hungry, she'd eat. Later, he watched her lean forward onto her knees, fold her hands as best she could with the shackles on, and pray. It appeared that she was adjusting to the notion of her return.

In the morning he saw that the plate he'd left for her was empty, licked clean. *So*, he thought.

10

For the next couple of days they saw no sign of Brown's party. They kept to the back roads, traveling slowly and in a westerly direction, and avoiding the heavily trafficked Boston–New York turnpike. Some of the roads were hardly more than cow paths that meandered through fields and woods. They ran into hedgerows and laurel thickets so dense they had to stop and retrace their steps; they got entangled and cut themselves on brambles and briars. And everywhere they confronted the ubiquitous New England stone wall, which seemed to Cain, at least, like a labyrinth designed by these blasted Yankees to trap them and prevent them from ever returning home. One time they were crossing a swamp, and Little Strofe had gotten sunk up to the stirrups in muck. The others had to throw him ropes and pull him out. By the third day, Preacher was starting to grumble about their lack of progress. "Hell, we'll never get home at this rate." He was for abandoning this course and heading directly south, returning to Richmond by the shortest route, even if it meant going through New York City. Cain, though, worried that Brown's party might come upon them if they returned to the main road. There they'd be outnumbered and outgunned, and would stand little chance in a direct fight. He thought they should continue proceeding west and cross the Hudson well north of the city, perhaps head out as far as Harrisburg before turning south into Virginia. Anyone following them wouldn't suspect that.

"They ain't coming after us, I tell you," Preacher said as they stopped at a crossroads. One sign pointed south toward New Haven, another north to Hartford. Preacher wanted them to turn south. "We done put the fear a God in them Yank sons-a-bitches."

"I wouldn't be so sure," Cain said, picking a sharp-edged beggar's-button that had gotten tangled in his pant leg.

"They ain't gonna risk their hides again for this pair," he said, indicating the two runaways with a dismissive flick of his derby-capped head.

"You don't know these Yankees like I do," Cain advised. "That Brown is a fanatic."

"I know he ain't got much stomach for a fight," Preacher said with a laugh. "You see the way them boys cut and run when the lead was a-flyin'?"

"I wouldn't be so sure," Cain said. "Besides, we're more likely to run into abolitionists if we take the turnpike."

"Dang, I ain't never seen such a old lady as you, Cain. Frettin' over ever' little thing."

"Looks like we could save us two days' travel if we head south," Strofe piped up as he looked over his maps. "Follow the coast. Take the ferry across Staten Island to Bayonne."

"New York has its vigilance committee, too," Cain cautioned.

"I'm just lookin' to get us home sooner."

"Maybe you ought to listen to Mr. Cain," Little Strofe said.

"And whyn't you keep your snout out of it, brother? You don't know what the hell you're jabbering about."

"But he does."

"You do what you want," Cain warned Strofe. "You run into trouble, you can tell Eberly it was your idea. I'm taking the girl and sticking to the back roads."

With that, Strofe backed off on the notion, and they continued on as they had.

Cain was never not aware of Rosetta riding behind him. He had taken off the shackles so she could hold on to him as they rode. Each movement of the horse, each dip or rise in the road, shifted her in ways that made him conscious of her presence all over again. When they climbed a hill he could feel her hands clutching the fabric of his shirt, pressing into his paunch, her body leaning sharply into his. When he forded a stream or had to slow down suddenly, he would feel her arms tighten around his waist ever so slightly. When she herself realized she was doing this she would pull away from him, and that, too, he was aware of. He objected when she slid backward too far, onto Hermes's kidneys, a particularly tender section for any horse, but especially on an Arabian. When she sat hard on the horse he would pin his ears back in annoyance or kick out or snort his displeasure. Cain would have to remind her to slide up toward him more, which she seemed indisposed to do. And once when Cain had stopped to feed him, she must have kneed him as she was dismounting and he scooted sideways, causing her to fall to the ground.

"You all right?" he asked.

She didn't answer. She got to her feet and dusted herself off.

"He doesn't like to be kicked like that."

"Tell him it ain't my idea to be on him in the first place," she replied.

Mostly they rode in silence, though now and then he'd ask if she were thirsty or if she had to relieve herself, or tell her to hold tight as they crossed a fast-moving stream. Cain, still chilled from getting wet, resorted frequently to sips of laudanum as a curative. At one point he turned to Rosetta and offered the flask. "Here," he said.

"I don't partake of spirits," she replied.

"It's medicinal. Good for what ails you."

"That stuff doan do a body no good."

"How would you know?"

"There used to be this slave name of Willy. He work on Mr. Eberly's plantation. He took to drinking corn licker and drank hisself into an early grave."

"Suit yourself," Cain said as he took another sip before putting the flask away.

Late one day they came upon a lonely farmhouse set back a ways from the road. They decided to stop and inquire if they might water the horses. The house was in bad repair, the roof missing shingles, the front steps rotted and sagging. Several windowpanes were broken and had pieces of oilcloth covering them. Discarded farm equipment littered the front yard, which had not been touched by a scythe in ages. A rusty plowshare, several broken wagon wheels, various hoes and rakes and spades—all were scattered in the high grass as if they'd been left there one evening after a day's work long ago and simply forgotten. Just off the porch were the scattered remains of a recently slaughtered Rhode Island Red chicken, its bright, bloodstained plumage strewn over the grass. The barn, too, was in shambles, with the front door hanging off its hinges and much of the chinking cracked and falling out.

As they rode up, a fierce-looking black dog, tied to a post in the front yard, took to barking viciously at them. It yanked on its chain until it was hoarse. Little Strofe put a rope on his two hounds and held them on a tight leash as they drew near.

An old woman sat on the porch in a rocking chair. She seemed to be soaking her feet in a bucket of water in front of her. She stared at them as they came up, but for some time she didn't make a move nor did she offer a word in greeting. She looked almost in a trance. Cain had an odd notion that she'd been waiting for them. She had wild gray hair that was uncovered and uncombed, and a filthy apron over an equally filthy dress of homespun. Bone thin, her eye sockets and jaws sunken in shadow, the old woman had the distracted look of a person not completely in charge of her wits. Cain could see that she wasn't quite as old as he had at first taken her for. She was perhaps in her sixties and might at one time have been a handsome woman, with strong, even features, though now she appeared mostly done in, bankrupt of some inner life force.

"Hush," she cried finally to the dog. When the dog continued its racket, she said, "I should have seen to you already." Then she lifted her feet out of the water, picked up the bucket, and carried it to the edge of the porch, whereupon she tossed the water at the dog. The dog immediately stopped barking and cowered, though it did let out one or two deep-throated growls before falling silent and lying down on the grass. The woman turned her attention back to the riders.

"Can I help you, gentlemen?" she asked.

"We were wondering, ma'am," Cain began, "if we might water our horses. And if you could spare them some feed, too, we'd gladly pay you."

She looked at him, then at the others, taking note of the shackles on Henry's wrists. She leaned sideways to look around Cain and gaze on the girl in the saddle behind him.

"Are they runaway slaves?" she asked.

"Yes, ma'am," he replied.

"Then I guess that'd make you gentlemen slave catchers?"

"That it would. We could move on if you'd prefer."

She stared at Cain, then glanced back over her shoulder into the house. She stood there, hugging her thin arms around the dry husk of her body. "That's for your conscience to puzzle over, not mine," she said.

Wordlessly she led them back to a water trough out near the barn. She pumped water from a pump and then showed them where the hayrack was.

"Don't have any oats or corn. That's all been used up."

"This will be just fine," Cain said.

"How about yourselves? Are you boys hungry?" she asked. "I don't have much, but you're welcome to share what food I have."

"We'd sure appreciate a home-cooked meal, ma'am," Strofe said.

Later, they sat at her kitchen table, all of them except the two Negroes, whom Strofe had manacled to a chestnut tree over near the barn. The house had a peculiar smell to it, a cloyingly sweet odor like burned leather. Before they ate, the old woman bowed her head and said grace. "Thank you Lord for the bountiful food we are about to eat." Though she put some food on her own plate, she hardly touched it. Now and then she'd look over her shoulder into a back room, the way a person might watch for the arrival of a stagecoach, as if she was expected somewhere at a certain time and didn't want to be late.

"This is mighty good," Strofe said to the woman.

"Just chicken stew."

"Are you all alone here?" Cain asked.

The old woman hesitated for a moment, as if it were a question she'd never contemplated before and the implications of its answer led her out in several dizzying directions at once. "Why . . . yes, I am."

"Who helps you around the place?"

"My sons used to. But with the banks' failure, they had to pack up and move out west. I manage all right."

While they were still eating, she got up and fixed two plates, and brought them and a pitcher of buttermilk out to the runaways.

"The hell's that stink?" Preacher said. "Smells like she got her a dead rat somewheres about."

The old woman was gone for a long while. Cain grew suspicious finally and got up and followed her out. He found her seated on the grass, talking to the two Negroes while they ate. As he approached, they fell silent. Behind them the sun was setting, casting long orange spears of light over the branches of the chestnut. The old woman's frizzy hair caught the sunlight and glowed like a dandelion seed on fire.

"Everything all right, ma'am?" he asked, squatting down. He glanced over at Rosetta, who traded looks with the woman before angling her head down toward her plate.

"Just chatting," the old woman said lightly, struggling to stand.

Cain offered his hand to help her up. Hers felt like a small broken-winged bird, and she was as light as a feather pillow. As they headed back to the house, she paused and turned toward him. "May I ask where you're bringing them?"

"Home," Cain said.

"That's a peculiar thought," she said. "Whose? Yours or theirs?"

Cain had never thought about it in such terms before.

"Virginia," he replied.

"What is your name, young man?"

"Cain."

"Like in the Bible," she said, the faintest blush of a smile turning her face almost coquettish. She seemed to be flirting with him. "That your Christian name?"

"No. Augustus is."

"May I call you Augustus?"

"Whatever you'd like, ma'am."

"My name is Hettie. You would be about my older boy's age, Ephraim. He was tall and broad through the shoulders like you. A fine-looking boy. Not so heavy as you."

Cain nodded, amusing the old woman.

"She's hardly more than a girl," she said, tossing her head back toward Rosetta. "Such a comely young thing to be chained up like a dog."

"She would run if not for the chains. She's tried it before."

"Wouldn't you in her place?"

"I suppose."

"Any feeling creature would."

"Thing is, ma'am, I have a job to do."

"Don't we all have jobs to do?" she said cryptically. "You almost couldn't tell from just looking at her."

Cain assumed the old woman was talking about how light-skinned she was.

"You won't let anything happen to her, will you, Augustus?" she said, more statement than question.

"I have to bring her back, ma'am, if that's what you mean. I have . . ." He was going to explain his situation, but he said only, "Obligations."

"But you'll see that no harm comes to her," she said.

"Of course."

She looked at him, her loose eyes momentarily catching hold of his.

"Can I trust you, Augustus?"

"That all depends."

She reached into the pocket of her apron and took out a small cloth change purse. It jingled with coins. She handed it to him.

"Would you see that she gets that?"

"She's a runaway. She's not supposed to have money."

"But you'll see that she gets it all the same."

She looked up at Cain with those wild eyes of hers.

"Are you sure you don't need it, ma'am? All alone like you are."

"I am beyond needing very much of anything in this life, Mr. Cain. There is just me. And the dog," she said, glancing over at the animal who lay sleeping on the ground. "And we have plans. You'll see that she gets it?"

Finally, he said, "I'll see that she gets it."

They went back inside, and while Cain finished his meal, she cleaned up from dinner. As she worked, she hummed a tune, a sad, lilting air.

"What's that you're humming, ma'am?" Little Strofe asked.

She turned from drying the dishes, her expression vacant. "It's called 'Lilly Dale.'"

"We had something very much like that back home. But we called it ''Neath the Chestnut Tree.'"

"Yes, that's 'Lilly Dale.' It goes by several names." The old woman went back to her dishes, but now she commenced to singing in a high, fluttering voice that clutched at the back of one's throat.

> "'Neath the chestnut tree,
> Where the wildflow'rs grow,
> And the stream ripples forth
> Thro' the vale,
> Where the birds shall warble
> Their songs in spring,
> There lay poor Lilly Dale."

When she finished she said, "You're welcome to stay the night in the barn. The roof leaks, but it's not supposed to rain tonight."

"Much obliged, ma'am," Cain said.

Later, she led them out to the barn, carrying a lantern to light the way. When she got them situated, she headed back up to the house. Cain followed her up. At the front porch he removed his billfold and said, "I'd like to pay you for your kindness."

"It wouldn't be a kindness if I took your money, now would it?" she said. "But I will ask a favor of you."

"I'd be happy to oblige if I can," he said.

"It is in the manner of moving something. Something that's too heavy for me."

"Would you be needing it moved now, ma'am?"

"No. It can wait till morning," she said absently, looking at him with those loose eyes of hers. In the lantern light, they shone a soft gray, and they made him think of someone else.

"Well, thank you for the food, ma'am. Good night." He tipped his hat and turned to leave, but she suddenly grabbed hold of his wrist. The coldness of her touch caught him by surprise. It sent a shiver coursing through him.

"Ma'am?" he said.

"Have you ever been smitten, Augustus?" she asked, slowly relaxing her grip.

"Smitten, ma'am?"

She laughed girlishly, and he saw beneath the hard years and the wrinkles the pretty girl she'd once been. When she laughed like this, he suddenly knew who it was she reminded him of. Not so much in the appearance of her, but in the way she acted, her manner. The woman made him think of his mother.

"In love. So in love you thought your heart would burst in your chest."

He scratched his beard, unshaven now for days.

"I suppose."

"It's not something one has to suppose. You would know if you had ever felt it. A body has not lived if he has not loved."

"Yes," he confessed after a while. "I was in love once."

"What happened?"

"She died."

"How?"

"They killed her."

"I'm so sorry."

"It was a long time ago. I've almost forgotten."

She stared at him and smiled sadly, as if she'd caught him in a lie that they both knew. "When it happened, were you all torn up inside?"

Cain shrugged. "I suppose. What I mostly felt was an urge to kill those that did it to her."

"You poor man," she said, touching his shoulder gently. "Love is God's greatest mystery. It's not something one can ever understand, nor ever live without. Remember that, Augustus." She fell silent for a moment, looking up at the house. "Love entered my life when I was fifteen. This man walked me home from a dance. He was a widower who lived on the next farm over from us. His wife had gotten a fever and died young and he'd never remarried. He was a good deal older, had grown children older than me. I had seen him before, not much to look at. He had a nice smile, though, and calm eyes. Like an evening sky in summer. And I liked his walk. Not a strut like that of some men, but a determined gait. He stood at my front door on a night just like this, and he took my hand and asked if he could kiss me. I didn't say yes, but he kissed me just the same. I thought of slapping him for being so forward, but my heart knew I was in love. I knew right then I would love him for all of my days and that if he wouldn't have me I would curl up and die."

She paused for a moment. Now it was Cain who asked, "What happened?"

"We married. I came here and lived with him for almost fifty years. I gave birth to three boys and a girl. The youngest two I saw buried out in back of the house." He waited for her to finish her story, but her eyes grew vacant as she stared off down the road, just the way she had when they'd come riding up earlier that day.

"Good night, Augustus."

"Are you all right, ma'am?"

"I am fine. Remember not to let anything happen to the girl."

"I shall try."

"No, don't try," she commanded. "See to it."

"I will, ma'am," he replied. "Good night."

After securing the two runaways to a horse ring in the tack room, the four men turned in.

"Crazier'n a hoot owl, that old biddy," said Preacher.

"She just old," Little Strofe offered.

"She gives me the willies," Preacher said. "She's the sort who'll sic the ab'litionists on you, sure as shootin'."

The others soon fell asleep, leaving Cain to thrash about awake. He had to agree with Preacher. He felt something was amiss with the old woman. The wary-hunter part of Cain wondered if she might indeed be an abolitionist who would sneak out after they were asleep and turn them in. But the other part, the one who'd confessed to having loved someone, worried about her. So he got up and quietly made his way out of the barn and up to the house, where he saw a light inside. He crept up to the window and peered in. It was her bedroom. The old woman sat on the side of the bed in her nightgown, combing her long gray hair and putting it in braids. She had a mirror in front of her that she turned this way and that, inspecting herself. He never imagined such vanity from an old lady, but she looked like a schoolgirl before her first dance. Then he saw what lay behind her in the bed: the sleeping form of a man. He lay on his back, his eyes closed, his hands under the covers. Cain wondered why she'd lied about being alone. Maybe the man was a lover and she didn't want anyone to know about him. Or maybe he didn't help around the place, merely slept in her bed. In any event Cain figured it wasn't any of his business; he backed quietly away from the window and headed to the barn.

When he woke with the first cockcrow in the morning, Little Strofe was already up and about, tending to his dogs.

"The old lady up yet?" Cain asked.

"Ain't heard a thing up there," he replied.

Cain left the barn and headed quietly up toward the house, retracing his footsteps from the night before. The black dog, he realized, was no longer barking. It lay in a dark heap at the end of its chain, its mouth open, its tongue swollen and lolling out onto the ground. Cain didn't have to, but he went over anyway and nudged it once with the toe of his boot, just to be sure. The animal was stiff and lifeless. He then headed back up to the house and knocked on the door. Receiving no reply, he opened it and walked in. The smell from the previous night was even stronger today—sharper, more concentrated, a pronounced sour tang that turned the stomach. Cain followed his nose toward the back room. As soon as he pushed open the bedroom door, he saw them—the old woman on the left, next to her the man he'd spotted sleeping the night before—lying side by side on the bed. While they might have looked to the casual observer as if they were merely an old couple sleeping, Cain knew immediately, they were both as dead as the dog. The old lady had died within the past few hours; her body was still somewhat pliant and not fully cold, more just cool to the touch. When he lifted her lids, her eyes were vacant but still those of a human being. The man, on the other hand, had been dead for much longer. His face had begun to collapse, and he already exuded the rank corruption of death. He was much older than the woman, though it was hard to assign an age to him now. Cain assumed then that the woman had probably poisoned the dog just before she did herself.

Only later did he find the note on the bureau, scratched quickly in a shaky hand.

April 23, 1857

Dear Mister Cain,

The favor I would ask of you is if you would see to it that my husband and myself have a proper Burial. You'll find our family Plot out back, where our two youngest children have been laid to rest. There are spades and picks in the barn. You needn't dig two Graves, as neither Father nor I are very large nor are we of a particular nature. We will be just fine resting together for Eternity, if Providence so wills, as we have for many years in this our marriage Bed. Thank you very much for your kindness. And please be sure to remember what I said about the girl.

Yours sincerely,

Hettie Atkins Burch

P.S. There is a side of bacon in the smokehouse. You're welcome to it.

When Preacher heard what Cain was proposing, he balked at it. "We're gonna dig their *what*?"

"Their grave," Cain said.

"Ain't none of our affair," he said. "I say we leave 'em and get the hell out of here before somebody comes 'round and finds us with them. Who's to say they won't think we kilt 'em?"

"It's not a C-Christian thing to leave 'em unburied," Little Strofe said.

"I don't give a shit. What's that crazy old biddy to us?"

"She fed us and put us up," Cain said. "It's the least we can do."

"Least *you* can do. I don't figure I owe her a dang thing."

"Suit yourself then," Cain said.

Cain and the Strofe brothers took turns digging the grave out in the family plot, while Preacher went over to where the two Negroes sat chained to the chestnut tree and stretched out and took a nap. The spring day turned sunny and warm, and they worked up a good sweat hacking through the rocky New England soil. When the grave was deep enough, they headed up to the house to fetch the bodies. However, on the front porch, the brothers fell to arguing over what to do next. Strofe thought they'd already wasted enough time and was just for throwing the two in the hole and covering them up as fast as they could, while his brother took the position that they ought at least to prepare their bodies and wind them in shrouds, since they didn't have proper coffins.

"You cain't just stick 'em in the g-ground like that," Little Strofe said.

"Why not?"

"Ain't decent. They ought leastways to be wrapped in a shroud."

"I ain't washin' a couple of dead strangers," said Strofe. "You want to do it, then be my guest."

They went back and forth. Finally a voice said, "I'll prepare the bodies if you want."

They turned to see Rosetta, who sat underneath the chestnut tree.

"I done it before," she said.

They unlocked the shackles and led her inside. She asked for some soap and water and rags. She undressed the old couple and set about washing them. Cain stood in the bedroom and watched as she went about her business. The pair looked pathetic in their nakedness, shriveled and gaunt, their skin pocked and of a bluish white hue. They looked like plucked and long-dead chickens lying on the bed. Cain thought: *So this is all that it comes down to.* Rosetta, though, didn't seem to mind in the least. She washed them and then got clean clothing from the chiffonier in the corner of the room and dressed them. She worked briskly, as if from experience, but Cain noticed that her movements were also tender and filled with compassion. From the dresser she found the woman's wedding ring, and she placed it on her finger. When she'd finished dressing them, she took a pair of sheets and used them for shrouds.

"I'll need some rope," she said to Cain.

He went out to the barn and returned with rope, which she used to wrap around the shrouds in several places, holding them in place.

"They're ready now," Rosetta said to Cain.

The men carried the two bodies out to the grave and lay them in, first the man and then the woman on top of him.

"Oughtn't we to s-say some words?" Little Strofe asked.

"What words?" his brother said.

"A prayer."

"You've a mind to, ain't nobody stopping you."

"I ain't no preacher."

He turned to Cain. The only thing Cain could think of was a proverb his mother used to read to him from the Bible: *For they eat the bread of wickedness, and drink the wine of violence.*

"We're wasting time," replied Strofe. He grabbed a shovel and was about to begin, when Rosetta said, "Wait." She stepped forward and recited the Twenty-third Psalm:

> *"The Lord is my Shepherd; I shall not want.*
> *He maketh me to lie down in green pastures . . ."*

When she finished, they began burying the two. As Cain threw shovelfuls of dirt on them, he thought of their conversation the previous night. About his promise to the woman. And about the mysteries of love.

11

They continued to ride west, toward the rolling hills that undulated across the western part of Connecticut and into New York State. They passed farmers driving wagons to market or children walking to school with their satchels slung over their shoulders or, in one case, a doctor in a sulky pulled by a fast bay trotter. Cain stopped the man and inquired if he might take a look at his wound, which the doctor did, pronouncing the stitches as professionally rendered as those of a surgeon. Mostly, though, it was the solitary rider or lonely pedestrian they came across on these back country lanes, some seemingly as intent on not running into fellow travelers as they. They would furtively slide by on the road with barely a nod, the brim of their hats pulled low to shade their faces. One morning they passed a well-dressed, middle-aged Negro man wearing a double-breasted paletot and felt bowler, lugging a well-worn portmanteau. When he saw them, he tried to slip into the woods, but it was too late.

"Just hold it there," Strofe called. When they were close, he asked, "Where you going, boy?"

"Nowhere," the man said. "Just up da road a piece."

"How far to the New York border?" Cain asked him.

"Ain't far, suh," he said, in that fawning way Negroes had with white men on horses. He nervously eyed Little Strofe's dogs. "Two day."

He looked at Rosetta, then Henry.

Preacher stared at the man's hat, which was similar to the one he himself wore.

"Where'd you get that hat, nigger?" he asked.

The Negro shrugged.

"I'm askin' you a question, boy?"

"Done bought it."

"Well, you give it here." When the man hesitated Preacher said, "You hear me, boy? I said give it here." The man took his hat off and handed it to Preacher. Preacher removed his own hat and compared the two. He even tried the Negro's hat on for size. It fit him much better than his own.

"I think I'll keep it. Here," he said, tossing his hat to the black man.

"I doan want your hat. I wants my own."

"Hit's a fair trade," Preacher said. "Now you take and git on out a here, you know what's good for you."

The man gave Preacher a surly look but he turned and started walking. As he went he mumbled under his breath, "*Swanga.*"

"What's that you say, nigger?" Preacher asked.

"Nothin', massa," the man replied without turning back. Once past them, the Negro broke into an awkward run down the road, lugging his portmanteau.

Just after they'd crossed the New York border, they stopped at a general store in a small out-of-the-way village to buy tobacco and whiskey, and for Cain another bottle of laudanum. Besides the store, the place amounted to only a couple of shabby unpainted houses, a small Baptist church made of logs, a blacksmith shop, and a feed and grain operation.

"How far to Dobbs Ferry?" Cain asked the owner, a tall man with a large gold tooth that seemed stuck to his lower lip.

Scratching his crotch, the man glanced out the window, as if he'd never been asked the direction to anyplace in his life.

"That's a good question," he replied.

Just as they were mounting up to leave, a party of men on horses came riding in. Dust from the road kicked up around them, and the air wavered in the midday heat creating an almost miragelike image.

There were four men on two bay horses, a swaybacked, broke-winded nag, and a black gelding with four white stockings and white hooves. The latter horse was three-legged lame, its hooves a mess, all broken up. Cain wondered if the man bred the horse or if he had been stupid enough to purchase one with four white hooves. Shuffling on foot behind the four men were a half dozen Negroes. They wore shackles hand and foot, and around their necks heavy iron collars with hooked prongs sticking out to the sides, some with bells attached. They were tied neck to neck by lengths of rope, the lead Negro's rope held by the last of the riders, who tugged them along at a brisk pace. If one fell, they would all fall and get dragged along. Cain had seen such arrangements before and didn't approve of them.

"Well, would you looky there," Preacher said. "Fellow slave catchers."

"Blackbirders," countered Cain, who'd been checking the cinch of his saddle. "Don't tell them anything."

Cain knew their sort. He'd had experience with blackbirders and he liked to steer clear of them. Despicable men of low character, they roamed about preying on any Negroes they could find, freemen or runaways, it didn't matter to them. In the South they kidnapped slaves legitimately traveling on an errand for their masters or freed Negroes with papers, which they'd confiscate and destroy. In the North, they haunted the black sections of large cities, waiting for a drunken Negro to wander into their clutches. They captured women and children, gray-haired old grannies, Negroes who'd been free their entire lives, and they'd put them in irons and march them down to the auction houses in Baltimore or Richmond or Charleston. They never carried warrants, and the law meant nothing at all to them.

"Why not?" asked Preacher.

"Just keep your mouth shut."

They came riding up to the store and stopped, the dust carrying beyond them into the faces of Cain and the others. The Negroes were a haggard-looking bunch, scrawny, poorly fed. Mixed in among them were two women, one of whom had been branded on her face—the mark of a runaway.

"How do," said the leader, a stocky, red-faced man with a powder burn beneath his right eye. His greatcoat was open and on his hip he carried a brace of blunt-barreled Tranter revolvers. He was on one of the bays.

Cain touched a finger to his hat in greeting.

"Where'd you get them niggers?" Preacher asked.

"Here and yonder," said the leader, smiling. He stared at Rosetta, standing beside Cain. "Where y'all headed?"

"Virginny," Preacher piped up.

Cain looked over at him, but Preacher was occupied by the other slaves.

"Why, we're going the same way," said the ruddy-complected leader. "We're bringing these here niggers down to Baltimore, to the block. What say y'all and us throw in together?"

"Thank you," Cain said, untying Hermes from the hitching post. "But we're fine as it is."

"You might want to reconsider," the man said.

"Yeah. Why is that?"

"Those abolitionists are everywhere hereabouts. What was that feller's name, Bell?" he asked, turning to the rider on his left, the one who rode the black gelding.

The man, who had a long dark beard with two streaks of pure white down the middle like the back of a polecat, was concentrating on chewing a fingernail. "What feller would that be?"

"The one we heard tell was looking for some folks took off with one of his runaway niggers."

"How in tarnation would I know?" the other snapped.

"That goddamned abolitionist. The one from out in Kansas."

"You mean Brown?"

"That's it. Brown. We heard he was riding down toward New York City. Asking along the way for any sign of some slave catchers he was after. You wouldn't know anything about that, now would you?" The man grinned, glancing first at Henry, then at Rosetta.

"Don't know anything about that," Cain said.

"But you see my point. We'd be better off throwing in together. Safety in numbers and all that."

"The man makes sense," Preacher said, glancing at Cain.

"No," Cain repeated.

"We're on the same side, mister," the leader advised.

"What side would that be?"

"The side of the law."

"Whose law?"

"The one that says a man's property can't be taken from him by some nigger-loving Yankee."

"And I suppose you have warrants for every one of those Negroes you got there?"

"That would be none of your business."

"Like I said," Cain repeated, "thanks all the same, but we're fine."

"But—" Preacher started.

"I *said* we're fine," Cain said, tossing a harsh look at Preacher.

The man looked from Preacher to Cain, then smiled. He was missing one of his front teeth.

"Well, boys," he said with mock indignity, turning to look at his comrades, "we can see when we're not wanted. Just trying to be hospitable is all." The one with the skunk beard laughed. Glancing at Rosetta again, the leader said, "That there is one fine-looking nigger wench you got."

Cain mounted, then reached down and pulled Rosetta up behind him. Then he wheeled Hermes around, nearly bumping the man's bay.

"I bet she'd fetch a goodly price at auction," the leader said.

"You boys have a good ride back," Cain said.

Later that day they stopped at a stream to water the horses and rest for a while. It had turned unseasonably warm for April, and they were all sweating profusely. Strofe had taken off his boots and was soaking his feet in the stream, while his brother lay on the cool grass with his hat over his face and slept. Having placed a feed bag filled with oats on Hermes, Cain was now busy currying him. He watched as Preacher sauntered over to where the two Negroes sat manacled on the ground near a rotted cedar stump.

He squatted down. "Wanna drink?" he asked, offering Rosetta his canteen.

"Already had one."

Preacher took off his new derby, then removed the blue kerchief from his neck and wiped his face with it. "Sure is a hot one. Ain't never pictured the North this hot. 'Least not in April."

Rosetta looked off toward the stream.

"Here," he said, extending the kerchief toward the girl. "You could use it to cover yourself."

She shook her head without looking up at him.

"G'won and take it," Preacher said.

"I don't want it," she replied, her voice low but firm.

"You done lost yours and I'm offering you this one. Take it."

"I told you, I *don't* want it," she repeated more emphatically.

"What's the matter, I ain't good enough to give you something?"

This time she glared at him. "You ain't got nothin' I want."

"Don't you get cheeky with me. Ain't nothin' I hate more than a uppity nigger."

"I *ain't* being uppity," she said. "I just don't want your damn kerchief."

"You watch your tongue, girl," he said, pointing a finger menacingly at her.

She looked at him scornfully.

"You hear me?" he asked.

Cain stopped brushing Hermes and looked over at Strofe, who was pulling on his boots. He was going to intervene, but Strofe beat him to it.

"All right, Preacher, that'll do."

"No, this here nigger's got to learn her some respect," he said. "Eberly don't want to do it, somebody got to."

"Leave her be," said Strofe. "You lay a hand on her and Mr. Eberly'll hear about it."

"You think I'm scared of that old coot?"

Rosetta smiled at him and said, "If you ain't, you're dumber'n you look."

Preacher reached out and grabbed her roughly by the shoulder.

"What you need is to be brought down a peg or two. Somebody oughta learn you some manners."

"And I suppose that'd be you?"

"You damn right. Nobody else seems to have a mind to."

Then she said something that surprised Cain a little. Staring coolly at Preacher, she said, "If'n I told Mr. Eberly you grabbed like this, he'd have you whupped."

"Hell, he would," Preacher scoffed.

Rosetta smiled at him. "Whup you just like a field hand."

Cain could see both the anger and the humiliation in Preacher's eyes. He wanted to hurt her.

"You hear me, Preacher," Strofe called over to him. "I said that's enough, you want to get paid."

Preacher continued to stare at Rosetta. Finally, he stood and walked over to his horse and began to saddle him.

"Tha's what wrong with this damn country," Preacher said.

"What's that, Preacher?" Little Strofe asked.

"Why, they ain't no respect is what. Niggers is running things."

As they were getting ready to leave, Rosetta asked Cain, "Could I wash myself? I ain't washed in a while."

"Maybe later. We got to get moving on." Once they were mounted and riding, he turned to her and said, "Would Eberly really have him whipped?"

"He'd kill 'im on my account," she said with something akin to pride.

They skirted New York City well to the north, crossing the Hudson at Dobbs Ferry and angling southwest through New Jersey's flat tidal marshes and pinelands, passing the small farms that supplied the big metropolis to the east. Though the afternoon sky was cloudless, a light haze hung in the salt-scented air, giving to everything the soft-edged look of things recalled in memory. Just outside of Paterson, Preacher's horse came up lame, and they had to ride into the city to find a livery. While there, Cain rode over to a general store to buy some sugar for Hermes and some whiskey for himself.

He asked the clerk, a blond fellow with thick, rubbery lips and yellow pigeon eyes, if he'd seen a band of about ten men ride through.

The man pursed his fat lips, like he was trying to fart.

"They'd be led by an old man on a white plow horse," Cain explained.

"There was some federal troops went through yesterday."

"No, these would have been civilians. They were heavily armed."

The man shrugged as he wrapped Cain's things in paper.

"I'd like to get a bar of soap, too," Cain told the man.

That evening they made camp in some woods near a railroad bridge over a broad, slow-moving tidal river. Several times they could hear the whistle of the train as it approached. For supper, Little Strofe fried up some corn pone and what was left of the side of bacon the old woman had left them, though it had started to smell like unwashed feet.

Preacher took one mouthful and spit his food onto the ground. "Dang, I'm sick and tired of your fixin's."

"If you d-don't like my cookin', whyn't you d-do it yourself," Little Strofe replied, growing bold enough to stand up to Preacher.

"M-maybe I will."

Preacher got up and went over to his horse and began to saddle him.

"Where you goin'?" Strofe asked him.

"Git me some decent grub for a change. 'Stead of his damn hog slops."

"You ain't back by morning, we leave without you."

"Don't you worry none. You ain't cuttin' me out a my share of the re-ward."

After he was gone, Cain took two plates of food and brought them over to where the girl and Henry sat manacled to trees several feet apart.

"Here," he said, setting the plates down beside them.

Rosetta took her plate but didn't start eating right away. She stared out over the river.

"Can I wash," she asked him. "I feel unclean. You know . . . woman's troubles."

He hesitated, wondering if it was just a trick of hers to escape.

Finally, he went over to his saddlebags and got the bar of soap he'd bought. He told Strofe he was taking the girl down to the river so she could wash herself.

"You think that's a good idea?" said Strofe as he took a sip from his bottle of applejack.

"I'll watch her."

"You oughtn'ta coddle them like that." Then he shrugged and said, "She runs, it's on your head."

From his vest pocket, Cain took out his key and unlocked Rosetta from the tree. She still had a pair of shackles on her wrists.

"Can I take a bath, too?" Henry asked.

"You sit tight," Cain told him.

"These here irons been galling my wrists, massa. They all bloodied."

"I'll look at them later."

He led Rosetta through some bushes down toward the river. The water was high and sluggish here and gave off the faint scent of the sea. Behind them, the sun had set, and it was getting on toward dusk, though with the quarter moon coming over the river there was plenty of light to see by. Evening had brought out the peepers and their metallic racket. Bats were dipping and wheeling in the air above the river, going after insects. A big fish broke the surface of the water near the shore, its ripples widening out. And eastward, through the haze, Cain could spy the lights of the city, like a gigantic riverboat all lit up and sailing through the evening.

"Here," he said, handing Rosetta the soap. She stood there, holding out the shackles to him.

"I can't hardly wash myself with my hands tied, now can I?" she told him. "'Sides, where I gonna run off to?"

"Last time you tried to swim away."

"You saw how good I was at that," she said, a hint of a smile softening her mouth just a little. "And if'n I did try to run, you can always shoot me with that gun a yours. I bet you're pretty good shootin' unarmed women."

He knew she was trying to get his goat and he wouldn't let her.

"Then again, you wouldn't get your re-ward for bringing me

back. And Mr. Eberly be mad at you. Wouldn't do to make him mad, now would it, Cain?" It was the second time she'd called him by his name.

"That'll be enough. That mouth of yours is going to get you in trouble someday."

"My mouth say what my heart tell it to. Tha's something my mama taught me."

As he unlocked the shackles, he asked, "I suppose you'd prefer to be back with those Howards."

She shrugged noncommittally.

"They treat you all right?"

"What's it matter to you?"

"It doesn't. It's just that Eberly didn't want anyone laying a hand on you."

"No, he wouldn't," she said, staring at him. "I liked the Missus just fine. Mr. Howard had him hungry eyes. Like a lot of white men."

When the shackles were off, she turned and walked down to the water's edge. Sitting on a piece of driftwood, she began to undress. She first removed the heavy brogans and stockings, then reached behind her and untied the apron. Standing, she unbuttoned her dress down the front, slid it over her angular shoulders, let it fall and stepped out of it. She folded the clothes neatly, placed them in a pile on the wood, and stood wearing only her cotton shift, which came to her calves. With a toe she tested the water, and Cain saw an unmistakable shiver course through her. Though the spring evening was warmish, the water had to be pretty cold still. Finally, she waded in. As she went deeper, she lifted the hem of the shift so it wouldn't get wet. When she was in up to her waist, she turned and looked modestly over her shoulder, back up the bank toward Cain. In deference to her silent request for modesty, he half turned away, keeping her still in the corner of his vision. Only then did she lift the undergarment completely over her head; she balled it up and tossed it back toward the bank. With her back to Cain, she wet the soap and began to wash herself. She moved her hands in short, efficient circles, not luxuriating in the act of bathing, but harshly, as if it were a form of self-flagellation. She washed herself, he felt, the way she might wash her master's clothes, with a perfunctory brusqueness.

He tried to keep her in the periphery of his vision as night came slowly on and softened the edges of all creation. He didn't think a man ought to look at a woman in such a vulnerable position, even one who might run on him. And yet, as he remained half-turned away, he felt this to be some sort of test of will, a temptation he felt bound to renounce in order to prove to himself, and perhaps to her, too, that he wasn't common, that he *wasn't* like Preacher or the Strofes as she had suggested, or even like old man Eberly for that matter. That he was different. That all southerners, all white southern men, weren't the same, that they weren't all tainted by the indelible stain of their peculiar institution. That there were a few white men of integrity, of principle still, who wouldn't take advantage of her simply because she was a slave and a woman.

Yet as he watched her out of the corner of his eye, her naked body just a short ways off, he told himself he wasn't some harem eunuch, either. That he was a man, too, a man who hadn't had a woman in weeks. And there she was, her dark, naked body wet and glistening in the half-light, so full of life and vitality. Finally, he said the hell with it. He gave in to what he told himself would be one quick look, turning his gaze full upon her. But once he saw her he found it hard to avert his gaze. She had a gravity that pulled him toward her. She was tall and slender, long-legged, small-breasted, narrow through the waist. At the same time, she was muscular, sinewy as a racehorse, her flesh hard and taut as if, at some point, she had been not a house servant but a rugged field hand. She was slender through the hips, and while he saw only the outline of her buttocks above the water, they were full and round. She gave the impression of a resilient strength, and he thought back to their fight in Boston. He thought, too, of what Little Strofe had said, that she was a wild one, and he understood now how lucky he'd been to have subdued her without either one getting badly hurt. She ducked her head beneath the water and washed her hair, some of the plaits coming undone, then soaped up her face and shoulders, her breasts, her belly. She ducked her head a second time, rose up out of the river and shook herself, crying out, "Oh, Lordy." When she was done, she turned and came walking out of the water, now without benefit of the shift. Her small breasts were high and firm, the nipples erect from the cold water, wet and shimmering in the semidarkness. Cain thought, *Jesus*. Indeed, she was a fine-looking woman. Cain's eye was drawn to the darker shadow between her legs and he felt shamed as a rumbling commenced down between his own legs. He understood now why the old man had wanted her back so badly, why he'd pay so much to have her returned: *Bring her back*, he'd both commanded and pleaded. And Cain knew, too, that he was no better than him, no better than the others, either. He was just a man like any other, with the same sort of dark urges and appetites, though he tried to cover them beneath a gloss of education and this thing he liked to call honor.

As he watched her come walking out of the river like a dark Venus emerging from the ocean, he noticed it: her belly. The slight swelling of it, the enlarged curvature below her navel. It was the only thing about her that wasn't lean and hard. Though he'd only seen mares and sows in such a state before, he thought with complete certainty, *She's with child*. He considered how he'd fought with her, twisted her arm and thrown her roughly over the saddle, ridden with her like that for miles. How he'd pulled her out of the flooded river and dragged her up onto the bank. How he'd pushed on her back, trying to force the water out of her lungs. How easily she could have lost the child or endangered her own health.

Suddenly, he realized several things at once. They came to him like one of those pictures in which you connected the dots and then all at once could recognize the thing for what it was. First, what the old woman had said to him back there, how Rosetta didn't look it. He now understood that it didn't have to do with how light skinned she was but with the fact that she was carrying a child. And then he realized, perhaps what Eberly was talking about when he said she'd stolen something from him, something that he wanted back. Was it his child? Was that why he'd wanted her back so badly?

Rosetta happened to glance up and catch him watching her. For a moment she didn't look away but returned his stare, modesty no longer a concern. Now she stared at him almost in challenge.

"Fancy what you see?" she called up to him. He continued for a moment to look at her. "Well, do you, Cain?"

Embarrassed, he turned finally and looked away.

She dried off with her shift, and when she'd finished dressing, she came up the bank barefoot, holding her shoes and stockings and the wet shift balled under her arm.

"I thought you said you had female trouble," he told her.

"I do."

"How can you have female trouble if you're carrying a child? You *are* pregnant, aren't you?"

She just stared at him.

"You should have told me," he said.

"What difference it make to you?"

"Why in God's name would you risk fighting with me if you're pregnant? Or jumping in the river. You could've gotten hurt. Could've lost the baby."

With her hand, she calmly wiped a drop of water away from her face.

"Because I *am* carrying this child is why. I rather die than go back there. Than bring this one back there, too," she said, one hand pointing off in the direction of *back there*, the other protectively rubbing the dress over her stomach.

"Is it his? Eberly's?"

She looked out over the river. The distant lights of the city shimmered in her eyes. He noticed the ball of muscle in her jaw tense, then relax, then tense again, as if she were chewing on something tough.

"It his."

"Does he know about it?"

"Oh, he know, all right," she said scoffingly.

"How about the other one? Israel."

"That his, too. Was. He sold my baby off 'cause I run away with him. 'Cause I wanted him to grow up free."

"Is that why you knifed him?"

She laughed, a high bitter laugh. "You damn right. Just wisht I'd killed him is all."

"Eberly said you stole something of value of his. Was he referring to the child?"

She pursed her lips. "I reckon so."

"If it was so valuable to him, perhaps he'll let you keep this one."

"*Let* me keep it? Talkin' 'bout my own flesh and blood. Besides, he figures he owns me and anything tha's mine."

Cain had never talked to a captured runaway like this before, and he found it troubling. Yet he wanted to say he thought such a thing despicable, for an owner to treat his slave that way. He wanted her to know how he felt, though, of course, he couldn't. That would have been a breach of trust on his part. He loathed the man, the sort of owner he represented. Still, he felt a certain obligation that went deeper than money or his personal feelings or even the law. Instead, he said simply, "I'm sorry." It was the second time he'd said that to her.

"What you sorry for?"

"For having to bring you back . . . to that man."

"He's not a man. He's a monster."

"I heard he treated you well."

"He treated me like his whore. Like something he bought and paid for. I ain't no more than a saw or a half acre of tobacco to him. Figured he could do what he pleased with me."

"But you fared better than most."

"He never laid a hand on me, if that's what you mean. Not in anger anyhow. But they's other ways of making a slave feel like a slave. Mr. Eberly he was a fine upstanding gentleman," she said with obvious sarcasm. "He never got his own hands dirty. He let Strofe or somebody like Preacher do it for him. He usta have them cat-haul runaways."

Cain frowned. He had never heard the term before.

"It when they tie a rope to a cat's tail and put the creature on the back of a slave. Then they pull the rope real slow, so the cat sinks its claws in. Another time he had Strofe flog this little runaway girl. She weren't no more than twelve. They tied her down on the ground. But on account of her being with child they dug a hole in the ground for her belly to fit. Mr. Eberly didn't want to damage a healthy slave child. Then they whup her so hard she give birth. Baby come out right in that hole."

Cain glanced out over the river. "I gave him my word."

"Your word! Huh," she snorted. "How much Mr. Eberly payin' you for your almighty word?"

"The money's part of it. I won't deny that. But it's more than that. It has to do with honor."

"Honor," she said, laughing in his face. "He done bought and paid for you just like me."

"He doesn't own me," Cain snapped. "Nobody owns me."

"Oh, he own you, all right. Difference 'twixt me and you, Cain, is I know it and you don't."

"I have to bring you back. I don't have a choice."

"Ever'body gots a choice," she said. "Only person don't is this young'un inside me. He don't have no choice. Can't choose not to come into this world. Or to come. People got to choose that for him."

"You think you have that right? To choose for him not to be born."

"Eberly may own this body," she said, patting the material over her breasts. "But he don't own what's inside me. Not my heart. Not my soul. That's more'n you can say, Cain."

"Let's go," he said. He'd had enough of her jabber. He put the shackles on and led her back to camp.

Once again, Henry complained that his wrists hurt. Cain squatted down and inspected them. They were in bad shape. The skin was rubbed raw from the irons and was beginning to bleed.

"Them shackles way too tight, massa," Henry said.

"They can't be loosened."

"Maybe you gots a bigger pair."

"Maybe you ought not to eat so much," Cain replied irritably. Still, he went over to his saddlebags and got some horse liniment and a rag. He removed Henry's shackles and poured some liniment on the rag and swabbed Henry's wrists with it.

"There, that better?"

"Any chance I could take me a bath, too?"

"No," Cain snapped. "What the hell do you think this is? Now stop your damn bellyaching, nigger."

He was suddenly fed up with both of them. Strofe was right. The more you coddled them, the more they expected. They were runaway slaves. Nothing more. Problems arose when you forgot that. His father had been right, about the difference between white and black. To go against it was to go against the natural order of things.

He lay down on his bedroll and looked up at the stars. The pounding in his head had returned, so he took out his flask and tried to drown it under a sweet haze.

A muffled noise came to him. Cain opened his eyes and sat up, alerted by the sixth sense he'd acquired over the years as a hunter. He pulled his gun, quietly crawled from his bedroll, and crouched, gazing into the darkness as his eyes adjusted. As he moved through the camp, he could see by the dappled moonlight filtering through the trees the recumbent figures of Strofe and his brother, sound asleep and snoring. Preacher, though, was still gone. He made his way over to where Henry lay sleeping, the blanket wrapped around him, his head tipped back against the tree, his mouth open. When he turned to check on Rosetta, however, he saw that she was gone. The shackles had been unlocked and lay near the tree. *Damn*, he thought. The last thing he wanted was losing a couple more days having to hunt her down.

He was about to wake the Strofes and tell them of her escape when he heard the noise again. A low, muffled sound, as of an animal in pain. Cain listened closely, trying to get a read on its source. He decided it was coming from down toward the river. He moved stealthily through the high grass, toward the sound.

When he got close, he saw something on the ground. By moonlight he made out two figures, one on top of the other, the white of naked haunches glowing in the night. It was Preacher, Cain knew immediately. His trousers were down around his ankles and he had Rosetta pinned on the ground. In one hand he held the big bowie knife pressed to her throat while with the other he was trying to lift the hem of her dress. She struggled against him, trying to hold her dress down.

"Hold still, damn you," Preacher hissed at her.

"Please don't," Rosetta pleaded in a whisper.

"Hush up, girl. Ain't agonna warn you again."

Cain crept up on them, put the Colt to the base of Preacher's skull, and cocked the hammer. Through the metal he felt Preacher's body stiffen.

"Make a wrong move and I'll kill you dead," he said. "Now drop the knife and get up. Slowly."

Preacher did as he was told. Standing with his trousers and underdrawers wrapped around his ankles, he wobbled unsteadily, the liquor fumes strong as turpentine.

"Can I leastways pull up my pants," he asked.

"Go ahead."

He pulled up his pants, buttoned his fly, and tugged his suspenders over his shoulders. Then he smiled at Cain, that evil snake-grin of his.

"Just havin' some fun," Preacher said.

Do it, Cain thought. He knew it would come to this sooner or later, that, as Hamlet said, "it be not now, yet it will come."

"Gonna kill a white man just havin' hisself a little fun with some nigger wench?" Preacher taunted. "What sort of man are you, Cain?"

"Shut up."

"Hell, I seen the way you look at her."

"I told you to shut up," Cain warned, feeling the pressure of his index finger on the trigger. *Do it*. He glanced over at Rosetta, who had sat up and was straightening her dress. The bodice was ripped, and by the moonlight he could see there was blood on the material.

"You think you're so high-and-mighty, Cain. I weren't doin' nothing you ain't thought a doin'."

"Shut up."

Preacher grinned knowingly at him and winked. "Me and you, why, we're—"

That's when Cain struck him with his gun barrel, hard, a sockdolager of a blow to the temple. Preacher collapsed like a thousand of brick. He lay there as if dead, blood pouring out of a gash along his hairline and down over the wine stain on his jaw.

Cain holstered his gun, then went to see about Rosetta. Squatting down, he asked, "Are you all right?"

"He hit me," she said, touching her nose, which was bleeding. Cain pulled his handkerchief out of his pocket and held it to her nose.

"Squeeze that until the bleeding stops. Did he . . ."

She shook her head.

Cain still had his key for the shackles, so he assumed that Preacher had lifted the other one from his saddlebags when he wasn't watching. He'd probably been planning this for a while.

"Can you stand up?"

Rosetta nodded.

Suddenly, she looked over Cain's shoulder and cried, "Watch out."

He started to turn when the flat side of Preacher's knife caught him flush across the cheek. The blow dazed him, and he stumbled and fell onto the ground, landing on his stomach. Cain reached for his gun, but Preacher was too fast. He pounced on Cain's back like a feist dog; he grabbed Cain by the hair and pulled his head back, pressing his knife to his exposed throat.

"G'won and try it, and I'll bleed you like a hog," Preacher hissed.

Cain could feel the razor sharpness of the knife, the prickle of it snagging his skin like a briar.

"Take the gun out with two fingers and give it here."

Cain removed his gun, slowly, and the man grabbed it from him.

Preacher whistled. "That's a right fine gun. Think I'll just keep it, since you won't be needing it no more."

"You kill me, you'll have to explain what happened."

"Hell, I'll just say you was drunk and with your bum leg and all you slipped and fell in the drink and drowned yourself. Simple as that. Nobody'll give a damn anyhow. You and your fancy gawdamn ways. Plus more re-ward for the rest of us."

While he was talking, out of the corner of his eye Cain could see the girl a short distance away. She slowly got to her feet and, crouching, began to back into the woods. She made eye contact with him briefly, her gaze filled with a meaning he couldn't decipher. He thought it might be, *You got what you deserved*. Then she turned and vanished into the night without a sound. He thought of saying, "She's getting away," if for no other reason than to momentarily distract Preacher. But he remained quiet. He knew she had only a slim chance of success, of eluding the dogs. He remembered she'd told him she would rather die than bring her baby back to Eberly.

"Problem with you, Cain," Preacher said, "is you think you're better'n ever'body else."

"Go to hell."

"That's where you're bound. Truth is, you ain't worth the cost of a bullet."

Cain closed his eyes. He pictured the wounded men that day on the battlefield of Buena Vista, as the Mexicans went from man to man silencing them with their bayonets. If he had died then, it would have made some kind of sense. Fighting and dying if not for a cause he understood, at least with men whom he admired. But this? Funny, he thought, how fate had picked him out to live that day, only to die here and now, in some place he didn't know, for a reason he couldn't fathom. It was all so strange. Yet he'd lived enough to realize men seldom get to pick the manner or time of their deaths, or whether or not it all made sense to them.

"All right, Preacher," came Strofe's voice. "Put it away."

Strofe came walking up holding a lantern in one hand, his shotgun in the other.

"The bastard deserves killing," Preacher cried, pressing the knife harder against Cain's throat.

"I mean it," said Strofe, sticking the barrel of his shotgun into Preacher's back. Behind Strofe was his brother with his musket also aimed at Preacher.

"L-let him up," he said.

Preacher hesitated for a moment, as if he were still debating what he was going to do. Finally he leaned down to Cain and whispered in his ear, "Remember. Me and you got us a score to settle once this is over."

He released Cain and stood.

"Try something like that again," said Strofe, "I'll kill you myself."

Preacher spat on the ground, then stormed off toward camp.

Cain rolled over and sat up. He touched his cheek, sore from where Preacher had struck him with the knife blade.

"You all right, Mr. Cain?" asked Little Strofe.

"Yeah, I'm fine, Mr. Strofe," he replied as the man helped him to his feet. He glanced out over the river toward the lights of the city. The entire night sky seemed ablaze with its incandescence, glowing like a comet. Then he remembered Rosetta. He wondered how far she'd get, and how long it would take them to find her. He thought he might even give it till morning before they began their search. If she were clever—and he knew she was that, all right—and lucky, she might even make New York by daybreak. All she had to do was follow the light. And if she reached the city before they captured her, it would be like looking for a needle in a haystack. Then again, he thought about what he owed Eberly and the promise he'd made to him, and he felt it might be best to go after her tonight, while her tracks were fresh and the dogs could follow her more easily.

"The girl?" he said.

"What about her?"

"She ran."

"And lucky for you she did," Little Strofe explained.

"What do you mean?" Cain asked, confused.

"Was her w-woke us up and told us what Preacher done to her. And was about to do to you. She come a second later and you m-might not be here."

"Where is she?"

"Right over yonder," replied Little Strofe, tossing his head behind him.

Cain looked past him and saw Rosetta standing there. She had her arms wrapped around herself like she was cold.

Only then did Cain understand that he'd misread the look in her eyes earlier.

12

For the next several days they rode west through the flatlands of New Jersey. The weather continued balmy for mid-April, and by midmorning Cain would have to remove his coat and vest, and roll up his shirtsleeves. Even then he felt the sweat trickling down his back where Rosetta pressed up against him, collecting where her hands held his stomach. The farther they got away from the ocean, the more the air turned dry and clear, smelling of pine and hemlock, and the freshly turned earth of farmlands now under plow. The sky unfolded in a sweep of delicate blue, fragile as the porcelain figurines Cain's mother used to have on her bureau. Seagulls were slowly replaced by a raucous band of crows that followed them for several miles, cawing at them as if they were intruders in their private place. Not far from a town called Hopatcong, the dogs jumped a big buck in a thicket and bolted after it.

"Louella. Skunk," Little Strofe called to them at frequent intervals.

As the day wore on with no sign of them, Cain could see him growing worried.

"They ain't usually gone this long," Little Strofe said.

"They'll be back when they get good and tuckered out," Cain tried to reassure him.

"I hope so. I'd hate to have anything happen to them."

Henry's wrists continued to look bad, even infected. Little Strofe found some snakeweed and made a poultice and applied it to the wounds, but they seemed only to get worse. They took to leaving the shackles off except at night, and then placed them only around his ankles.

Preacher didn't speak to anyone. Now and then he might look across at Cain and stare at him, his small dark eyes narrowed to a slit of unadulterated hatred. He ate his meals alone, taking his plate and going off by himself. He rode silently at the back of the group and didn't even offer his usual complaints about which way they went. He reminded Cain of a rattler that was getting itself all curled up, ready to strike. Cain was now convinced he'd made a mistake in not getting rid of him when he'd had the chance. Even more so now, he felt he would have to watch his back.

As they rode along, Cain felt a subtle but definite shift in things. He couldn't put his finger on exactly what it was, but the change was unmistakable. Of course, it had something to do with that night, with Preacher and what had happened. But it was more than that. He felt it in his spine as he rode along, in an acrid metallic taste in his mouth that even several swigs from his flask couldn't leach away. Even the day itself seemed to mirror the change that had come over Cain. The sunlight, ruthless as a scythe, swept harshly across road and field and forest; it was tinged an odd yellowish green, like the charged air right before a summer storm, filled with premonitory warning. It stung his eyes, as it would those of a man who'd been kept in a dark cellar and then brought suddenly into the bright light of day. And yet, he was not blinded. In fact, just the opposite. He saw everything in such detail—the edges of a chestnut leaf, the purplish black feathers of one of those crows perched on a fence post, a stone along the road shaped like an old man's head. All of creation stood out with such stark, austere clarity, it was as if he'd never seen any of it heretofore.

He remembered right before his mother died, she had sat up in bed and grabbed his wrist so hard he thought she meant to hurt him. Her pretty gray eyes shone with an agitated fever and were sighted on something only she could see. "Augustus," she cried. "Oh, Augustus.

It is all too much." That's what he felt now—that it was all too much to look upon.

He thought it might have had something to do with his coming so close to death, yet several times before he'd nearly died, and he'd not felt anything like this. He thought this odd feeling had more to do with Rosetta. Now as she rode behind him, her hands pressing against his belly, he felt an awkwardness he'd not felt before. Perhaps it was his knowing that she was pregnant, that she was carrying Eberly's child, a life she wasn't sure she wanted to bring into the world and certainly not back to Virginia, to that monster, as she'd called Eberly. Or maybe it had to do with the fact that she'd had a chance to run, to save herself and her baby, and hadn't, that she'd chosen to wake up the others and save him from Preacher's knife.

Why had she done that? he wondered. Especially after she said she'd kill him if she ever got the chance? It didn't make sense. Now he felt an obligation he didn't want to feel, a weight he didn't want to carry. He told himself he had a job to do and he was going to do it, that all other considerations were secondary. Of course he felt sorry for her. Any person with half a heart would, no matter that she was a runaway slave. And he felt only contempt and scorn for Eberly. What he had done to her was beneath what a man ought to do, especially a southerner and a supposed gentleman, and after this was all over, after he'd been paid his money, he had a good mind to tell the old son of a bitch exactly what he thought of him. Now Cain understood what Eberly had meant about this situation calling for someone with discretion. Someone to keep his secret quiet, that's what he wanted. Despite this, the girl was still his legal property, and he, Cain, was obliged to return her, as he'd given his word to do, whether he liked it or not. He didn't make the rules. He wasn't the one who'd written the law. Besides, there was the not-so-trifling matter of his horse and the five hundred dollars he would make. He needed that money. It would give him a new start.

As he rode along, he was also troubled by something Preacher had said to him that night, that he'd seen the way Cain had stared at the girl and knew that Cain wanted to do the same thing to her that he had tried. Don't pay him any mind, Cain cautioned himself. He was a fool, his appetites little better than those of an animal. Still, Cain couldn't get the notion out of his mind. How *had* he looked at her? Sure, she was a fine-looking woman. He'd have to have been blind not to notice that. From time to time when he was growing up on his father's farm, Cain would take heed of some young slave wench. When the women washed their clothing down at the creek or when one lifted the hem of her dress to carry apples and he'd catch sight of a shapely calf—he noticed them. Sometimes it was more than noticing them. Sometimes he'd picture them as he lay down at night in the darkness of his bed, picture them as he took hold of his growing hunger. Yet that was only normal. Besides, unlike Preacher or Eberly, he'd never acted upon what he felt. So what if he'd noticed Rosetta? Any man would, no matter what color he was.

Around noon the next day, they stopped for lunch at a pretty green lake surrounded by hemlock and spruce trees. Cain led Hermes down to the water's edge and helped Rosetta from the horse. She stood there, waiting for him to get the shackles out of the saddlebags. Instead, he took out the horse's feed bag and filled it with oats.

She sat on a rock. "He a fine horse," she offered.

"Yes, he is," Cain replied proudly. He thought of telling her that it was because of this animal that he had come after her in the first place. That he cared enough for Hermes and didn't want to lose him. That unlike the Strofes or Preacher, who did all this out of mere pecuniary reasons, for the money or because it was their job, his reasons were somehow more noble—he did it out of the love for his horse. But he had to admit to himself that he wanted the money, too. And then there was the fact that the *only* thing he'd ever been any good at was catching slaves, and he wanted to show up a man like Eberly, a man who looked down upon him. Rich, powerful planters like Eberly came to him with their tails between their legs to ask him to bring back their valued possessions. He knew all of this was true, too.

From his pocket, he took out the money purse the old lady had given him.

"Here," he said.

"What's this?" Rosetta asked suspiciously.

"The old lady we buried. She wanted you to have it. There's nearly ten dollars there."

Rosetta opened the purse, shook the coins out onto the palm of her hand.

"She had her a good heart. How come you giving this to me?"

"Because it's yours."

"You coulda kept it."

"I'm not a thief."

He removed the cinch and took off the saddle and the blanket and began to brush the horse. After a while, he stopped and glanced over his shoulder at her. "I want to ask you something. And I want you to tell me the truth," he said.

Rosetta looked at Cain, waiting.

"Why did you do it?"

"Help bury her?"

"No, not that. Why did you wake up the Strofes? You could have run."

"Wouldn't a got far," she said with a laugh. "Not with them dogs after me."

"But you could have tried to get away," he said. "You had a chance. Just like the chance you had in the river."

She jerked her shoulders up toward her ears, then let them fall slowly downward, one shoulder at a time.

"You said you'd kill me if you got the chance," he reminded her.

"I still might," she said, her face expressionless, so he couldn't tell if she meant it or not.

"You had the chance to run and you didn't. Why?" he asked again. "I thought the last thing you wanted was to go back there."

"It is," she replied. "But I got to ponderin' on what you said last night."

"What was that?"

"'Bout whether I got the right to choose whether this chile gonna be birthed or not. More I got to ponderin' on it, more I thought you're right. How it ain't my choice. Never been mine. It God's choice. His will to do as he wants. Only thing I can do is protect this life I'm carrying."

"What does that have to do with you not running?"

"You saved my life. Twice. In the river and then again last night," she said.

"So you figure you owe me?"

"Not for me," she replied, raising her eyebrows. "If it was just me, I'da let him cut your throat, Cain. Mine, too, for that matter. But I owe you for my chile. For saving his life. Let me tell you something. When I found out I was with child again—with *that man's* child—first thing I thought of was doing away with it. I didn't want no part of it. No, sir. Didn't want his seed growing in me. Not again. But then I got to thinkin' how it wasn't my baby's fault. And how it was mine own child, not Eberly's. How if God decided to put life in me who was I to say no to it?"

Cain looked at her and then nodded his head, not so much in agreement as because he didn't want to know all this about her life. "For whatever reason you did it," he said, "I want to thank you."

"Oughta be thankin' God. He the one saved you."

"You saved me."

"Just like a white man to think we can save ourselves. Y'all so used to thinkin' you're in charge of things."

She smiled at him again, this time without the note of irony, then glanced out over the lake. He stared at her. In the light of day her skin shone a warm golden color with reddish highlights on her cheeks and forehead. And her eyes seemed to keep changing hue, depending on the light and time of day, and her moods, which, he had begun to realize, were as unpredictable as the weather. Now they were lighter, a soft turquoise blue. She was, it suddenly struck him, beautiful, and he felt a familiar but long-dormant sensation move inside him, faint yet sure as the far-off rumble of a train. Was he no better than Preacher? Than Eberly? Did he want to possess her, to own her in the way men owned women of any color?

"So we even now," she said, glancing up at him.

"What does that mean?"

"Just mean we is, is all."

He wasn't sure if she was suggesting that she would put aside the hatred she'd previously harbored for him, accept her fate and no longer fight it; or if she was giving him fair warning that, if the chance presented itself, she would still kill him with impunity. He scrutinized her face, trying to read her intent there. Yet a cloud happened to pass overhead at that moment, making her expression all the more inscrutable.

That evening only one of Little Strofe's dogs came straggling into camp, its tongue hanging out, and looking the worse for wear. It was Louella. There was no sign of Skunk. The bitch's back leg and foot were bloodied, and she was limping badly. When Little Strofe knelt to inspect, he found that her hindquarters had buckshot in it.

"Some sumbitch shot her," he said, incredulous, his eyes watering. "Why would anybody want to s-shoot her?"

Cain got his box of medical supplies and picked out the buckshot with a pair of tweezers. The dog stared up at him and made low whimpering sounds. "Hit's all right, girl," comforted Little Strofe, who held the dog while Cain worked. "Where's Skunk? What happened to 'im?" When Cain was finished removing the lead, he washed and cleaned the wounds, poured some whiskey on them.

For the next several days as they rode south, Little Strofe continued to call for his missing hound. "Skunk," he'd yell. "C'mon, boy. Here, boy." After trying that for a while, he'd change tactics. "Dang you, Skunk," he'd call. "I'm gonna whup your mangy hide when you git back, I swear." Yet as the days passed without any sign of him, the chances of his returning looker bleaker. One night Cain found Little Strofe washing pans down by a creek. He was crying. Cain squatted down beside him.

"He's got a good nose," Cain said. "It wouldn't surprise me if he followed our trail, Mr. Strofe."

The man nodded, unconvinced. "Always did g-give me problems, that dog. He was the runt of the litter, Mr. Cain," the man confessed. "I had to take a bottle and feed him by hand."

"Don't give up hope."

"I reckon," the man replied, but Cain saw the doubt in his eyes.

They continued southwest, crossing the Delaware at Phillipsburg and heading into Pennsylvania. The Quakers, Cain knew, were almost as hardheaded and belligerent as the Boston abolitionists when it came to slavery, and they would need to be cautious. He'd heard stories about those who aided and abetted fugitives, even resorted to violence to further their cause. Like the one about the sweet old lady who'd scared off a couple of slave catchers with a load of buckshot they ended up having to pick out of their backsides. For all their peaceful, God-fearing talk, they could be as brutal as any overseer or slave trader.

They rode past Allentown and Kutztown and Reading, heading for Harrisburg, where they would eventually turn southward toward Virginia. The country unfolded in a series of green rolling hills, fertile pastureland filled with dark-faced Jersey cattle, and fields newly planted with wheat and corn. Along the way, they came upon the neat, well-kept farms of the Amish, whom they saw working in the fields dressed in their black clothing. Outside a small town called Womelsdorf, they met an older couple in a covered, two-wheeled trap heading off to church. Cain stopped them and asked how far it was to Harrisburg. The man, who wore a straw hat and a long beard, told them in an odd German accent it was two days' ride. He glanced at the two Negroes and gave the reins a sharp crack.

For a long while they followed a narrow washboard road that wound its way through a mountain gap of mixed hardwoods and pine. Trees were beginning to form buds, and on some of the lower slopes the dogwoods were in bloom. Earlier they'd passed a large dead rattlesnake along the side of the road that a crow and several turkey buzzards were fighting over. The crow, smaller by half, had held its own, seemed even to have had the upper hand. Behind him now, Cain could hear Little Strofe and Henry arguing about snakes. They were debating whether a rattler or a cottonmouth was the more dangerous.

"You can s-step on a cottonmouth 'fore you knows he's there," said Little Strofe. "Leastways with a rattler you can hear him."

"I knew a overseer in the fields once got hisself bit on the leg by a big ole rattler," said Henry. "He drop down dead by the time he lift up his pant leg."

"Huh!"

"Hit's true. I seen him. Drop right down dead."

"Ever'body knows the orneryest snake is your c-cottonmouth. Them critters downright mean."

They continued debating the merits of their respective positions for several miles. As they rode along, Cain developed an itch in the middle of his back that was driving him crazy.

"Would you do me a kindness?" he asked Rosetta. "Would you scratch my back?"

She paused for a moment, then started to scratch it lightly.

"Lower. And harder," he instructed. When she finally hit the spot, he cried, "Oh, God."

She lifted his shirt and inspected his back. He felt her fingers, cool as alcohol, running down his spine, and he shivered.

"They look like jigger flea bites," she told him. "You got you any guncotton in your medical box?"

"No," he replied.

"That's what you need. That or turpentine. I'd get them bites, Momma'd put guncotton on them."

About two hours before nightfall, they reached the top of a long mountain pass. Cain stopped and got out his spyglass and scoped the road behind them as far as he could see. For the past two days he'd had the uneasy feeling that they were being followed. He'd had no evidence to go on, save for a feeling in his gut, but that same feeling had saved his neck on more than one occasion, and he was loath to ignore it. Yet he saw nothing. He waited for Strofe and the others to catch up.

"Why don't you go on ahead," Cain told them. "I'm going to set here for a spell and watch our flank."

"You ain't still worried about Brown, are you?" Strofe said to him.

"Better safe than sorry," he replied. "I'll catch up with you before nightfall."

As Preacher rode by, he was heard to say, "Hell, he jess wants to be by his lonesome with that bitch."

Cain decided to let it go.

He held Rosetta's hand as she slid off the back of Hermes, then dismounted himself. He shackled her wrists and led the horse into the woods a little ways and tied him to a tree. From his saddlebags he got his spyglass and the canteen, before heading back to the road.

"Here," he said to Rosetta, handing her the canteen. "Sit still and don't move." With his spyglass he scoped the road they'd taken through the valley. He could see for miles. Nothing.

So he sat down on the ground and removed his flask and had a sip.

"You got kin?" she asked.

"My father and brother have a farm out in the western part of Virginia," Cain explained, surveying the valley below. "A place called Nottoway Chase. That's where I grew up."

"What about a mother?"

"She died when I was a boy."

"They own slaves, your folks?"

"Some. Not many."

"One's too many. How 'bout you? You got you a wife?"

"No."

"How come?"

"I don't know."

"Ever come close to gettin' married?"

"I was engaged once."

"What happened?"

"What the hell is this?" He wasn't used to anyone let alone a runaway asking him so many questions. He thought of telling her just to shut up. But, oddly, he didn't mind talking to her, telling her about himself, his life. He couldn't say why. Perhaps it was that he wouldn't see her again. "I had to go to war down in Mexico."

He knew that, at best, it was only a kind of truth, something smooth and polished to a high sheen that made the telling of it easier.

"How about you?" Cain asked. "Did you have any other family?"

"Just my momma and my boy. And this one here," she said, touching her belly.

"What about your father?"

She snorted. "Never had me no father. Can I axe you something, Cain?" she said in an undertone.

He turned toward her. "That all depends."

"How come you with these men?" She tossed her head in the direction that the others had ridden.

"What do you mean?"

"Why you doin' this? Takin' folks back to their chains."

"It's my profession. It's what I do."

"But me and Henry ain't never done nothing to you."

"Doesn't matter. You're a runaway, and it's my job to see that you're returned."

"So it's just the money to you?"

"The money's part of it," he said to Rosetta. "I'm in Eberly's debt. He could make things very difficult for me if I didn't bring you back."

"You ain't like them others, Cain," she said to him. "Preacher and the Strofes. They stupid and low-down mean and can't do no better than this. But you, you got more in you. You got learnin'. Brains."

"I thought you said I was just like them."

"I'm thinkin' maybe I was wrong about you."

"Or maybe not. Maybe I am no better than them."

"Tha's just you lettin' yourself off easy," she told him.

"What's that supposed to mean?" he asked.

"If you don't count yourself no better'n them, then you don't have to live up to no more. It makes things a whole lot easier for you."

"That'll be enough," he told her.

"You don't like when the truth hits too close to home, do you, Cain?" she offered.

"I said, 'enough.' Now damn it, shut up."

When he turned back to watch the road, he saw, about a mile distant, the swirling dust from a party of riders. He grabbed his spyglass and had a closer look. There were about six men, riding hard in his direction. The leader rode a dappled gray horse, and he was spurring him violently. When they got closer, he recognized the same figure he'd seen back at the river. Dressed in black, his long gray beard sweeping behind him as he galloped along the road, coming on like the apocalypse. That goddamned Brown. He had with him only half the party now. Cain figured perhaps some of them had given up and returned to their other lives. Or maybe they'd split in half, with the other group following the road along the coast. In any event, they were onto them. They'd reach him in a few minutes.

"Son of a bitch," cried Cain.

"What's the matter?" Rosetta asked.

"It's that fool Brown."

"Who's he?"

"Henry was working for him. He's an abolitionist. Stay down," he cautioned her.

He hurried over to his horse and got his Sharp's, then returned and took up a position behind a boulder at the side of the road. He rested the barrel on the boulder and adjusted the rear sight, waiting for the riders to come into range.

"You gonna kill him?" asked Rosetta from behind him.

"Hush up," he told her as he cocked the hammer.

"What'd he ever do to you?"

"I told you, 'hush.'"

He figured if he killed Brown, the others might be discouraged and turn back. At the very least, there would be one less to worry about. He waited patiently for them to come within range. When he'd tell people back home what he'd done, they'd probably make him a hero. The man who'd killed Osawatomie Brown.

After a while, he said, "Don't you think he'd kill me if he got the chance?" Rosetta didn't say anything. "Do you know what he did to men out in Kansas?"

When he turned to look at her, she was gone.

"Goddamn it," he cursed.

He turned back to the riders. Though they were still not yet in range, he fired anyway, just to scare them off and give him time to catch Rosetta. The shot had the desired effect. The riders pulled up and scattered into the trees. Then Cain turned and ran off into the woods after Rosetta. He stopped momentarily and listened. He could hear her running through the woods. He followed the sound.

She hadn't gone more than a few hundred paces before he caught up to her. He grabbed her by the shoulder, gently but firmly. She didn't fight him.

"I thought you weren't gone to run again?"

"I never said that. You 'spect me to just go on back to that man without a fight?"

"You could get hurt. The baby, too."

"And goin' back won't hurt me?"

"Let's go," he said. "They'll be coming soon."

They hurried back to his horse and took off.

When he reached the others, Strofe said, "We heard a shot."

"That was me. Brown's on our trail," he said, looking over at Preacher.

"How far back are they?"

"A couple of miles maybe."

They rode hard for a while. Just before it got dark, Cain had them turn off onto a shallow stream that headed south. They followed that for some time so their trail couldn't be picked up, and when it was too dark to ride through the thick woods, they stopped and made camp. They didn't light a fire, so they had to eat a cold supper. They took turns standing guard.

The next day they broke camp early. They continued heading south until they came to a narrow one-lane road and then headed west again. Cain kept looking over his shoulder to their rear, expecting Brown. But they saw no more sign of him, and that feeling in his gut that someone was following him lessened, then disappeared completely.

Later in the day, they were rounding a bend in the road when up ahead Cain spotted a large black caravan stopped. The entire wagon listed to one side like a ship taking on water in a storm. As Cain drew near, he saw that the right rear wheel had broken, two sections of felloes had caved in and snapped the spokes attached to them. On the side of the wagon was painted in large scarlet letters, DR. DELACROIX'S INDIAN MEDICINE SHOW, and below that a placid scene of an Indian village. Off to the right was an advertisement for a bottle of something called Sagwa, which was billed as a "blood, liver, spleen, and kidney renovator." Hitched to the front of the wagon was a pathetic-looking Missouri fox trotter, far too slight an animal to pull such a large vehicle by itself. The poor creature appeared thoroughly used up and about to drop in its traces. Behind the wagon, they came upon a small misshapen man, dangling by his short arms from a long wooden tree limb he'd jammed under the rear axle. He'd used a wooden barrel as a fulcrum and was trying to raise the wagon, but it was still too heavy and he was too small to get the thing to budge. In fact, when they came upon him he was still suspended in midair, several inches above the ground.

"Good day, gentlemen," the little man offered in a squeaky voice as he dropped down from the pole. He brushed his hands on his woolen trousers and smiled up at them. He was extremely small, not a hair over four feet, and dark-skinned as a Mohammedan. He had a neatly trimmed Van Dyke beard, a too-large mouth of exceedingly white teeth, and a face as big and round as a pie. He was dressed in a burgundy frock coat whose tails nearly touched the ground and a broad riverboat gambler's hat. His short legs were bowed like those of a chimpanzee, and he walked in a kind of back-and-forth shuffle. The other thing about him was that he had a crooked back that made him cant to the right, just like the wagon, and over his left shoulder rose a hump like that of a dromedary. All in all, he was an odd cut of a man.

Cain wondered what the little fellow had been fixing to do, even if he had been able to get the caravan off the ground. He didn't appear to know the first thing about changing a wagon wheel, hadn't unhitched his nag of a horse, hadn't so much as trigged a wheel to keep the caravan from rolling forward on him. Off in the woods a short ways, a campfire burned, and suspended over it was a pot with something simmering. Whatever it was, it smelled savory.

"It is my great good fortune to have met with fellow southerners," the man said in a deep southern accent that Cain felt was more than a little contrived. He spoke formally, as one would who tried to give the impression of learning and erudition. "I have had nothing but bad luck ever since I crossed north of the Mason-Dixon."

"Us, too," lamented Strofe.

"As you can see, my wheel has been utterly exfluncticated, leaving me in something of a pickle."

"Need some help?" Little Strofe asked.

"Indeed, if you would be so kind," he replied. "It seems I have neither the heft nor the length needed to move this burden of mine." He smiled broadly, parading his white teeth.

They dismounted and began to help him. As the other men worked, the small man stood looking on, offering no shortage of advice on the best way to change a wagon wheel—how they had to lift the load higher by moving the fulcrum closer to the axle or how they ought to be careful, as he was carrying valuable medical supplies. Still, in an hour's time they had the new wheel and hub on, and the caravan righted and ready to go. When they'd finished, the crookback man thanked them profusely for their help.

"Dr. Chimbarazo," he said to them, bowing at the waist.

"Who's Delacroix then?" Preacher asked.

"The late founder of the company," the small man explained. "A man of singular genius and vision. He taught me everything I know."

"Was he as sawed off as you?" Preacher joked.

Though not quite a dwarf he was but a few inches shy of it, mostly owing to his high-heeled boots and to the inordinate length of his forehead. His features were as coarse as those of a bulldog, and his dark eyes were drowsy, as if he had just woken from sleep, and of a striking russet color mixed with golden spots like the side of a brown trout.

"You a nigger?" Preacher asked.

"Hardly," the little man replied, indignant. "I will have you know that I am the proud inheritor of Castilian and Roman blood. My mother's side is one hundred percent pure Eye-talian. Can trace its lineage to the Borgias, renowned poisoners and popes," the man said with a little laugh. "And my father is a direct descendant of Rodrigo Díaz de Viver, better known to the world as the Cid," Dr. Chimbarazo bragged.

Cain could see that the little fellow was your typical traveling charlatan, a garrulous blatherskite, as noisy as a magpie and just as bothersome.

"Well, you sho'nuff look like a nigger," Preacher insisted.

"I assure you that my blood is as pure white as your own, sir," the man replied. Turning to Cain he asked, "How may I repay your largesse?"

"No need," said Cain.

"Wait," the small man said, holding up a stumpy finger. With surprising nimbleness, the crookback scrambled up the steps leading into the caravan's back door. In a moment, he reappeared with a slender bottle containing a golden brown liquid.

"Have y'all ever tried Indian Sagwa?" he asked. When they said they had not, he launched into a lengthy discourse on the salutary effects of the tonic he held in his hand. "It comes from natural spring waters taken from a cave in the great north woods, and has in it secret Indian herbal remedies passed down from time immemorial. Think about it, gentlemen. Why is it that the lowly savage who leads such a brutish existence is able to live illness free. One word—Sagwa. It works for every ailment known to man. Whether a consequence of bad blood, a diet deficient in meat, or impure living, any illness will fade away with a daily dose of what I hold here in my hand. It is especially efficacious," the small man rambled on, "for sufferers of scrofula, eczema, sores of any kind, skin eruptions, impetigo, venereal disease, gout, rheumatism, malaria, dyspepsia, piles, consumption, ear infections, disturbances of the pancreas, night sweats, insomnia, depression, as well as all diseases originating in the liver or spleen. Its efficacy is particularly noted for hard stools, and is guaranteed to keep the bowels in regular working order."

"That there work for the flux?" asked Strofe.

"Stopper you up like a cork in a bottle," the man replied. "It is the perfect remedy for overstimulation of the intestines. Just one teaspoon will have you functioning normally in twenty-four hours. Why, sir, your bowels will be restored to those of a child."

"How much do it cost?"

"It retails for two dollars a bottle. But, as you have done me a good turn, I will let you have it for a mere one. Plus, I will throw in, at no extra cost, a bottle of Dr. Delacroix's patented Indian Prairie plant oil, which aids in digestion."

Strofe removed his coin purse and took out a dollar. As the man reached up to receive the money, Cain took notice of the small six-shot pepperbox the crookback carried in a shoulder holster underneath his frock coat.

"And, of course, all Dr. Delacroix's products have a money-back guarantee," the small man said. "If y'all are not satisfied, just return what you don't use to the address on the bottle for a full refund."

"Do you have any ointment for cuts?" Cain asked, thinking of Henry's wrists.

"Why, of course." Again, the small man disappeared up into the wagon and came out with a small jar in his hand. "Indian Miracle Salve. This works wonders on all cuts or abrasions or eruptions of the epidermis, and is equally good for the megrims. Just apply to the temples and your headache will disappear in moments."

As Cain paid the man, he caught how he stared up at Rosetta standing off a ways.

"Is the lovely Ethiope your property?" the man asked.

"No," replied Cain.

"Heavens," Dr. Chimbarazo said. "Such pulchritude I have never laid eyes on in the Negroid race." Turning back to Cain, he added, "To repay your kind generosity, please stay and partake of my humble repast."

Since there was only an hour or so of daylight left, Cain consented.

The man had cooked up a heaping stew with bits of squirrel and rabbit and some sort of meat that Cain couldn't put a name to. Whatever it was, the stew was good and filling, and it left their mouths buzzing with its piquancy.

"That's a right fine stew," Little Strofe said, complimenting the man.

"An old Spanish recipe of my mother's," the man said. "Handed down through generations. In the battle of the Armada against the English, they ate of the very same meal aboard ship."

"Thought you said it was your pappy's side come from Spain?" Strofe said.

"I'm afraid you're mistaken, sir. My dear mother, rest her soul, is a direct descendant of Rodrigo Díaz de Viver. Who was to become famous as the Cid for driving the infidels from Valencia."

Strofe, who'd drunk some of the Indian Sagwa, leaned to one side and let out with a loud exhalation of gas. "'Least I don't have the runs no more."

"I told you it would cure your intestinal problems."

Later that night, the crookback got out a deck of cards and began to play solitaire.

"You up for a friendly game of poker?" Preacher asked.

"I've been known to wager a copper now and then," the little man said, smiling.

"But I ain't usin' your deck," said Preacher, taking out his own. "And I don't play unless one-eyed jacks is wild."

Strofe and his brother agreed to play as well. Dr. Chimbarazo proved to be a skillful player of the game of poker, one who, Cain could tell, was used to parting hayseeds and hawbucks and untutored farm boys from their money. Cain did take note, however, that when the crookback grew unsettled about a situation, he would suck on his lower lip like a babe. Still, by the end of the evening the crookback had skunked them; he'd won a large pile of gold and silver coins.

"Hell, I'm out," Strofe said.

"Me, too," added Preacher, eyeing Dr. Chimbarazo. Later, Cain would hear him grumbling about that "cheating little nigger," but other than that, he didn't do anything.

"How about you, sir?" the man said to Cain.

Cain had been sitting there going it strong with the laudanum and was feeling no pain. He knew better than to get into a game of cards with such a fellow as the crookback without a clear head.

"Thank you. No," Cain said.

Every once in a while the crookback would glance over at Rosetta, who sat manacled to a tree near Henry. He'd lick his lips greedily, the way a man dying of thirst would on seeing a glass of water just out of reach.

In the morning as they saddled up, Dr. Chimbarazo took Cain aside. "May I have a word with you, sir?" he said.

Cain and the crookback walked over to the far side of the caravan. The man reached into his coat pocket and offered Cain a cigar, which he declined. He smiled up at him and stroked his goatee pensively. Only then did Cain realize that the white teeth were fashioned from ivory.

"My last assistant deserted me some time ago. Ran off with a cooper who came to one of our shows. Belinda May was the creature's name. She was in all respects quite unsuited to the demands of being my assistant. Dumb as a rock. However, she was a sweet young thing who drew customers like moths to a flame. Besides which, Belinda May made up for her lack of native intelligence by being skilled in ways especially useful to a bachelor on the road for long periods of time."

He offered Cain a conspiratorial smile at this.

"What does all this have to do with me?" Cain asked brusquely.

"Of course, more matter and less art," the man said. "Well, since she left I have been quite busy bringing relief to the suffering and hope to the hopeless, and have not had the opportunity to enlist the services of another assistant. I wonder if I might purchase your enchanting Negress there," he said with a nod toward Rosetta.

"She's not mine to sell."

"I assure you I would be willing to pay her owner more than a fair price for such a fine specimen."

"I said, she's not for sale."

"Very well, then," the crookback said, nodding pensively. "Perhaps, sir, we might still work something out that would be to the advantage of both of us."

"What are you talking about?"

"As you can imagine, it gets rather lonely traversing the countryside, and I have had only myself to relieve my masculine needs, which are, despite my stature, quite formidable," he said. "I have not had the pleasure of a female's company in nearly two months' time. To put the matter bluntly, sir, I am in desperate need to fornicate."

Cain looked at the man and frowned.

"I would like to rent the services of the wench."

"Rent her?"

"I would, of course, be willing to pay you handsomely," he said as he removed his billfold. "You could pocket the proceeds, and no one would be the wiser. We would both be well pleased with the arrangement. Shall we say ten dollars for an hour's service?"

Cain turned and started to walk away, but the man hobbled after him and grabbed his coat sleeve.

"Fair enough," Dr. Chimbarazo said. "Let us say twenty-five then."

Cain turned on the little man savagely. "What do you take me for?"

"Come, come, my good fellow," the crookback offered with a laugh. "You are, after all, a slave catcher."

"I'm not some damn pimp," Cain said, yanking his sleeve away from the man's grasp and once again starting to walk away. However, the little man was, if nothing else, persistent. He hurried after Cain, caught him just as he was about to round the caravan.

"I can see that I've offended you. My sincerest apologies. It's just that I've never found myself so smitten by the fairer sex. I'll go you fifty dollars, sir. Besides, she will get as good as she gives, I assure you. Any woman who lies with Dr. Chimbarazo is not left unsatisfied. That comes with a money-back guarantee, as well."

The man thought this last comment funny and chuckled, his mouth all gleaming white teeth.

Cain suddenly lost his temper. He grabbed the small man by the throat, hoisted him into the air, and slammed him hard against the caravan. The crookback tried to wriggle out of his grasp but Cain held him firmly pinned there. The small man reached for his pepperbox, but Cain easily twisted it out of his hand and swatted him across the face with it. His broad gambler's hat was knocked to the ground. Cain squeezed the man's scrawny neck until his eyes bulged and his lids fluttered rapidly, and he appeared on the verge of passing out. Relenting finally, Cain relaxed his grip a bit so the man could breathe.

"Give me one good reason why I shouldn't thrash you all hollow," he said.

"Please, don't," Dr. Chimbarazo pleaded in a raspy voice. "I have a sick old mother depending on me at home."

"I thought you said she was dead?" Cain replied.

"She's near on to death," the man pleaded. "Could pass at any moment." He went on to explain that if anything were to happen to him it would certainly be the end of her. Though he knew it to be a cock-and-bull story, Cain nonetheless let the man drop to the ground. He fell to his knees, hacking and coughing, fighting for breath. Cain bent and picked up his hat and shoved it onto his large head. Grasping him by the collar, he escorted the man roughly to the front of the caravan and said, "Get your ass going before I change my mind." The crookback hurriedly climbed up into the seat of the caravan. He took hold of the reins but turned toward Cain and asked, "May I have my gun back, sir?"

"Consider yourself lucky to leave with your life. Gitup!" Cain said as he slapped the horse's rump.

The caravan started off down the road in the opposite direction. Cain looked at the ugly-looking pepperbox in his hand, its six stubby barrels like a nightmare of Vulcan's. He was going to heave it into the woods. He'd never liked that sort of gun. For a small thing it was unwieldy, and with all those barrels it misfired as often as not. And you couldn't hit a bull in the ass if you were holding on to its tail. Still, he thought better of it and decided to shove it into his boot.

13

When they crossed the Mason-Dixon line into Maryland, Preacher took off his derby and waved it about. "Hell's bells," he cried. "We's back home, boys." Then he stood in his stirrups, pulled down his trousers, and, aiming his fish-belly-white rear end toward the north, farted loudly. This proved a bad omen.

Shortly after this, Preacher's horse threw a shoe and he had to double up with Strofe until they could find a livery. After that, Strofe was hit with a new wave of stomach cramps that made him groan in pain. Then they passed a farm whose house and barn had recently burned to the ground, leaving its dozen sooty-faced inhabitants to camp under a chestnut tree, in the branches of which a hoot owl sat plain as day, going *whooo . . . whooo*. Little Strofe said everyone knew that sighting a hooty owl in broad daylight was a sure sign of bad luck. He took some salt from his saddlebags and tossed it over his left shoulder, but it wasn't enough to prevent the omen from working itself out. What had been a clear, pleasant day soon clouded over. The skies mushroomed with a greasy blackness tinged with gold and green, and there hung in the air the hard smell of axle grease and burnt hair, and before anyone could say "Catch a weasel asleep," it began to rain. Heavy drops exploded when they struck stone or earth, stinging when they met with flesh.

The April rain continued unabated for several days, a cold, leaden downpour of apocalyptic proportions. It flooded rivers and creek beds, hollers and low-lying fields, washing away the newly planted crops. The swollen rivers flowed over their banks and scooped up all manner of things: trees and fence posts, chicken coops and corncribs, and even the occasional cabin, and sent everything careening downriver in a churning brown stew. They saw the dead and bloated bodies of horses and pigs and cattle being swept along. In one flooded river just east of Hagerstown, they saw floating along a small log cabin, on the roof of which lay a red-haired woman buck naked. She looked like some damsel out of a fairy tale, waiting for the kiss of a lover.

"Damn. Looky, there," cried Preacher. "If only I could swim."

She didn't move, not even when they called to her, and no one knew if she was dead or alive. On the same river they saw just the steeple of a church, with the bell still in it and clanging away, as if calling people to service. The rain turned the hilly back roads of the Maryland panhandle into treacherous quagmires where the horses lost their footing, slipping and sliding as they plodded along. Once, as they were descending a steep hill into a valley of small farms, Strofe's Percheron, a clumsy animal under the best of conditions, tripped and fell headlong down the incline, pitching Strofe into the muck. Even with their oilskins on, the damp leached into the bones of the six riders, and neither fire nor whiskey nor exertion could drive it out. Cain feared he would never be warm again.

"Ain't felt my feets since Harrisburg," lamented Henry, who sat shivering on the back of Little Strofe's mule.

"Hit's the end of the world," Little Strofe said.

"You speak da trufe. Ain't never seed such a low-down, mean-spirited rain."

"Wouldn't s'prise me one b-bit to see old Noah hisself come sailing by in his ark."

The one good thing—Cain knew it would make Brown's following their trail nearly impossible.

The horses and the mule plodded dumbly along, no doubt wondering at their masters' lack of sense to be out in such conditions. Little Strofe's remaining dog, Louella, trotted along with her thin, lizard head hung wretchedly between its shoulder blades. It was hard to tell whether she was more affected by the loss of her companion or by the sheer inhospitality of the weather.

They were forced, finally, to seek shelter at an inn. The owner, of course, wouldn't take in Negroes, so he put all of them up in the barn out behind the inn. Built in the Dutch manner, the barn proved to be quite comfortable, tight and dry, with piles of hay to sleep on and the yeasty smell of grain mingling with the sweet pong of cow manure. All in all, it suited them just fine. Not only did they appreciate getting out of the cold rain, but they also savored the respite from the daily grind of travel, giving their backsides a much-needed rest from the pounding of the saddle twelve hours a day for all those weeks. They spent the next three days mending harnesses and repairing boots, sewing clothing, drying out and oiling saddles, reloading firearms, washing clothes, shaving, even trimming their hair and beards. With some lye soap, Rosetta washed in the horse trough and then set about braiding her hair. While oiling his gun, Cain watched her unawares. She happened to look up and catch him, and he pretended sudden interest in his revolver.

Henry, who'd worked in the tannery on Eberly's plantation, knew his way around shoes and boots, and with some nails and a hammer he scrounged up from the barn, he set to work repairing the footwear of those who'd worn holes in their boots. They all enjoyed the break, all, that is, save Preacher, who grumbled about wanting to get back to Richmond, since he was, as he put it, "randy as a old tomcat." He couldn't wait to spend his share of the reward money getting good and corned, and seeing a certain whore by the name of Sweet Nance. Little Strofe, still troubled by the disappearance of his dog, occupied himself by playing his Jew's harp. He would sit there alternately playing and then petting his one remaining dog and staring glumly out into the rain, wondering what had happened to Skunk. The ointment Cain had put on Henry's wrists had seemed to work; the wounds from the shackles were almost healed. Strofe had less success with his purchase. Dr. Delacroix's Sagwa tonic didn't help him a whit, and, if anything, seemed to aggravate his intestinal troubles. The flux had him running to the outhouse out in back of the barn every ten minutes.

"I shoulda knowed he was just a charlatan," Strofe complained as he held his guts and canted to one side to issue a loud fart. "Aaaah! God-dang it all!"

"Oughta send the bottle back to that lil sawed-off feller," Preacher offered. "Git your money back."

"You really think somebody's gone be waitin' on the other end?"

"Maybe you ain't took enough of it yet," said Preacher, who sat there rubbing the blade of his knife over a whetstone.

"Looky," he said, holding up the empty bottle. "I plumb drank the whole thing." He heaved the empty bottle out into the rain, where it hit a rock and shattered. "My guts is on fire."

"Could be you got yourself worms," Preacher offered.

"How the hell would you know? You ain't no doctor."

"My brother had worms real bad. Liked to died from it."

"Just shut up."

"Ever' time he shat you could see them wiggling around in his dung."

With that, Strofe got up and hurried out into the rain, making for the outhouse.

Preacher stayed away from Rosetta, avoided her completely, which was easy to do, as he wasn't responsible for her in any way. He treated her as if nothing had happened between them. But even though he didn't speak a word to Cain, now and again he'd shoot him that malevolent, gat-toothed grin of his. Those deep-set, black eyes would narrow and just a hint of that snakelike smile would harden his mouth, as if to tell Cain he hadn't forgotten his threat.

Cain's leg ached with the dampness. He'd run out of laudanum and there was nothing to do but wait until they got to a town where he could buy more. He felt, as he always did when he ran out, irritable and out of sorts, his skin itching, his hands seeming to jump around of their own accord. He tried to occupy himself with Milton, reading by lantern light. He was to the part where Satan took the form of the serpent to trick man into betraying God. While he preferred the earlier sections better, where Satan appeared noble and majestic in his rebellion, he nonetheless appreciated Milton's insight into the twisted mind of the fallen angel. It was a far shrewder understanding of psychology than that offered by any alienist or phrenologist.

> *foul distrust, and breach*
> *Disloyal on the part of Man, revolt*
> *And disobedience: On the part of Heav'n*
> *Now alienated, distance and distaste,*
> *Anger and just rebuke, and judgement giv'n,*
> *That brought into this World a world of woe.*

As he chanced to look over at Preacher so intent on sharpening his knife, for a moment he was struck by the possibility that *he* was the serpent in their midst, the one waiting to lead them to ruin. But then he told himself that was just a fanciful notion of a soul with too much time on his hands. They were all fallen creatures already, himself no less than the others, and they hardly needed someone like Preacher to lead them astray.

Now and then he'd glance over at Rosetta, who sat on a pile of hay, sewing. At night the two Negroes were chained to the cattle stanchions, but during the day they were allowed to move freely about the barn. The past two days he noticed how she'd been sick, vomiting when she woke up. When he inquired about it, she told him it was just morning sickness. She had asked him for a needle and thread, and she occupied herself with mending her clothes, which were now dirty and threadbare. She was a skilled seamstress, her fingers moving quickly and assuredly as they worked the needle through the thick homespun material. He found himself staring at her belly, thinking of Eberly's child growing there. Would he sell this one off as well, to punish her for running away again? What sort of man did that? Got a woman pregnant, then sold off his own child, his own flesh and blood. But perhaps this time he wouldn't. Perhaps the child was the valuable thing he wanted back, more so even than his concubine. Occasionally she'd look up and their eyes would meet for an awkward moment. There was no longer in her gaze that sharp, accusatory look with which she used to view him before. Now he considered it simply a look of wistful longing. He thought, too, about what she'd said to him a few days before. How he wasn't like the others, how she'd been wrong about him. He wondered if that was true.

The inn owned several Holsteins that stood dumbly eating silage from the feed trough, their enormous heads locked in stanchions. A young German milkmaid who worked at the inn would come out morning and evening to feed and milk the cows and to muck out the barn. She also carried out heaping platters of eggs and grits, sausage and fried bread for them to eat, as well as pitchers of fresh buttermilk to drink. It was a welcome change from the cornmeal and dried fish and salt pork they'd been used to for the past several weeks. The German girl wore a white bonnet tied primly under her plump chin and a long filthy apron that came well down below her sturdy knees. She was a solid thing, with fleshy arms that could easily carry two full buckets of milk balanced on a yoke over her broad shoulders. Her wide face was as rosy pink as the cow's teats she pulled on. She would smile modestly at the men but would speak only a few words of broken English when she came into the barn.

"What's your name, darlin'?" Preacher asked her.

"Katarina," she replied shyly, with a heavy accent.

"Whyn't you come over here and set a spell on my lap."

"*Ich muss arbeiten.* Vork," she said, and went about milking the cows.

"I got me something you could work on," Preacher joked.

She came in from the rain once with two heavy platters of food that were almost slipping out of her hands.

"Let me help you with that," Little Strofe said, grabbing one of the platters from her and bringing it over to a workbench near the tack room.

"*Danke,*" she said.

"You're all wet."

Her shawl and bonnet were soaked from the rain. When she took off her cap her long blond hair unraveled and fell to her shoulders. She looked pretty and younger even with her head uncovered. Sixteen, seventeen. Little Strofe hurried off to get a rag from his saddlebags and gave it to her so she could dry off.

"Where y'all from?"

"*Deutschland,*" she replied, dabbing her face and head with the rag.

"Where in tarnation is that?"

She tried to explain with hand gestures where she'd come from. As best they could, Little Strofe and she talked as she milked the cows. Later he helped her bring the full buckets into the inn. After that, every time she came out, he would go over and sit by her and keep her company as she did her work. She seemed to like his presence, would smile and blush when she saw him. Sometimes the others could hear them giggling like a pair of schoolchildren. Little Strofe seemed quite taken by the young girl.

"Looks like your brother got hisself a sweetheart," Preacher said to Strofe.

The last evening they were there, Little Strofe approached Cain and said, "C-could I ask you something, Mr. Cain?"

"Of course, Mr. Strofe."

"You think I might could borrow your razor?"

"Certainly." Cain went over to his saddlebags and took out his razor and a bar of soap. The small, stocky man headed out back to the watering trough and washed and shaved himself and put on some clean clothes. When he returned, Cain hardly recognized him. Clean-shaven, his face smooth and pale, shadowed a dark blue where his beard had been.

"Why, you look like a new man, Mr. Strofe."

He smiled good-naturedly.

That night after the German girl was finished working, she and Little Strofe met out in the root cellar behind the barn.

"Think your brother's diddlin' her?" Preacher asked Strofe. He was staring out a window toward the root cellar.

"Ain't none of my business. Yours neither."

"If'n he's gettin' his wick wet, I say good for him. That's what that boy needed."

"You leave him be," ordered Strofe, who was now beginning to take a more brotherly attitude toward Little Strofe.

Later that night, his brother came running back through the rain into the barn.

"So, you get you any pussy?" Preacher asked, chuckling.

"Shut your d-damn gob," Little Strofe cursed, turning on Preacher.

"Who you tellin' to shut up?"

"I w-won't have you t-talkin' like that about K-katarina," he stuttered nervously, shaking a fist in Preacher's face.

"You'd bes' watch who you're threatenin', boy. Hell's bells, I'm just funnin' with you. Don't get yourself all in a lather."

After he'd made his point, Little Strofe went over and lay down beside his dog. He petted Louella and spoke to her softly. Soon he was snoring.

Cain closed his book and put his glasses in his vest pocket. He got up stiffly and hobbled over to where Rosetta sat sewing on a pile of hay. He held the key up and said, "It's time." She finished the stitch she was sewing and got up and went over to where the stanchions were and sat down in front of the cows. One of the Holsteins leaned down and smelled her hair, and Rosetta absently swatted its nose. After Cain had locked her wrists in the shackles, he called over to Henry, who was at the workbench hammering nails into the heel of one of his brogans.

"Let's go, Henry."

"Almost done here, massa."

"Well, hurry up." Cain looked down at Rosetta. She had her shawl wrapped around her shoulders, and she looked pale and tired, as if the trip had worn her down, drained something out of her. "You all right?" he asked.

She nodded.

"There are more blankets in the tack room. I could get you one if you wanted."

"I'm fine."

He squatted down in front of her. In an undertone so the others couldn't hear him, he said, "What I told you the other day. About why I didn't get married."

"You said you had to go to war."

"Well, yes. That wasn't all true."

"You didn't fight?"

"No, I fought, all right," he explained. "It's that I didn't *have* to fight. That was just an excuse. I went off to war so I wouldn't have to marry her. I got cold feet and ran off one night. Never came back."

"You ain't seen your family in all these years?"

"No. My father disowned me. And my brother went ahead and married the woman I was supposed to," he said with a laugh.

"That makes you a runaway, too, Cain."

"I suppose it does."

"Only thing, nobody huntin' you down and bringin' you back," she said, shaking her chains for emphasis.

"They wouldn't want me back."

"That woman. You didn't love her?"

"No. Not the way a man ought if he's going to marry her. I suppose I could have done worse. Her father was very wealthy. My old man always expected I would marry her, and I no doubt disappointed him mightily. Maybe it was a mistake."

"But you couldn't marry her," she said.

"No. I would have grown to hate her. And she to hate me."

He thought about what the old woman, Hettie, had talked about, the night before she killed herself. The nature of love. About being so in love you thought your heart would burst. He had never felt anything close to that for Alexandra.

"So you did the right thing," Rosetta said.

"For the wrong reasons."

"What you mean?"

He didn't know why he was telling her any of this. She was just a runaway slave. Another man's property. He realized that he'd never talked about this before with another soul.

"I ran off like a coward. I couldn't face her. Couldn't face my father."

"Goin' to war ain't what a coward does," she said.

"In my case it was."

Rosetta turned her head and looked up at him at an angle. Her mouth, he noticed, was no longer held taut but allowed to assume its natural fullness; suddenly, he had an odd yearning: he wanted to trace his fingertips over her lips, to feel their softness. When he looked back up at her, it was as if she could read his thoughts.

"Sometime," she told him, "doin' the right things for the wrong reasons is all we can do. We just got to trust that's what God had in mind for us."

"I'm not sure he had anything in mind for me."

"Oh, he got something in mind for ever'body," she said. "Even a low-down soul catcher like you, Cain."

He nodded, though he wasn't sure he subscribed to the notion that God had any sort of plan for him.

"Henry," he called, "get your ass over here. Now."

The Negro came shuffling over carrying his shoes in his hands and sat down near Rosetta.

"You want to put your shoes on before I put the shackles on you?" Cain asked.

"No, they's some nails I still gots to tamp down," Henry replied. "Can I have more of that balm, massa? It work real good on my cuts. See," Henry said, showing his wrists.

From his saddlebags, Cain got the jar of Indian Miracle Salve and handed it to Henry. When he was finished slathering it on, he said to Cain, "My ankles startin' to hurt now. You can put them shackles back on my wrists. They's all healed."

Before leaving, Cain looked at Rosetta.

"You 'member what I told you about God," she said to him.

Mr. Cain," a voice burrowed augerlike into his sleeping skull. "Mr. Cain, wake up."

Groggy, Cain opened his eyes to see Little Strofe's homely face hovering over him. "What?"

"He done took off."

"Who?"

"Henry. He's gone."

Soon they were all awake. They found the shackles still attached to the stanchion and still locked, but now they held no black wrists. Cain saw hunks of grease and a light residue of blood smeared on the metal of the shackles. So that's why Henry had been so intent on fixing his shoes, he thought. He was planning on taking a trip. And why he hadn't put them back on, either. He didn't want to make any noise when he crept out in the night. Cain looked out the open barn door to see that the rain had finally stopped, and that sun had broken partially through and was spilling weakly onto the muddy earth, pale as goat milk.

"Damn nigger used that grease you give him to slide his wrists out," Strofe said to Cain. "I warned you not to coddle 'im that way."

"I wasn't coddling him," he said. Still, he thought, he should have seen it coming.

Rosetta sat there, still shackled to the stanchion.

"He say anything to you about this?" Cain asked her.

She shook her head.

"Nothing at all?"

"If he'd had, you think I'd still be here?" she snapped at him.

"What do we do now?" wondered Little Strofe.

"What the hell do you think we do?" his brother replied. "We go after him. He can't a gone that far."

"What about her?" Preacher said, pointing at Rosetta.

Strofe glanced at Cain. "We'll just have to take her along," he offered.

Cain hesitated, then said, "You think that's a good idea?"

"Why not?"

"What if we run into Brown and his boys? Or some other abolitionists that Henry might lead us to. Then what? If something were to happen to her, I doubt your boss would be very happy."

The big man stood there, scratching his beard. "So what do you got in mind?"

"I say one of us starts back with the girl. After Henry is captured, the others can meet up with him south of here."

"And I reckon that somebody would be him," complained Preacher. He didn't say this to Cain but directed his comments to Strofe, who turned and looked expectantly at Cain as if for an answer.

"I'm the one responsible for her," Cain said.

"Now just wait a doggone minute," Preacher said. "Why does *he* get to take her back while the rest a us got to go traipsing after the other nigger?"

"Just take it easy," Strofe said, trying to calm him.

"Whyn't we draw cuts to see who stays with her?" Preacher offered. "Or better yet, whyn't Cain go after Henry and the three of us take the girl back?"

"You're not coming within ten feet of her," Cain warned him.

"That a fact?"

"It is."

"Now both of you, hold your horses," Strofe commanded.

"We're supposed to trust him with her?" Preacher challenged. "Hell, you seen the way he looks at her? We all of us have. And how the two a them are always talkin' and whisperin' and such."

"Just shut up," exclaimed Strofe. Then to Cain, he said, "Mr. Eberly don't want nobody laying a hand on her."

"What is that supposed to mean?"

"He just don't, is all."

"I'm not the one tried to rape her," he said, looking over at Preacher.

Strofe thought for a moment. "All right. Where we gonna meet up?"

Cain told him Fredericksburg, which was about halfway and on the same road to Richmond. There was an inn he'd stayed at several times when he'd gone north hunting runaways. Down near the Rappahannock. The Rising Sun Tavern.

"We'll meet there," he told them. "I'll wait for you. If, by some chance, you get there before me, you wait for me."

"All right, brother," Strofe said. "Fetch your dog."

"One minute," Little Strofe said. He ran out of the barn, heading for the inn. When he came back in a few minutes, the German girl was with him. They hugged once in the courtyard, then he turned and headed into the barn. He unleashed the dog and had her smell the shackles, fixing Henry's scent good.

"Awright, girl," he said. "Steboy."

The tawny-colored hound took off out of the barn baying wildly. Cain watched the other three men mount up and ride off, following the dog's lead. Little Strofe turned several times and waved to his girlfriend and she waved back. Preacher hadn't gone fifty yards before he halted, turned his horse around, and came galloping back, almost as if he'd forgotten something. He rode right into the barn, right up to Cain.

"You," he said, his small black eyes glowering, the red birthmark on the side of his face seeming almost to smolder, "don't think I ain't wise to you."

"Oh, yeah?"

"Tha's right. You may a fooled them with your big talk and fancy ways. But I seen through you from the first." He glanced past Cain toward Rosetta. "And just remember, when this is over me and you's got a score to settle."

With that, Preacher wheeled his blue roan about and bolted, the horse's hooves kicking up packets of mud in its wake.

PART THREE

Wo, if it come with storm, and blood, and fire;
when midnight darkness veils the earth and sky!
Wo to the innocent babe—the guilty sire—Mother
and daughter—friends of kindred tie! Stranger and
citizen alike shall die!

WILLIAM LLOYD GARRISON, *THE LIBERATOR*

14

Cain rode south with Rosetta seated behind him, crossing the Potomac at Harpers Ferry. Swollen with rain, the Potomac and Shenandoah rivers surged down through the narrow mountain gaps, converging below The Point and flooding low-lying buildings. Having been gone for nearly two months, as Cain passed over the B&O viaduct into Virginia, he felt something tight and hard rise up in his chest. He told himself it was merely a physical ailment, dyspepsia perhaps, or the effects of having run out of laudanum. But he wondered if it could be a touch of homesickness. He'd never felt this before and he thought it bespoke a change of heart. Perhaps the South meant more to him than he had ever imagined. As they rode down Potomac Street, he spotted a druggist's shop and pulled up in front of it. He helped Rosetta down, then dismounted and tied the reins to a hitching post. From the saddlebags he got out the shackles.

"I ain't going nowheres," she said.

"You just tried to run on me."

"You think I'd try in broad daylight?"

His answer was to put shackles on her wrists and attach her to the hitching post. "I'll be right back."

When he came out of the druggist's, he walked a few doors down and went into a bakery and bought two meat pies as well as a mason jar of fresh milk. Then he unlocked Rosetta and led Hermes over to a grassy area beside a church where they sat on the ground in the shade. It was midmorning, sunny and warmish, and the sky shone a perfect blue above the rocky heights that surrounded the town.

"How are you feeling?" he asked her.

She shrugged.

"Here," he said, handing her one of the pies.

"I ain't hungry," she replied. "My stomach's all jouncy."

"Take some of this then." He offered her the bottle of laudanum he'd just purchased. "It'll settle your stomach."

"That stuff ain't good for the baby," she said.

"Not eating ain't good for the baby, either. At least drink some milk. Babies need milk to grow."

She looked over at him and snorted.

"What you know 'bout babies, Cain?"

In truth, he didn't know much about them.

"I know they need milk."

"What you so worried about me for?" she said, smiling to show her teeth, which were white and straight as piano keys. "'Fraid you won't get that re-ward if'n I get sick?"

"You got to think about your child."

Her smile vanished and her gaze turned solemn and distant. "You don't hafta tell me that. All I been thinkin' 'bout is this here chile."

She conceded finally and drank from the jar in a desultory fashion. She'd barely taken a sip before she was struck by sickness again. Leaning over, she vomited a white, frothy liquid onto the ground. She retched violently several times.

"Can I get you anything?" he asked.

She shook her head. "It'll pass by and by," she replied as another wave of nausea convulsed her. While she was retching, he noticed, for the first time really, how grubby and frayed her clothing was. Her dress ragged and stained, her stockings hanging down around her ankles. He went over to his saddlebags and got a rag. Then he walked over to a water trough and wet it.

"Here," he said, handing her the rag, "use this to clean yourself."

When she glanced up, she appeared pale, and her breathing was labored.

"Morning sickness don't last but a few weeks," she said. "Like it say in the Good Book, 'In sorrow you gonna bring forth children.'"

Soon her breathing leveled out and she took another drink of the milk, a small sip. She swallowed and waited to see how her stomach would react to it.

"Feel better?" he asked.

"Some." After a while, she gazed out over the town, toward the river and beyond to the high cliffs. Looking up, she shielded her eyes against the bright sun. "It's a right fine day."

"That it is," Cain agreed.

"What would you be doin' on a day like this?"

"What do you mean?"

"If'n you wasn't bringin' back a runaway. If you could do what'ere you wanted to."

Cain shrugged. What would he be doing? he wondered.

"When it was nice like this, my momma and me usta do the wash. Stoke up a big fire and boil the water in the kettle. Throw in the lye. Me and her would talk, about this and that, get to laughin' about something. She always said there wasn't nothin' smell better'n new-washed clothes. And she was right. I love the smell of clothes hanging out to dry." Rosetta glanced down at her own soiled garments. "You know what they'd get me to thinkin' of?"

"What?"

"Clouds."

"Clouds?"

"Uh-hm. When I was a little girl and I'd look up at the clouds, all white and fluffy, I thought they must smell so clean, so fresh. That nothin' in the whole wide world could be cleaner than them. So what about you, Cain? If you had all day and nothin' to do."

"I used to like to ride up high somewhere, and set there and read."

"All by your lonesome?"

"Yes."

"You strike me as somebody likes to be by hisself."

Cain thought of replying, but right then a thin, slump-shouldered man happened to step out of the church. He wore a black preacher's hat, and he carried a satchel like a doctor, and when he saw them sitting there on the church grass he walked over to them.

"Good day, sir," he said to Cain, smiling broadly to show a mouthful of long yellow teeth. "I'm Reverend Covington."

"Good day, Reverend," Cain replied.

"Are you new to town?"

"Just passing through."

"What seems to be the problem?"

"No problem. We're just resting here for a moment."

The man stared at Rosetta, nodding his narrow skull. "Indeed. The evils of drink are indeed pernicious. More so with your Nigro. Despite years of civilizing influence, that inherently wild African blood is unleashed by the corrupting influence of alcohol. I have seen it all too often. As it says in Leviticus—"

But Cain wasn't in the mood for a sermon. "She's not drunk," he corrected. "She's with child."

"I see," the man said, pursing his lips so that they looked like a pair of worms twisted around a fishing hook. He gave Cain a castigating look.

"No, you don't see," Cain snapped at him. He thought of explaining but decided it was pointless.

"There is a Nigro church just down by the river," the man offered.

"She's not fixing to go to church," Cain explained. "Just looking to set a spell."

"I'm afraid she's not allowed on church grounds."

"We'll be moving on directly, Reverend," Cain told him.

"She can't stay here."

Cain looked up at him. "I said, we'll be moving on just as soon as she's able."

"You need to move on now, sir. Or I shall have to notify the constabulary."

Cain stood and took a step toward the man, who fell back nervously when he saw the look in Cain's eyes and the size of the gun that he carried on his hip. "I told you she's sick. We'll be moving on just as soon as she's feeling better."

"It's all right," Rosetta said, wiping her mouth on his old shirt and getting shakily to her feet.

"You're supposed to be a man of God?" Cain said to the minister, clenching his fist.

"Leave it be, Cain," she offered. "It ain't worth it."

He gave the man a last scornful look before turning away. He mounted, then helped her up, and they rode on down the street.

"You sure got you a temper, Cain," Rosetta said to him.

"I don't abide fools and hypocrites."

"That temper gone get you in trouble one day."

When he saw a general store, he stopped. He got out the shackles and secured her to a hitching post. Then he went inside to buy some provisions. He purchased bacon and flour and cornmeal, some oats and sugar for Hermes. While he was paying the clerk, he spotted a dress hanging behind the counter. It was a blue calico garment with long sleeves, buttons down the front, and something frilly at the bodice that caught Cain's fancy. It made him recall the first time he'd seen Rosetta, standing outside of that shop window in Boston, staring in at the dress. The only Negro woman he had ever really known in any substantial way was Lila, and to save his life he could not have described a single article of clothing she'd ever worn. She had clothed herself as they all did, in what he'd thought of simply as "Negro garb," some sort of dull homespun material, sturdy and innocuous. Back then it would not even have entered his mind that a black woman cared a lick for what she put on her back.

"Can I see that?" he asked the man. The clerk got the dress down for him and Cain held it up in front of himself, trying to judge whether it would fit her. The only garment he had ever purchased for a woman was a scarf he'd bought for Eileen McDuffy. He told himself that Eberly wouldn't want her dressed in rags, like some lowly field hand. That she should be looking proper when they rode into Richmond. He figured, too, that Eberly would reimburse him.

"What size is your wife, sir?" the clerk asked.

"Oh, it's . . . I'm not sure," he replied.

"You could have her come in and try it on."

"I don't believe that will be necessary. This looks about right."

Rosetta was tall, broad shouldered, and the dress appeared made for a woman of some height, so he went ahead and bought it, along with a shift and a pair of wool stockings, and another shawl for the cool mountain evenings. The clerk wrapped it all in brown paper and Cain paid him and went outside.

"Here," he said to Rosetta, handing the package to her.

"What's this?"

"I figure you needed some new things to wear."

Impatiently, Hermes nudged Cain's arm, letting him know that he could smell the sugar in the sack. "Here you go, boy," he said, giving him a piece. Then they mounted up, and headed out of town.

They rode all day, stopping briefly in midafternoon to feed and water the horse. Spring was in full bloom. Up among the hills the dogwoods were flowering, a flashy display of pinks and whites and lavenders. The air smelled sweetly of wild grapes and honeysuckle, tulip poplar and mountain ash. The evenings had grown milder, descending on the earth like a soft, dark blanket. At night they could hear the dull whir of crickets, and the North Star, the one the runaways used to lead them to freedom, blazed in the sky behind them like the lone eye of some nocturnal creature. They made camp at a creek beside an abandoned gristmill. Cain lit a fire and began to cook their dinner, bacon and corn pone and coffee. He wasn't much in the way of cooking, but being on his own for so long he'd learned to make do. What he lacked in skill, he more than made up for in meals that filled the belly.

"Why don't you try on your new dress?" he said to Rosetta.

"I thought you were saving it for when we got back."

"Go ahead and try it on now."

She took the package and headed off into the woods to change. He told her not to wander too far off. She was gone for a good long while, and twice he'd called out to her to make sure she was still there.

"Ros—" he began to call again, but stopped when he saw her standing at the edge of the woods. She stood there in her bare feet, her toes digging into the earth, her head angled slightly downward, unsure and awkward as a girl going to her first dance. He was surprised by the transformation the dress had wrought in her. The rigidity with which she confronted the world—the stiffness of her shoulders and spine, the firmness of her mouth—had sloughed off and she looked young suddenly, and soft, a girl whose only thought was the precious feel of the new dress on her skin.

"I didn't know what size you took," he said, for want of something else.

"It fit just fine. It'll need letting out some through the belly shortly," she said, touching the material over her stomach. "Well?" she asked. "How's it look?"

"Turn around," he said.

With her arms outstretched, she pirouetted slowly, as if she were dancing to some music he couldn't hear. For a few seconds they both almost forgot why they were there, forgot that her skin was black, his white. It was as if they were just a man and a woman, and behaving in the quite normally awkward way of two people in such a moment as this. Cain felt something flutter inside of him, as if a butterfly had somehow gotten trapped in his chest. *Why, she looks lovely*, he thought.

Though all he said was, "It becomes you."

"I'll go take it off now."

"No, wear it," Cain said. "Throw those other rags away."

"Why?"

"Because it looks good on you."

She pursed her mouth cynically and stared hard at him. "You wantin' Mr. Eberly to see he got his money's worth when you bring me back?"

"No," he said peevishly, in part because he knew she was right. "I just thought you could use it."

"It wasn't on account you wanted to show me off to him?"

"Take the damn thing off if you want," he snapped at her. "Throw it away for all I care. I was just trying to do you a kindness."

She stared across at him. Finally, she said, "I shouldn'ta said that. Thank you."

He nodded grudgingly.

Later, after they'd eaten, they sat quietly near the fire. Rosetta worked on plaiting her hair while he sat there oiling his gun, though it didn't need for oiling. The silence between them solidified, grew dense as molasses. He wondered what had caused it, then realized what it was—the dress. Rosetta acted differently in it, moved differently, tentatively, not as innocently or naturally, as if it had made her feel different, self-conscious in a way she'd not been before. And somehow he felt different, too, around her. More so even than his having seen her naked or realizing she was pregnant, or the business with Preacher, they were now both aware of the other's physical presence in a way they had not been before. He wondered if the dress had been such a good idea.

"You think they'll catch Henry?" she asked after a while, more to break the silence than anything else.

"I reckon so," he replied, looking up from his gun. "You sure he didn't say anything to you about where he was going?"

"Not a word. I wouldn't a tole you anyhow. I ain't a blabbermouth like him."

"Eberly was of the opinion Henry and you ran off together."

"We run off at the same time, not together."

"Eberly was very concerned that Henry might have done something with you."

"Huh! You think I let that nigger touch me? But maybe I should of. That would rile him good. He wouldn't want nobody gettin' what was *his*."

Cain glanced across the fire at her. He watched her plaiting her hair, deftly weaving it with her fingers. He had always told himself his business was just to bring them back, safe and sound. To get paid and be on his way. What happened to them after that was not his concern. They could run away again for all he cared; in fact, that suited him just fine, for then he could go off and catch them again and make more money, which had happened more than a few times.

Despite telling himself not to, he asked, "What do you think Eberly'll do with you?"

She drew her lips taut but didn't say anything.

"You cost him a pretty penny," he said to her. "Not to mention the inconvenience and the worry."

"Worry?" she snorted.

"He was plenty worried, all right."

"That man just used to gettin' what he wants."

Again he asked, "What do you think he'll do with you?"

"Ain't no concern of yours. You'll get your money, don't you worry."

"I'm just asking is all."

She lifted her shoulders and let them drop mechanically. "He don't like to be disrespected."

"I saw that. Will he punish you?"

"He won't lay a hand on me. That ain't his manner. But he'll get even, one way or the other."

"What of the child?"

"I don't like to think about it."

"Maybe this time he wants it, too. He said you stole something of value of his."

"What I stole from him was me," she said. "It's *me* he wants back."

"But it's his child, as well."

He saw the muscle in her jaw knotting itself. As he watched, he saw tears squeeze out at the corners of her eyes and slide down her face. It was the first time he'd seen her cry, and he could tell it was something that cost her a great deal.

"All right if I go down and wash myself?" she asked.

Cain nodded. He finished oiling his gun and put it away in his holster. The night had gotten cooler and his leg began to act up. He took off his boots and lifted his pant leg and began to massage his calf. When Rosetta returned, she wrapped a blanket around her shoulders and sat opposite him.

"Where'd you get them scars, Cain?"

"The war."

"Lordy."

From his pocket, he removed the bottle of laudanum, pulled out the cork stopper with his teeth, and took a sip, feeling the numbing warmth fan sweetly out inside him.

"Don't you know that stuff ain't no good for you, Cain?"

"It takes the pain away."

"Sometimes pain's a good thing."

"It always struck me as something to be avoided."

"It makes you know you're livin'." He thought then of what the young Indian girl had done to his hand when he thought he was dead, squeezing the flesh so that he felt the pain of being alive.

"How'd you get started on that?" Rosetta asked.

"It's a long and not particularly interesting story."

"Ain't got nothin' better to do."

Cain looked across at her, her eyes watery and diffuse now from her having been crying. He took another swig, stoppered the bottle, and put it away in his pocket. He'd never told anyone about the war before. In part because he was embarrassed by his desertion, *both* of his desertions: his running off *to* the war and then his running *from* it. But then he thought, *What the hell*. In a couple of days, she would be back to her life and he would be heading out west and they'd never see each other again.

So he told her about the war, the battle of Buena Vista, how the Mexicans sent wave after wave of men to their deaths. He told her how easy it was to kill a man, just about the easiest thing he'd ever done. How finally he'd been hit by grapeshot and then waking up and listening as the wounded around him were executed by the enemy. How he thought he'd be next, and only by a stroke of luck had they stopped before they got to him. How he'd been able to crawl off behind a rock. How the Indian girl appeared out of nowhere and brought him to her hut up in the mountains and nursed him back to health. How he'd foolishly felt the call of duty and turned himself in and the months he'd spent in prison. How it was the doctor there who gave all the wounded laudanum. How he'd come to depend on it like a nursing calf does a teat. He told it all to her. All except for what he'd felt for the girl and what had become of her.

Rosetta, however, must have sensed that he'd held back something. When he was done talking, she looked across the fire at him and a vague smile played across her mouth.

"What?" he asked.

"The girl?" she said.

"What of her?"

"You didn't say what happened to her? Did you go back there?"

"Yes," he replied. "When I got out of prison. She was already dead by then."

"How?"

"They killed her. The Mexicans."

"Why?"

"For befriending the gringoes."

"And what did you do?"

"How do you know I did anything?"

"You ain't the sort of man let something like that go."

He nodded. "I found one of the men responsible for her death. A priest. It was him that got the townspeople riled up. I went into the church when he was praying and slit his throat."

"You killed a man of God?"

"He wasn't a man of God. Any more than that fellow today was. If there's a hell, he's got a front-row seat."

"Then what'd you do?"

"I left Mexico."

"You never went back home?"

"Couldn't. Not after what I did. And, like I told you, my father had disowned me."

"Tha's right. You suppose to marry that rich woman but you run away."

He nodded.

"You love that Indian girl?"

"No," he lied. "It was just something that happened."

"But you blamed yourself for her death, didn't you?"

"I suppose," he said, staring into the fire until he could almost see the girl's face in the flames staring back at him. "She wouldn't have died if I hadn't come into her life. Or if I had stayed."

"You don't know that for sure."

"Maybe I could've protected her."

"Some things you can't protect against."

"I could've tried. I could've at least died trying."

"Sometimes dying is the easy way out. Sometimes it harder to go on living."

He shrugged, unconvinced.

"Lookit me, Cain. I tried to protect my chile and no matter what I done, it wasn't no use. Sometimes things's just gonna happen, and they ain't nothin' you can do about it. And the only thing you can do is keep on livin'."

He wasn't sure if she meant her first child or this one she was carrying. Or whether she was talking about her trying to escape and his bringing her back. And then he decided it didn't really matter. He felt suddenly exhausted, as if all the weeks of journeying, all the nights sleeping on the damp ground, the long days in the saddle, the rain and snow and cold, the fights with Preacher and with her, being shot at and knifed and the near drowning—as if all of it had only, right at that moment, caught up with him. He felt old and dried up and worn down, felt like a man who had traversed a great desert, and when he'd reached what he thought was the other side discovered only more desert, that it went on endlessly. He was tired of all this, tired of hunting runaways, tired of dealing with men like Eberly. Tired of the whole bloody thing.

"I'm done talking," he said.

He got up and walked over to Hermes and got the shackles. A thought, however, occurred to him: what if he left them off, just let whatever was going to happen, happen. If she took off, she took off. And if she did, he could strike out for California now. Wouldn't even go back to Richmond. Just pack his things, take what little money he had, and go. He had his horse. He figured he could get by somehow or other. He always did. Win a few games of poker, hire himself out if he had to. Just leave. Of course, Eberly wasn't the sort of man who would take such a betrayal lying down. But the hell with him. Then again, he warned himself that that would be just plain foolish. She was worth five hundred dollars cash to him.

Five hundred! Plenty enough to see him out to California and then some.

When he returned, she watched him as he shackled her to a birch tree close by the fire. She didn't say anything. He spread two blankets over her.

"You warm enough?" he asked. "It's going to get cold tonight."

"I'm fine," she said, staring up at him.

Then he got his own bedroll and unfurled it on the other side of the fire. He crawled under the blanket, pulled his hat low over his face, and closed his eyes. But tired as he was, sleep, he sensed, would still take its sweet time. He thought about what she'd said, how sometimes living was harder than dying. The getting up and going on each day. Perhaps there was some truth to that. Somewhere in the night an owl hooted.

"Cain," Rosetta said after a while. "You sleepin'?"

"No."

"Me neither. What you gone do with all that money you get for bringin' me back?"

"I don't know. Maybe I'll head out west."

"What of catching slaves?"

"I think I am well shut of this profession," he said with a weary laugh.

"I don't think it's one that you were cut out for."

"No?"

"Uh-uh. You don't seem to have you a knack for it. If I could go anywhere I wanted, I think I'd like to try Paris, France."

"Why is that?"

"I saw me a picture of it once. All these women wearing high hats and long fancy dresses. And one of 'em was a Negro, dressed up just like white folks."

15

He woke in the morning to a strange silence. He didn't hear her breathing nor did he smell what had become her familiar musky scent. With his eyes closed he thought, *What if she had escaped, like Henry?* What would he do?

But before he had a chance to decide, she spoke up. "Want I should make us some coffee?"

He opened his eyes and sat up, his head feeling soft and runny, like an undercooked egg. The morning had broken some time before. The sun was already painting the treetops a pale color, like tallow.

He looked over at her. "How long have you been awake?" he asked.

"Hour. Maybe more."

"Why didn't you wake me?"

"I ain't in no hurry to get back to my cage," she said with a snort. "'Sides, you look like you could use the rest."

He unlocked the shackles, and she set about building a fire while he headed off into the woods to relieve himself. His thoughts from the previous night, he realized, were nothing more than those of an overtaxed mind. He had a job to do.

Rosetta poured him a cup of the strong, bitter-tasting coffee.

"You hungry, Cain?"

He nodded, and she set about making bacon and warm ashcakes.

When it was done, she handed him a plate of the fixin's. It was good, and he ate with some spirit this morning. She sat there with the shawl draped over her head and shoulders, drinking from a cup.

"Thought you were a house nigger," he said. "Where'd you learn to chop wood and make a fire like that?"

"When my momma be up to the massa's house, it was left to me to cook and get the fires going in the fireplaces."

"How are you feeling this morning?" he asked.

"Better. Who's TJ?"

"My brother. Why?"

"You said his name in your sleep. He the one married that woman you were s'posed to?"

"That's right."

"You hold that against him?"

"Why should I?"

"Some men be mad they own brother got what was intended for them."

"He saved me from that life. I should be ever grateful to him."

He glanced over at her. She looked up from eating and seemed about to say something, but then she looked away.

After breakfast, they packed up and headed out. Cain figured they had maybe three days' ride to Fredericksburg, and another day after that to Richmond. Four days. Four days and he'd be done with this.

A s they turned southeast toward the sea, they rode through country that became flat as a skillet. They passed fields where Negroes were working, plowing behind mules, setting tobacco, hoeing, chopping wood. They rode through small towns with people whose accents were familiar, people who barely gave a second look to a man bringing a Negro back to servitude. In the evening, they camped just outside a place called Bryon Creek. They put up in a stand of birches on the banks of a narrow tidal river that smelled of salt and mud and dead fish. Cain had shot a small doe with the Sharp's and Rosetta had cleaned and dressed it; now it was roasting on a hickory spit over the fire. The odor of seared meat smelled good, and Cain looked forward to a thick venison steak. Rosetta had scoured the woods and come up with a pile of greens that she boiled with salt.

After he'd eaten until he couldn't eat any more, Cain got his saddlebags and brought them over to where his bedroll lay. He withdrew his Milton and put on his glasses.

"What's that you always readin'?" Rosetta asked.

"A poem."

"What about?"

"God and Satan," Cain replied. "I'm at the part where Satan tempts Eve."

"Gets her to eat that apple, I reckon," Rosetta said.

"Yes."

"Wasn't for that apple, we wouldn't a had all these troubles. Pains and heartache and tribulations—all 'cause a that ole apple. Could you read me some?"

"If you'd like."

Cain opened the book and began to read where he'd left off:

"But he thus overjoy'd, O Fruit Divine,
Sweet of thy self, but much more sweet thus cropt,
Forbidd'n here, it seems, as onely fit
   For Gods, yet able to make Gods of Men:
And why not Gods of Men . . ."

When he'd finished reading, Rosetta said, "A man write that?"

"Yes," Cain replied.

"White man?"

"Yes."

"Figures."

"Why?"

"Only a white man would want to be a god."

Cain chuckled at that.

"One thing I never could figure out about that story," Rosetta opined. "How come it always the womenfolk leading men down the wrong path? Why not the other way round?"

"I don't know," Cain said.

"The way I sees it, it's the menfolk more often than not that's to blame. There was this one slave down on Mr. Eberly's plantation. Jonas. A man with growed children working in the fields already. Old. Older than you, Cain," she said with a straight face. "This Jonas had him a wife, a good woman name of Letty. But he had him a roving eye. He took a fancy to this one young girl, Charity. She weren't but fourteen and kinda slow. Born that way. Didn't matter to Jonas, though. He got her with child. When Letty found out about it, she took to yelling and screaming at poor Charity, hitting on her and calling her a black nigger whore for sleeping with her man. As if it her fault what her husband done to her. Letty went to Mr. Eberly and made up some story about the girl stealing from the smokehouse. Got her fifty stripes."

"How old do you think I am?" Cain asked.

"How old?" Rosetta glanced over at him, looked him up and down, as if seeing him for the first time. "Cain't never tell with white folks. Fifty?"

"Fifty!" Cain scoffed. "Hell, I'm not forty yet."

"It's all that liquoring you do. Saps the life out of a body. You ain't a bad-looking man, Cain. For a white feller," she said, smiling. Then she glanced down at the book he was holding. "Why you readin' that anyway? You don't even believe in hell."

"I don't believe in it as someplace with fire and brimstone, if that's what you mean. But, like Mr. Milton, I believe we can make our own hell. Satan says the mind can make one place into the other."

"Sometimes I think I already been there. Not just in my mind neither. Could you read me some more? I like the sound of it on your tongue, Cain."

They were sitting near the fire, Cain reading to Rosetta about Satan's trickery, when several men on horseback came riding into camp. The horses, Cain saw, had been ridden hard, were well lathered, their nostrils flaring. The first thing Cain recognized was the black gelding with the four white stockings, its lameness now even more apparent. It shifted its weight to the left side and now gingerly pointed its right front hoof. When Cain glanced up, he saw the man with the long, streaked beard and, beside him, the red-faced one with the powder burn under his eye. The blackbirders they'd run into back in Connecticut. Only now, they were without their booty of Negroes. Cain wondered what had brought them here. He supposed it could have been just a coincidence. They were all headed south. Then again, he'd always been reluctant to put his trust in happenstance. He knew why they were here—Rosetta.

"Evening," said the ruddy-faced leader, tipping his hat.

Cain nodded but didn't say anything.

"We saw your fire," said the one with the skunk beard. "That venison sure do smell good."

"You're welcome to some before you move on," Cain said, making his intentions clear.

"Thankee kindly," the man replied, getting down from his gelding. Two of his companions dismounted as well, and the three of them fell upon the carcass of the deer, hacking off thick slabs of meat with their knives and tearing into them. The leader remained on his bay, holding the reins with his left hand. He stared down at Rosetta.

"Have we met somewhere before?" he asked Cain, scratching his chin. Cain knew that the man recognized him, that he was just pretending.

"We have," Cain replied. "Up north."

"Oh, that's right," the leader said, his eye on Rosetta. "I do recollect that pretty nigger gal you got there."

"I thought you were headed for Baltimore. This is a little out of your way, isn't it?"

"We got sidetracked with other business," the man replied, smiling. He had a broad, square face and a wide mouth full of crooked, broken teeth. "Where are your friends?"

"They went into town," Cain said.

"That a fact?"

"They should be back directly."

"Funny thing is, we were just in town and we didn't see them. They'd be two heavyset fellows and a scrawny blond one with a birthmark on his neck? Bell," he called to the bearded man, "you see those fellows that were with this here gentleman?"

The one called Bell looked up from his eating, his beard slick with grease and dark blood that shone in the firelight. "Ain't seen nobody fit that description."

"Well, they were there," Cain insisted. "And they'll be back any time now."

The leader looked down at Cain and nodded. Finally he dismounted and walked over toward the fire. He was shorter than he appeared in the saddle, perhaps only five eight, but broad shouldered and thick through the middle. Not fat, but solid and imposing in the manner of a well-fed Angus bull. The three others were sitting close by the fire, intent on eating.

"Move," he commanded. When they didn't make way for him fast enough, he gave one man a firm kick in the butt.

"God dang it, Clayton," the man cried. "What'd you have to go and do that for?"

"I said move."

Grumbling under his breath, the man quickly made room before he was kicked again.

The one named Clayton squatted and took hold of one of the doe's front legs and twisted it roughly, bone and tendon and cartilage snapping. Then he withdrew an onyx-handled clasp knife and with his left hand severed what continued to attach the leg to the body. Still squatting on his haunches, he started to gnaw on the joint, holding it with one hand, the other dangling at his side. Cain watched his jaw muscles working as he tore off hunks of meat and chewed them with his snaggle teeth.

"Yessirree, this here's right tender venison," the man said. "My compliments to the chef. I figure that must be you?" he said, glancing across at Rosetta.

She looked over at Cain.

"You don't have to ask him. You cooked it, didn't you, girl?"

Rosetta nodded.

"See, I don't bite. I bet you cook for your master?"

She just stared at him.

"I bet you do a lot of things for him," he added.

The man's greatcoat was open, exposing the pair of Tranter revolvers. They were of British make, ugly blunt weapons but good at doing damage at close range. Cain glanced over at the others, did a quick inventory. The bearded one carried a small-caliber Smith & Wesson pistol on his hip, a five- or six-shot revolver, and he had about him the look of a man who knew how to use it. One of the remaining two, red-haired, soft and jowly, showed a single-shot Navy pistol sticking into the waist of his britches and a knife in a sheath slid down into his boot. The third, a thin, wizened old man with a bad cough, had his coat buttoned up, and Cain couldn't tell what all he carried. He turned his gaze back to the one called Clayton, figuring whatever would happen would start only with his blessing.

As discreetly as he could, Cain lowered his right hand and pretended interest in a twig on the ground. Casually he released the leather loop holding the hammer of his Colt, then left his hand poised there. The movement did not go unnoticed by Clayton, who eyed Cain suspiciously. Suddenly the man reached toward his coat pocket. In an instant, Cain drew, cocked his gun, and pointed it at the man.

"Hold it!" Cain commanded. The others stopped eating and turned to look at Cain. Skunk beard made a move for his gun and Cain turned the Colt on him, and would have shot him if the leader hadn't called out.

"*Whoa!*" he cried. "Just hold your horses, the both of you. Bell, don't do a doggone thing." Then, to Cain, he said, "Easy with that thing, friend. I was just fixing to offer you something to drink. No call to draw on me like that. We don't mean you any harm."

"Take it out," Cain said. "But real slow."

The man cautiously withdrew his hand from his pocket.

"See," he said, holding in the air a pint of some clear-colored liquid. "Just moonshine. Bell's pappy made it. Didn't he, Bell?"

"Best licker you ever did drink," skunk beard said.

Gradually Cain released the hammer of his gun and let his arm drop to his side. He held it there for a few seconds, his instincts still warning him that he hadn't been wrong. Finally, though, with no other evidence to go on, he holstered the weapon but didn't take his eye off Clayton.

"Here," the man said, passing the bottle across to him. "You could use you some."

Cain hesitated, then accepted the bottle and took a drink. His heart was pounding, and so he took a second. The liquor went some way to quietening it.

"Appreciate it," Cain offered, extending the bottle back to Clayton.

"Give the girl a drink. She looks like she could use it, too."

"She doesn't drink liquor."

"Never saw a nigger refuse free liquor," Clayton exclaimed, accepting the bottle and taking a drink. Then to skunk beard, he said, "You ever see a blue-eyed nigger, Bell?"

"Can't say I have. Then again, she don't look like she got much nigger blood in her," the other replied. "Pass that bottle over yonder, Clayton."

"You bringing her back for auction?" the leader asked Cain.

"No. She's a runaway," he said, glancing over at Rosetta. "I have papers for her from her owner."

"A fine-looking wench like her would fetch a goodly price on the block."

"Her master hired me to bring her back."

"I can see why he'd want her back, too," he said, looking over at Bell and winking. Clayton had been working on a piece of gristly meat for a while and he finally gave up and spit it into the fire, where it popped and sizzled. "How much he paying you?"

"Enough."

"Three hundred?"

"I don't see as that's any business of yours," Cain said.

"My business is—"

"I *know* what your business is," Cain interrupted.

"How's that make us any different from you, friend?"

"I have a warrant for what I do. I don't go grabbing any Negro I can lay my hands on and selling them downriver."

The man grinned at this, the action pushing his fleshy cheeks into round balls under his eyes and exposing the missing front tooth. He stared across the fire at Cain. His eyes were heavy-lidded and dark as calf liver. In them was a smug look, that of someone holding a pair of aces to your jacks and just waiting for you to bid into his hand.

"You call it what you want. It comes down to the same thing. We both make our living peddling flesh."

"Clayton," the red-haired man interjected.

"Shut up."

"I got to piss."

"Well, go piss then. You looking for me to hold it for you?"

The others laughed raucously and teased the man with obscene gestures. The red-haired man got up and plodded off into the birch trees.

"Tell you what, friend," the leader said to Cain, "I have hard cash." He patted his coat over his breast. "Name your price."

"I told you she's not for sale."

"Hell, everything on God's green earth is for sale if the price is right. So go ahead and name your price."

"Not in this case, friend," Cain replied, giving the other back the same smug smile.

"You're just trying to drive up her value. I respect that. You're a businessman just like me. How's four hundred sound to you?"

"I can't sell her to you."

"All right, I'll go five hundred. That's cash on the barrelhead. Right here and now."

"I promised I'd bring her back."

"A man of integrity," Clayton said, his tone laced with a sarcastic edge. "That's the problem with this here country. Nobody has integrity anymore. Everybody's just out for himself. Even our beloved president. Hell, all the cotton interests have old man Buchanan sewn up tighter than a drum. You think he cares a fig for the South? He just knows where his bread is buttered. No integrity left nohow. I'll tell you what. I'll go you five hundred and fifty dollars cash. That's my final offer. That'll buy you a lot of integrity." He looked over at the skunk beard and winked again.

"You must be hard of hearing. I said, she's not for sale," Cain repeated flatly.

"All's you would have to do is tell her owner she escaped. You could pocket the money and be on your way, friend."

"I'm not your friend," Cain snapped. "And I think it's time you boys be on your way."

Clayton looked over at the other two and smiled. "But we haven't finished eating yet."

Cain watched as the man ate some more from the joint of meat. He kept the other two in the corner of his eye and tried listening for the one who'd gone off into the woods, but he couldn't hear a thing in the darkness.

"I said, you need to leave."

"All right, I can see your game, friend," offered the leader.

"Game?"

"You drive a hard bargain. But I'm feeling in a generous mood. Six hundred then. And that's my final offer. After all, I got to have some room for profit. We both know that's more than fair."

"You and your no'count boys get your asses on those horses and get the hell out of here," repeated Cain, watching the man's hands. "Now!"

"You know, I'm sorely disappointed in you, corncracker," Clayton said, shaking his head.

"Is that so?"

"Here I am, making you a generous offer—more than generous—and you got to treat us like dirt." The leader turned to the one named Bell. "What did I do to deserve such treatment?"

Bell laughed. "Ought to teach the corncracker some manners, Clayton."

"Friend, I didn't have to offer you a plug nickel. I could've just taken her and been off. Instead, I try to treat you fair, and here you go disrespecting me."

Cain tried to work out how he'd play this. Just like in a poker game, he always tried figuring out what would happen, who was holding what, who would make the first move, who was bluffing, who he had to pay attention to. He decided he would shoot the one named Bell first because he seemed to pose the greatest danger. After that, he'd go for the leader, who, he'd noticed, did everything with his left hand. Even though he had two pistols, his left hand was still holding the deer leg, and he'd have to drop that first to go for his gun. The old man would be easy. What gave Cain some pause, though, was the red-haired man in the woods. There was no telling where he was and what he'd do when the shooting commenced.

Cain watched as Clayton tossed the uneaten portion of the leg bone into the fire and let his hand drop down toward his thigh.

"Don't move it any closer, friend," Cain warned him.

"Why not?"

"Because I'd have to kill you."

The man laughed, exposing his broken, snaggle teeth. "I don't know if you noticed, but you are outnumbered four to one," he said.

"I told you, my friends will be back any minute."

"We've been on your trail for the past two days, and we know the other three left a while back to hunt the runaway."

"Which they ain't agonna find," said Bell cryptically.

"So it's just you, friend," Clayton offered.

Cain nodded, knowing that his bluff had been called, and it was time to show what he was holding.

"Well, chew on this, friend," Cain said. "No matter what happens, I'll be sure to kill you."

"Is that a fact?"

"It is."

The man nodded thoughtfully. "Nobody has to get hurt. Let us have the girl and we'll be on our way."

"That's not going to happen."

The other men exchanged knowing looks. Cain saw something grow cold and hard in the man's dark eyes. Clayton swallowed hard, as if he were trying to swallow a stone. At first, Cain thought it was fear, the fear of knowing he was about to die. He'd seen that look before in men's eyes. A sort of dreadful anticipation, where the breath tastes of carded wool, and the belly and balls contract in preparation for the inevitable end. He'd felt it himself that day at Buena Vista, waiting to die. And there'd been a few times since, when he could taste his end. But this time he realized too late his mistake, that it wasn't fear at all that he saw in the man's eyes.

"Behind you, Cain!" Rosetta cried.

Drawing his gun, Cain spun around. A split second before the cudgel the man wielded came crashing down on him, just missing his head but smashing into his left shoulder, Cain fired. The bullet struck the red-haired man just below the nose and went crashing on through his brain and out the back of his skull, before lodging in a birch tree behind him. The wounded man stood there for a moment staring down at Cain in utter surprise, spitting teeth and fragments of bone, trying to curse, but his mouth was filled with blood, and the only sound that slipped out was a wet-sounding gurgle. The man was dead already, but his body was too stubborn to give in to the notion yet.

Cain spun back around just as a bullet bit viperlike into his side, bringing scalding nausea with it. He managed to cock his gun and take aim at the leader when another round smashed into his skull just above his left temple, setting off a fierce clanging in his head. He shuddered and his eyesight failed him as he fell down in darkness.

16

From the sulfuric-scented gloom came a deep-bellied growl followed by the savage scraping of teeth on bone. The air around him hung heavy with the stench of ash and excrement, blood and burnt flesh. *Hell* was the thought that impressed itself on his slowly returning consciousness. He figured he'd died and gone there. The gnashing of teeth and the sweet stink of burning flesh suggested he had crossed the river Styx and entered the realm of shades, and when he opened his eyes what he saw only seemed to confirm his impression. In the predawn murkiness, he was able to make out a pair of large, hairy beasts just a few feet away, fighting over the remnants of what appeared to be a limb. With their jaws locked on it, they pulled in opposite directions, contending fiercely over the nearly fleshless appendage. They snarled and shook their heads back and forth, their shoulders and haunches tensed. Looking beyond them, he saw a third gnawing on the remains of a slender carcass that lay in the ashes of a fire. And, from behind him, he heard the jaws of yet another. Lying on his left side, Cain turned his head slightly to look back over his shoulder. There he was met with the most gruesome of scenes. Some sort of grayish hound had its muzzle buried deep in the belly of a dead man. When it withdrew, from its bloody jaws hung a string of glistening entrails. His head rapidly clearing, Cain realized that it wasn't hell after all, and that the creatures were merely a pack of wild dogs, no doubt lured by the smell of a meal.

Cain's movement brought him suddenly to the attention of the dogs. The two fighting stopped and stared at him. One of them, a long-haired black mongrel with a bad case of the mange, dropped the bone and turned squarely on Cain, its head lowered between its thin, pointy shoulders. It growled at him, baring its fangs. They all stood there for a moment, confused and frightened by this meal come suddenly to life. The other dog of the fighting pair, some sort of black-and-white terrier with stumpy legs sticking out of a rotund body, took a couple of cautious steps toward Cain, its ears flattened against its narrow head. Cain reached for his revolver but found his holster empty. The other dogs, emboldened by the terrier's lead, slowly advanced on Cain, moving with the tentativeness of a group of school-yard bullies not completely sure of their advantage.

"Ha!" he screamed at them, waving his right hand about. But his cry had little effect. They continued closing in. The black mongrel circled to his left, as if to outflank him while the dog to his rear held his ground, like a dutiful soldier having been given orders to cut off the enemy's path of retreat.

"Go, you bloody bastards," he cried again, but they continued to close in on him.

He looked around for a stick or rock, some weapon with which to defend himself, then remembered the pepperbox. He reached down into his boot and, to his utter amazement, found it still there. The blackbirders had overlooked it. He took careful aim at the one closest to him, the black dog, and squeezed the trigger. The gun made only an ineffectual *click*. "Damn," he cried, cursing the crookback, who'd probably used cheap percussion caps. The dog continued slouching toward him, his head now so close Cain could smell the dead-meat odor of its foul breath. He pulled the trigger a second time, and now the gun crackled. The .32 caliber bullet ripped into the dog's muzzle, just below its left eye. The animal sneezed once, as if he'd snorted some pepper, shook its head, then dropped to the ground, its legs splayed outward to the sides.

The others proved, as bullies usually do, to be cowards. They hightailed it, running through the stand of birches, one of them still clutching a piece of bone in its mouth.

When Cain tried to raise himself up, his head commenced to pounding as if several cannons had gone off nearby, and he nearly passed out. He touched his temple, his hand coming away greasy with blood. He could feel a wide gash there, running from the left temple across to the middle of his forehead. But he felt no hole into his skull, and the bone beneath felt solid and unbroken. He guessed that the bullet had just glanced off his skull, though he hardly took this for luck. When he sat up, he felt a pain like a branding iron on his left side, just at the point of his last rib. He'd been hit there as well, he figured. He made a cursory inspection to see if he'd been hit anywhere else. As he leaned forward he was struck by a wave of nausea. He waited until it subsided a little and then rolled over onto his knees, and caught his breath, before slowly trying to stand. He saw the red-haired man lying a few feet away, his mouth gaping open, as if he still had something more to say. His face was covered in blood. His shirt was torn and his belly ripped open, part of his intestines pulled out and lying on his trousers. Beside him lay the cudgel he had intended to knock Cain's brains out with. Cain bent at the waist and vomited a stream of sour bile and last night's undigested venison.

He made his way down to the river, his legs unsteady as those of a brand-new foal, and dropped to his knees. His throat was parched, so he cupped his hands and drank copiously from the briny-tasting water. The nausea returned, making him vomit several more times. When it had passed, he washed his face, trying to rinse the wound on his head. Then he sat on the banks and removed his coat and shirt. The chill of morning made him shiver, bringing goose bumps to his skin. He inspected the wound in his side. It was still oozing blood, not a good sign, but at least the bullet hadn't hit a major artery, or, he hoped, a vital organ. And the color was a bright, clear red, suggesting that it had missed his bowels, which would, he knew, have spelled a slow and painful death. He'd seen men gutshot in the war, and it wasn't a way he preferred to die. He dipped his shirt in the water and cleaned the wound as best he could. It was a relatively small hole, probably from one of the pair of .32 caliber Tranters, he guessed, the concave edges neat and well defined. An entry wound. He felt along his back but couldn't find where the bullet had exited. He stuck his index finger into the wound, moved it around. He could feel where the bullet had struck and broken a rib. When he pressed it, the rib gave way and sent a bright shimmer of pain flashing through him.

"Sweet Jesus," he cried.

He looked in his coat for the flask of laudanum, but it was gone. They'd taken it, too, the bastards.

He stood a little too fast and his head swirled, and he had to wait till the dizziness subsided. When it did, he took his time walking back up to the campsite. He looked around for his saddlebags, hoping for the comfort of his bottle of whiskey or, at least, to find some rags for his wounds, but they were nowhere to be found. Lying on the ground, however, was his copy of Milton. He picked it up and walked over to a nearby pine tree. With his pocketknife he scraped some pine tar off and opened the book and smeared it on a page. It was where the Archangel Michael was engaged in deadly combat with Satan. Cain sat on the ground and ripped the page out and pressed the pine-tar-covered paper to the wound. He'd seen this done before to stanch bleeding. Then, with his knife, he cut his shirt into strips, tied the strips together, and wound them to make a single long cord. He placed a piece of his shirt over the paper, then, over that, tied the cord around his torso to keep the bandage in place. Only when he'd finished his doctoring did he realize he was cold, and he pulled on his coat. He checked for his billfold but wasn't surprised to find that missing, too. They'd taken Hermes, as well as his gun and his blackjack, but he wasn't thinking about any of that right now. What he was thinking about was Rosetta, and how he would go about getting her back. He pushed the pain away and started to work out possibilities, to sift and organize, to fashion a plan. He figured they probably had a half day's lead on him. Plus he didn't have a horse. He slid open the barrels of the pepperbox and checked to make sure he had four shots remaining. Then he snapped it closed and shoved it into the pocket of his trousers.

In the road he knelt and looked for their trail. He was able to spot Hermes's distinctive hoofprint, and he knew someone was riding his horse, as Hermes had a different gait when not being ridden. He figured Rosetta. The trail headed north, and he followed it for a time before losing it near the town amid the many other hoofprints and wagon wheel tracks in the road. He had to backtrack until he picked it up again, as the four riders left the road and cut through some woods toward the northeast. At first, he was stumped at this move but then realized where they were headed. Baltimore again. No doubt to one of the many slave auctions held down near the docks. He'd worked for several of the slave traders in that city, wealthy and powerful men like Austin Woolfolk and Early King, and even for a woman, Hope Hull Slatter, one of the most brutal slaver dealers of them all. They'd purchase Rosetta and put her aboard a slaver bound for the New Orleans market, where she'd spend the rest of her days on some cotton plantation being abused by some new owner. And before that, he knew the three blackbirders would get drunk and have their fun with her. Cain knew all of this.

He tried running, but his side hurt too much, so he had to limit himself to an awkward, sideways half jog, half walk, like a crab at low tide. With each stride his head throbbed and the wound in his side contracted like a fist that slammed into his ribs and lungs, almost knocking the breath from him. He thought at any moment he would collapse, but he forced himself to keep putting one foot in front of the other, trying to establish a rhythm that would take over and lead him on. He was sure the pain couldn't keep up this intensity, and if he could just wait it out he could beat it. But that strategy proved wrong, for the pain, if anything, became worse. Several times it doubled him over, and once he fell to his knees and retched up a yellowish bile. At least there was no blood in it, though, which he took as good news. The pain formed in his mind a kind of adversary, something animate and separate from himself, whose goal was not only Cain's death, but also his total surrender. And he'd decided that, though it might eventually kill him, he would not succumb to it. Several times he cursed it and called it names—son of a bitch, bloody bastard, whoreson knave, scoundrel, dog, swine, eater of rat excrement—feeling that, by personifying it, he could make it something manageable, something able to be defeated.

As he moved along he began to work up a good sweat. He removed his coat and tied its arms around his waist. He shuffled along bare chested, the brisk morning air actually feeling good on his burning skin. After a few miles he stopped by a stream and drank some water and washed his face. The wound in his side had soaked through the paper, so he tore out another couple of pages of Milton and shoved them under the cord he had tied around himself. He then started off again, this time, he realized, moving slower. He knew it would be hard to cut their lead on foot no matter how fast he moved, but he figured this would have to do until he could come up with a better plan.

He followed the trail through woods and thickets, over streams and low-lying fields, the smell of the ocean getting stronger as he went. It was little more than an old game trail or Indian path that the blackbirders were taking, and they probably knew it well from their trade. Still, they didn't appear to be in a hurry. The horses' hoofprints did not bite deeply into the ground, nor were the strides those of animals moving much faster than a walk. They were the tracks of men who had nothing to fear and who purposely took their time, as if on a Sunday jaunt. Cain pushed himself onward, figuring his chances of catching up to them were slim, but at least he would not give in to the pain.

Around midmorning he found himself plaguey weak from hunger. As he passed an apple orchard, he went in and looked on the ground for last year's fallen fruit. He found a few brown, wormy apples that the deer had missed, and he tore voraciously into them. The soft meat exploded in his mouth into a watery paste but did little more than titillate his hunger. Down the road a piece, though, his spirits revived a little when he spotted some Guernsey cows grazing in a pasture. A quarter mile away was a farmer's house and barn, but he didn't see anyone about, so he climbed over the worm fence and cautiously approached several of the cows eating off by themselves.

"Here, bos," he said, having grabbed a handful of grass and extending it in a kind of bovine greeting. "It's all right, bos."

Yet as he got close, the animals spooked and took off, running in their clumsy sort of way across the pasture. He saw one, though, off by herself under an elm tree. She appeared big with calf. Cain slowly made his way over to her. When he reached her, he patted her flank and reassured her.

"Nobody's going to hurt you, girl. Just want to borrow some of your milk."

She turned her bulbous eyes to look at him, then went nonchalantly back to munching on the grass. He lay down between her legs, took hold of one of her teats, and pulled a squirt of milk into his mouth. The liquid was sweet and warm and life giving, and he didn't think he'd tasted anything so good in all his days. He hadn't quite quenched his fill, though, when he heard a voice calling out. Sitting up, he saw a man up near the barn, holding what appeared to be a hoe. The farmer was running at him full tilt. Cain decided against waiting and trying to explain his situation to the man. Instead, he thanked the cow and took to his heels. He cut across the road and disappeared into some woods. Soon, the farmer gave up.

Cain cut back onto the path a half mile away. After walking for an hour, he came at last to an actual road. Here the four riders had turned to the north along it. Cain followed them. The wound in his side had begun to bleed and throb again, and he was forced to stop and tend to it. Although his forehead felt hot, he found himself shivering, so he put his coat back on. While he was seated there at the side of the road, an older couple approached in a buckboard wagon filled with supplies, and when they saw him, they stopped. The man had a long gray beard and the black garb customary of Quakers, and the woman wore a poke bonnet. He was thin and gristly while the wife was plump as a pullet. Cain asked them if this was the road to Baltimore, and they said it was. Then he asked if three men and a Negro woman had passed them. They said they had not seen anybody fitting that description.

"Why, you are hurt, sir," said the man.

"I'm all right," Cain replied.

The husband got down to see if he could help Cain. He was frail-looking and walked with a decided stoop.

"I think not," the man said. "Can you stand?"

"Yes."

"Why don't you get on the back of our wagon and we'll take you to have your wounds attended to."

"Dr. Caulkins is just a few miles distant," interjected the woman from the wagon.

"I can't stop," Cain said. "You wouldn't happen to have any cloth you could spare, would you, ma'am? My dressing needs changing."

The woman got down from the buggy and waddled over to where Cain sat. She bent down and took a portion of her petticoat and tore it off. She had her husband get a canteen of water from the wagon. She poured water on the cloth and set about cleaning his wounds. First the one on his head and then the one in his side. Up close he saw that she had grayish eyes, the color of morning fog in the mountains.

"The wound to your head doesn't appear grave," she explained. "But the other one is in need of doctoring. It may be infected." Placing a hand to his forehead, she added, "Goodness sakes, you are burning up, young man."

"Let us take you to the doctor," the husband insisted.

"Thank you, but I have to be moving on."

"But you are sick," said the woman.

"I'm well enough."

"You are either running from something that frightens you or toward something that beckons," the woman said.

"Some of both, I suppose."

"Are you sure you are strong enough to travel?"

"I don't know. Thing is, I need to try. Would you have any whiskey, ma'am?"

"I'm afraid we don't condone liquor of any sort, even for medicinal purposes. But take the water," the woman said. "And wait." She stood and hurried over to the wagon. She came back with biscuits wrapped in oilcloth. "In case you get hungry." They were still warm, and it was obvious she had just baked them to bring someplace or other.

"Thank you," he said, standing.

"Whatever you're after, it must be very important," she said.

"It is."

Then, as he turned and started hobbling away, the woman called after him, "Good luck. May the Almighty be with you."

Late in the afternoon, he came within nose distance of a hog farm. Its sour stench stung his nostrils a full mile before he'd even reached it. His feet were aching, and the wound in his side had started a funny sort of cadence, similar to a heartbeat but deeper and slower. *Thug . . . thug. Thug . . . thug.* He wasn't sure what this meant, but he deemed it not a good sign. As he reached the hog farm, which sat right up against the road, he saw a Negro working in one of the pens. He was pouring a bucket of swill and potato peelings into a large trough. Cain stopped and called to the man. The Negro came sauntering over, taking his time. He looked Cain up and down and then whistled.

"Looks like you got into it with the wrong feller, mister."

"How far to Baltimore?" he asked.

"Day and a half. But not in your condition."

"You happen to see three white men and a Negro woman ride by this way? They'd have had a big horse with a blaze face."

The man was middle-aged, with wisps of gray in his beard. He wore a kerchief around his neck and a sweat-stained slouch hat pulled down low. He had yellow eyes, and they stared at Cain with the suspicious look that slaves always gave to white men asking questions.

He shrugged.

"It's important. I believe they're going to sell the woman at the slave auctions in Baltimore."

The man took his hat off and wiped his forehead with a hand. "Ain't nothin' new 'bout that. They's always going by here with slaves in tow."

"But they stole her."

"She b'long to you?"

"No."

"Then what bidness it a yours?"

"I'm trying to keep her from being sold."

The man stared at him with his jaundiced eyes. "So's you can bring her back to her massa and c'lect the money."

"You don't understand," Cain said. "I'm trying to help her."

"Help her?" the man repeated, jeeringly. "Ain't never seen no soul catcher that was any help to a slave."

"Did you see them?"

The man shrugged again.

"I don't have time for this," Cain said, laying his hand on the butt of the pepperbox in his waist. "Did you see them?"

The man's expression didn't change at all with the implied threat.

"I only want to help her," said Cain. "She's with child."

The man gave in to a half smile, showing a gleam of gold tooth. "So dat it."

"No, it's not what you think. I just have to keep her from being sold. Did you see her? Please."

The Negro continued looking at him. Finally, he said, "Three men pass by 'round noon yestidy."

"They have a light-skinned Negro girl with them?"

"Yessum."

"How were they riding. Hard?"

The man shook his head. "Average, I reckon."

"Would you know where I could get another mount?"

"You lookin' to buy one?"

"They took all my money, everything I had."

"Horses like slaves. You want one, you gots to pay for it."

"I will when I get my things back."

The Negro laughed. "Ain't the way it works. You pays first and then you gets what you want." Cain got the impression that he liked toying with him.

"Please," Cain said. "I don't have much time."

"We ain't none of us do," the man said, scratching his beard. "Mr. Henderson up the road a ways, he got him some horses. You might could find yourself one there. His place just before the river."

Then the man leaned toward him, as if he were wary of being overheard, though there was not a soul in sight. "He got him a coupla mean-ass dogs. You'll want to be mindful a them. Remember, none a this you heard from me, mister."

Cain thanked the man and moved on.

He reached the farm at twilight but waited until it was fully dark before making a move. It was set back from the road about a half mile. There was a main house and barn, several outbuildings, acres upon acres of rolling pastureland, with woods behind leading down to the river. Cain was upwind, and he didn't want those dogs to get his scent and commence to barking. So he circled around and, by the light of the stars, made his way along the river, then approached from downwind, through the woods. He quietly entered the barn through a back door. It was dark inside and he tripped over something and nearly fell. Several of the horses stirred in their stalls. He lay still for a moment, letting the noise settle, permitting his eyes to get used to the darkness. Luckily, he hadn't alerted the dogs. He got up and made his way cautiously over to the stalls. As much by feel as by sight, Cain tried to pick a horse with some grit. He slipped his hand into the stalls and felt each horse's neck and shoulders. There were several large plow horses, strong but plodding animals, a blaze gelding who tried to nip him when he placed his hand on the horse's withers, a bay whose neck was too thin for its squat body. He finally settled on a strong-looking roan mare. She wasn't that big, only thirteen hands or so, but she had a good chest and legs, and she looked like she could run some. He went over to the tack room and grabbed a bridle, a blanket, and a well-worn saddle, then returned to the mare.

"It's all right, girl," he reassured her. "I'm just going to borrow you."

She remained calm as he tacked her up.

Before he left the barn, he happened to find a hatchet on a workbench, and he slipped that in his trousers' waist. Then he led the horse out the back and through the woods toward the river. When he was some distance from the house, he pulled himself with difficulty into the saddle and, by starlight, picked his way carefully through the tangle of trees and undergrowth. He'd almost reached the river when he heard the dogs commence to barking. This was followed by other noises, the startled, angry voices of men calling to one another in the night. At the riverbank, he paused for a moment to take stock of things, assessing the distance across and the water's speed, and picking out an especially high pine tree on the far bank that would serve for purposes of navigation. Then he led the mare down into the river. When the water reached his thighs, he shuddered and slid off the horse, to allow her to swim freely. With his right hand Cain clutched onto a handful of the horse's mane, while in his left, he held the pepperbox aloft so the powder wouldn't get wet. The horse didn't hesitate at all but moved confidently into the river. She was soon over her head, swimming hard, instinctively keeping her nose upriver against what proved to be a strong current.

"Atta girl," he said, urging her onward.

He kept his eyes on the pine tree, using it as a beacon. As he moved through the dark water, his body slowly grew accustomed to the cold. In fact, he actually found the water refreshing, and his wounds, for the time being, almost ceased to ache. The water seemed to act as a poultice, soothing and comforting and restoring him. Above the river, to the east, he could see the night sky filled with stars, scattered like grains of salt over a black tabletop. They appeared so low he felt he could almost reach out and pick them up, put the salty particles on his tongue. He recalled the night sky in the desert in Mexico, how cold and clear and orderly the universe had seemed to him then, not the chaotic doings of men but the perfect physics of sky and space and objects. Several notions pressed in upon his mind as he crossed the river. He thought of what the old couple had said to him, that he was either running from something that scared him or toward something that beckoned. He thought of what the Negro swineherd had told him, that he only wanted to find her so he could bring her back for his own profit. And then, he thought of what Hettie, the woman back in Connecticut, had said to him the night before she took her own life: *Remember not to let anything happen to Rosetta.*

The mare came out on the far bank and shook herself. Cain placed his foot in the stirrup and pulled himself into the saddle again. As he rode up the bank through some tangled undergrowth, he startled a covey of quail. They exploded in a confusion of wings as they darted in all directions. When he made the road, he took off at a full gallop, able to make out the way ahead only by starlight. He pushed the mare for all she was worth. She wasn't as smooth-gaited as Hermes, but she had a powerful hind end and a generous nature, willing to give all she had and then some. She lowered her head and lengthened her stride, and Cain got up in a half seat and held her high on the neck, whispering to her.

"Gitup, girl," he said, making clicking sounds, urging her onward. "Gitup, girl."

He rode her hard through the night, stopping only once to let her drink some water from a creek. When Cain dismounted, he felt feverish, sick to his stomach. The burning, throbbing pain in his side had come back with a vengeance. He retched a few times, managing to draw up only a thin bile. When the nausea passed, he felt suddenly exhausted, felt an irresistible urge to lie down on the ground and sleep, perhaps for just a few minutes, just enough to catch his wind. But he knew that if he did, he might never get up, so he forced himself back in the saddle and rode on, guided only by the stars and the occasional light of a house or cabin. The mare had more than proven herself to be a good, dependable animal, so he gave her her head while he leaned forward onto her withers and surrendered to his weariness. Into her ear, he whispered, "Take me to her, girl." The rhythmic motion of the mare's gait gradually eased the pain some, and he found the lathered smell of the horse soothing. A hush fell over the night as he rode headlong into it. Somewhere along the line, he must have drifted into a drowsy, somnolent state that wasn't quite sleep, for he could still feel and smell the horse under him.

Still, he jerked awake, clutching the reins just before he'd have fallen off the horse. It was still dark, but dawn was pushing up against the night. He could tell by the way things were getting edges, separating themselves from the anonymity of night. He heard, too, the early cries of mourning doves off in the woods. He kicked the mare into a gallop and rode hard for some time. "Just a little more, girl," he said, prodding her on. She'd already given him all she had, and he hated to push a horse beyond its limit, but he had no choice. He came up over the crest of a hill, and daylight spilled suddenly across the eastern horizon like a cool fire burning the treetops. He paused, squinting against its radiance.

The mare looked back at him, as if to ask if they were through, but he kicked her again into a gallop and she rode on unstintingly. Fortunately, they had been riding only for a short time when, off in a stand of black locust trees on the side of the road, he spotted a dull reddish gleam. As he approached, he saw that it was the dying embers of a campfire. He dismounted quietly and tied the mare to a locust. Drawing the pepperbox, he crept slowly up to check things out. On his way into the woods, he saw horses penned in a makeshift corral made of ropes and branches. He recognized the black horse with the limp and the swaybacked roan and the two bays, but he didn't see Hermes. He cocked the pistol and removed the hatchet from his waist, and thus armed, quietly entered the camp.

Several empty bottles littered the ground, and the camp had the familiar sugary stink of corn liquor. He saw the three sleeping forms tucked beneath their bedrolls. They emitted the sodden, deathlike snores of men who'd collapsed into sleep after a night of riotous behavior. Rosetta lay next to the leader, the one named Clayton. He had his right arm draped over her. A blanket haphazardly covered the pair's legs, yet Cain could see her blue dress, or what was left of it. It was torn across her chest, exposing her shoulders and breasts. Cautiously, he squatted down and looked at her, to see if she was all right. She wasn't moving at all. Her face was toward him, but it was in shadow, and for a moment, he thought her asleep, perhaps even dead. But then he saw her blink several times in the predawn light. A message? he thought. Was she trying to warn him of something? Then he saw that she wasn't blinking so much as she was throwing her gaze down toward her left wrist. That's when he noticed the shackle. He followed the chain from her arm and saw that it went to Clayton's right wrist. The bastard had chained her to him in sleep so she couldn't run away. In reply Cain nodded and put his finger to his lips. With her chained as she was to him, Cain knew he would have to take care of this one first, or Rosetta would be in danger.

He crept around behind the leader. Raising his hatchet, he was about to bash his head in when he heard a noise behind him. Spinning around, Cain saw that it was the one with the skunk beard. He had sat up and was staring at Cain from fifteen feet away.

"Who the fuck—"

Cain fired. Though he'd aimed at the man's face, the weapon shot low. The round smoked through his beard and entered just above the Adam's apple. The man grabbed at his beard frantically, as if a wasp had gotten caught in there and was stinging him. Then he began coughing, spitting up blood. Despite the wound, he was still able to reach for his weapon, and Cain had to expend another shot. But this time he adjusted for the gun's shooting low. The second round took him flush in the middle of his forehead and the man tottered momentarily, then collapsed like a bale of wet cotton, spilling over onto his face. Now the old man came running at Cain with what looked like an ancient cavalry saber. Before he could get close enough to do him any harm, Cain fired, striking him in the chest. The old man swore once, then fell to his knees as if in prayer. He still had enough left in him that he tried to raise the saber. With his boot, Cain shoved him backward, and he toppled over onto the ground and lay still.

Awakened from what must have been a drunken stupor, the one named Clayton had had a chance to scramble to his feet. However, he found himself entangled in the chain attaching him to Rosetta, and it took him a few seconds to get free. When he was finally unencumbered, he made the mistake of going for the gun in his right holster but found that wrist still attached to Rosetta, who remained on the ground, a deadweight. By the time he thought to reach for his other Tranter, it was too late.

"I'd rethink that if I were you," Cain warned, sticking the pepperbox in the man's face.

"Hell, you're just going to kill me anyway."

"Maybe. But I will for certain if you go for that gun."

This seemed to hold out some promise for the man and adjusted his thinking accordingly. He pursed his lips and nodded, then let his hand drop at his side. His body seemed to untense itself.

"You're a mighty hard fellow to kill, friend," the man said.

"Some have tried before."

"You got more lives than a damn cat." Then, looking over toward the old man on the ground, he called out, "Pap? Hey, Pap?" When he didn't get a response, he looked at Cain. "Why'd you have to go and kill the old man?"

"He was fixing to do me some harm," Cain said.

"He couldn't hurt anybody. He was just a sick old man."

"Should have had the sense to get himself a new profession then, one less demanding."

"You corncracker son of a bitch." The man didn't cry, but his eyes got runny and he clenched his jaw, then hawked something up and spit it on the ground. "There wasn't any call to shoot him."

"Shut up," Cain commanded. "Where's my horse?"

"Sold it."

"Who to?"

"Traveling medicine man. His horse was all used up."

"Little broke-back fellow? Dark skinned?"

The man seemed amazed at the fact that Cain had guessed correctly. "That be him. Dr. Some Damn Thing or Other. Full of gabblement."

On the one hand, Cain was struck by the coincidence. Then again, everything seemed to have a hidden connection on this trip.

"Where was he headed?"

The man shrugged.

Cain pressed the barrels of the gun against the man's forehead. "I'm not going to ask you a second time."

"West," he replied. "Said something about heading out to Hagerstown. That's why he was in the market for a horse."

"That better be the truth."

"Got no reason to lie to you, friend."

"And stop calling me friend."

Cain looked down at Rosetta. She was half sitting, half lying on the ground with her knees bent, her left arm awkwardly pulled up by the chain.

"I want to know something else," Cain asked the man.

"What's that?"

"Did you take advantage of her?"

The man named Clayton smiled. "You referring to this here bitch?" he said, rattling the chain so that it yanked Rosetta's arm into the air as if she were a marionette and he a puppeteer.

"I asked—did you touch her?"

It was light enough now that Cain could see the smug look in his reddish brown eyes. The look of a man who held another man's innermost secret in the palm of his hand.

"You mean did I fuck her?" The man glanced at Rosetta. "Why don't you ask her yourself?"

Cain looked at her, noted the cold anger in her eyes, the flesh around them drawn taut, the hard set of her mouth. Then he turned back toward the leader.

"Go ahead, girl," the man said. "Tell him. Tell him how we all took turns with you. Tell him how much you liked it."

He turned back toward Cain and, with a smug grin, said, "Now I see why her master wants her back so much. I never had such a good piece of tail, black or white, in all my born days."

It was as if the man had a hankering to be killed, so Cain decided to oblige him. Staring into his eyes, he squeezed the trigger.

However, there was just a thin metallic click. The man's expression changed rapidly in the course of a split second: it went from one of shock, to that of fear, to something akin to unexpected joy, the sort a person has on finding an unanticipated coin in his pocket. Then he started laughing like one who'd lost his faculties.

"Mister, you just ran out of lives."

As he went for his gun with his left hand, Cain lunged forward with the hatchet, swinging it in a short, vicious stroke, as if he were splitting a piece of ironwood kindling. The hatchet caught the man at the hairline, and the blade settled deep into his brain. Blood spurted out, coursing down his face. He shuddered once, then stiffened, his spine arching, his arms and legs extending rigidly. He held that position for the briefest of moments, then his muscles went limp and he dropped straight down into himself, collapsing as if his bones had turned to jam.

Cain went over to check on the old man. He wanted to make sure he wasn't playing possum, so he kicked him with his boot. The man didn't move. Then Cain returned and squatted down in front of Rosetta.

"You all right?" he asked.

She stared at him silently, the rage glistening like diamonds in her eyes. Then, as if she had just realized she was still manacled to the dead man, she let out with a terrible screech, and began yanking frantically on the shackle, trying to free herself.

"Wait," Cain told her. "Let me get the key."

He rifled through the dead man's pockets until he found the key, then removed the shackle from her wrist. As soon as she was free, instead of getting as far from the body as she could, she crawled closer and rose up on her knees so that she was staring down at the dead man. Cain watched her uneasily. Her jaw was set, and her eyes filled with a chilling sort of malice. It put Cain in mind of the time back in Boston, when she fought him. "Rosetta," he said. But she didn't seem to hear him. Then she grasped hold of the hatchet, still buried in the man's skull, and pulled it out and raised it over her head. She slammed it down into the dead man's face. She did this over and over, crying out, "You white buckra." Soon his face was nothing more than a bloody mess. Cain thought of stopping her, but he figured it would be better to let her get it out. After a while she tired and stopped of her own accord. She knelt there, breathing hard.

Cain came over and put his hand on her shoulder. She spun on him with the hatchet, as if she would strike him as well.

"Whoa," he said, raising his hands in surrender. "Take it easy."

She stared at him for several seconds, her hollow-eyed expression that of a lost soul. He noticed that she had several small scrapes and bruises on her face, a welt over her eye, as if from a fist. Then suddenly a change came over her. She went limp and fell to the ground. Hugging her stomach, she began to cry, great heaving sobs that convulsed her. Cain squatted beside her, not knowing what to do. Finally, he put his hand on the back of her head and stroked her hair.

"You're safe now," he said.

After a while, her crying slowed, then stopped altogether. Still her ribs quivered and her breathing was erratic.

"Everything's going to be all right, Rosetta."

"Easy for you to say," she hissed at him.

"I'm sorry," he said, continuing to stroke her hair. "Is the baby all right?"

"I don't know. I ain't no doctor."

Cain stood and went over to the horses. He rummaged through the saddlebags until he came up with a shirt and a kerchief. He grabbed a canteen off the pommel and returned to her.

"Drink some," he told her. Then he took the canteen back and poured some water on the kerchief and began to gently wash her face. When he was done, he handed her the shirt and said, "Here. Put this on."

"I don't want their things on me," she said.

"You're shivering. Put it on." When she hesitated, he said, "Please. Just until we can get you something else."

She relented finally and put it on. Then he managed, with some difficulty, to pick her up and carry her away from the carnage, over to a tree near where the horses were tied.

"Sit here," he said. "I'll be right back."

She clutched his hand. "Don't leave me."

"I'll be right over there. I have to take care of some things. Just sit still."

Cain went over and searched the bodies. He found his gun and blackjack on the body of the bearded one, then located his flask on the old man. The man had had it in his breast pocket, and it now had a bullet hole clear through it, right through the Augustus part of his name. He took it anyway. From the body of the one named Clayton, he found the money purse the old woman had given Rosetta and took that, too. He also confiscated one of the Tranters, sliding it into his boot, but his Sharp's rifle was gone, probably sold off somewhere. Cain couldn't find his own billfold, but he did locate the leader's, and assumed his own money was mixed in with the other man's. The whole thing came to a little shy of two hundred dollars, and he wondered what the fool had given Hermes away for. He also understood then that the man had never had the money to buy Rosetta in the first place, that from the start he'd planned on killing him and stealing her. Not that it mattered much now, though it did make his killing of four men a little easier to accept. As he searched the man's body, he kept his eyes averted from the raw thing that had been his face.

When he'd taken everything that was his, he grabbed hold of the man's leg and dragged him deeper into the woods. He came upon a ravine, twenty feet below, which was a marshy swale that seemed a fitting place for the blackbirders to rot for eternity. Before he shoved the first body over the edge, he cursed him for good measure. Then he heaved the pepperbox after him, figuring the thing had nearly got him killed and he wasn't going to push his luck. He returned for the other bodies. He'd finished with the bearded one and had pulled the old man to the edge. Under his coat the man wore a homespun wool shirt Cain thought he could put to use, despite the bullet hole and blood. He'd just started unbuttoning it when the old man suddenly opened his eyes and cried, "Lord, Jesus?"

Cain jumped back in surprise. "I thought you were dead."

"What in tarnation you doin'?"

Just then Cain heard the sounds of people approaching along the road. A half mile off, he saw a farmer's wagon and behind it, several men on Percherons. The old fellow commenced to crying out. "Help! Help me!" Cain grabbed him by the throat and finished him off. When he was certain that the man was dead once and for all, he removed his shirt before depositing him with his son and the other blackbirder. Then he put the shirt on and hurried back to where the horses were tied. He picked out the stronger-looking of the two bays and the mare he'd stolen, before releasing the other horses and sending them galloping off into the woods.

Turning to Rosetta, he said, "Somebody's coming. Can you ride?"

"Never rode no horse on my own before," she replied.

"What I was asking was, are you well enough to ride?"

"I reckon I can," she said, standing up, although she was wobbly on her feet.

"We need to cut dirt. I'll take the bay. You ride the mare. She's spirited but easy." As he helped her up into the saddle, their faces came within inches of each other's.

"You expectin' me to thank you, Cain?"

"I'm not expecting anything."

"Well, good, 'cause I ain't about to. If you hadn'ta come huntin' for me to begin with, none a this woulda happened," she said, glancing off in the direction of the camp.

The iron in her spirit had returned, and in some odd way, he was grateful for it. She would need it for whatever would happen next.

Cain struggled to pull himself up into the saddle. In all the commotion he'd almost forgotten the wound in his side. Now he was aware of the pain again, a sharp gnawing in his side, but he took hold of the reins of the mare and headed off at a gallop. He wanted to put some distance between himself and this place. Though he'd killed in self-defense, you never knew how something like this might turn out if he were connected to their deaths. The way his luck was running, he'd be brought before a judge who was kin to one of these men.

They headed west, toward Hagerstown.

17

The flatlands of the coastal plain slowly altered as the countryside grew hilly again. The day turned warm and humid, a gummy haze hanging in the air and coating their bodies like a drunkard's sweat. It seemed they had ridden in a large circle; Cain recognized some of the landmarks they had passed several days earlier—a certain rock in the shape of a cat's head, a stream meandering through a field, the burnt-down farm with the family still camped out under the chestnut tree. For a while he held the reins of the mare, pulling it along behind him. Soon, though, Rosetta got the hang of being in the saddle, and he let her ride along on her own. Now and again, he'd glance back at her to see how she was doing. She remained silent, her face a mask of stoic inscrutability. He couldn't help but think about what the blackbirders had done to her. And he knew it was true that if he hadn't come after her, none of this would've happened.

They crossed over a pebbly-bottomed creek, and he pulled to a stop.

"I figured you might have need to wash yourself," he said to her.

They dismounted, and he led the horses into the woods, where they couldn't be seen from the road. In the saddlebags, he found a piece of lye soap and an old rag, and he gave them to her. He allowed her some privacy by heading up the creek a ways. With the jouncing of the ride, the wound in his side had begun to bleed again. He could feel the warm blood oozing down his waist, soaking his pants. He removed his shirt, the one he'd taken off the old man, and then the bandage, and inspected the wound. It was black and puffy, nasty-looking. He washed it as best he could with the cold creek water. When he was done, he retied the now filthy bandage and put his shirt back on, and returned to get Rosetta.

She'd gotten dressed and was sitting on the bank, her shoes off, her knees drawn up and her arms wrapped around them.

"Do you feel better?" he asked.

She threw him a sideways glance and frowned.

"It take more'n a little water to wash this foulness off a me."

He nodded. He didn't know what to say, didn't know what a woman felt after something like that. "How's the baby?" he asked again.

She sighed. "It kickin' up a storm."

At noon, they came upon a small hill settlement—livery, Baptist church, gristmill, a general store, a few unpainted shacks that perched on the steep banks of a fast-moving creek. Cain pulled up in front of a dry goods store, and they dismounted. Before he headed into the store, he shackled her. Once inside, he bought cotton cloth for bandages, a new shirt, a bottle of whiskey, some foodstuffs, gunpowder, miscellaneous supplies.

"You have any laudanum?" Cain asked the clerk.

"Don't carry it. What in blazes happened to you, mister?" asked the clerk, who chuckled as if Cain's wounds were a source of amusement to him. He was a slight man missing both front teeth, no doubt, Cain guessed, from someone's fist. As he spoke, he had a habit of permitting his tongue to slide into the open space, so that his speech had a wet, lisping quality. "That blood on you?" he asked Cain.

Cain nodded. "You got a doctor here?"

"Did. Doc Bryerly."

"He's not here anymore?"

"One of his patients shot him dead last fall." The man paused for effect, wanting Cain to ask why. Cain could see he was not going to get anywhere until he did.

"On account of?"

"On account of the feller caught him operatin' on his wife, if you catch my drift." The man leaned conspiratorially toward Cain and then snickered at his own joke. "Yep, ole Doc Bryerly was near on to eighty, but he was still a spry old devil. Back up in the hills they's all sorts of young'uns with his stamp on them."

"Is that so?" Cain said.

The man nodded smugly, proud of their local doc.

"You got any live doctors?"

"Closest is Hagerstown."

"How far is that?"

"Day's ride. In your condition, I'd figure on two. They's Black Maddy," the man offered.

"Who might she be?"

"Nigger midwife does some doctorin'."

"Where does she live?"

"On the pike west of here. You come upon a swamp. Her shack is just beyond that in the woods."

As he paid the man, Cain asked him, "You see a short fellow in a big caravan come through these parts?"

The man threw his head back and laughed, his tongue flickering out like a corn snake's.

"Uppity little fellow with a hunchback? Yeah, he rode through here a couple days back. Selling his medicines and such. I could see right off he was nothing but a charlatan."

"Was the caravan pulled by a chestnut stallion with a blaze?"

"In fact, it was. Right fine horse. You have cause to be after him?"

"You might say."

Cain collected his supplies and left. After releasing Rosetta, they mounted up and headed out.

Midafternoon they stopped to water the horses at a small creek in a notch between two mountain peaks that looked like the profiles of a pair of old men arguing. Cain's mouth was parched, and he knelt near the water and dipped a hand and drank. His hand, though, was trembling so much that little of the water reached his mouth, so he bent and put his face right into the creek and drank liberally. He removed his shirt and lifted the soaking bandage to check on the wound. It was swollen considerably, the flesh around it turning a dark purple color like uncooked calf's liver.

"Here, let me look at that," Rosetta said to him, pushing his hand away and inspecting the wound herself. "Lordy. Whyn't you tell me you was shot this bad, Cain?"

"Nothing to be done about it."

"Could a found us a doctor."

She stood and went over to his saddlebags and got some clean rags. When she returned, she soaked them in the water and washed away the dried blood.

"Easy," he cried at her rough touch.

"Stop your bellyachin'," she replied. Then she put her face down to the wound and sniffed. She wrinkled her nose and said, "That there's infected, Cain."

"Since when did you become a doctor?" he said to her.

"I done enough doctorin' to know that needs tending to."

"I'm all right."

"You ain't all right." She placed her hand to his forehead. "You feel like a skillet."

"We should get going," he said.

Rosetta shook her head. "You fixin' to kill yourself, Cain? We need to get you to a doctor right quick."

"The fellow back at the store said the closest was in Hagerstown. A day's ride."

"You ain't gonna make another day in the saddle."

"He said there was a midwife by the name of Maddy. Just past a swamp along the way. She did some doctoring."

She rinsed the bloody cloth in the water and dabbed his forehead with it. Then she gathered some moss from nearby trees and applied it to his wound.

"That'll draw out some a the poison. But that bullet's got to come out. The sooner, the better."

Before he saddled up, he put on the new shirt he'd bought and then got the bottle of whiskey from his saddlebags and took a long sip. The wound still pained him, so he took another, without bringing much relief.

They continued on for the rest of the day, heading up into the mountains. Toward sunset, the road entered a dense forest of tall hemlocks, majestic trees whose limbs hung out over the road, forming a kind of tunnel. As they headed into it, Cain was put in mind of the beginning of *The Inferno*, where Dante is entering into Hades: *I found myself within a forest dark.*

The road appeared to him to waver and undulate, to be a thing not made of solid earth. Cain had grown progressively worse—his skin pallid and feverish, and he shivered so hard his teeth chattered. However, if he leaned forward over the pommel, he found that the pain in his side was to some degree lessened, so he dropped the reins and rested his head against the horse's warm, lathered crest.

When Rosetta saw him slumped over like that, she rode up ahead.

"Cain. Cain!" she called, nudging his shoulder. Yet her voice arrived in his brain garbled, as one heard from underwater. She got down off the mare and led both horses into the woods at the side of the road. She helped Cain from the saddle, and he leaned on her for support as she guided him over to a cushioned bed of hemlock needles where he collapsed in a heap. "I'm cold," he said. So she fetched his bedroll and spread a blanket over him. She squatted above him, looking down at him with a scornful look on her face.

"What?" he asked.

"Tole you, you needed to get that bullet out."

"You like to be right, don't you?"

"You're in a fix now," she said.

"I've been in them before," he replied stubbornly.

"So how you gone get yourself out of this one?" she said, smiling almost vindictively.

"Don't you worry, I'll figure something out."

"How 'bout I ride on ahead and get help in Hagerstown."

"No."

"Why not?"

"Too dangerous," he explained, his voice hardly above a whisper.

"I'll be careful."

"Somebody catch you on a stolen horse, what do you think is going to happen?"

"I can tell 'em my massa sent me to fetch help."

He shook his head. "They'll suspect you're a runaway making up some story. I can't let you go."

"If I don't, you gonna die."

"I can't let you."

She stared down at him, searching his eyes. "What's the matter, Cain? You worried I'll take off and leave you?"

He just stared up at her.

"That it, ain't it? You worried I won't come back. That you'll lose the re-ward money."

A fresh wave of pain shot through him then, turning his body rigid as the ache stiffened his muscles.

"I can't let you go," he repeated.

"Huh!" she scoffed. "How you fixin' to stop me, Cain?"

"I'll stop you," he said. He reached under the blanket for his Colt, but she easily wrested it out of his hand and pointed the big gun at him. Then she looked down at him and laughed cruelly, a side he'd not seen in her before.

"How it feel, Cain?" she said.

"How's what feel?"

"You bein' at my mercy now. The high-and-mighty soul catcher don't look so big now."

He just looked weakly up at her.

"I ought to put a bullet in you, after what you done. You and ever' other one like you."

He saw that pent-up rage flare up again, the sort he'd seen when she'd taken the hatchet to the blackbirder's face. The sort he'd noticed in other Negroes, silent, deadly, waiting to get a taste of revenge on the white man.

"Like I tole you before, you didn't have to come after me," she said. "You *chose* to."

"I didn't want them selling you downriver."

"I ain't talkin' 'bout that," she snapped at him angrily. "I mean, you didn't have to come after me in the first place. You didn't have to bring me back to that man. You *chose* to do that, Cain."

He started to say something, but she cut him short.

"And I don't want to hear 'bout your blasted word. 'Bout honor or any a that bunkum every white southerner talks about like it was gospel. Ever'body got a choice," she said, her voice taut as a bow string on a fiddle. He thought of their conversation that night on the riverbank back in New Jersey, about everybody having a choice. "You made your choice to come after me and you got what you deserve. Ain't got nothin' to do with me." When he remained silent, she said, "By rights, I ought to leave you here to die." She stood and walked a few feet away, staring off into the darkened woods. Then she turned around and came back over to him. "Tell me one good reason why I shouldn't get on that horse and take off out a here and never look back. And don't go sayin' you saved my life. We'd neither of us be in this fix if'n you'd minded your own damn business."

"I suppose I couldn't blame you if you did."

"Damn right, you couldn't blame me. I got this child to think about. I don't need to be obligin' myself to some man gonna bring us back to slavery. Some damn *white* man. No matter what he did for me."

"You're right," Cain said.

"'Course, I'm right."

"Can I ask you one favor before you go?" Cain said.

"All depends," she said, the anger slowing.

"Could you build me a fire?"

"You want me to build you a fire?"

"If you would. And put a pan of water on to boil."

"What you fixin' to do?"

"Make some coffee. I'm cold and I'd appreciate a cup of warm coffee."

Rosetta stood there for a moment, debating. Then she shook her head and set about building a fire. When she got it going good, she headed off into the woods with a canteen in search of water. She returned after a while, filled a pot with water, and put it on the fire to boil. Then she scavenged for kindling and put it in a pile within Cain's reach.

"There," she said. "That should hold you awhile. You be needing anything else, Cain? 'Fore I go."

"Bring my saddlebags over here."

She brought the saddlebags back and placed them on the ground beside him, then she stood there with her hands on her hips, looking down on him. He glanced up at her silently.

"Don't be lookin' at me like that," she said.

"Like what?"

"Like you doing. I don't owe you nothin'. Not one damn thing."

"Never said you did."

"Good. Just so we straight on that."

He nodded.

"I be going now," she said. "You just remember—that bullet in you is your own doin'."

"Sure," he replied. "If you see any riders, you make sure you take to the woods. And don't trust anyone. Even if they tell you they're Quakers. If you make Hagerstown, you turn north. Just a few miles and you'll cross the Mason-Dixon line. You'll be in Pennsylvania, but don't let your guard down. There'll be blackbirders all along that stretch. Stay off the main roads. And here," he said, pulling from his boot and extending toward her the smaller Tranter. "I'll trade you this for the Colt. It's easier to handle. Ever fire a gun?"

"I know which is the business end," she said.

"It still kicks pretty hard, so hold it with two hands and aim low and for the body. Don't look a man in the face before you shoot. Harder to shoot somebody if you look him in the eyes."

"Don't you worry none," she scoffed, shoving the gun into the pocket of her dress. "It comes to it, I won't have no trouble shootin' a white man."

"No, I don't suppose you would," he said, and tried to form a smile. "You have that money purse I gave you?"

"I do."

He reached into his pocket and withdrew his billfold. He removed some bills and gave them to her. He thought she might be too proud to accept them, but she took them and stuffed them into her pocket with the gun.

She nodded a thanks, then went over to the horse and mounted, as easily as if she'd been doing it every day of her life.

"Take care of yourself, Rosetta," he called to her.

"You, too, Cain," she replied. Then, almost as an afterthought, she added, "If'n I run into that Maddy, I'll send her back to you."

"Sure," he replied. But both of them knew it was just something she said so she could leave him with a free conscience.

With that, she took off into the darkness. Soon the horse's hoofbeats faded to silence, and Cain was alone.

He built up a good fire. He wanted it to last the night, keep away animals in case he fell asleep or passed out. From his pocket he removed his clasp knife and from the saddlebags got the box with his gun supplies and took out the bullet mold. He dropped the knife and the bullet mold into the pot of boiling water, then took two long drafts of whiskey. After that, he removed the bandage to expose the inflamed wound. With a piece of cloth he grasped the handle of the knife and put it over the fire, heated it until the blade was red-hot and he could feel the warmth creeping back up into the handle. Then he lifted it out of the flames and, without giving his resolve a chance to weaken, he placed the flat side of the blade flush against the wound.

The breath went out of him as if he'd been kicked by a mule, and he screamed like a banshee.

He continued pressing the blade against his flesh, cursing to high heaven. He cursed all manner of things, living and dead, animate and inanimate: the trees and the hills and the night air simply because it was there, the blackbirder who'd shot him, Tranter for making the gun that he'd used to put the bullet in his side, Eberly for sending him on this mission, Misters Clay and Webster for writing the blasted Fugitive Slave Act. He even cursed God for fashioning Africans in the first place, figuring if there were no Negroes there wouldn't be slavery and he would have had some other vocation in which he was less likely to be gutshot. He wasn't making much sense, but the pain had muddled his thoughts, narrowed his mind to a fine point in which subtle distinctions didn't matter. When the ache in his side and the sickening stench of his own burning flesh overcame him, he rolled onto his right and vomited. After a while the sickness passed,

and he was able to catch his breath. Then before his will or strength
failed him, he went back to work.

With the cloth he picked the handles of the bullet mold out of
the boiling water. They were shaped like a pair of pliers, with a sharp
pincer at the end for cutting lead sprues. During the war he'd once
seen a surgeon extract a piece of grapeshot from a wound using a
bullet mold when he hadn't had regular surgical tongs. Cain pressed
them against the wound, trying to force the ends into the hole, but
it was too small. So he picked up the knife again and started cutting
along the grain of the muscle, enlarging the opening. He got only a
short way, though, before he was overcome by pain, and he passed
out. He came to in a few minutes and tried again. He got a little
farther before he passed out once more.

When he awoke, he tried again, and this time he was able to open
the hole wide enough for the bullet mold to enter. He pushed the
mold into the incision, following the track of the wound. He probed
around, searching for the lump of lead that had bitten into his flesh.
He had to do it more by feel than by eye, as the angle was too sharp
for him to see, and besides blood seeped out and coated everything.
Twice he had to stop and mop up the blood with the cloth, before
plunging the mold back into the wound. It felt like the fingers of
death reaching right into him, trying to grab hold of his very soul and
yank it out of his body. Still, he kept at it with a single-mindedness
that blunted the pain somewhat. He told himself that he needed to be
careful not to damage his internal organs and end up making things
worse than they already were, though he didn't see that as likely. He
was about to give up on the entire notion when, beneath the broken
rib, down toward his kidney, he felt something hard and compact,
and it made a clicking sound against the metal mold. After several
attempts, he was finally able to snag it with the pincer ends and pull
it out. When, at last, he held the bloody .32 caliber ball up to the
firelight, he was filled with something akin to pride. The lead bullet
looked like the eye of some creature fashioned by Hephaestus. He
put the ball into his coat pocket, thinking that, if he were somehow
to survive this, it would make for an interesting conversation piece
over a whiskey ages and ages hence.

The thought of whiskey prompted him to take a sizable drink from his bottle. He was weakened and shivering so badly now that he could barely hold the bottle to his lips without spilling it. Then he splashed some directly onto the wound, as he'd seen the doctors do in the war. After that he packed the wound as best he could with cotton cloths to stanch the flow of blood, which was considerable. He was exhausted, his limbs weary and leaden. He lay back on the soft ground, staring up into the gritty darkness overhead. He couldn't see stars or sky, and felt saddened that he would die without ever having seen them again.

As tired as he was, though, his mind was very clear and alert, more so perhaps than it had ever been. Yet he wasn't afraid. More disappointed than anything. It wasn't dying so much that troubled him as it was having left things so unfinished, so many loose ends. His beloved horse in the hands of some scoundrel who'd work him till he dropped in his traces. His never having realized his dream of going out west, starting over, making a new life for himself. Most of all, the business with Rosetta. Part of him, even now, wanted to complete what he'd started, finish his job, see to it that she was brought safely back. But another part felt differently. This part knew something with the certainty that comes only to a man facing the imminent prospect of his own demise: he wouldn't have brought her back. Though he'd not been aware of it, somewhere the idea must have been brewing in him for a while. Maybe as far back as that night he had watched her bathe in the river and come walking out of the water like some Venus emerging from the ocean's foam, when he learned that she was carrying a life inside her. Maybe even before that, from the very first time he'd seen her in the streets of Boston gazing into that window at the dress.

He thought it odd that this decision had come to him only now, but then again, maybe that's why he allowed himself to think it—when it was no longer in his power to decide her fate one way or the other. In any case, he marveled at the change in himself, this sudden alteration in his thinking. Not only would he *not* have returned her, he actually found himself hoping she'd make it to freedom. For one thing, it let himself off the hook—his having captured her and brought her south would no longer matter. For another, in an odd way it pleased him that Eberly wouldn't get what he'd paid for. He pictured Rosetta riding through the night. He saw the wind in her face, blowing her shawl back, her urging the horse onward, the fear and hope mingling in her eyes, the baby inside her jouncing and wondering what all the commotion was. He pondered her chances of making it to freedom. Not much, he knew, but one in a million was better than going back to Eberly. And she'd already made it once, so she was not someone to underestimate. If he were a praying man, he'd have prayed for her. Then again, if he were that, he'd have prayed for himself, too.

Something else came unbidden to him then, the sort of revelatory notion that comes to a man when he has a glimpse of the abyss, when all the restraints that had bound him to a life and a certain view of the world are cast off and he is momentarily freed to think his own thoughts for once. It was a curious notion, one that both confused and yet made everything suddenly clear to him. Above all, he knew that the *only* reason he even entertained it now was exactly because he would never have to contemplate its actuality. Still, for a moment he let himself picture her once more, the soft tension of her mouth, the strange, ever-changing blue of her eyes, the way her burnished skin shone in the firelight. In his mind he reached out and touched her face lightly, almost the way the blind man had touched his own face. *Yes*, he thought. Then, because the image pained him so, he pushed the whole notion from his thoughts, willed it back into whatever dark recess of his heart had given rise to it. And then he remembered what the blind man had said to him. How if he made the wrong choice things would go hard for him. He had and they did.

Help her, he thought. *Please help her.*

The last thing he recalled, the last thing he felt he would *ever* recall, was the tremulous cry of a screech owl wafting through the night. *Who-who-who?* it cried.

For some time, Cain slipped in and out of consciousness. All manner of peculiar images swept by him. One moment he was sitting on the side of the bed, brushing his mother's hair, the next he was watching a woman lying completely naked on the roof of a cabin that floated by on a surging river. There was even a frightening series of bloody visions of the men he'd killed, both in and out of war. They all stared at him as a body, with the silent, accusatory eyes of the damned. The last dream he had was of the Indian girl. She lay beside him in the hut, her warm body naked against his. She felt so real, so palpable, her skin like a wildfire against his own. When he shivered with cold, she held him tightly, pressing him against her. *Cain*, she whispered hotly into his ear. *Cain*.

When he came to finally, it was dark. The fire blazed nearby, but he nonetheless shivered with cold. His mouth was parched, and his head drummed to its own sullen beat. When he moved a little to his left, he felt his side flare up with pain. As his eyes focused, he saw, sitting across from him, a small, shriveled form squatting on its haunches. An old woman. She was as black as coal, her tiny face as furrowed as a prune. She wore a white kerchief wrapped about her head, and extending from her mouth was a long corncob pipe. Leaning over the fire, she stirred something in a scorched pot. For a moment, he thought he was still dreaming and that she was the Indian girl's grandmother. But then she spoke, and he realized he was awake.

"For a while there, young feller, I thought you was a gone coon," she said to him.

Cain tried to get hold of one of the thoughts fluttering around in his head, but they eluded him and he just stared across the fire at her.

"You done a fair job a doctorin' yourself," the old woman said. Without straightening, she moved crablike over toward him and squatted beside him. She put a cup of some awful-smelling liquid to his mouth and helped him to sit up. "Drink this."

Cain was so repulsed at the smell, he turned away from it.

"You ain't out the woods yet. Drink!"

The liquid tasted as bad as it smelled, and he had to fight gagging when he swallowed. He then thought of Rosetta. He tried once more to speak, but he had no more luck this time.

"Hush," the woman scolded. "Get you some rest."

Whatever she'd given him made his eyelids grow heavy. In a little while he was asleep. He dreamed once more that the Indian girl had come and lain with him. He could feel her naked body against his, warm and sweet as whiskey, her arms wrapped around him, hands rubbing his chest.

When he woke again sometime later, the old woman was gone. In her place, Rosetta was squatting near the fire. It was light out now, though the sun was hidden behind a mist hovering close to the ground. She was turned at an angle away from him, chopping wood, and didn't see that his eyes had opened. He watched her for a moment. He noticed her hands, how finely made they were, long and thin, with fingers like those of some highborn mistress, but also how strong and supple they were, how they moved with such deliberateness and assurance as she wielded the hatchet, the same one she had used on the blackbirder's face. Then he looked at her profile, the fullness of her mouth, the slight overbite she had, the smoothness of her honey brown skin.

"Morning," he said.

"Well, look who it is," she replied, turning toward him, a faint smile framing the corners of her mouth.

"Didn't think I'd see you again," Cain said.

"I was thinkin' the same thing about you."

He brought his right hand up in front of his face and looked at it, turned it this way and that, as if seeing it for the very first time, the way an infant is dazzled by its own limbs.

"I had some dreams," he offered.

"That you did. You were talkin' up a storm."

"I dreamt you had turned into an old lady."

She looked over at him and chuckled. "Wasn't no dream, Cain. That was old Maddy. And lucky for you, I found her."

Rosetta explained how she'd come upon the cabin near a swamp on the road to Hagerstown. How she'd told the old lady that lived there of a man who was dying, pleading with her to come back and help her. When Maddy first laid eyes on him, she'd said, "Chile, you brung me all this way for a *white* man?" Yet she stayed and tended to

Cain's wounds. Made him poultices from dogwood trees and linden roots, from herbs she had brought in a leather pouch, boiling them and putting them on his wounds.

"She kept telling me you were done for. But God musta heard my prayers."

"Where did that Maddy go?"

"Had to midwife a woman in labor. But she said she be back."

"How long have I been out?"

"Goin' on four days."

"Jesus!" he said, trying to raise himself. As he did, he felt the stabbing pain in his side commence again, like the bite of a small feist dog. "Damn!" he cursed.

"Jess set still. You ain't ready to go nowhere," she said to him.

"My horse—"

"You never mind 'bout your horse. Maddy said for you to stay put till she got back." From a pot at the edge of the fire she poured a cup of a brownish liquid. Then she came over and squatted next to him. "Here. You're suppose to drink this."

She held up his head and tipped the cup toward his mouth.

"What in the Sam Hill is that?" he said, wincing at the taste.

"Drink it all up you want to get better."

He looked up at her. In the hazy morning light, her eyes were smooth and soft. He thought then of the dreams he'd had about the Indian girl.

"I dreamt of that Indian girl," he said.

"Yeah," she replied, having him drink more of the awful-tasting brew.

"I was cold, and she came and lay down beside me."

Rosetta smiled. "What she look like?"

"She had long dark hair. Dark eyes. Her skin was soft, the color of acorns."

"She pretty, this dream girl a yours?"

"Yes. She was pretty."

He realized that he was hoping to make Rosetta jealous. But she only looked down at him and offered a cryptic smile.

"What?" he asked.

"Wasn't no dream," she said. "You was shakin' real bad. Maddy said I should get under the blanket and warm you."

He looked at her, confused for a moment, then exclaimed, "That was you?"

She smiled at him, nodded.

After a while, he said, "What made you come back?"

"Damned if I know. Drink some more," she told him curtly. She held his head up again. "Wasn't that I didn't give it serious consideration, Cain. When I come to Maddy's place, I thought hard on jess keepin' on going. Heading north. I come this close to doin' it," she said, holding her thumb and forefinger a hair's distance apart.

"What changed your mind?"

"Just plain stupidity, I guess."

"Did you think I wouldn't bring you back?"

She snorted, shook her head. "I figure you gonna do what you have to. But my coming back hadn't a thing to do with you, Cain. It had to do with me. I thought, Rosetta, you can't just leave him to die. That wouldn't be right."

"This from the same woman who said she'd kill me if she got the chance."

"Killin' you was one thing. Leavin' you to die was another. And not after how you come to be shot on my account."

"I thought you said it was my own fault for coming after you?"

"It was. But I figured you didn't have to risk your neck to find me. I prayed to God, askin' him to tell me what to do. I was goin' back and forth when some patrollers come riding up. I took to the woods until they passed. Then I got to thinkin' 'bout my chances of makin' it to freedom on a stolen horse. Figured not much. So it's lucky for you them patrollers come by when they did, Cain."

What had been so clear the night he was alone and thinking he would die, no longer seemed so clear now. Could he just turn her loose? Let her go free? There were certain considerations that he had to weigh now in the harsh light of day. He started to say something, but she told him firmly, "Hush up and drink some more."

Over the next couple of days he slowly began to recover, gradually regaining his strength so that he was able to stand and walk a little. The old woman, Maddy, rode in on a black mule to check on her patient.

"You lookin' only half-dead now," she joked, smiling to show gums that didn't boast a single tooth.

Cain was lying near the fire. She lifted his shirt and checked on the wound in his side.

"Comin' along. Look like you gonna pull through after all, young feller."

"He a stubborn one," Rosetta said.

"Chile," the old woman instructed Rosetta, "g'won down to the creek yonder and fetch me some water."

After Rosetta had left, the old woman turned to Cain. From the fire she took a piece of kindling and lit her pipe. She stared at him for a while with her dark, gummy eyes.

"I reckon I'm looking at a soul catcher," she said after a while. "Is you?"

"I am," Cain said.

"If she'd a tole me at first, I'da let you die."

"I'm grateful you didn't."

"Ain't me you need being grateful to." She looked off in the direction where Rosetta had headed.

"I have responsibilities," he said.

The old woman snorted. "Responsibilities? That girl done gave you back your life."

"Don't you think I know that?"

"You don't act like you do. She said you a good man. That you ain't like other white folks."

Cain shrugged.

The old woman frowned so her entire face seemed to collapse in on itself. "Well, is you?"

"Am I what?"

"A good man."

"I don't know."

"You know what her massa done to her?"

"Some."

"And you gone bring that poor girl back to him?"

"He could make things hard for me."

"For you! And what you think it be like for her? Going back there. You know that girl's with chile?"

He nodded.

"That baby doan deserve to be born a slave. It's drunk of freedom, and slavery would only taste of gall in its mouth."

"That wasn't my doing."

The old woman smiled, exposing her pointed pink tongue. She tapped her pipe clean on a rock. "It all white folks' doing. Every single one a you to blame for it."

"Wasn't me put that baby in her."

"Maybe not. But bringing her back there you might as well."

"I've been more than fair to her," Cain said.

"Fair?" the woman exclaimed. In one sudden motion she pulled a knife from her boot and placed it against his throat. "You listen to me, soul catcher," she hissed, her eyes flaring with anger, her wrinkled face turning hard as stone. "I could make sure you don't bring her back. I killed white men before. Don't mind doing it again neither. Wouldn't take but a flick a this here knife and we wouldn't even be talkin'."

Cain could feel the blade against his throat. His gun was under the blanket, but he didn't have the strength to fight her.

In the next second, though, her face changed, softened. With her other hand, she reached up and stroked Cain's cheek lightly. Her hand was hard and calloused, yet smooth as a piece of sanded pinewood. He thought of Lila's hands.

"But she says you a good man and I'm willing to believe her."

Just then they could hear Rosetta approaching. The old woman slipped her knife back into her boot.

"How's he doing?" Rosetta asked.

"Just fine," the old woman replied, staring down at Cain.

They ate supper together and then turned in for the night. As he lay there, Cain thought of the blind man's prophecy again, that two souls would be entrusted to his care. At first he'd thought it had meant the two slaves. Then later, when he learned that Rosetta was pregnant, he thought perhaps it meant her and her unborn child. But now he wasn't so sure. Maybe one of the souls the blind man had meant was his own, which he thought peculiar, as he didn't reckon on having a soul to save. Still, it was a thing to ponder on.

In the morning Maddy got on her mule.

"You set tight for a while, young feller," she warned Cain. "Don't wanna go opening up that wound of yours."

"Thank you," Rosetta said.

"Take care a him," Maddy said to her. "See that he stays out a trouble." Then, to Cain, she said, "Think about what I said. And don't go gettin' yourself shot up no more."

18

It was several more days before Cain was strong enough to ride. Even then, Rosetta reminded him of what Maddy had told him, that the wound could open up and start bleeding again. But Cain figured that the little crookback already had nearly a week's head start on him, and he worried about ever seeing Hermes again.

"You wanna go killin' yourself over some horse?" she cautioned him as they rode along.

"He's not just some horse."

"That's the thing I can't figure, Cain."

"What's that?" he asked.

"You white folks put your niggers in chains, work them till they drop, flog them near to dying. But then you go and risk your neck for a dumb animal."

They rode west toward Hagerstown, Cain on the bay, Rosetta beside him on the mare. She would ride for miles without so much as a word. He'd glance over at her, and she'd be staring straight ahead. So quiet was she that he sometimes almost forgot she was there. He even found himself missing Little Strofe's mindless prattle. Except for the ache in his side, the journey was almost to his liking. The day stretched out sunny and seasonably warm for May, the slowly greening mountains outlined against the pale blue of the sky. Lilac and mountain laurel, dogwood and rhododendron bloomed along the lower ridges. Now and then, he'd spot a red-tailed hawk or an eagle, circling lazily over a field. As they approached the small town of Thurmont, the sky turned preternaturally dark, as if by a sudden eclipse, and the air stank foully of fire and ash. There was a metallic taste in Cain's mouth that reminded him of the way the air in war tasted. They soon learned the cause. At the base of a mountain was an iron foundry with several smokestacks belching black smoke. Behind the foundry, an entire mountainside had been stripped bare by mining. In the road, they passed miners and colliers and founders trudging off to work. They stopped to ask several if they'd seen a man come through fitting Dr. Chimbarazo's description. The workers who spoke English at all did so with a heavy German accent. None had seen the little crookback.

Around noon, though, they came upon a teamster driving a wagon pulled by a couple of Belgians. The wagon was filled with barrels of whiskey.

"You see a stumpy little fellow in a black caravan pass this way?" Cain asked the driver. "Calls himself Dr. Chimbarazo."

The man, about Cain's own age, had reddish blond hair and was stoutly built; he wore leather sherryvallies over his pantaloons and a dark slouch hat.

"Passed him about four days back," the man explained. "Tried to sell me some of his elixirs."

"Which way was he headed?" Cain asked.

"West. Toward Hagerstown."

"Did you take notice of his horse?"

"Bay colored if I recollect."

"And his face."

"Blaze."

"What are the chances I could relieve you of some of that whiskey you're toting?" Cain asked the man. He'd not had a drop of whiskey or laudanum in several days and had worked up a considerable hankering. "I'd be happy to pay for it."

The man got down from his seat and walked over to Cain.

"Do you have something to put it in, friend?"

Cain emptied out his canteen.

"Use this," he said.

The man went around to the barrels and filled the canteen, then walked back over to Cain. Before he gave it to him, he had a healthy sip of it himself, wiped his mouth on his hairy forearm.

"There you go."

Cain had a drink of the whiskey. "That's right fine liquor." He started to reach into his pocket to pay the man, but the other held up his hand.

"My compliments."

Cain thanked the man, and they continued on their way. As he rode along, he would take a nip now and then from the canteen. After a while, the pain in his side no longer concerned him as much.

"I thought you give up that poison," Rosetta said to him.

"Well, you thought wrong," he replied.

"That's the devil's drink."

"Me and the devil have been boon drinking companions for some time."

"Eberly used to get slewed on that."

Cain looked over at her, waiting for more. But she fell silent.

They rode on for several more miles before she spoke again. "I have to stop," she said as they rounded a curve in the road.

"We need to push on."

"I'm hungry."

"Looks like a creek up ahead. We'll stop there."

When they reached it, they dismounted and made camp beneath a sycamore tree, just beginning to leaf out in the spring weather. While Rosetta started a fire, Cain led the horses down to the water. He hobbled them, then got his canteen and took a drink, savoring the strong bite of the bourbon whiskey. He stood staring down into the creek, which was clear and sandy bottomed, with minnows darting about like thoughts in an addled brain. Like his own thoughts now. He glanced back over his shoulder at Rosetta, who was chopping wood. In the back of his mind, he heard the voice of Maddy: *That girl done gave you back your life.*

Later, when lunch was ready, Cain sat across from her, eating corn pone and salt pork. He hadn't yet gotten his appetite back, and the food merely filled up a space within him. Rosetta, though, ate voraciously, tearing into the salt pork and wiping up the grease with the corn pone and then cutting herself another piece. She must have sensed he was looking at her.

"What?" she asked, glancing up at him.

"I didn't say anything."

"With you, Cain, it's always what you ain't sayin'."

He took another sip from his canteen. "What did you tell that woman?"

"What woman? You mean Maddy? Didn't tell her nothin'."

"She knew I was a slave catcher."

"Anybody could see that. Leastways, any Negro."

"What else did you tell her about me?"

"Nothin'."

"She said you told her I was a good man."

"Might of. What difference does it make?"

"I'm not."

"You sure do like to think that," she scoffed. From the skillet she picked up another piece of fried corn pone and took a bite out of it. "I usta think you put yourself above them others, the Strofes and that Preacher fellow. That you were high-and-mighty, like Mr. Eberly."

"I'm not a *damn* thing like him," he hissed, taking offense.

"See," she said, smiling that her comment had struck a nerve. "And you're right. You're not. But that's just what I mean, Cain. You have a good heart. Thing is, you want to go and deny it. It's easier that way."

"You don't know a thing about me."

"That's where you're wrong, Cain. I know you. Maybe better'n you know yourself. You like to pretend you don't have a heart. That you're hard like a stone. That nothin' bothers you. You ain't the only one neither. Lots of folks, especially white folks, find it easier to deny their goodness than go through the trouble of doing what they know's right. You think most white folks, even most white southerners, don't know ownin' another human being is dead wrong?"

"Most I know believe in it."

"That's a lie. You know that well as I do. Not in their heart of hearts. It's just that it's easier to tell themselves they believe it's all right. If they didn't, they'd have to give up ever'thing they believed in, everything they got on the sweat and blood of Negroes, and that, they ain't ready to do. That's the way most people live, buryin' things down deep inside them. Take you, Cain."

"What about me?"

The fire started to smoke, and she jabbed at it with a stick. She stared across it at him, her eyes narrowing to gray slits.

"What's buried in your heart, Cain?" she asked.

"Nothing," he replied, taking another drink from the canteen.

"Ever'body's got something buried. Something they won't tell nobody. Tha's why you drink that poison, ain't it?"

"I told you why. I drink it on account of the pain in my leg," he replied.

"Huh! It's about that Indian girl, ain't it?"

"You don't know what you're talking about," he snapped at her.

"You loved her, didn't you, Cain?"

"No," he said, then paused. "It was a long time ago."

"You loved her and then you blamed yourself for her dying. Tha's why you drink that stuff."

"I told you, I don't know."

"Sure you do," she challenged.

"That'll be enough," he said.

She shook her head, smiled at him.

"What?" he asked.

"Whenever you don't want to talk 'bout something, you say that's enough. Like you can just stop yourself from thinkin' on it."

"How about you?" he asked. "What do *you* have buried?"

"I'm a slave, remember. I can't own nothin'. Not even secrets."

"You must have something."

She looked at him evenly. "You wouldn't want to know, Cain."

And he knew she was right. As he took another sip from the canteen, an image slipped into his mind, something that disturbed him like a foul smell: it was of Eberly's hands on her. He saw his pale, clean, old man's hands, riddled with blue veins, roving over her smooth skin, touching her, exploring her, impressing his ownership of her body upon her, the way a cowhide or a chain or a brand did. It was the first time he'd actually allowed himself to picture such a scene. He couldn't say why he pictured it now, but he did. And this made him think again of what she'd suffered at the hands of the blackbirders. A sick feeling welled up in him, one composed of rage and of anger, and of something else, too. He realized it was jealousy, the sort a man gets when the thing he most desires is possessed by another.

He scraped his remaining food into the fire and stood, walked over to the horses. The mare nudged his arm, looking for something to eat. From his saddlebags he got out some oats and fed her by hand.

In a little while, Rosetta followed him over. She stood there, gazing distractedly into the stream.

"I ain't never told nobody this," she began. "Ain't so sure I want to be tellin' you, neither."

He glanced over at her and waited. He wasn't sure he wanted to hear what she had to say. She didn't look at him as she spoke, just kept staring down into the water.

"My momma and me live in the slave cabins, down near the tannery. That when the missus still living, before he move us up into the big house. My momma was a fine-looking woman. Prettier'n me. Eyes the color of molasses. And strong. She could work as hard in the fields as any man. She learned herself to read the Bible and she taught me, too. About the Israelites held captive by that old pharaoh. How they waited to be led out of bondage. Before Mr. Eberly started to take an interest in her, there was a slave name of Solomon used to come around. He was kind, used to bring her things. She liked him a lot. I did, too. But then Mr. Eberly took to visiting her after it was dark. When he did, Momma make me sleep on a pallet on the floor. She told me, 'Stay there, Rosie. And hush, chile, no matter what you hear.' Mr. Eberly and the missus didn't have no children of they own. Later, the missus caught a fever and died. That when he move Momma and me into the big house, so he could have her all to himself. Had us a room right behind the kitchen. He come to her there at night. There wasn't no pallet for me to sleep on, so I lay in bed, right beside them. I turned my back to them, kept real quiet. Tried to sleep. But I couldn't help hearing him making noises, grunting on top of her. Smell him, too. A liquored-up smell. Sometimes she would hold my hand while he had at her. Later, she'd hug me, tell me, 'It all right, Rosie. G'won to sleep.'

"After some years, I grew up. Started to become a woman myself. When I commenced to bleeding, started to grow breasts, that when he took notice of me. I be doing chores around the house, cleaning and such, and he give me this look, the kind men do to something they have a hankerin' for. Momma saw the way he look at me, too. She tell me be careful, Rosie, not to let myself be alone with him. So I tried being careful, kept out of his way, never looked him in the eye. Momma even rubbed cat pee all over me so I smell bad and he wouldn't want to come near me." With this, she stopped and gave out a brittle little noise, part laughter, part sigh. "But that didn't stop him. No, sir. This one time I was in the kitchen scrubbing the floor on my hands and knees. I was about twelve. Mr. Eberly come in the house after he was out riding. He smell of the drink. I remember the way he'd get with Momma when he was all liquored up. Low-down mean. Not hitting mean, that wasn't his way. He left that to others. But mean the way some men can be just looking at you or talking, make you feel like you're dirty. He come up behind me and bent over and started touching me. My back and shoulders, stroking my hair. Saying how pretty I was. How I was turnin' into a right fine-looking woman. My momma come in the house then with a pile of clothes she'd been washing, and she see Mr. Eberly touching me. She say to him, 'Please don't do that, massa.' She say that I just a girl still. She begged him. 'Please, massa, leave her be.' Said he could do anything he wanted to her but to leave me alone. His eyes got the way they can get, cold and hard as iron."

Here Rosetta's voice changed. Cain was surprised at how much it became the haughty, aristocratic southern voice of Eberly. She obviously knew that voice intimately, knew its every nuance and pitch. "'Every damn thing on this plantation,' he said, 'is mine. Every last board and nail, every shred of clothing you wear. Every morsel of food you put into your mouths, all of it's mine. And that includes every one of my niggers and everything that's theirs. And I'll do any damn thing I please with any one of them I please. Do you understand?' 'Don't do that, massa,' she said, but that only got him more riled up. He walked over to me and grabbed the front of my dress. 'This here dress is mine,' he cried, ripping the front down so I was half naked. I tried to cover myself but he grabbed my breasts hard, so they hurt. 'These are mine, too.'

"I didn't want to cry but I couldn't help it. Mostly on account of seeing my momma. She had this sorrowful look on her face, that she was shamed she couldn't protect her daughter. But then she tell Mr. Eberly if he didn't stop touching me, she'd kill him. I thought, *Oh, God, no.* Massa swore then, pulled his gun out, and went over and put it against her head. 'Who are you going to kill?' I was crying, begging him not to do that. I said, 'Momma, just go. I be all right.' But she looked him in the eyes and said it again, 'You touch her, I'll kill you.' He tried to laugh it off, but you could see it troubled him, her saying that. 'You think you can kill me?' he said. 'You know you couldn't do that.' Then he changed suddenly, put the gun down and stroked her cheek gently with the back of his hand. She stare at him cold like. 'You touch her, I'll come into your bedroom and cut your throat while you sleeping,' she said. And he knew she was speakin' true. His eyes turned fierce again, and he stormed out and got some of his men. Strofe and a few others. He had Momma taken out and tied to the whipping post. Had Strofe cowhide her with a hundred lashes. She was half dead when they finished.

"He wouldn't let me go tend to her. 'Stead he brought me back inside and took me right there in the kitchen. Push me down hard on the floor and yank up my dress. He was drunk and rough. That first time, I thought I'd 'bout die. When he finish, he got up and pulled up his trousers. He said, 'I didn't want some field nigger spoiling you. Now you're a woman, Rosetta. My woman. And don't you forget it.' Next day, he had Momma brought to the auction block in Richmond and sold her downriver. From then on, I stayed up in the big house with him. He told me he loved me, that he loved me more than anything. Huh! What he felt for me wasn't love. He made me feel lower than dirt. Love don't make you feel like that. Funny thing is, it turned out he was right about one thing. He got me to feeling that I was just a piece of property. *His* property. Worth no more than the heel of his boot. I was fourteen when my chile was born. His, though I never felt that it was. I named him Israel, like in the Bible: 'I arose a mother in Israel.'

"Then one time Mr. Eberly was playin' cards with some a his huntin' friends. He call me and tole me to fetch him another bottle of licker. Israel was sick at the time, had a fever, and I didn't want to leave him alone, so I had him on my hip. I brung him into the room where those men was sittin' and Mr. Eberly he was fit to be tied. He took me aside and said I was never to show my baby around like that again. I said, 'But he's your own blood.' He got so mad I thought he would hit me. 'Stead he said if I did that again he'd sell Israel downriver, just like he done my momma. He held that over my head. Anytime I done something he didn't like he would say he gonna sell Israel downriver. If I made his eggs too hard. If I didn't polish the silverware just so. Anything. So I made up my mind I was gonna run away with my baby, so he couldn't ever take him away from me. And one night I finally did it, I up and run. I didn't get out of the county before they catch me. As punishment, Mr. Eberly sold my baby off. Tha's when I knife him. My only regret is I didn't kill him."

She fell silent then. Cain saw that her jaw was set in anger but that tears were sliding silently down her cheeks. He saw that the telling of it had hurt her, deeply, profoundly, as if its excision from somewhere deep inside her had wounded her as much as the bullet's removal from his side had him. There was something else now that he felt, something that he had managed to bury all the years he'd worked as a slave catcher, telling himself he was just enforcing the law, just doing the bidding of other men who had made the decisions about right and wrong. A thing he knew to be akin to guilt. That which flowed from having white skin and being a man in a world fashioned to meet the needs and desires of white men.

"I'm sorry," he said. She remained still. He reached out and lay a hand on her shoulder. "Rosetta."

Finally, she glanced over at him, the first time since she'd begun to speak.

"I'm sorry," he repeated.

"You and me both, Cain. You and me both."

The sun was just sliding behind the western mountains when they reached Hagerstown. Cain was dog tired, his side aching. Not a sharp pain, just a dull reminder that he'd pushed himself too hard. What he had a hankering for more than anything was a soft bed to lie in and a bottle of whiskey. They rode along a run-down part of town, past a number of unpainted and weary-looking buildings—a general store, a livery, a leather goods shop, an undertaker's, several other businesses. The people they passed stared at them, mostly eyeing Rosetta, a Negro on a fine horse. He stopped finally in front of a squalid-looking doggery. It was housed in a lean-to attached to a feed and grain business. Out front a crudely painted sign said only WHISKEY 2 BITS.

"I'll go in and inquire if anyone has seen him," he said to Rosetta. "You stay here with the horse. I'm going to put the shackles on, so nobody wonders what you're doing here."

Then he went inside. The place smelled yeasty, from the feed business next door. It was empty, save for some old loafer who sat at the end of the bar, which was made of a single rough-hewn pine plank set atop a pair of sawbucks. The barkeep, a tall, raw-boned fellow, stood behind the bar, eating pickled pig's feet from a large jar, sprinkling them liberally with salt. He had about him the look of one who'd recently faced a major disappointment he had not yet acclimated to. His eyes were tinged with yellow and unfocused, his mouth held in a fixed attitude of sullenness. When he saw Cain come in, he seemed, more than anything, annoyed that his repast was about to be disturbed.

"Whiskey," Cain had to call over to him.

Perturbed, the man shoved the rest of a pig's foot into his mouth, got a label-less bottle from behind the bar, and came over and poured Cain a drink in a filthy glass.

"Two bits," he said by way of greeting.

"Any place I could get a room?" Cain said.

"There's Tanney's boardinghouse over on Church. You want anything to eat?"

"What do you have?"

"Pig's feet," the man replied.

Cain shook his head. "You wouldn't happen to have seen a small crookback fellow come through here?"

"We get a lot of folks passing through on the pike."

Cain shook his head. "He'd have been driving a big black caravan. If you'd seen him, you wouldn't forget."

The man shrugged, went back to his eating. He seemed to eat more out of obligation than hunger, the way a body took medicine.

Cain downed his whiskey and started to leave. It was then that the old loafer at the end of the bar called over to him.

"Fellow calls himself Dr. Chimpanzee?" the man said with a snort.

"Something like that."

"His wagon was over near the railroad depot. He was peddling his cures."

"He still there?"

"That I couldn't tell you. Just a half mile past where you're headed."

"Much obliged, friend," Cain said. He left money on the bar to buy the old man a drink and headed out into the street.

He and Rosetta found the railroad depot easily enough. Nailed to a bulletin board near the entrance, a large handbill advertised: COME SEE DR. DELACROIX'S WORLD-FAMOUS INDIAN MEDICINE SHOW. Below was a list of all the maladies that Dr. Delacroix's various tonics and balms and ointments were guaranteed to cure. In a vacant lot just behind the depot, Cain spotted the familiar black caravan. The traces were, of course, empty, and when Cain knocked on the small back door, there was no sign of Dr. Chimbarazo within.

"Now what?" Rosetta asked him.

"I'll find him."

First, though, as daylight was rapidly fading, he decided he'd better find a room. They rode back to Church Street where he located the boardinghouse named Tanney's. As they dismounted, a wide-hipped, red-haired woman came strolling out onto the front porch. She carried a bucket of slops, which she tossed into the alley on the side of the building.

"What can I do for ye?" she asked with a heavy brogue. Her low bodice exposed a sizable portion of large, wrinkly bosom, and from beneath her jaw hung fleshy pink wattles. By the lantern light on the porch, Cain saw that she had comely green eyes and might have been pretty in her day, but that day was so long gone that it was hard to tell. He asked if she had a room.

"Aye. Dollar a night. Another two bits if you'll be wanting food," the woman said. She glanced at Rosetta. "And what of your nigger? There's the barn out back."

"I was hoping for a room for her?"

"Huh! I run a respectable place," she said, offended. "There's the Hampton Hotel. They take in blacks."

He wasn't about to lose sight of her again. From his vest pocket he took out a silver half eagle and handed the coin to her, an amount equivalent to five times what the room cost.

Raising her eyebrows, she looked at the coin, then at Rosetta, weighing her conscience against the money. "'Course, a gentleman needs his diversions," she said, smiling lewdly, showing several missing teeth. "Bring her round back, though. But mind ye, 'tis between us."

"Could she have a bath?"

"So it's a bath she'll be wantin' now," she scoffed, giving Rosetta a sneering look. "If it got out I had a black nigger in the tub, they'd never set foot in it again."

Cain took out another coin and handed it to her.

"I'll find some soap and a basin for her."

In the room, he told Rosetta, "You wait for me here. I want your word you won't try to run again."

"My word?" she said, raising her eyebrows.

"Yes. Promise me."

"You are the most contrary man I ever did meet, Cain," she said. But finally she agreed not to run.

"Lock the door and don't let anyone in except for me. Understand."

"When you comin' back?" she asked.

"Just sit tight."

Then he headed for the door.

"Cain," she said, her voice insistent.

He turned toward her. She took two steps and stopped, her hands out in front of her, the way a person would walk in the dark, fearful of falling. He noted, too, something in her eyes, something he could not quite decipher. Fear for herself? Concern for his welfare? Then he thought, What if something were to happen to him, say somehow he was connected to the killing of those men, and he was arrested. What would become of her?

"You comin' back, ain't ya, Cain?" she asked, as if reading his thoughts.

"If I'm not back by morning, you go over to the livery we passed earlier."

"What are you talkin' about?"

"I'm just saying in case something were to happen to me."

"What's gonna happen to you?"

"I'm just saying if something did. The horses will be there. Take the mare. She's sound, has a smooth gait. Won't give you any trouble. Sell the bay for whatever you can get. Like I told you already, head due north, but stay off the main roads."

"Cain?"

"But I'll be back."

"You'd better."

As he shut the door, he heard her cry out, "You be careful, Cain."

Riding over to the livery, he thought that there was nothing stopping her from bolting. Then again, she could have done that anytime while he was sick. Once more, he wondered why she hadn't. She'd said it was because she couldn't just leave him to die. And yet, she'd nearly killed him herself. He couldn't make sense of her. She was, he felt, a most peculiar creature. In fact, he'd never encountered a slave like her. He'd never encountered *anyone* like her. Sounding in the back of his head were Maddy's words: *That girl done gave you back your life.* She'd saved his life not once but twice already. In some ways he wished she hadn't, that she'd left him to die. It would have been simpler that way. Now he felt obligated, felt he was in her debt, and he didn't like being in anyone's debt. Not hers or Eberly's or anyone else's for that matter. He half hoped that when he returned, she'd have slipped away. Then he wouldn't have to decide what to do. He'd made up his mind about one thing at least: if she ran, he wouldn't go after her. No matter what happened, he wouldn't hunt her down again. He was through hunting down runaways.

But there was something else, too, that troubled him, something that went back to the night he thought he was going to die. Not about Rosetta the runaway slave, but about Rosetta the woman. When he felt certain he was about to die, he'd permitted himself to entertain the notion, but he hadn't died, and now he was thinking it again. He recalled the look in her eyes up in the room, and he thought, too, of how her body had felt against his when he was feverish, how she'd warmed him that night and kept him from dying. Though he didn't want to admit it, there was something more than obligation at work here. It wasn't something he could deny any longer.

By now it was fully dark, the sky peppered with stars. The street-lamps along the main street had been lit and the smell of coal oil was heavy in the air. He found the livery owner tossing hay into the stalls. He told the man, a thickset fellow with bushy gray side-whiskers, that he wanted the horses fed and curried, and that he thought the mare had a loose shoe. He'd heard it clinking as the day went on. He told him that his servant girl might be coming by in the morning to fetch his horses for him, and the man was to let her have them, no questions asked. Cain paid him in advance. As he was about to leave, he heard a familiar sound coming from somewhere in the back of the barn. He walked along, looking into the darkened stalls. In the last but one, he spotted a large horse with a blaze face looking out at him. Even in the dark, he could tell it was Hermes. On spotting him, the horse came right up and pushed his muzzle forcibly against Cain's shoulder.

"Hey, boy," he said, overjoyed at his good fortune. Hermes's long tongue ferreted around in his coat pocket, searching for sugar.

Cain walked back over to the livery owner.

"Where did you get the chestnut stallion?"

"A fellow is boarding him."

"About so big?" Cain asked, holding his hand out waist-high.

"That be him."

Cain mulled over his options. He could tell the man the plain truth, that the horse had been stolen, that it belonged to him. But then again, in the world in which he operated, he knew the plain truth was often as slippery as an eel, and as likely to bite you. He didn't have a bill of sale, a shred of proof that the horse was indeed his. Who's to say that the livery owner would take his word over that of the crookback. Or he could simply stick his gun in the man's face and just take the horse, then and there. That would be the simplest thing to do. But of course they'd get up a posse and come after him. He thought of how ironic it would be if he got hung for stealing his own damn horse. No, he'd have to come up with a better plan.

"Where's the owner?" Cain asked.

"He's staying over at the Hampton."

Cain inquired directions to the place, which turned out to be across town. Before he left the livery, he went back to the stall where Hermes was. He scratched the horse along his muzzle. "Don't you worry. I'll be back for you," Cain promised.

Then he made his way to the Hampton on foot. The squarish, wood-sided building was three stories high with a mansard roof and a porch out front. Before he went in, he checked his Colt as well as the Tranter he kept in his boot. He wasn't sure what he'd do when he found the crookback, figuring he would make it up as he went along.

Inside, he went up to the front desk, behind which a gray-haired Negro wearing a tie and waistcoat sat reading a newspaper.

"I'm looking for a man," Cain said. "He's about so high. Has a hump on his back."

The old man looked up from his paper, eyeing Cain suspiciously. "What's your business with him?"

"I need to talk to him."

"Ain't seen him."

"I owe him some money," Cain lied. "He's expecting me."

The man's expression changed immediately. "In that case, last door on your right," the Negro said, flicking his thumb in that direction. "Make sure you knock first."

Cain walked down the hall and knocked on the last door on the right. It was opened a crack by a bull-necked Negro with a scar that started on his forehead at the hairline and angled down over one gray, sightless eye.

"What you be wanting, mister?" he asked.

"I have business with Dr. Chimbarazo," he explained.

"What sort?"

"It's private."

"Doc's busy," explained the Negro.

"I wanted to buy some of his medicine."

From behind the door he heard the crookback's familiar squeaky voice. "I will be at my wagon tomorrow during regular business hours."

"It's an emergency."

"Show him in," the crookback said.

The scar-faced Negro opened the door and allowed him to enter. Cain found himself in a dimly lit, smoky room where half a dozen men were seated around a table playing cards. They were all black, save one, a ruddy-faced man with a dark, broad-brimmed hat. They turned as a group and stared guardedly at Cain when he entered. Through the haze of cigar smoke he spotted the man called Dr. Chimbarazo on the far side of the table, looking like a child in a grown-up's seat. He had a pile of coins and bills sitting in front of him, a pile larger than that of all the others combined.

Cain made eye contact with the small man. If he recognized Cain, he didn't let on.

"Now what's the nature of this emergency," the small man asked.

"I'm here for my horse," Cain said.

"Your horse?" the small man repeated, frowning.

"Yes, you have him."

"Do you know anything about this feller, Doc?" said the ruddy-faced man, who was seated to his left. He had a big Army dragoon in a holster on his hip, the only person so armed. He seemed to be on familiar terms with the crookback.

"Never saw him before in my life," Dr. Chimbarazo replied. Cain couldn't tell if he was lying or actually believed they'd never met.

"I think you need to turn around and leave, mister," said the white man, who had flat, undertaker eyes. When Cain didn't make a move, he added, "That'd be right now."

"He has my horse and I've come to get him back," Cain said.

"I'm afraid you're mistaken, sir," the crookback replied.

"No, I'm not. You have him. A chestnut stallion with a blaze. I saw him over at the livery."

"Nonsense. I paid cash for that animal," the small man said. "Bought it fair and square."

"Where's your bill of sale then?" Cain asked.

"I'm not under the slightest compunction to show you anything."

"It's my horse. If I have to, I'll go to the law," he threatened.

The crookback smiled, showing his too-white ivory teeth, and glanced over at the red-faced man.

"I'm the law here," he said, pulling back his coat to expose a badge. "Sheriff Huneycutt. You got any proof that the horse in question is yours?"

"I'm telling you it's my horse. It was stolen from me."

"Are you accusing this gentleman of common thievery?" the sheriff asked, barely keeping a straight face. The other men snickered at this.

"Ask him if he knows the horse's name?"

The other men looked at Dr. Chimbarazo, waiting. Instead, he reached into the inside pocket of his frock coat and pulled out a piece of paper, and handed it to the sheriff, who opened and read it silently.

"Says here he bought and paid for the horse, mister."

"That piece of paper doesn't mean a damn thing," Cain said.

"Looks fine to me," the sheriff replied. "What's your name, mister?"

"Cain."

"You have a bill of sale says any different, Mr. Cain?"

Of course, he had no such thing.

"He got that from the men who stole it from me," he explained to the sheriff.

"Who'all was supposed to have stole it from you?"

"Four men back east. They robbed and shot me, took my horse. Left me for dead. Blackbirders. They stole a runaway I was bringing back."

The crookback stared at him hard, as if trying to puzzle out where he'd seen Cain before.

"Got word t'other day they found some men dead over near Gaithersburg," the sheriff said. "By the looks of it, somebody robbed and killed them. Stole one of their horses. You wouldn't know anything about that?"

"No," Cain replied.

"What sort of mount you riding?"

"Like I said, they stole my horse. I'm on foot," he lied.

"Looks like you got the wrong sow by the ear, mister," said the sheriff. "If I was you, I'd head on out of this town before you run into trouble."

"All right, I'll buy him from you," Cain said. "I'll give you fifty dollars."

"He's not for sale," said the little man.

"A hundred." The man shook his head. "A hundred and fifty then."

"I told you he is not for sale."

Having used up his patience, Cain took an angry step toward the little man. He wanted to throttle him. But the large Negro with the scar put a hand on his shoulder. "Friend, you oughta listen to the sheriff and get on outa here 'fore you find yourself in a whole heap o' trouble."

Cain figured he could go back over to the livery that night and take what was his. But as if reading his thoughts, the sheriff said, "Doc's horse turns up missing, I know who to come after. We don't take kindly to horse thieves around these parts."

Cain leveled his gaze at the crookback, then turned to leave.

"Hold on a moment," said the small man. Cain turned and found the man staring closely at him. Slowly, a smile of recognition creased his dark features. "Ah, yes. Now I remember you. You have changed a good deal but you're the man I met on the road. The one with the lovely runaway." The man's face then turned suddenly hard and his eyes flashed with anger. "You pistol-whipped me, you villain."

"You had it coming," Cain said. "You pulled a gun on me. I should have killed you outright."

"Do you still have the girl?" Dr. Chimbarazo asked.

"That's no concern of yours."

"Where are your friends?"

Cain didn't want to admit he was alone, in case the crookback and some of his cronies followed him later and tried to get even.

"They're camped outside of town. They're expecting me."

Once more Cain turned to leave, and once again he was stopped.

"I've an idea," the small man said. "You want your horse back? How about if we play for him?"

Cain paused, turned around once more.

"Play for him?" he asked.

"Yes. Just you and me in a game of poker."

"If I win, I get the horse?" Cain asked.

"How much money do you have to wager?" Dr. Chimbarazo asked.

Cain paused for a moment, wary of confiding to a gambling opponent exactly how much he had available. "Enough."

"I figure my horse is easily worth four hundred. A truly exquisite animal," the man said with a straight face.

"I know his worth," Cain snapped.

"Do you have four hundred to put up?"

Cain shook his head.

"Let him play a few hands then," said one of the other gamblers, a thin, yellow-faced Negro wearing a stovepipe hat. "Give him a chance to win some of that cash you already took from us, Doc."

"Yea, yea," the other men taunted. The crookback stared across at Cain and smiled in a curious sort of way.

"Very well then. I shall give you a chance to win a few hands, and if you reach that amount I'd be willing to put up my horse. Are the terms agreeable to you, sir?" he asked.

"Fine by me," replied Cain, who sat down and took off his coat.

"I'll have your sidearm, mister," the sheriff commanded, reaching for Cain's weapon in his holster. Cain grabbed hold of the man's wrist.

"Nobody takes my gun," Cain said.

"I be givin' it to him, friend," said the scar-faced man. When Cain looked up, he saw that the scar-faced Negro was pointing a large-caliber double-barreled derringer at his face. He let go of the sheriff's wrist and the other removed his weapon.

"A Walker," the sheriff said, admiringly. "They ain't but a few hundred of these made. Were you down in Mexico, son?"

Cain nodded.

"So was I. Where'd you fight?"

Cain told him Monterrey, Resaca de la Palma, Buena Vista. Immediately, the sheriff's attitude changed. He started calling him "son."

"Is that where you got that limp, son?"

The crookback stroked his Van Dyke and looked across at Cain. "Check his person, Sheriff. He may be in possession of another pistol."

"I have to search you, son," he said. When he hit the wound in his side Cain flinched visibly. "Sorry," he said. Eventually he discovered the Tranter in his boot.

"I'll have to take that, too," the sheriff told him.

Cain took a seat and the yellow-faced Negro poured a glass of whiskey and slid it across the table to him.

"Here you go," he said.

"You gotta watch the doc," explained another Negro, a stout, coal black man who sat to Cain's left. He wore spectacles and smoked a stogy. "He'll honeyfuggle you five ways to Sunday."

The other men laughed.

19

They played seven-card stud with a twenty-dollar betting limit to start. The yellow Negro acted as dealer. He had quick, unctuous hands, which Cain watched closely to make sure he was dealing from the top of the deck. The other men sat looking on, drinking and laughing, occasionally making comments. When Cain won the first couple of hands easily, they teased the crookback.

"He's gonna skunk you, Doc," the sheriff said.

"How's it feel to lose?" added the bespectacled Negro.

Dr. Chimbarazo merely looked across at Cain. "Deal the cards, Mr. Sprague," he said stonily to the dealer.

Of the next three hands, Cain took two more. In the last he'd had three kings, one in the hole and two faceup. The crookback had two pairs showing, jacks and sixes, and he boldly raised Cain each round, upping the pot to well over one hundred dollars. Wanting to nurse what cash he had, Cain could ill afford to lose that much in a single hand, and his opponent was obviously aware of that and trying to convince him he was holding the jack or six of a full house. Cain would normally have played it safe, gone with the odds and folded. But he'd had a feeling the small man was bluffing, and against his better judgment, he stayed in and matched him raise for raise. As it turned out, he was right. The small man's two pairs were all he had. Cain's opponent was a clever gambler, the sort who gave away nothing in his demeanor, not in his gestures nor his eyes, not in the way he surveyed his hole cards or threw in a gold eagle to raise. With each hand, he remained impassive, giving off neither the smug gleam of anticipated victory nor the faint tang of fear that some gamblers exuded like the musk of a wounded animal. And not once did he suck on his lower lip, as he had when playing with the Strofes and Preacher. He won and lost with perfect equanimity, and Cain knew he would have to be careful.

Overall, though, he was feeling pretty good about things. He was nearly $150 to the good and needed only a few more winning hands to have enough to wager for his horse. But then, feeling cocky, he got careless, bet far too much on a pair of tens, and promptly lost to the crookback's three treys.

"Told you, you gonna have to watch him," the bespectacled man said.

After that, Cain played with, what was for him anyway, unusual circumspection. Even when he won the next hand, taking in nearly two hundred dollars, and Dr. Chimbarazo offered to play with no betting limit, Cain replied with uncharacteristic caution. "I'd just as soon keep it as it is," he told his opponent.

They played another half dozen hands, with Cain winning twice as much as he lost. He soon had more than enough to wager for his horse.

"I'll play for Hermes now," he said.

"For who?" asked the crookback.

"My horse."

"You mean *my* horse. Very well."

To the others, Cain added, "Y'all are my witnesses. If I win, the horse is mine, free and clear."

"I'll see that Doc abides by the rules," said the sheriff.

So they began the last hand.

Cain anted up four hundred dollars, the agreed-upon value of the horse, while the crookback put up the sham bill of sale. With each successive round they raised each other another twenty dollars. For Cain, things started out on a positive note. Of the first three cards he was dealt, he found himself in possession of a pair of tens, both faceup, and a queen in the hole. Dr. Chimbarazo, though, quickly followed with a second ace to match one already faceup. He looked across the table at Cain's pair of tens and gave off the faintest hint of a smile. But it was, Cain believed, a hollow smile, one meant more as a bluff than a sign of genuine confidence. Nonetheless, the small man raised him the maximum each round. Cain was sure he was bluffing and matched his bet. He felt even better when, on the next round, he drew another lady to go with the one already in his hand. *Two pairs.* He glanced across at Dr. Chimbarazo, who was now sucking on his lower lip. *Yes,* he thought. *I have the little bastard now.* Immediately after that, though, Cain began second-guessing himself. What if he were holding a third ace in his hand? What if Cain were to lose everything? Still, he figured if he was going to strike out for the West as planned, he'd need a good horse as well as enough funds, both traveling money and a grubstake once he'd arrived. He had a feeling, though, something in his gut that made him feel lucky. This time it was Cain who raised his opponent. The small man counted the money sitting in the pile in front of him. It was barely enough to stay in the hand.

More confident than ever, Cain offered, "You still want no limit?"

Dr. Chimbarazo stroked his goatee.

"Will you take a bank check, sir?"

"Cash."

"These men will vouch for me."

"Doc's good for it," said the sheriff.

Cain thought for a moment. Even if the crookback cheated him with the check, he figured he'd get his horse back and still stand to come out of the game with almost a thousand dollars in winnings.

"I'll let you make it out for whatever I bid. Not a penny more."

"That's very decent of you, sir. No limit then. Deal the cards, Mr. Sprague."

Cain felt he had him right where he wanted him. On the next-to-last round, he couldn't believe his luck—he drew a third queen, giving him a full house. Unless the crookback was holding four aces or had a full house himself, Cain couldn't lose now. So he took all of his remaining money and pushed it toward the center of the table.

The small man raised his eyebrows, looked at his cards, and then across at Cain. He sighed and brought his lips together in a pout.

"Are you going to stay?" Cain asked, smiling.

"Just a moment, sir," he said.

Finally, Dr. Chimbarazo took out his checkbook and wrote a draft for the exact amount that Cain had bid.

"I match your bid, sir," the crookback said.

The final round of cards was dealt. His opponent glanced at his last hole card and then at Cain.

"I call," Cain said.

However, instead of showing what he was holding, the little man said, "It's my bid." He reached into an inner pocket of his coat and took out a billfold, from which he removed a stack of bank notes.

Cain stared across the table at him in disbelief.

"What the hell's this?" he asked.

"It's my turn to bid," said the crookback calmly. He removed several bills and tossed them in the pot. "I raise you five hundred."

"You said you were broke," Cain cried.

"I said no such thing, sir. I merely asked if you would take a bank check."

"And I let you, assuming you didn't have cash."

The small man shrugged, pursing his lips.

Turning to the other men, Cain said, "He can't do that."

"Doc never said he was out of cash," replied the dealer.

Cain then looked to the sheriff.

"That's right, son. He didn't."

Suddenly Cain realized he'd been had. The little man had tricked him. He didn't have anywhere near five hundred to bet. It was the crookback who was smiling now.

"Your bet, sir," he said to Cain. "Or are you going to fold?"

Cain saw not only his grubstake vanishing before his eyes, but his horse, as well. Now he'd never get to California, unless he brought the girl back and collected the reward. Everything he'd hoped for, everything that had been within his grasp, was now slipping through his fingers. He was about to fold when the crookback said, "Of course, there is one other possibility."

"What's that?"

"You could put up your runaway."

Cain stared across at Dr. Chimbarazo, wishing he'd snapped his neck when he'd had the chance. He shook his head.

"You *do* have her still?"

Cain remained silent, thinking.

"I would permit you to put her up against my wager in full."

"She's not mine to bet. She belongs to a Mr. Eberly of Henrico County, Virginia."

"Are you quite sure?"

"I'm sure," Cain replied, pushing away from the table and rising. "I'll have my weapons now," he said to the sheriff.

"You'd bess pick 'em up in the morning, son," the sheriff said. "Give you a chance to cool off."

Cain turned and started for the door.

"How about for just one night with her?" the crookback offered.

The other men whistled or clucked in astonishment.

"Lordy, that must be some kinda woman," said the dealer.

"Never thought I'd see the day Doc lost his wits over poontang," added the stout Negro. "And colored poontang at that."

The others laughed.

Cain hesitated with his hand on the doorknob. He wondered what the small man was up to—all of that for just one night? It didn't make sense. Either he was dead sure of what he was holding or Rosetta had some powerful hold on him, one that went well beyond dollars and cents. He'd seen men gamble wildly for such things before. A favorite hunting dog. A piece of land that wasn't worth beans to anyone except them. Some mining claim that had long been panned out. Could the crookback have been so all-fired-up for Rosetta that he'd lost his wits? If so, Cain was sure he could beat him. When men played with their hearts, or their cocks, instead of their heads, they were easy marks. Then again, perhaps the man's dare was merely cold calculation, the certainty of the victor. Cain thought for a moment. He warned himself not to, that what he was planning was dangerous. Then again, he couldn't think of another way to get his horse back and keep Rosetta safe.

"What's it going to be?" the crookback asked again. When Cain still didn't reply, the little man said, "Suit yourself," and reached out to draw in his winnings.

"Wait," Cain said, turning back to the table. "Just one night with her?"

"Just one night," he replied, a malignant gleam in his dark eyes.

Cain took a seat.

"First," the small man said to Cain, "I will need to know where she is."

"She's with the others outside of town."

"How do I know you're telling the truth?"

"You have my word," he said, glancing at the sheriff.

"He's a veteran. His word's good enough for me," the man replied.

"Very well. But if you lose, I shall require you to produce her immediately," Dr. Chimbarazo said, looking at the others at the table.

"Don't worry," said the sheriff.

"I just want some assurance," the little man countered.

"We'll make sure he holds up his end."

"And I have her until daybreak," the man added.

Cain had worked out a plan in his head if he lost. He would bring the crookback and whoever accompanied him on a wild-goose chase into the woods and lose them, then double back and get Rosetta and take off. It was a plan not without risks, but he saw no other way of getting his horse back. And he sure the hell was not going to give Rosetta over to the little son of a bitch. He'd kill him first. He'd kill them all if he had to.

"Stop yakking and let's play," Cain said.

"All right, show us what you got," said the little man.

Taking a deep breath, Cain turned his hole cards faceup.

"He's got a full house, queens and tens," said the dealer. "What're you holding, Doc?"

Cain stared across the table at the crookback. The smug, ivory smile on his round pie-face rapidly faded, changing first to incredulity, then to embarrassment, and finally to rage. His mouth hardened in anger and his eyes turned into small hard things, like acorns. Then he turned his hole cards faceup.

"His full house trumps your three aces, Doc," the dealer said.

"He . . . he cheated," the crookback stammered.

"Now, Doc, he whupped you fair'n square," said the sheriff.

When Cain reached to pick up his winnings, including the bill of sale for Hermes, the crookback fumbled for something in his vest. But the sheriff had already drawn his big Colt dragoon and placed it against the small man's temple.

"I don't think you want to do that, Doc."

The crookback froze while the sheriff reached his hand into the other's vest pocket and came out with a small-caliber coat pistol.

"Son," the sheriff said to Cain, "I'd suggest you take your winnings and get on out of here."

Cain scooped up what he'd won, shoving the bills and coins into his pocket. Before he left, he turned to the sheriff and said, "I think I'll need my guns, Sheriff."

The man gave them to Cain and he left.

A s he hurried across town, he kept looking over his shoulder. He purposely headed in the wrong direction for a time, just in case some friend of Dr. Chimbarazo's tried to follow him. Again, he heard the words of the old Negress Maddy: *That girl done gave you back your life.* It was true—she had. And in more ways than she could have imagined. Then he thought of Eberly. He knew the old man would try to make things difficult for him. He was not the sort to give up once his mind was fastened on a thing, as it was on getting Rosetta back. Plus with a man like him, there was pride involved. There was always pride. He'd get a warrant out for Cain's arrest as a horse thief, send a posse out after him. If caught, he could hang for that alone, though Cain suspected the old man would never let him be brought in. If he got his hands on him, he'd deal with him himself. And he would make Cain pay, all right. In the same way he did his Negroes.

Then he thought of the way Eberly had looked as he stood in the doorway of the whorehouse. His stone cold eyes softening for a moment as he'd said, *Bring her back.* At that moment, Cain felt, it was more than dominion or ownership, more than simply wanting to see his will imposed on the world. More even than the desire to have a favorite plaything, a mere bauble returned to him. It was something deeper and more profound, something akin to love, if a man such as Eberly could actually be capable of loving something. He saw Eberly standing there, his gaze wistful and downcast, his haughty demeanor having abandoned him, leaving him as forlorn-looking as a child who'd lost its mother. Then, for some reason, Cain pictured Rosetta as he'd first seen her in the streets of Boston, staring into the shop window, with that sad, pensive look on her face. She'd reminded him of someone then, the high, strong cheekbones, that indomitable expression of hers. And just like that the thought that had been lingering in the back of his mind for some time now became clear.

He climbed up the stairs and into the room where Rosetta was still sleeping. From the bureau, he got the oil lamp and lighted it. She was turned toward him, her mouth open slightly, and he held the lamp close to her face, inspecting it. She roused with the light.

"Cain?" she muttered, holding her hand up to shield her eyes. "That you?"

"I want to ask you something," he said to her.

"What's the matter?"

"You don't have to answer if you don't want to."

"What?"

He placed one hand on her shoulder. "Is he your father?"

"What you talkin' about?"

"Eberly. Is he your father?"

But he already saw the answer in Rosetta's face. In all of her features, the angle of jaw and cheekbone, the line of her brow, the almost patrician cut of her nose. There was the unmistakable stamp of Eberly. She looked up at him, then rolled away from him, ashamed.

Cain placed the lamp on the bureau and sat down on the side of the bed. He hesitated, then reached out and lay his hand on her shoulder. She flinched at his touch, so he withdrew it.

"It's all right," he reassured her. Her back was to him, so he couldn't see her face. "Did he know?"

She snorted in disdain. "Oh, he knew, all right. He knew."

She fell silent for a while. Cain placed his hand on her shoulder again, and this time she left it there. He waited. He noticed the fine velvety down on the back of her neck, as soft as lamb's wool. The way her shoulder blades rose and fell with her breathing. When she began to talk, it was as if something inside had broken and its contents came spilling from her. He could actually feel the movement of it in her shoulders, the pouring out of what she'd kept locked up inside. He recalled then how she'd said everybody had something buried deep within them, something they couldn't tell anyone.

"I think he liked that I was his," she began, her voice flat, devoid of emotion, as if she were reciting someone else's story. "Not just some slave he owned but *his*. His flesh and blood. That he owned me in every way a man can own something. When he be in my bed, he usta whisper in my ear, 'You my girl? You my sweet little Rosetta?' It made me hate him all the more."

She went on like this for a while, telling Cain how her father would rape her. The things he did to her. Made her do to him.

When she paused, he asked, "How did you find out? Did your mother tell you?"

"No. She wouldn't never a told me. I heard talk around the plantation for a long time. The other slaves saying this and that. About Mr. Eberly and my momma. About me. They's always talk and I figure they just jealous on account of how he treated us special like. I didn't set no store by it. Didn't know the truth till later, when Momma was already long gone and I'd given birth to my boy. One day I was down at the tub washing the clothes. Israel was with me. He follow me everywhere. He was such a sweet little boy. Solomon, the man who used to bring my momma sweet potatoes, he happened by. He said, 'Mornin', Miss Rosetta,' and he look down at Israel. Then he said my little brother gone be a right fine-lookin' man. I said, 'What you mean, my brother? This here my son, my boy Israel.' He said, 'That young'un's your son *and* brother both.' At first I didn't know what he gettin' at. Then, when I finally did, I stared at him like he just slapped me. But something inside me *knew* it to be the truth. I guess I always known it, too. After that I take to looking in the mirror and couldn't help seeing Mr. Eberly's face staring back at me. It was like I had the thing I hated inside me, and no matter what I did I couldn't never get it out. And whenever I look at my little Israel, I felt so ashamed. 'Course I'd felt shame before. Tha's what a slave's life is—shame. But never like this. To know he was my father and that he was layin' with me, touchin' me that way. That he was my son's father, too. It made me feel dirty, like I'd fallen in the pig mire and I was covered with it and no amount of soap and water would ever clean me of it. You want to know the truth about why I ran, that's why. Sure, I wanted to save my baby. Have him grow up in freedom. But I also wanted to set myself free. I didn't want him touching me no more."

When she finished, she fell silent, and for a moment he thought she was sleeping, but then he could tell that she was crying softly, could feel her shoulders gently quivering, as if with cold. Her body seemed drained of everything, a hollow shell lying there. Cain, too, felt suddenly emptied. And at the same time, he felt filled with something else—shame. He felt shame for having made a deal with that man. For having caught her and brought her back in irons. For having treated her like an animal. For having nearly gotten her killed. For what Preacher had almost done and for what the blackbirders had done. Most of all, he felt ashamed of the color of his skin. It was something he had never before really thought about. He was a white man, that was who he was, who he'd *always* been, but he'd never thought about that, sort of the way a person is never really aware of the air he is breathing or the ground under his feet. It was just something *there*, something he possessed. Now his skin felt too tight and hot about his flesh and bones, like a sunburn, squeezing him from the outside, so that he was painfully conscious of it.

"The bastard," he said under his breath. If he'd had Eberly there he would have killed him with his bare hands. He'd have grabbed him by the throat and choked the life from him the way you'd wring a chicken's neck.

"Cain," she said, without looking at him.

"Yes."

"If I was to ax you to do something, would you do it?"

"If I can," he replied.

Of all the things he imagined her asking, the one he didn't expect was the one she asked. "Would you hold me?"

He stared down at her for a moment. Then he removed his holster and put it on the bureau, started to lie down on top of the covers.

"No. Here," Rosetta said, lifting the covers. He pulled off his muddy boots and lay down next to her. She wore her shift and had her back to him, but she reached behind herself and found his hand and took it and draped his arm over her side. She held on to his hand tightly with both of hers, pulling him toward her, into her. She was tense, all her muscles drawn tight as fiddle strings. He could feel her shivering, and then, after a time, slowly beginning to relax. He could smell her hair and skin, a pungent yet vaguely sweet scent like the smoke from an applewood fire. Though he tried not to, tried to fight back the feeling, he felt himself becoming aroused. It was not something he could help. He was, after all, just a man—a man who had not been with a woman in a long time. *Yet, if this is what she wanted, why not?* he thought. And hadn't he wanted her as well, wanted her ever since he'd laid eyes on her in front of that store in Boston? It was more than plain, animal need, though it was that, too. It was part of that confession he'd made to himself the night he thought he was going to die, when all the rules he'd lived by had fallen away, and he was no longer a slave catcher or a white man or a southerner, and Rosetta wasn't a runaway slave belonging to someone else, when he was simply a man and she just a woman, a woman he happened to have fallen in love with.

"Rosetta," he whispered hotly into her ear. Yet when he kissed her on the neck, he felt her flinch and stiffen again.

"What?" he asked.

"Jess hold me," she said.

"I thought . . ."

"I jess want to be held, Cain," she said. Then she added, "Feel."

She slid his hand down so that it came in contact with the ripe swelling of her belly, and she pressed it firmly there. He could feel something faint but sure, a kind of insistent murmur like the beating of a spring rain on a roof. He could feel the beating of it in his hand. Neither said a word, and after a time he heard her breathing level out and become rhythmic, felt her hands release their tight lock on his, and he knew she was asleep. He thought of removing his hand but he kept it there, over the child that she was carrying, Eberly's child. He stayed like this for a long time, holding her, not moving for fear of waking her, listening to her breathing, taking in her scent, thinking about what he'd admitted to himself, thinking of the sheer oddness of it all.

What in the hell are you doing? he thought. Sometime just before he fell asleep, it came to him. What he would do. It was clear now. It was all very, very clear.

20

W here is he?"

Hands shook him roughly awake in the still, predawn darkness. Instinctively, he reached for his revolver on the bureau, but it wasn't there. He felt instead the hard, cold mouth of a gun barrel pressing the hollow of his cheek.

"Hold still, slave catcher," the same voice came again.

Someone lit a lantern and Cain squinted against the sudden light. When his eyes had adjusted, he found himself staring down the business end of a .54-caliber Perry. The bitter odor of saltpeter and sulfur still wafting from its barrel suggested it had been discharged quite recently. The gun was attached to a tall, rawboned man wearing a plug hat pulled low on his forehead. He was bearded, his sharp, handsome features appearing as if hewed from stone. Standing behind him in the small room several other men had crowded in, all armed with muskets and pistols, a couple even with long machetes that hung in scabbards attached to their belts. They brought with them the strong tang of horseflesh and sweat, of long days in the saddle. Across the bed from the man with the Perry was another man, younger, red-haired, with a sullen mouth that looked almost bruised. More finely fashioned than those of the first, his features nonetheless linked him as a brother. He held a Springfield rifle pointed at Cain's chest.

"Move on peril of your life, slave catcher," said the tall man.

"Dr. Chimbarazo send you?" Cain asked. He thought perhaps that the crookback had decided to repossess the money he'd lost and to send some hill ruffians to get it, perhaps even to try to take Rosetta from him.

"I was sent by the Almighty himself," the tall man offered. "Where is he?"

"I don't know what in Sam Hill you're talking about, mister."

With this answer, Cain had the gun barrel shoved more forcibly against his cheek, this time hard enough that it jammed against a back molar. Through the metal he could feel the *glub glub glub* of the man's pulse.

"I'd be careful with that thing if I were you," said Cain, staring coldly at the man.

"Friend, if I were *you*, I'd start talking and be quick about it," said the red-haired man, prodding him in the side with his rifle.

"I am going to ask you once more," repeated the tall one. "Where is he?"

"Where the hell is who?"

"Henry," intoned another voice from the shadowy corner of the room. After a moment, the owner of the voice stepped from the gloom into the brilliance of the lantern. He was an old man, his gaunt features exaggerated, thrown into disquieting chiaroscuro. Half his face was illuminated, the other half left in darkness. "I've come for my friend."

This one was dressed in black—hat, greatcoat, trousers. He stood ramrod straight, with a proud, almost arrogant bearing, and yet at the same time he gave the impression of one unconcerned about his mortal appearance. His coat had not been brushed in ages and was nearly threadbare, and for a belt he wore a piece of hemp. The gray hair sticking out from beneath the hat was wild and unkempt. A man of advanced years—though Cain guessed he was younger than he appeared—he had a weathered, gristle-thin face that seemed hacked from a piece of ironwood and a riotous expanse of beard that flowed down over his chest like ashes from a fireplace. His fierce, bullet gray eyes seemed to glow red at the edges. Something about him struck

Cain as vaguely familiar. Still, it took Cain a few more seconds before it came to him. And then, though he'd only seen him through his spyglass, he realized suddenly who the man was. The same one who'd been following him all these weeks, who'd shot at them back at the river. The Great Abolitionist. Osawatomie Brown.

"You're Brown?" Cain said.

"I shall ask the questions. Where is Henry?"

"I don't know."

"I am well aware that you slave catchers kidnapped him from my farm, and we have tracked you here." He cast his eyes at Rosetta, as if he'd just noticed her lying there. He gave her a quick sidelong glance, seemed about to say something to her, then let the thought go and returned his attention to Cain. "Are you denying you were one of them?"

"No. I'm one of them," Cain admitted.

"I told you, Father," said the red-haired man.

"So I ask you again, where is Henry?"

"He escaped and the others went off after him," Cain replied.

"He's lying," replied the red-haired man, an excited expression on his face. He was about five nine, with narrow shoulders and a soft face that had something of the boy about it still. He was the one Cain had seen behind the house, standing with his father that day. "He's got him hidden somewhere, Father."

"Son," Brown said with calm firmness.

"But he's lying, Father," the young man insisted. "I say we take him out and make him tell us where he is. He's already confessed to being a slave catcher."

"That will be enough, Oliver," the father commanded.

"But, Father—"

The old man turned his steely gaze on the son.

"Forgive me, Father."

Brown looked back at Cain. "Where are they?" he asked.

"I told you, I don't know."

"When did Henry run off?"

"If you've been tracking us you ought to know it was right after we crossed into Maryland."

"I do not believe you. I will ask you one more time," he said in a voice used to uttering pronouncements. The tall man looked at Brown, who nodded, and then he cocked the hammer of the Perry. Cain knew that at Brown's command, the son would not hesitate to pull the trigger then and there.

"Wait," Rosetta said, sitting up. "He's speakin' the truth. Henry run away."

"And who are you?" asked Brown, turning his gaze on her. His eyes slid down her body, pausing finally at her belly.

"I'm Rosetta. Me and Henry run off from Mr. Eberly's plantation at the same time."

"When did he slip away from the slave catchers?"

"Couple weeks back, I reckon," Rosetta explained. "Them others took off after him like he said. Ain't seen hide nor hair a them since."

"And what part have you in this?" Brown asked her.

"Part?"

"Did this man kidnap you, too?"

She hesitated. It was Cain who finally answered. "I had a warrant to return her to her owner, if that's what you mean."

He felt her nudge him under the covers.

"Tha's true enough," she agreed. "He did take me. But he saved me, too. Wasn't for him, I'da been dead not onct but twice."

"You don't have to lie. He can't hurt you anymore. You're safe now," said the younger Brown.

"Ain't no lie. It's the truth. He saved me."

"He's a slave catcher just the same," the red-haired man said.

"He ain't like them others. He's a good man."

"Slave catchers are an abomination in the eyes of God," the son said. He glanced toward the old man, as if for approval. "What are we going to do with him, Father?"

Brown stood there for a moment, thinking. Then, turning to another man, he commanded, "Bind this one and bring him along."

"At least let me put my boots on," said Cain, looking at Brown.

The others turned toward Brown, and he nodded, then left the room.

As he was led away, Rosetta called after them, "Don't you do nothin' to him. Y'hear me. You leave him be."

They headed down the stairs. Behind the boardinghouse, in the blue-toned light of early morning, Cain made out some dozen horses, tended to by a couple of men.

"What're we gonna do with him, Captain Brown?" asked one of them, a burly man with wide muttonchops.

Another, a scrawny lad of fifteen, cried, "Can I shoot this one, Cap'n?"

Brown silenced the men with a single movement of his upraised hand. From a sheath at his side hung a long machete. Cain wondered if the weapon was the one he'd used to hack men to death in Kansas. Taking hold of the rope that bound Cain's hands behind his back, Brown pulled him roughly along, leading him out behind the barn. The man wasn't as big as he had appeared while Cain was lying down. In fact, he was of average height, lean and hard muscled, with the shoulders and arms of a common laborer. He pulled Cain along with a strength that belied his relatively modest size. Suddenly, he stopped beside a water trough, at the edge of a corral. The air was punctuated by a sharp, manure smell. Still holding him fast, Brown gazed up at the sky, looking at it the way a farmer would for rain. Toward the east it was already turning a milky gray, but to the west it was still a gunmetal blue shot through with stars. Brown turned and leveled his gaze on Cain.

"Get on your knees," he told him.

"Like hell. If you've a mind to—"

With his boot, Brown gave a vicious kick, which struck the back of Cain's right leg, and at the same time yanked downward on the rope. The effect brought Cain immediately to his knees.

"Son of a bitch," Cain cried.

"How does it feel to be bound like a slave?" the old man asked him, squatting beside him.

"Go to hell."

"Where you shall shortly be, sir."

"If you're fixing to kill me, do it and dispense with your abolitionist lectures," Cain countered.

With one hand Brown grabbed Cain by the hair and jerked his

head back, while with the other he drew his machete and placed it against his now exposed neck. "*I* shall decide when you are to die," cried Brown. He was so close Cain could feel his warm breath on his face, the sour smell of his body. He held him there for several seconds, then slowly relaxed his grip on his hair. "I should be home tending to my farm instead of hunting down men like you. Is this your full-time occupation?"

Cain turned his head slightly so that he was looking at Brown. "It has been of sorts."

"A man ought to be engaged in real work. Not living off the sweat of another."

"I reckon there's some truth to that," Cain conceded.

"Have you ever had cause to kill a man, Mr. . . ."

"Cain."

"Ah," the old man said, his eyes gleaming almost playfully. "An apt name for a slave catcher. Have you had occasion to kill your fellow man, Mr. Cain?"

"I have killed men before."

"It is not something one ought to take lightly."

"I have never done it save when I hadn't any choice."

"Which is as it should be. The face of every man I have ever killed haunts my dreams." Brown's gaze turned distant and hollow, as if he were looking into his very soul. "I will take each of those faces to my own grave. And yet, if I had it within my power, I would slay every last southerner, every owner and agent, even the innocent babe at its mother's breast. All who profited from the sweat and blood of the Negro. I would lay waste to the South. Do you understand, Mr. Cain?"

As he said this, Brown slashed at the air in front of him with the machete: *woof, woof, woof.*

"Sounds like a fair amount of killing to be done," Cain said.

"This country needs a lot of killing."

"Are you so sure all those who would have to die would be deserving of it?"

"No, sir, I am not," Brown conceded. "But I would kill them just the same, and leave it to God to sift the innocent from the guilty."

"Like those men out in Kansas?"

Brown's demeanor changed immediately, his eyes ablaze like those of a man staring into a furnace. The old man turned savagely on Cain, though it didn't appear as if he were actually seeing him, but something far off in the distance.

"I would kill them ten times over if I thought it would end this. I would kill you with no more thought than a man would give to crushing a flea."

"Then let's get to it and stop all this blather."

This seemed to incite Brown even more. "You think I wouldn't," he cried. "You think I would hesitate to cut you down like the dog you are?"

"No, I'm sure you would," Cain said. "May I ask a favor of you first?"

"What?" said the other impatiently.

"Would you see to it that the girl is safe?"

The old man continued staring at him for several seconds. Slowly, another change seemed to come over him. His eyes gradually lost the fire in them and they appeared to focus on Cain, to really and truly see him, as if for the first time. He appeared then as a man for the first time, and not some avenging angel.

"Did you put her in that way?"

"No. That was someone else's doing, not mine."

"You were in bed with her."

Cain thought of explaining things, but he saw how useless that would be, that it would make him look like some coward trying to save his hide. Instead, he offered only, "It's not like that."

Brown permitted himself a sly smile. "Then you are an even greater fool than I'd taken you for. Were you planning on bringing her back to bondage?"

Cain shook his head. "I was, at first. But now . . . No."

"You reckon this will save your pathetic neck?" Brown said.

"No. But it happens to be the truth."

"You expect me to believe that?"

"I expect you'll believe what you've a mind to, and nothing I say is going to change that."

Brown rose to his feet, bringing the machete up and over Cain's head. "Any last wishes, Mr. Cain?"

"No." Then he thought for a moment and said, "Just make sure she gets to safety."

Cain closed his eyes, waited.

Instead of the *woof* of the blade, what he heard was, "Which way were you headed, Mr. Cain?"

"What?" he asked, confused.

"Before I came. Which way were you headed?"

"I . . . I was planning on going out to California."

"And the girl? What of her?"

"I was going to bring her along until I reached a free state."

Brown was silent for a moment. Cain chanced looking up at him. The old man stood there, gazing off over the rooftops. He seemed to be chewing on some private thought that gave him pause. Then he turned and looked down at Cain.

"You remind me a little of my son Frederick, Mr. Cain."

"Is that so?"

"It is. About the eyes. He was a good son and he gave his life for the cause. Tell me, Mr. Cain, if I were to let you go, I'm not saying I shall, but if I did," the old man said. "Do I have your word that you will not return her to slavery?"

"I don't know as my word much matters now. But yes, you have my word."

"I lived for a spell in Ohio," explained Brown. "There is a freed Negro settlement by the name of Gist out there."

"I've heard tell of it."

"It's on your way. They give aid and comfort to runaways. You might try there."

At that Brown used the machete to cut the rope tying his hands.

"I'll give it some thought," said Cain, rubbing the feeling back into his wrists.

"The girl was right," Brown said. "You are not like the others."

He offered his bony hand, and Cain shook it.

"You might could try Fredericksburg," Cain told him.

"How's that?" Brown asked.

"If you're looking to get Henry back. The others were supposed to be waiting for me there. A place called the Rising Sun Tavern."

Brown looked at him, touched the brim of his cap in thanks, then turned and started walking toward the others.

"I'll need my gun, sir," Cain said to him.

"Why?"

"I might have occasion to kill those who would bring her back to bondage."

At this the old man smiled.

They'd been riding in silence for a spell when Rosetta finally spoke. "What'd you tell that fellow Brown made him let you go?"

Cain was on Hermes while Rosetta sat astride a sorrel gelding he'd traded the livery man for, swapping both the mare and the bay in exchange. While the livery man had gotten the better of the deal, Cain figured it wouldn't look good if they were stopped with a pair of stolen horses, one being that of a murdered man. They'd lit out of town fast, Cain wanting to put some distance between himself and the crookback in case the little man had thought of getting back what he'd lost.

"I just told him the truth," Cain replied.

"Which was?" she asked.

"That I wasn't bringing you back."

He felt the weight of her stare.

"When did you come to that decision?"

"A while back."

"And when was you plannin' on tellin' me, Cain?" she said, raising her eyebrow playfully.

"Soon," he replied, looking over at her.

She glanced back over her shoulder at the rising sun. "We traveling west. Where to?"

"Ohio."

"Ohio?" she exclaimed. "What's there?"

"The Gist Settlement," he said.

"What manner of place is that?"

"A freed slave village."

He'd never been there himself but he'd heard about it. The place lay somewhere out in the wilds of Ohio. Like Timbucto, it was a refuge for former slaves. The land was bequeathed by a wealthy Englishman, Samuel Gist, who, upon his death, had not only freed the slaves from his Virginia plantation but also provided them with land out in Ohio where they could resettle. People back home in Richmond spoke of the crazy Gist and how he'd left his fortune to his slaves.

"Why we goin' there?" she inquired.

"Because you'll be safe there."

"Cain," she said. When he ignored her, she repeated. "Cain."

He kept riding. Rosetta kicked the gelding and rode up ahead of him. She then turned the animal into his path so that he was forced to stop and look at her. "How come you ain't bringin' me back?"

"Would you rather I did?"

"'Course not. I'm just curious why you changed your mind."

"I'm not altogether sure."

She stared at him fixedly. In the daylight, the resemblance between her and Eberly was unmistakable. He only wondered why he hadn't seen it before.

"Was it account of what I told you?" she asked.

"I suppose that had something to do with it. I couldn't bring you back to that man."

"That the only reason?"

"What difference does it make?" he said. "You just ought to be glad I'm not."

"'Course I'm glad. I just don't understand why you changed all of a sudden. He won't take this easy, you know."

"I know."

They rode on. Over the Appalachian Mountains the morning had broken sharp and crisp. The last stubborn traces of fog lingering in the hollows and blanketing the fields scurried off before the approach of the day's heat. Cain was hoping they could make Cumberland by nightfall the next day. They were following the National Pike, busy this time of day with fellow travelers—wagons filled with goods making for the eastern markets, lumbering Conestogas carrying entire families westward, stagecoaches jouncing and swaying as they surged past, headed in both directions. Every now and then they'd have to make way for someone driving a herd of cattle or pigs or sheep. Once, in a small hamlet called Shady Glen, they had to give way for an entire schoolhouse that was being pulled down the pike. It had been loaded on the beds of two wagons placed side by side and was being transported by two teams of half a dozen oxen each. Another time, Cain spotted off in the distance a large group of men on horses, approaching at breakneck speed. He didn't like the looks of them, so he and Rosetta slipped off into the woods. Hidden, they watched as the men stormed by, spurring their mounts in hot pursuit of something.

"Slave catchers," Cain said to Rosetta.

"You think so?"

"I'd bet money on it. Eberly may have already sent men after us."

Cain figured with any luck they could make Gist in a fortnight. He planned on heading due west to Morgantown, then angling south for New Martinsville or Parkersburg, one of those river towns where he would cross the Ohio into free territory and then try to find the Gist Settlement. He knew, though, that as he approached the river and a free state, he would need to be careful. There were plenty of runaways with the same notion. They used the river as a compass north, following it up from Tennessee and Kentucky. And wherever there were runaways, there would be slave catchers and blackbirders.

At noon they came to a small hamlet where two smaller roads converged with the pike. There was a Baptist church and a dry goods store. Cain went into the store and bought some provisions for their trip: salted fish and jerked beef, a wheel of cheese, some dried peaches, coffee and salt and sugar, bandages, a can of lard, sacks of meal and flour, horse feed and some sugar for Hermes, as well as sundry other supplies, including a bottle each of whiskey and laudanum, his first in some time. They continued on for a ways before stopping in front of a large, empty building, set back some distance from the road. It was two stories with a horse barn in back and, by the looks of it, had been an inn that had fallen on hard times. An ornately carved but now weathered sign over the front door said WELCOME. They dismounted and made a fire off to the side. After he'd seen to the horses, Cain sat and took off his shirt and removed the bandages over his wound. He poured some whiskey on a rag and began to clean it. His side was still tender from the broken rib, and when he breathed deep it hurt, but the wound was finally on the mend.

"Here, let me do that," Rosetta said, taking the cloth from him. "Gimme that bottle of yours."

He handed her the flask of laudanum, and she uncorked it and poured a little on the cloth. As she worked on him, washing away blood that had crusted at the edges of the wound, he watched her. Her long, slender hands moving expertly. He could still remember the feel of her skin and her smell as he lay next to her the previous night. He thought of what Brown had told him: that he'd been a foolish man to have done nothing. He'd felt he'd done the right thing, the decent thing, despite the fact that his body had told him otherwise. Now he wasn't so sure. Maybe he was just a fool.

"It comin' along just fine," she said, dabbing at the wound. "You just gotta make sure you don't go gettin' yourself shot up no more."

"I'll try my best not to."

Cain took the bottle of laudanum from her and had a sip. He hadn't had any in a while and he appreciated the way the liquid warmed and filled his chest.

"You know that stuff gonna kill you one a these days," she warned.

"If it's not by a bullet," he said offhandedly.

"A bullet's faster."

"What are you so concerned for?"

"Somebody gotta be, since you so all-fired-up to kill yourself."

"Why don't you let me worry about that?"

"You ain't doin' such a good job keepin' yourself in one piece, Cain. Remember, Maddy put me in charge of seein' that you stay out of trouble," she said, smiling playfully.

He started to move before she was finished, and she said, "Hold your horses. I ain't done yet."

She ran her finger down the scar over his chest. "Where you get this one?"

"That was from a runaway, too."

"Serves you right. You ever think you picked the wrong line of work, Cain."

He looked at her and smiled. "It has occurred to me."

Then she put on a fresh bandage and tied it around his torso.

Later, as they were eating lunch, Rosetta was chewing a piece of jerked beef when she stopped suddenly and sat up straight, her ear pitched, as if listening for some distant sound. The expression she wore was a mixture of concern and delight.

"Oh my," she said.

"What?"

"Just felt this little one move," she said, rubbing her stomach in small circles. "This chile kicks harder'n a mule. Funny, most the time he so quiet, I almost forget about him."

"How far along are you?" he asked.

He saw a change come over her eyes. Perhaps it was the attempt to avoid thinking back to the night of the child's conception, and he regretted having asked her.

"Five months, near as I can tell."

"What're you going to name it?"

"Bad luck be namin' a child 'fore it's even born. Besides, what if it's not a male child?" She took another bite of food and fell silent for a time. "What you think Eberly'll do?" It was, Cain noted, the first time she hadn't called him Mister Eberly.

"What can he do?"

"You don't know him," Rosetta said, wagging her head.

"We're a long way from Richmond."

"He ain't the sort of man to take no without a fight."

"You let me worry about him."

As he reached out to cut a piece of cheese, Rosetta took hold of his hand. She glanced down at it, turned it palm up, staring at it as if it were something of sudden interest.

"What?" he asked.

She put her own hand next to his. "Funny," she said. "Our palms ain't so different in color."

He looked instead at her face.

"You ever wonder, Cain, why all this fuss on account of one person's skin being lighter than another's?"

"It's not that simple." He thought of what his father had told him about slavery, about being a southerner, about the honor of one's race. He thought about everything he'd been taught growing up. He thought of what he had seen in the eyes of slaves and in the eyes of masters, too. "It has to do with money and owning things. Nobody likes to give up what's theirs, and they'll fight like hell to keep it. Like with my horse. And I suppose it's got something to do with what people are used to. They like things the way they've always been. They don't like to change." As he spoke, Rosetta continued to hold his hand, to run her thumb along the creases in his palm, as if she were reading it.

"Fear, too, I reckon," he said.

She snorted disdainfully. "What white folks got to be 'fraid of?"

"You. What we've done to you. What you'd do to us if you ever got the chance."

When he'd finished, Rosetta screwed up her mouth.

"I have to go pee," she said.

She headed out behind the abandoned structure. Maybe it was the talk of her being pregnant, but Cain noticed, for the first time, how she was beginning to walk differently now. More slowly, not so much tentatively as with the motion of one who carried something of priceless value, her feet spread out and her arms a bit more out to the sides for ballast, with a heft in her hips she had not had before. Yet the change, he admitted to himself, made her all the more lovely. She still had the grace and power of a mare about to foal. He marveled at her. Watching her lifted his heart, made him feel lighter, less earth-bound than he could ever recall feeling.

While she was gone, he started to saddle the horses. He thought of Eberly again, and his good mood quickly darkened. The old man would never give her up, he knew. He'd use all of his money and his power and his connections to hunt her down, to search for her—and Cain, too, for that matter. Only a bullet would stop him. After all those years of being the hunter, Cain knew he would now be the hunted.

A half-dozen riders approached from the east. They were the same ones that had passed them earlier in the day. Cain removed the leather loop holding down the hammer of his gun.

"How do," said one of them, nodding to Cain. He was an older man, in his fifties, with a dark, wispy beard, the sallow complexion of one used to the night, and small glistening-black eyes like a raccoon. Hanging from the pommel of his saddle were a pair of shackles. "We're looking for a runaway," the man said. "Young nigger gal."

Cain gave a furtive glance toward the woods and, in a voice that was almost a shout, said, "Haven't seen any niggers in these parts."

"You sound pretty sure, fellow."

"I am," he cried.

"Hell, you don't have to yell," the old man replied. "I ain't deaf. You by yourself?" He glanced at the other horse, the saddle on the ground. Cain followed the man's gaze as it took in the gelding, then glanced back into the woods behind Cain.

"Yes," he said, continuing to saddle Hermes.

"What's the other horse for?"

"I'm fixing to sell it."

"Saddle, too?"

"Everything. Why, you looking to buy?"

"No, just curious. Where you headed?" the old man asked.

"West."

"Just west?"

"That's about the size of it," Cain replied.

"Where you comin' from?" asked one of the others, a jowly man wearing a red cap that resembled a fez.

"I don't reckon that's any of your business," Cain replied.

"You wouldn't be on the run from the law, would you?"

"I've told you all I'm going to tell you." Cain stopped readying the horse and turned and stared at the man.

"We're patrollers hired by the county, and we have the right to ask you any damn thing we want to," said the jowly man.

"Is that so?"

Finally, the old man interrupted. "That'll be enough, Earl. Thank you for your time, mister," he said to Cain. "If you see any niggers fitting that description, you contact the sheriff."

"I'll be sure to," Cain replied. "By the way, you know the name of the runaway?"

The man shook his head. With that, they spurred their horses and galloped off toward the west.

Cain wondered how they'd tracked them this far west. Perhaps the sheriff back in Hagerstown had told them Cain had a runaway with him that belonged to Eberly. Or maybe it was the little crookback, who would, of course, be looking to pay him back any way he could. Whatever it was, they were now on his trail. Only when they were gone a while did Rosetta emerge from behind the house.

"What did they want?" she asked.

"They were looking for a runaway girl."

She gave him a nervous look. "They say who?"

Cain shook his head.

"We ought to get off the main road for a while, though," he said.

21

If they were on his trail, he would need to lose them, so they cut into the woods to the south, rode through a dense hardwood forest just beginning to leaf out in the fine spring weather. They passed between alder and beech, tulip tree and ash and hickory, oak and maple. The sweet fragrance of wildflowers hung thickly in the warm May air: elderberry and honeysuckle, dogwood and mountain laurel, jack-in-the-pulpit, wild columbine, and pink lady's slipper. He made zigzagging lines across creeks and over sharp ridges, skirting narrow ravines two hundred feet above surging mountain rivers. Sometimes they had to wade through swamps, other times negotiate bramble thickets so tightly packed they had to dismount and walk their horses.

At dusk, they pitched camp beside a waterfall surrounded by cedar trees, which exuded a strong, resiny smell. For supper, Rosetta fried up some fish and corn pone, and with the flour and peaches and lard she made a peach pie. Cain ate like a man condemned.

"That was good," he said, rubbing his belly.

"I guess so. You had three pieces," she said with a smile.

"Where did you learn to fashion a pie like that?"

"My mother. She was a good cook. She made all of Eberly's meals. He said she was the best cook in Henrico County."

Cain hesitated before asking, "You never heard from her again?"

She shook her head. "I heard she was sold to a cotton farmer down in Georgia. Don't know for sure, though."

Later, as the mountain night turned cool, they sat close about the fire, Cain on one side, Rosetta on the other, trying to draw such warmth as they could from it. Overhead, the night sky was frantic with stars, while somewhere off in the distance came the piercing howl of a wolf. His leg ached fiercely from the cold. The pain there had been overshadowed of late by the wound in his side, but now that that was on the mend, the leg, like a willful child, began calling for his attention. He'd finished the laudanum a while back and so took a long drink of whiskey.

"What you fixin' to do after you bring me to Ohio?" Rosetta asked. "You still of a mind to go out west?"

"I sure can't go back to Richmond," Cain replied. "I was figuring I might give California a try."

"What's there?"

"There's still a lot of gold to be had."

Rosetta raised her eyebrows and snorted in a way he'd come to know, a certain affectation he found almost agreeable. "I can't see you with no pick and shovel, Cain."

"Why not?"

"I can't is all. There was this one slave work on the plantation. Joshua. He was a big talker. Always goin' on how when he run off, he gonna head out to Californy and dig him up some of that gold."

"A lot of men have had the same notion and come up empty."

"But you reckon it'll be different with you?"

Cain shrugged. He thought of something his father had once told him. How a man doesn't get to pick his life—it picks him. Maybe that was true. Maybe that was the thing he'd never understood.

He said, "There's more ways to strike gold than digging it out of the earth."

"You figurin' to part it from those that do?"

"Seems a might easier that way," he said with a smile.

"Still, it won't be easy out there by your ownself," Rosetta said.

"I'm used to being on my own. I'm turning in. Good night."

The next day they reached Cumberland by midafternoon, and since there were still a few more hours of daylight remaining, they pushed on before stopping for the night. When they made Keyser's Ridge the following day, they headed due west toward the Ohio River. Rosetta's horse threw a shoe, and Cain ended up having to put her on Hermes while he walked her gelding. It took them four more days to arrive in Morgantown, Virginia. Cain stopped at a livery where he had the horses tended to.

"How far to New Martinsville?" he asked the owner, a fat man with a greasy, off-kilter smile.

"All depends. Five days if you go south through the valley toward Fairmont. Three if you head up Pentress and Dunkard Creek way. But this time a year you never know 'bout the road up there. The bridge in Ralston is out a lot," replied the man.

They camped just south of the town. The next day Cain started out heading southwest, generally following the dark, undulating Monongahela River as it seemed to writhe and double back on itself like a stepped-on rat snake. They were soon overtaken on the road by first one and then an hour later a second band of riders approaching hard from the east. Each time Cain and Rosetta were barely able to slip into the woods before the riders came surging past. By the looks of them Cain guessed they were slave catchers. He decided not to take the chance of staying on the main road but, instead, cut northwest directly toward New Martinsville. The path from there through the mountains was of poor quality, muddy and rock strewn, with a number of sections little more than untended cow paths while, over some swampy parts, there were only corduroy roads made of rough saw logs laid side by side in the muck. Although it was slow going, the journey was uneventful. They saw no more riders. The days passed pleasantly enough for spring weather in the mountains—the mornings cool with dew covering the ground, the afternoons sunny and humid, a haze sitting along the valley floors like raggedy muslin. One afternoon they were caught in a sudden downpour, which ended as abruptly as it had begun.

"Look," Rosetta said, pointing toward a rainbow ahead. It spanned the peaks of two mountain ridges like a colorful bridge. "When a rainbow's in front of you, it's good luck."

Some of the dogwoods and rhododendrons along the lower mountain slopes had already bloomed, garish explosions of red and lavender and white. Overhead, turkey buzzards and the occasional red-tailed hawk rode the air thermals. They passed through deep gorges made of limestone, rising five hundred feet on either side. Along this route they met few travelers—mostly farmers or teamsters bringing goods to or from Morgantown, an occasional Negro driving hogs. In a valley, they passed coal miners trudging off to the mines, their faces permanently blackened, their eyeballs white and startled-looking. One of them called out, "What's a nigger doin' riding a horse?"

One morning in a winding holler deep in the mountains, they came upon a woman dressed in white, standing by the side of the road. From a distance she looked to be holding something in her arms. For a moment Cain thought she was a mirage, a trick of sunlight. But as they approached, he saw that she was not a specter at all but real flesh and blood, a sickly-looking, bone-thin woman, her face gaunt and haggard with a deathly bluish pallor to it. Her head was uncovered, and a tangle of wild, strawlike hair billowed around her, cascading down the front of her blouse. Her eyes were lackluster and blank. It was hard to affix an age to her. She could have been anywhere from twenty to forty, but Cain leaned toward the opinion that she was younger than himself. Her filthy blouse was partially open, and one weary-looking breast was attempting to nurse what appeared to be an infant. You couldn't see the child, as it was swaddled in a fancy white tablecloth with lace at the edges.

Cain had seen folks afflicted with it before, and one look at the woman told him she had the cholera.

He reined in Hermes but didn't dismount. He wanted to keep a safe distance. The woman was hanging on to life by a thread that was badly frayed; she didn't look like she'd last out the hour. She seemed to be staring out over the valley at something in the distance.

"Morning, ma'am," he said. "What happened to you?"

She turned her blank gaze full upon him, but it seemed to take her eyes several moments before they were able to get him in focus.

"We all been sick . . . with the bloody flux," she said. She spoke slowly and with great effort, pausing several times to catch her breath. "Me and my . . . husband and the young'uns."

"Where are the others?" Cain asked.

"Back yonder," she said, letting her head loll to her right, toward where a narrow cart path disappeared up into a holler.

"You have family back in there?"

She wagged her head in the affirmative.

"Had. They's all dead. I sent my oldest boy . . . for help. But that was a while back. Hit's just me . . . and the baby now," the woman said, glancing down at the child she held.

"When I come to a town, I'll send help back for you," Cain offered. Then turning to Rosetta, he said, "We ought to be moving on."

"Cain!" Rosetta hissed at him.

"What?"

"We can't just leave 'em."

"What would you suggest?"

"She's all alone."

"You want to catch what she has?" Then, lowering his voice, he added, "Besides, she's not long for this world."

"I don't care. You can't just leave them to die."

"Think of your own baby, then," he said, staring at her. He turned his horse and said, "Let's go."

But Rosetta had already dismounted.

"Are you mad?" he cried.

However, she had crossed the distance to the woman. She took her by the elbow and led her back to a hickory tree and had her sit down, with her back to it.

"Bring some water," she instructed Cain.

He cursed, saw it wasn't any use, and so dismounted and brought over a canteen. As he got close to the woman he was sickened by the odor that emanated from her. Something beyond the foul stench of her disease, it was the ripe smell of death itself. Rosetta gave her the canteen, and the woman drank frantically from it.

"Easy," she said to the woman, touching her forehead. "She burnin' up."

Rosetta took the canteen from her, poured some water in her cupped hand, and wiped it across the woman's brow. The other sighed and laid her head back against the tree, then closed her eyes. She remained so still that for a moment it appeared as if she had already expired. Rosetta gently lifted away the cloth covering the woman's child. When she did so the source of the odor became abundantly clear. The infant had been dead for some time, and the warm, humid weather had already put it in a severe state of decay. Cain thought he would retch.

Rosetta, though, didn't so much as flinch. "What's your name, honey?" she asked the woman.

She opened her eyes, glanced around curiously, as if surprised to be on this earth still. "What?"

"What's your name?"

"Maggie."

"When did your young'un take sick, Maggie?"

"I don't re'klect. Near on to a week ago. She won't . . . take any milk."

"How 'bout you give her over to me."

"No!" she cried, her blank eyes becoming suddenly fierce.

"I ain't meanin' her or you no harm."

"You get away now, nigger," the woman said, doing something with the corner of her mouth that was close to a snarl.

"Jess take it easy, Maggie," Rosetta said, trying to calm her. "What the baby's name?"

The woman looked down at her dead child, the way a mother might look at a baby merely asleep, and said, "Emmie."

"Tha's a pretty name."

"She's my only girl. Been sleepin' a lot . . . on account of the fever."

"You want her to get better, doncha?"

Maggie glanced at Rosetta. "'Course, I do."

"We'll see that she gets to a doctor."

"A real doctor?"

"Yessum."

"Promise?"

"I promise."

The woman stared at Rosetta warily. Reluctantly, she handed the baby over to her.

"Keep her bundled up. She don't like . . . the cold none."

Rosetta handed the child to Cain, who took it and had to fight back another, stronger urge to retch.

"Cain, why'nt you see 'bout takin' that child to the doctor right quick," Rosetta said, throwing a conspiratorial glance in his direction.

He took the hint and said, "I'll find a doctor, ma'am. Don't you worry."

He carried the child over to Hermes, pulled himself into the saddle with one hand, and rode for a while. He stopped when he could no longer see them and dismounted. He grabbed the hatchet from his saddlebags, walked into the woods a short distance, and set the dead child on the ground. With the hatchet he flailed away at the earth, softening the rocky soil. Then, using the flat of the blade and his bare hands, he scooped out a shallow hole. When it was a foot or so deep he stopped. He wrapped the shroud securely around the child, laid it gently in the hole, and began to cover it. Once done, he gathered some rocks and placed them on the grave so varmints wouldn't get at it, at least not right away. After he was done, he chanced to smell his hands. They stank of earth and of death. Again the urge to vomit swept over him, but this time, like a man with a hangover, he surrendered to it. He bent and let his stomach try to expel the poisonous nausea rumbling down in his gut. When he was finished, he staggered over to a small pond and dipped his hands in, tried to wash the smell from them. No matter how hard he tried, though, they still stank. He thought of Rosetta telling him how hard it was to wash away the foulness she felt.

When he got back, Rosetta and the woman were gone. He followed their trail along the path up into the holler. A quarter mile in, he came upon a crudely fashioned, rough-hewn log cabin whose chinking was mostly gone and whose roof sagged pathetically. Off to the right were half a dozen freshly dug graves, with wooden crosses made of white birch limbs tied at right angles and sticking up from each grave. Cain wondered if the woman had dug them all herself. He went inside and found Maggie in bed, Rosetta sitting beside her, reading from a worn Bible. The place, too, smelled foul, of corruption and mortality. The woman's eyes were closed, and her sunken, open mouth emitted a raggedy breathing. Rosetta read from Psalms: *"Yea, though I walk through the valley of the shadow of death, I will fear no evil: for thou art with me; thy rod and thy staff they comfort me."* She glanced over at him and shook her head to let him know that the woman wasn't far away from her journey's end.

In an hour, it was over. This time, instead of a grave, Cain found some coal oil and poured it about the house. Then he lit a locofoco and set it all ablaze. As they rode away, they saw the flames shooting through the holes in the wood, taking over the roof, consuming the cabin.

"That wasn't very smart," Cain said as they rode west. "We could both get sick."

"They's worse things than dying" was all Rosetta said.

And he knew she was right.

Six days later, they reached New Martinsville. From a small rise to the east, Cain could see the town spread out below, the river to the west, and beyond, the free state of Ohio. Down at the river, he saw a ferry. Nearby, there were several men with rifles standing at the loading gate. He got out his spyglass and took a closer look. They appeared to be stopping people who had slaves and checking their papers before they'd let them board.

"What's the matter?" Rosetta asked.

"I don't know, but I don't like the looks of it."

Had word of their flight somehow gotten all the way to the Ohio River? It seemed unlikely, but then again, Eberly wasn't the sort to take defeat easily. If he'd gotten wind that they were headed west, he might have wired on ahead and alerted the towns along the river. He certainly had enough money and influence to bring to bear on their capture.

"What we gonna do?"

"We'll head south. Find somewhere else to cross."

Several years before, he'd tracked a runaway to Parkersburg, two days' ride to the south, so he was familiar with that town a little. There at least a railroad bridge crossed the river. And on the far side, in Belpre, Ohio, he knew there would be people who would help runaways on their way to freedom. They would probably know where the Gist Settlement was.

For the next two days, they rode south, keeping the river over their right shoulder. The Ohio was wide and deep this time of year, though in a couple of spots it looked as if a crossing could be attempted. However, he didn't like the notion of trying it now, in Rosetta's condition. He thought of her struggling that time in the river up north, and almost losing her. Besides, even if they could make it over, he wouldn't have the faintest idea where the settlement was.

On the afternoon of the second day, the sky suddenly grew overcast and a rain began to fall. At first a light spring drizzle, it soon turned into a downpour, cold and mountain raw, flogging all beneath its wrath like a cat-o'-nine-tails. Off across a field that had once been under plow, Cain spotted an abandoned cabin.

"Come on," he said to Rosetta.

The structure had obviously been uninhabited for years. All of its windows had been broken, and its roof sunken in like an old man's mouth. A tangle of blackberry and dewberry vines had crept up along the sides of the cabin and seemed almost to be pulling the house down into the earth like bony fingers. The front door, attached now by only a single rusted hinge, squawked loudly when Cain opened it. Inside, the place smelled of bog and earth and the lives of small varmints who had taken up residence. Water dripped from various holes in the ceiling, and one section had been fire scarred. Still, a section of floor over near the well-made stone chimney was relatively dry. While Rosetta set about making a fire in the fireplace, Cain brought the horses inside a lean-to attached to the house, so they'd be out of the rain. He hobbled and unsaddled them, then fed them.

"Good boy," he said to Hermes, feeding him a piece of sugar.

Tired, his leg aching from the cold, Cain warmed his hands over the growing fire. Rosetta had scrounged around the cabin for wood, breaking up some old pieces of furniture that had been left behind. When the fire was blazing, Cain felt the muscles in his neck begin to uncoil.

"What you think happened to the folks lived here?" Rosetta asked as she began to make supper.

"Probably headed west like everybody else."

"I keep thinkin' 'bout that poor woman back there. Her family dead and gone. Dyin' all by herself."

"She didn't die alone. She had you," Cain said.

"I mean dyin' without people that love you. Family and such."

"I saw plenty of men in the war die all alone."

"I think that's the saddest thing there is. To die without your loved ones nearby. When I think of my momma, the thing that makes me saddest is thinkin' a her dying without me there."

"Maybe you'll see her again. Who knows?"

"I doubt it."

With a stick, Cain jabbed at the fire. "Is that why you came back to me? Didn't want me to die alone."

"I s'pose."

After they'd eaten, they spread out their bedrolls and lay down beside the fire. Outside, the rain blew fiercely against the roof, sounding like handfuls of sand peppering the shingles, while in the corners of the house the intermittent scurrying of small creatures could be heard.

"Would you read me some of that book, Cain?" she said. "About God and Satan."

Cain got up and went over to his saddlebags and took out his copy of *Paradise Lost*.

"Anything in particular you'd prefer hearing?"

"Don't matter. I like the sound of his words. What's his name?"

"Milton."

"Sounds like this Milton fellow was on speakin' terms with God."

Cain read the part where Adam forgives Eve for eating the apple.

> *"I with thee have fixt my Lot,*
>   *Certain to undergo like doom, if Death*
> *Consort with thee, Death is to me as Life;*
> *So forcible within my heart I feel*
> *The Bond of Nature draw me to my own,*
> *My own in thee, for what thou art is mine;*
> *Our State cannot be sever'd, we are one,*
> *One Flesh; to lose thee were to lose myself."*

Cain glanced up and saw her rubbing her stomach absentmindedly as she stared off into the darkness of the cabin. Her eyes were distant, wistful, and he could imagine her thinking of the other one, the child she'd lost. Every time she'd look upon the one she was carrying now, it would bring back the other, her joy and loss linked together as if by shackles. He wanted to say something, yet what could he, a man who knew nothing of what it was like to carry life and then have to give it over, a slave catcher who had for years dealt in the misery of others, offer to her?

Instead he said only, "We'll be in Ohio by and by."

She looked over at him and said, "I guess I oughta thank you, Cain."

"You don't have to thank me."

"But I do. I'm sorry for some a the things I said."

"It doesn't matter now."

Later, he was dreaming of oceans and long stretches of white sands. That's when he felt something moving against him, something warm and supple yet as unstoppable as a wave. He started to reach for his gun, but in the darkness still, he knew it was Rosetta. He felt her warmth, her body pressing into his, her scent strong and sweet in his nostrils as new-mown hay. He lay on his back and remained still, pretending to be asleep. He felt her cold hand on his chest, inching across his skin until it hovered right above his heart. He thought she wanted only the heat from his body, as she had several nights earlier. But her hand slowly moved up to his face. It slid over his features, delicately outlining his countenance, the gesture reminding him of the way the blind man had touched his face. Then he recalled again what the blind man had said to him, about having a choice to make. Had he made the right one? he wondered.

Rosetta leaned into him and feathered her lips across his cheek. Her breath was spicy, like warmed cider. When he still didn't rouse himself, she rose up, pressed herself against him, and kissed him full on the mouth. A stirring commenced in him.

"Cain," she said, reminding him of how the Indian girl had said his name, with a kind of innocent urgency. "Cain."

"I thought—"

"Hush," she told him. "You think too much, Cain. You want me or not?"

"Want you! I've wanted you since I first laid eyes on you."

She leaned down and kissed him again, harder this time. She pulled away a little so she might look down at him, to search his eyes. This time he responded, pulling her down into his embrace and kissing her back. In a moment they were at each other, tugging at buttons, pulling off clothes, struggling for the freedom of their nakedness. Frantically, hungrily, they threw themselves at each other. Cain felt in her a terrifying sort of desperation. He was reminded of the first time he'd met her, how she'd tried to kill him there at the bridge, that deadly force which had been unleashed within her. What he felt in her now came from the same source. It was a thing made up of equal parts anger and fear, desperation and yearning, and he realized now that it met its match in something in himself. For each of them, there was an elemental power deep inside, one that neither could have admitted to before this very moment but which now was struggling to get out. All that had been held back, denied, imprisoned in them, not just for the past two months they'd been together but for the entirety of their lives—all of that was suddenly let loose. He knew that he was crossing a line that he could never cross back over again. Just before their lovemaking came to an end, Rosetta cried out, her nails clawing at the flesh of his shoulders. Only then did she collapse into him, exhausted and spent.

He held her until he heard her breathing flatten out and he knew she was sleeping. He lay there for a time in the dark cabin, listening to the rain, pondering the meaning of it all. *Stop*, he told himself. Just as she'd said, he needed to stop thinking, to hold on to this moment tightly because he didn't know if anything like it would ever come his way again. He buried his face in the smooth, taut flesh of her neck. After a while, he gave himself over to the weariness of the long days they'd spent traveling. He felt the muscles in his neck and shoulders loosen, and then, like a man drunk on a fine claret, he allowed himself to slide into the deep comforting arms of sleep.

22

When Cain awoke, Rosetta was squatting before the fire, fixing breakfast. Silently, he watched her for a moment. He followed the outline of her back against the blue calico of her dress, how it dipped in at the waist before swelling to the luxuriant fullness of her haunches. He reached out and touched her, feeling desire rumbling to life in him again. She turned and smiled at him.

"Hungry, Cain?" she asked.

"Yes," he replied, smiling. "But not for food."

This time they enjoyed themselves in the leisure that was beyond hunger and need. They stood facing each other in the bright sunlight and he unbuttoned her dress slowly now, taking his time with each button, as if he had all the time in the world and each button was a thing of purest gold. When he had unfastened the last, Rosetta shrugged the dress off her thin, broad shoulders and let it pool at her feet. Something in his chest tightened as he gazed upon her brown nakedness, with its inviting secrets, its subtle nuances of swelling and recess, what in the darkness of the previous night he'd only been able to delight in by touch. When she started toward him, he told her, "No, wait." He wanted to savor the ripeness of her breasts, swelling with the life growing inside her, the strong, lean legs and firm haunches, the darker shadow below her belly. Even the bulge of her stomach was a thing amazing to him. Its smoothness fascinated him, and he reached out and slid his fingertips gently over its surface. She offered him a smile then, one filled with both a girlish innocence and a certain knowing wistfulness.

"You just gonna look?" she asked.

"You're beautiful," he said.

"By the time you get to it, Cain, I'll be a wrinkled old lady," she said, laughing.

Only then did he draw her toward him. They lay on the floor of the cabin and made love to the sound of the horses snuffling and the scraping of their hooves. When Cain looked over, he saw Hermes staring at him, as if conspiratorially. This time they moved slowly, not in the heat of need nor in the anguish of frustration, not trying to rid themselves of some terrible pent-up thing, but each trying to give the other something, a gift, a thing to share tenderly. When they were finished, they lay quietly in each other's arms, not exhausted or drunk with fatigue as they had been the previous night, but awake, more fully conscious of everything. Cain was aware of the beating both of his own heart and of hers beneath her ribs, of the smooth indentation of her lower back, the silky feel of the fine down along her cheek. It was, he knew, an altogether different thing than he'd ever experienced before, one both extraordinary and a bit unsettling.

Raising herself up so she could gaze down into his eyes, Rosetta placed a finger to his lips and said, "I love you, Cain."

After breakfast, Cain saddled the horses and they started off. The rain had let up, though the day was gray and overcast, with raggedy clouds strewn about the valleys and hollows like cotton batting. As they rode along now, he felt a transformation in the world around him, a deepening of all of its colors and sounds and smells. And he sensed a change in Rosetta, as well. She would glance over at him from time to time and smile that sad, knowing smile of hers. She carried herself with a new lightness, as if a weight had suddenly been taken off her shoulders. He, too, felt different somehow, more fully alive than he'd ever felt. And yet, in a strange way, he also felt a certain tension, a wariness of his changed state. It was as if he now carried within himself something infinitely fragile, a delicate thing that might shatter if he so much as stumbled, something both palpable and discreet, which he could sense as a pressure under his ribs on the left side, not far from where his wound had been. It made him cautious, in a way he was not used to. Not so much regarding himself—he'd always known how to fend for himself—but because of Rosetta. He wasn't altogether sure he liked this strange new feeling.

Late that afternoon, they reached the outskirts of Parkersburg. Cain saw the B&O railroad bridge that crossed the Ohio into the free town of Belpre and, down below it at the wharf, a steam ferry with side paddle wheels. With his spyglass, he noted, too, the men standing about armed with rifles and pistols. Some of them wore local militia uniforms, with the distinctive gray kepi headgear.

"Damn," he cursed.

"Now what?" Rosetta asked.

He led her a ways into the woods, then climbed a small hill. From here there was a good view of the town below, the ferry, the road they'd come in on.

"I'll go into town and ask around. You wait here." Before he left, he gave her back the Tranter, reminding her again to shoot low and to hold it with two hands.

"When you comin' back?"

"I'll be back before dark."

Cain rode into town. He stopped in front of a barbershop a stone's throw from the river. He went in and ordered a shave.

"What're all those men doing near the bridge?" Cain asked the barber, an older man with a head of white hair down to his collar.

"They're checking papers," the barber replied as he worked on Cain's beard.

"Why?"

"Heard tell they're looking for some runaway trying to cross over. Got the militia out and everything."

"All this for just one nigger?" Cain asked.

The man shrugged disinterestedly. "You'll be wanting a haircut, too?"

"Just the shave."

When the barber had finished, Cain glanced in the mirror in front of his chair. He hadn't seen himself for months and was a little surprised by the man staring back at him. He'd lost weight, his face thinner, the eyes more wearied, the lines around his mouth more deeply etched. He looked like someone who'd just awoken from a night of bad dreams. He paid the man and headed out into the street.

He left Hermes tied to a hitching post and walked down to the river. Several of the armed men standing on the wharf were talking among themselves. They paused to eye him suspiciously, then they fell to talking again. Cain made his way over to the ferry which was loading up for its next crossing. He went up to a young boy working on it and asked what the fare was.

"Hit just yourself?"

"Yes."

"Four bits."

Cain looked down at the muddy water. The Ohio here was deep and swift from the spring rains, with another river spilling into it just to the south. A half mile below the railroad bridge, a large island split the river in half. Maybe they could try to cross there. But with Rosetta in her condition he didn't like taking the chance. Besides, they'd probably be watching the banks for people crossing. Perhaps they might just continue south looking for a better place to ford.

As he was heading back up to his horse, he saw a one-armed Negro driving a team of oxen twitching a large pine log down toward the river. He was squat and powerfully built, with the empty sleeve of his right arm pinned to the shoulder. Cain approached the man.

"Afternoon," he said.

The Negro nodded but didn't turn his gaze downward the way most would on meeting a strange white man.

"You taking that log over to Belpre?" Cain asked.

"I is."

"I'm looking to get someone across to the Ohio side."

"They's the ferry ri'chere," the man said with a flick of his head.

Cain paused for a moment. "You wouldn't happen to know of those who might be able to help get someone to the North."

The Negro looked at him suspiciously, shook his head. "Doan know nothin' 'bout that, mister."

Cain took out a silver dollar and flicked it toward the man. With his one hand, the Negro snatched it out of the air but didn't deign to look at it.

"You sure?"

"Like I said, doan know nothin' 'bout that," he repeated, disdainfully flicking the coin back to Cain.

Cain stared at the man, then figured he'd take a chance.

"I know of a woman with child who needs to get to safety. She's got some soul catchers after her. Just asking for some help is all."

The man stared at him warily. He looked over his shoulders at the militia, then leaned in and said in a whisper, "Over yonder they's a man name a Stone. You ax for him. Mebbe he can hep you. Tell him you got some sheep you want delivered."

"Sheep?" Cain said.

"Yessum. Didn't hear nothin' from me," the man said nervously. Then he turned and headed off.

Cain headed back for his horse before walking down to the ferry. One of the guards asked what his business was over in Ohio. Cain replied that he was looking to purchase some sheep and the man let him pass onto the ferry. On the ride over he exchanged looks with the one-armed Negro, and when they disembarked, the man nodded to him.

Over in Belpre, he headed to the nearest saloon, figuring someone there would know the man. He sat at the bar and bought a whiskey, the first one he'd had in a week's time. He figured to have just the one.

"Where could I find a man named Stone," he asked the barkeep.

"South part of town," replied the other, a small man with hairy forearms. "Right across the river from the Little Kanawha. Can't miss it. A big white house with a red roof."

"Crazy fool's got himself a makeshift cannon aimed across at Virginia," said another man who sat a few seats down from Cain. He was pale skinned and wore a loose boatman's shirt he had not changed in some time. The barkeep laughed.

"You got business with that abolitionist son of a bitch?" the man asked Cain.

Cain ignored the comment and started to leave.

"Hey, I'm talkin' to you."

Rather than chance a scene, Cain kept walking out the door.

He found the place down near the river and turned into the drive. It was a grand house, something on the order of a southern plantation, two stories high with a long, tree-lined drive leading up to an elegant portico. Cain dismounted and went up to the door and knocked. A frail-looking, gray-haired man answered the door. At first Cain thought he might have been a servant.

"May I help you?"

"I'm looking for a man named Stone."

"What would you want with him?"

"I have some sheep to deliver."

The man, who had a long gray beard, looked him up and down, noting the gun on his hip. Then he glanced over Cain's shoulder out to the road.

"Come in," he said, ushering Cain quickly into the house. He led him into a parlor where he had him sit.

"May I offer you some refreshment?"

"Whiskey."

"I'm afraid I don't keep any in the house."

"I'm fine, then," Cain replied.

"So you have sheep to be delivered?" the man asked, sitting down opposite him. Though frail, the old man sat rigidly upright like a man in church, hands on knees.

"Yes."

"How many?"

"Just one."

"I didn't get your name."

"It's Cain."

"I have not had the pleasure of working with you before, sir. Where do you hail from?"

"Back east."

The man looked him over again, taking note once more of the big gun on his hip. "If I may be frank, you hardly look like a shepherd. Have you brought other sheep across the river?"

"No, this is the first time."

"I see," the old man said, bringing one bony hand to his beard. "Why have you decided to help the cause now?"

"I'm not interested in any cause," replied Cain, growing annoyed at the man's questions. "I only want to get one sheep across."

"We have to be careful. There are spies everywhere."

"I am looking to find the Gist Settlement. Have you heard of it?"

"Yes. It is about a week's ride west of here. Why?"

"I would like to bring someone there."

The man wagged his head. "You do not want to be going there now."

"Why not?"

"It's far too dangerous. The roads south and west of here are chock-full of slave catchers and patrols."

"I've noticed them. What's the cause of it?"

"They're after a runaway female."

"I heard. All this for just one girl?" Cain said.

"She's wanted for murder."

"Murder!" he repeated.

"Yes. She killed her mistress. Happened over near Elkins. From what I've heard, the mistress was beating her with a frying pan, and the poor girl wrested it from her and hit her back. Evidently it killed the woman. So the girl fled."

Cain smiled inwardly. All this time he'd thought it was Rosetta they were after. Turned out to be just a coincidence. He still had to be careful, especially taking a slave north across the river. They'd be suspicious.

"There is a five-hundred-dollar reward for her capture," Stone explained. "They've been scouring the countryside looking for her. Which has made things rather difficult for everyone."

"Would you help me?" Cain asked.

"I cannot help you if you're set on going west."

"I just want to see her somewhere safe."

"A woman runaway?"

"Yes."

"I would be willing to arrange transport north."

"How far north?"

"Canada. Where is she now?"

"Across the river."

"I have some sheep hidden away in the woods," the old man said, continuing with the absurd cover. "Tomorrow night I shall be bringing them on to the next station. If you can get her here by midnight, I will be happy to take her along as well."

"They're guarding the bridge and the ferry."

"Yes. You will need to be careful. They have patrols all up and down the river on both sides. If you don't have the proper papers for a slave, they will stop you. They are jailing any Negro without them. However, there is a man on the Virginia side that sometimes brings runaways across. Pettigrew. He's not one of us. He charges for his services."

"I can pay," Cain said.

Stone then described where the man lived in Parkersburg, a cabin in a wooded area down near the confluence of the Little Kanawha and Ohio rivers. He then stood and offered his hand to Cain.

"You will need to have her here by midnight or I shall be forced to leave without you. Godspeed."

Cain took the ferry back across the river. By now it was getting on toward dark. He rode down to the junction of the two rivers and, as the underbrush became so clotted with sweet briar and blackberry brambles, he had to dismount, tie Hermes to a tree, and go it on foot. In the darkness, he crept through the woods, getting entangled and cut up on the vines. He came finally upon a cleared area down by the water. By moonlight, he made out a cabin, built into the side of the bank with the back suspended over the water on stilts. Dense undergrowth grew up along the sides of the cabin. He saw a light in the window and smoke wafting from a chimney. In front of the place was a small garden patch, while off to the right was a ramshackle shed and chicken coop. Cain headed up to the front door and knocked.

"Whatchu want?" a voice called from within.

"I'm looking for Pettigrew."

"That'd be me. What's your business?"

"John Stone said you could help me. I have some sheep I need transported across the river," Cain said.

"Ain't interested."

"I'm willing to pay twenty dollars."

There was silence, followed by the sound of a wooden bar being slid across behind the door. The door swung in and Cain found himself facing an old fowling piece.

"Twenty dollars, you say?" said Pettigrew. Behind the gun was a thin, pale man, shirtless, wearing a pair of homespun trousers held up by suspenders. His skin appeared grayish in the dim light, and while his arms and face were skinny, he had a potbelly that sagged over his pants waist. A mangy white cat circled about his legs.

"That's right."

"What sort of sheep?"

"You interested or not?"

"C'mon in."

Inside, the place reeked of coal oil, corn liquor, and rotting fish. The man hung his gun above the fireplace, walked across the room, and grabbed hold of an empty hogshead. He rolled it out of the way and lifted up a hinged part of the flooring, which turned out to be a trapdoor. He glanced over at Cain and said, "I have to take precautions." Then he climbed down a ladder toward the river. Cain glanced around the sparsely furnished cabin. Besides the table and two chairs, there was a bed in the corner, at its foot a crudely made box fashioned of pine planks. It resembled a coffin. Pettigrew returned in a moment carrying a stone jug dripping water. He sat at a table made of a rough slab of cottonwood cut width-wise and propped up on four spindly legs.

"Well, set yourself down whilst I eat."

Cain sat across the table from Pettigrew. The man fell to eating a pile of fried catfish. His mouth made crunching noises as he broke bones and cartilage without seeming concern. He washed it all down with copious swigs of liquor from the stone jug. He didn't offer Cain any. The cat had jumped up on the table and was watching the man eat, biding his time.

"How come you cain't go by the reg'lar ferry?"

"This sheep needs special care," Cain replied.

"How many?"

"Just the one."

Pettigrew smiled, showing a handful of blackened teeth.

"You either running from the law or you got a nigger needs crossing. Wouldn't be that nigger gal they's after here'bouts?"

"No," Cain replied.

"When you lookin' to cross?"

"Tomorrow night."

"Hell," the man cried. "Too dangerous now. You tell Stone to wait a few days. Let things settle down a mite."

Cain got up, went over to a window at the back, which looked out onto the river. The river's dark surface gleamed in the moonlight like a piece of polished onyx. Below, nearly hidden by overhanging limbs and bushes, sat a dugout canoe in the water.

"I'm only wanting to get across that river," Cain said.

"You and ever' damn nigger south of the Mason-Dixon."

"All right. I'll pay you thirty dollars."

"They catch me, I'd go to prison. Naw, you wait awhile."

"No, it has to be tomorrow night."

Cain could see that the man had already decided he would do it and was now just trying to increase his price.

"All right," said Cain, "fifty dollars."

At this, the man stopped chewing. He looked across the room at Cain and his eyes narrowed.

"You make it a hunnerd and you got yourself a deal."

"A hundred dollars just to cross?"

"It's dangerous times. Take it or leave it, mister."

Cain removed his billfold and dropped fifty dollars on the table. While he was counting the money, Pettigrew's attention was drawn away from his plate, allowing the cat to move in on his dinner. When he saw it, the man swore and smacked the cat with the back of his hand, sending the thing sprawling onto the floor.

"Ain't but fifty there," the man said.

"The rest when we land on the other side."

Pettigrew took another drink from the jug. "Tomorrow night be here soon's it's dark. And make sure you have the rest of the money."

Riding back through town toward where Rosetta was waiting, Cain decided to stop at a saloon down near the river. He was thirsty and figured to have himself another drink, and mull things over. Everything had gotten so jumbled up, his mind streaked and his will flummoxed. That odd sensation he'd had up under his ribs since the previous night was still there. When he'd finished the first glass of whiskey, he had another and then another after that, hoping for some sort of clarity. He thought of some lines from Milton: *The mind is its own place, and in itself, can make heaven of Hell, and a hell of Heaven.*

It was late when Cain finally stumbled out into the street. As he mounted Hermes and turned east, he chanced to see several horses tied in front of an inn across the street. He noticed that one of the animals was gray colored in the moonlight, its hindquarters muscled and thick. Something told him he'd seen the animal before, but he was too drunk to pay it much mind.

As he approached the spot in the woods where he thought he'd left Rosetta, he dismounted and walked along on foot. He stumbled over something in the dark and fell headlong. As he lay on the ground, behind his ear he heard the distinctive click of a gun's hammer.

"That you, Cain?" Rosetta whispered.

"It's me."

"Where on earth you been?"

"I had to make arrangements," he said.

She struck a locofoco and lit the lantern she carried. She held it up in front of him. "You're drunk," she said, staring at him.

"So what if I am?"

"I was worried sick, and you out gettin' liquored up."

Before he knew it, he'd blurted out, "I don't need to answer to some . . ."

He didn't say some runaway slave, some white man's nigger bitch, but they both knew that's what he meant. She gave him a look at once angry and hurt, and turned and walked farther into the woods where she'd made camp. In silence she built a fire and began to cook supper, not even looking over at him.

"Plans have changed," he finally said.

"Yeah?"

"Yeah." He explained the business about the other runaway, that they had the militia out looking for her and that they couldn't use the ferry. Once across the river, he told her, they were going to meet up with a man who ran the Underground Railroad.

"He'll take you north," he explained.

"What about that place you talked of?"

"It's too risky. Not with all the patrols they have out on the roads. But he'll see that you get to Canada."

"Canada?" she said. "I don't know nothin' 'bout Canada."

"You'll be safe there."

"Why don't I go back to Boston, then? 'Least I knew folks there. There was other Negroes in Boston."

"You'd never be safe in Boston. You know that. He'd find you."

"Just take me back there."

"No. That's crazy."

"Then let me make my own way."

"I said no."

"Am I still your nigger slave or am I free?"

"You're going to do what I damn well tell you. And that's final."

They ate supper in an awkward silence. Cain sat there morosely sipping from his flask. He regretted the comment he'd made before. He didn't even know where it had come from. Just some ornery dark place that was buried deep in him. That place that all white men resorted to finally, ultimately.

"What about you?" she asked after a while. "Where you gonna go?"

"I told you. I'm heading west."

She pretended interest in the food on her plate. Then she looked across the fire at him. "Take me with you."

"What?" he said, looking up at her.

"Take me with you. I wouldn't be no trouble."

"How the hell am I going to take you with me?" he said.

"Why not?"

"Because it'd be too dangerous."

"I come all this way with you, didn't I?"

"And we both nearly got ourselves killed in the process! I tell you, it's too dangerous."

"You just want to be shut of me is all."

"That's not why. It's just that it's safer for you to go north with those Underground Railroad people."

"What about last night and this morning? Didn't that mean nothing? Or was that just sport? Havin' you a little fun."

"You know that's not true."

"No?"

"No!" Cain snapped at her. He wanted to tell her what he felt. He wanted to tell her that he loved her, loved her more than he'd ever loved anything. But something held him back, something turned his love to anger and to bitterness. "Don't you understand?"

"Only thing I understand is the man I love don't want me."

"It just wouldn't work, Rosetta. Out west is not going to be any different. They wouldn't let us be."

She got up and came around the fire and sat down beside him. She put her hand on his arm, got up so close he could smell her warm breath on his face.

"I could make like I'm your slave. Nobody'd have to know 'cept us."

"No," he replied.

"Listen to me, Cain. It could work."

"Just stop it."

"I'm willin' at least to try."

"I told you to stop."

"You're just afraid?"

"Afraid? Of what?" he hissed at her.

"It ain't got to do with nobody else. It's got to do with you afraid of being with me." She put the palm of her right hand against his face. "Please, Cain. I'm beggin' you."

"Stop it."

"Don't do this. We could be together, me and you."

She tried to hug him then, but he shoved her violently away and stood up.

"Godamn it. I said enough," he cried, staring down at her. "Tomorrow you're going north, and I won't hear any more about it. Do you hear me?"

With that he stomped off into the woods.

23

When Cain woke, a dull rattling commenced in his head, almost as if, while he'd slept, someone had poured buckshot into his ear. Shielding his eyes from the bright morning light, he tried to form spit to have something to swallow the foul taste in his mouth. Rosetta had already been up for a time, having made a fire and boiled coffee.

"You want coffee?" she asked just this side of surly.

"Please."

She poured him a cup and he sat up and took it.

"What time is it?" he asked, more just to break the silence than to engage in conversation with her.

"Figure 'bout seven. More riders come by earlier," she said with a nod toward the road below. "When we leavin'?"

"At nightfall."

They spent the day pretending nothing was wrong. Cain cleaned and oiled his gun, replacing the percussion caps, while Rosetta occupied herself with darning her socks. An awkwardness had set in between them, so that when they spoke at all it was like strangers sharing a stagecoach. At one point she looked at him, frowned, then said, "See you cut your beard," to which he replied simply, "Yes." Later on, he told her he was going to take the horses down to the river to water them. While he was there, he watched the traffic on the Ohio, some of it headed north to Pittsburgh, some south to Cincinnati. There were flat-bottomed crafts and scows, dugouts and droghers, barges filled with coal and lumber, as well as a long stern-wheeler headed upriver. On the other side, he saw a colored man behind a large draft horse plowing a field. Not a half mile away, freedom loomed like an impenetrable fortress.

He picked up some stones and skimmed them across the water. They danced on the surface for a while, slowed, then sank beneath the current. He thought about his conversation with Rosetta the night before. He couldn't take her with him. That was just plain crazy. It would just be too dangerous. Besides, a life together wouldn't work. He wondered if it was true, as she'd said, that he was afraid. Afraid of what people would say? Was he still, in his heart of hearts, a southerner, a white man? Despite everything they'd been through, everything he felt for her, could he never renounce that? Maybe his father had been right. Or was it simply that he was afraid of tying his life to another, losing his freedom by shackling himself to this woman? He couldn't say.

When darkness fell, he told her, "Let's go."

They circled around the town, keeping to the woods as much as possible. The night was pleasant and clear, with a nearly full waxing moon hanging above like the eye of a cat. They made their way toward the river and dismounted, walking the rest of the way. As they got down closer to the water they could hear the raspy chorus of frogs and the metallic drone of crickets. It was cooler down near the water. After a while, Cain made out the shack. A light shone inside. As they approached, Hermes neighed once and bobbed his head nervously. Cain froze. He drew his Colt and peered warily into the woods around him.

"What?" Rosetta whispered.

"I don't know."

They waited for several minutes. When nothing happened, he told her to wait there with the horses.

He crept up to the front door of the cabin and crouched in the darkness, trying to hear any noises that might be coming from inside. Nothing. He rose up and peered through the window, saw the man sitting at the table drinking from his jug. At that moment, Cain heard something behind him, and he whirled around. It was the cat, oblivious to how close it had come to losing all of its nine lives. The animal simply rubbed its nose against the gun's barrel. Finally, Cain stood and knocked. In a moment the door swung inward, and the man stood there, holding a lantern aloft.

"Wondrin' where you was," Pettigrew said. Glancing down at the gun in Cain's hand, he asked, "What's that for?"

Cain looked over the man's shoulder into the cabin. Only when he was sure it was safe did he holster the gun.

"We all set?" he asked the man.

"You got the money?"

"I do."

Pettigrew stuck out his hand. "Let's see it."

"We said when you get us across."

"*You* said. Things changed. You'll need to pony up now or we ain't goin' nowhere."

Cain didn't like paying in full before they were across, but the other man held all the cards.

"Where's your sheep?" the man asked, looking past him into the darkness. "We ain't got all night."

"I'll be right back."

When he reached Rosetta, he tied the horses to a tree.

"Come on," he said to her. They found Pettigrew back inside, seated at his table drinking from the stone jug.

"Want a nip?" he asked Cain.

"I thought you were in a hurry."

"We got us a little time. Set yourself down and relax," the man said, smiling unctuously.

"I want to get going," Cain replied. "I have an appointment on the other side."

"All in good time," he said, staring at Rosetta. "Now I see why you were so all-fired-up to get her across. Ain't she a likely thing."

"We need to go."

"Just hold your horses, mister," Pettigrew said, glancing toward the front window. "I'm waitin' on somebody."

"What?" Cain said.

"'Nother passenger."

"You didn't say anything about that."

"Didn't figure it was none a your business."

"I'm paying you good money."

"So's he," Pettigrew explained. "Don't get your dander up. Have a drink and relax. Maybe your nigger'd like a drink."

"I want you to take us across now."

"What say you to a drink?" he said, extending the jug out to Rosetta.

"I said *now*," Cain repeated. When the man just smiled at him, Cain drew his gun and shoved it in his face.

"Hey, now. Ain't no call for that."

Cain cocked the hammer.

"Awright, awright. Take it easy with that damn cannon," Pettigrew said, getting to his feet. He picked up the lantern and headed over to the front door. He set the lantern down on the floor and grabbed his coat, which hung from a peg near the window. When he picked the lantern up, he did something odd: it almost seemed as if he swung it back and forth in front of the window.

"What're you doing?" Cain asked.

"Nothin'."

"Get away from there," Cain said. When the man didn't move, Cain walked over to the window and shoved him away from it. Then he wrested the lantern from him.

"The hell you think you're doing?" Pettigrew exclaimed.

"Shut up."

"You can't come in my house and treat me like that."

With that, Pettigrew suddenly reached for something in his pocket, but Cain was able to club him with the barrel of his gun. The force knocked the man to the floor. Cain squatted and searched in his pocket, removing a single-barreled derringer, which he pocketed. Then he blew out the lantern and went back to the window.

Now that the cabin was dark, Cain chanced peering out into the night. Even with the moonlight, at first he saw nothing, but as his eyes slowly adjusted, he was able to make out the shed and the chicken coop, and some twenty yards beyond, the thick lumpy shapes of trees. He scanned the woods, for what, he wasn't sure. The night was still, silent save for the ratcheting sound of the crickets.

"Christ Almighty," Pettigrew moaned, rubbing his head. "You near'bouts broke my skull."

"I told you to shut up," Cain warned him. "Who's out there?"

"Nobody."

Cain continued to search the woods. He was almost ready to give up when, just to the right and behind the chicken coop, he thought he made out something, a lighter, almost silvery shape that slowly separated itself from the surrounding darkness of the woods. A horse, he thought. And then, next to it, gradually emerged the muted but distinct shape of another, and then another. Cain was able to make out a half dozen horses, all still saddled.

"Those your horses?" Cain demanded.

Pettigrew paused for a moment, rubbing his head. "They are."

"How come they're saddled?" Cain leaned over and shoved the barrel of his gun into the man's nose. "Who's out there?"

"Don't know what you're talkin' 'bout," the man said.

"Who were you waiting for?"

But right then, Cain's attention was drawn to a noise outside. He heard footsteps running through the woods.

"Help," Pettigrew cried. "He's got a gun on me."

Cain was going to strike the man again, but a voice broke from the sheltering darkness of the woods.

"Cain," it called. He sensed he'd heard it before, but for a moment, he couldn't place it. "Come on out and bring the girl with you."

"It's *him*," Rosetta said.

Eberly, thought Cain.

Then he was returned to the whorehouse in Richmond: *Bring her back*, Eberly was saying once again. And with that, Cain realized, suddenly, eerily, whose horse the silver roan was, the same one he'd seen the night before in town. If he hadn't been so drunk he'd probably have recognized it. Preacher's mount. Cain wondered how they'd found him, but now it didn't really matter.

He squatted down beside Pettigrew. He removed his pocketknife and opened the blade. Grabbing the man by the hair, he pulled his head back and placed the blade to his throat. "How many men does Eberly have with him?"

"I don't know," Pettigrew said. Cain yanked on his hair and the man cried out. "Jesus. Seven, maybe eight."

"How are they armed?"

"One feller had a Jennings. The rest I couldn't say."

"What did you tell Eberly?"

"Nothin'."

"Did you tell him I was meeting Stone?"

"No."

"I am going to ask you again and you had better tell me the truth."

"No. I swear to God, I didn't."

Cain thought for a moment. He knew he couldn't let the man go. If he hadn't already told Eberly about his plans for getting Rosetta across the river to Stone, he surely would now. Cain couldn't risk that.

Pettigrew must have caught something in Cain's expression. "You ain't gonna—" Pettigrew began. Yet with a flick of his wrist, Cain had drawn the blade sharply across his throat. Pettigrew tried to cry out, but what emerged from his mouth was only a surprised gurgling sound. He struggled to stand, as if that might somehow help him, but managed only to stagger forward a few steps before collapsing. The man's body continued kicking, scratching the floor, fighting for several seconds until what life remained in him leached out onto the floor, and finally it lay still. Cain didn't feel anything about having killed him. He would've killed ten men, a hundred, a thousand, to keep Rosetta from being taken.

"Cain," the voice said again. "There's no call for anybody getting hurt. You just bring the girl on out and I'll let you go."

He felt Rosetta's presence squatting behind him.

"What we gonna do?" she whispered.

He was silent for a moment, letting the dust of his thoughts settle. He tried to fashion a plan; that was always Cain's way. Finally, he came up with the only thing he could think of. Walking over to the back of the cabin, he rolled the hogshead out of the way and lifted the trapdoor cautiously and, with his Colt at the ready, peered down into the black water. Below, it was dark, yet from the moonlight he could make out a crudely built ladder that led down to the water. A canoe rested there, tethered to a tree. He was sure the thick undergrowth sheltered the ladder and the canoe from those up in front of the cabin. At least he hoped that it did.

Finally, he went back over to Rosetta. "You're going to go out and get in that canoe and head for the other side."

"What about you?" she asked.

"I'll be fine."

She snorted. "How you gone be fine? All those men he got out there."

"Let me worry about that."

"I want to stay with you."

"You can't stay with me," he said.

"Why not?"

"Because you can't."

"And you can't tell me what to do no more," she countered.

"Rosetta, listen to me."

"You listen. You don't own me, Cain. I can do what I want."

"And what you want to do is get in that canoe and leave. While you still have the chance."

"Ain't lettin' you stay on account of me. It's me he wants. I'll give myself up, then."

"Are you mad? After all we went through to get you here."

"Won't be having you on my conscience."

"Even if you give yourself up, you really figure he's just going to let me walk on out of here? After all the trouble I caused him? After what I *know*?"

"He might."

"You know him better than that. You know he's not going to let me go."

"Ain't gonna leave you, Cain," she said stubbornly. "I'll fight the bastard with you. I don't care what happens to me."

He took her firmly by the shoulders. In the dim light that seeped through the window he stared into her eyes, which were a pale, powdery gray.

"Listen, Rosetta," he said. "If you won't think of yourself, at least think about that child you're carrying."

"I am thinkin' 'bout it."

"I thought you didn't want it born into slavery?"

"I don't."

From outside came Eberly's voice again. "You send the girl out, Cain, and I'll let you go. You have my word as a gentleman."

"See," she said.

"He's lying," Cain told her. "He'll kill me and he'll take you back. You want that? Have him sell off this child, too. Or what if it's a girl child? You want her to be around him? You really want that?"

He knew he was being cruel, but there was no other way. She didn't say anything for a while. Soon he saw the tears running down her cheeks.

"When you get across, look for a big white house down near the river. Ask for a man named Stone. He's expecting you. You need to be there by midnight. You have the gun?"

She nodded.

"Try to be quiet. Use it only if you have to."

Then he took out his billfold and handed it to her. He went over to Pettigrew's body and searched through his pockets until he found the money he'd paid him.

"Take this, too," he said.

"Won't you be needing some?" she asked.

Instead of answering, he said, "You have to go."

Before she did, though, she threw her arms around his neck and hugged him.

"I love you, Cain," she said.

He brought her over to the trapdoor. "You wait here till I start shooting. Then you hurry down the ladder, get in the canoe, and paddle like hell."

"But—"

"Don't look back. Keep your eyes on the other side. That's freedom waiting for you over there. For your baby, too."

"But, Cain—"

"No, listen to me," he interjected.

She threw her arms around his neck one more time and clung to him. He finally had to pry her hands off.

"I love you," she said again.

He wanted to tell her he loved her, too, but he felt she had to have her head clear, her thoughts completely focused on getting away, not on him, not on what she was leaving behind. Instead, he leaned toward her and kissed her. "Be careful, Rosetta. Now get ready."

Then he turned and walked over to the fireplace. He located Pettigrew's old fowling piece, then felt around on the mantel until he found his powder horn and canister filled with buckshot. Not knowing he'd need it, he'd left his own ammunition back in his saddlebags. He headed to the front of the cabin and sat down beside the window.

"Eberly," he called out. "It's me. Cain."

He waited until he heard the old man's reply so he had some notion of where to aim. As soon as Eberly spoke, Cain flung open the casement and laid down fire at the noise, emptying his revolver. They didn't return fire. Glancing over his shoulder, he saw that Rosetta had slipped away.

When it was quiet again, he heard laughter. Then another voice from outside.

"Hell, Cain, you can't hit shit," Preacher taunted.

"Just bring her out, Cain," Eberly called. "I'm not interested in you. You bring the girl out and you can go about your business."

He assumed that Rosetta had gotten away; otherwise they wouldn't still be trying to negotiate with him. They'd have burned him out. He remained silent as he concentrated on reloading, using Pettigrew's powder and shot. This time, he was forced to fill the chambers with buckshot instead of .44 caliber lead balls. Though he'd never shot one himself, it would resemble a Lemat's revolver with its single shotgun barrel. He thought how it might actually work to his advantage. The buckshot wouldn't be as accurate, but it would throw a wide and deadly pattern better suited to close-in fighting, which he figured it would come to sooner or later.

When he was finished, he decided to fortify his defenses as much as he could. He crawled over and grabbed a chair and wedged it behind the door. Then he dragged the dead man's body and lay that against the door, too. It wouldn't stop them. It would only slow them down, but that's all he could hope for. Every second he could buy would give Rosetta a little more time before they realized their mistake. And as long as they believed she was in there, he didn't think they'd just fire indiscriminately into the cabin, for fear of injuring her. But when their patience ran out, they'd eventually come. Next, he made his way over to the table in the center of the room, set the jug of moonshine on the floor, and dragged the heavy piece of furniture to the corner farthest away from the door. There he tipped it on its side, with the legs set out away from the corner. The top was thick and would, he felt, stop all but a heavy-caliber rifle round. Then he went back over and grabbed the fowling piece and the jug and settled in behind the overturned table. He uncorked the jug and took a long sip of the copper-tasting liquid. It tasted foul, but it slowed his breathing and calmed his nerves some, so he took another.

"Hey, Cain," Preacher yelled. "It was you told Brown where he could find us, wasn't it?"

Cain didn't respond.

"Hope you're glad you got both a the Strofe boys kilt. Nearly got me kilt, too, you dirty sum'bitch."

He regretted the death of Little Strofe, but he figured it was a thing unavoidable.

"Cain," the old man called. "Listen to me."

He didn't reply for a moment. Then he figured he ought to keep him occupied. "What do you want?"

"You know what I want. I thought we had an agreement between gentlemen?"

"You're no damn gentleman."

"Let me come in and talk to her."

"Go to hell."

"Then send her out, Cain. I promise nothing will happen to her."

"Just like nothing happened to her before? And before that to her mother," Cain taunted.

"What did she tell you?"

"I heard all about it, Eberly."

"She fill your head with her pack of lies? Rosetta," he called, "what did you tell him?"

"She told me the truth."

"You come on out now, Rosetta, and I'll forgive you. You hear me?"

"She's not coming out," Cain yelled.

"You can keep the baby. You have my word. What do you say, Rosetta?"

Carrying the fowling piece, Cain crawled over to the front of the cabin. He poked the gun out the window and squeezed the trigger. He wasn't even sure the ancient thing would fire, but it did, kicking like a horse with a burr under its saddle.

"There's your answer, Eberly."

"This wasn't any of your affair, Cain," the old man called. "You'll regret this, I assure you."

After that, he heard nothing outside for a long while. He headed back over and got down behind the table. He reloaded the fowling piece, putting in an extra charge of powder and buckshot and ramming it snug with the ramrod. He balanced the gun on a table leg, so it was aimed in the direction of the front door. He'd only need to pull the trigger. As he sat there, he wondered if they'd come at him now or wait till morning. Darkness had its obvious advantages. But then again, Eberly would fear Rosetta's accidentally getting hit in the shooting. He figured they'd wait till morning. Then he checked the powder flask. Counting the rounds he already had in his guns plus the derringer, he thought he had enough for a dozen shots, fifteen at the most. He would need to be frugal from here on out, making each shot count.

As he sat there, he saw something white moving in the shadows along the cabin's wall, like a wisp of smoke. Pettigrew's cat. It came slinking cautiously up to Cain, pushing its nose against his leg, meowing.

"This is not a place you're going to want to be," he told the animal. The cat continued to press against him. When he went to pet it, though, the thing bit him on the hand. Cain swatted it, and the cat bolted, hiding somewhere in the darkness.

As he sat there, he took more swigs from the jug until it didn't taste so bad. He wondered where Rosetta was now, whether she'd made it safely across the river. If she could get to Stone's place, he felt good about her chances. Stone seemed both reliable and committed to what he was doing. He'd take her on to the next station, and from there someone would lead her on to the next and, if luck was with her, so on all the way to Canada. He'd never been there himself, but a few runaways he'd hunted had followed the North Star all the way there. While he knew that some slave catchers didn't even stop at the border, most would give up and turn back. It became too costly a proposition. The reward on the runaway wouldn't pay the expenses to bring him back. Rosetta and her child would be reasonably safe there, he felt, though who could say with somebody as single-minded as Eberly? Probably only death itself would stop him.

Rosetta had said they could have gone there together, the two of them, but Cain knew that would have been impossible, even in Canada. Nowhere in the world could they have lived in peace. Of course, it was perfectly fine to do what Eberly had done, to take a slave as a mistress, but a white man and a black woman living openly, freely as man and wife—no, people weren't ready for that. Still, he found himself trying to picture what a life with her would have been like—a simple life, himself in a field, behind the traces of a mule, plowing—*he*, a farmer! Working all day, as Brown had said a man ought, and then coming in toward evening, weary, sitting down to supper, Rosetta across from him. Also sitting there would be a boy. For some reason, he imagined a male child. He'd be striking-looking, like Rosetta, with her sharp features and matchless blue eyes. At night they'd sit in front of the fire, and he'd teach the boy to read. He'd show him how to ride a horse and to track and hunt—animals, that is. And to shoot a gun. Yes, that, too. Because the world was a dangerous place and he'd have to know how to protect himself and those he loved. Cain imagined sleeping beside Rosetta, making love, waking up in the morning with her next to him. He let himself imagine all of this now, perhaps because he knew it would never come to be. He would not leave this place, he knew. He regretted more than feared that fact. Yet, of all the many things he regretted in his life, the one he regretted most was that he had not told her he loved her.

Time passed. Bars of silvery moonlight now slanted at an angle through the back window, pooling wetly on the floor near the fireplace. The night grew cooler, and the insect noises ceased. Everything became very still. He craned his ears, listening, waiting. He felt as he had at Buena Vista, when he was wounded and he lay waiting for the Mexicans to come and finish him off. He felt tired and worn out, felt he could sleep for ages. He lay his head back against the rough log wall and decided to shut his eyes for a moment. When they came, he would need to be alert, ready.

He must have dozed off, for he jerked suddenly awake when a raspy noise sounded nearby. It was the cat, hissing at something. He sat up with a start, scanning the now dim light around him. The front door was still shut, but he could *feel* the presence of another in the room with him. As his eyes adjusted, he saw that the trapdoor lay open. Somehow they had found the back way in and slipped inside while he'd been sleeping. He made out movement near the fireplace, then slowly, the darkness took on a human form. A man, hunched over, carrying a big revolver, while behind him, another with a double-barreled shotgun. Cain quietly raised the fowling piece, took aim at the first figure, and fired for the middle of his body. The man didn't have a chance to utter a sound as the blast threw him into the wall behind him. With his revolver, Cain then turned his aim on the second figure and fired again. As this one fell, though, he managed to get off a blast of his shotgun. Most of the pellets were absorbed by the table but some managed to strike the part of Cain's left shoulder that had been exposed. The lead bit scalding pain into his flesh. The man on the floor still had some life in him, and he emptied his second barrel at Cain, who luckily had taken cover this time. Cain then leaned over the table, took his time, and fired another shot into the man, finally silencing him.

"Damn," Cain cursed, touching his wounded shoulder.

He didn't have time to linger on this, though. He knew others would follow these two. He put his handgun down, took up the fowling piece, and reloaded it, expecting more of Eberly's men to come at him at any moment.

Seconds ticked off slowly. He could see now that it was close to dawn. The darkness had leached out of the night, leaving behind a chalky blue like the light in a dream. Several figures rushed by the open window and he fired his handgun once. He might have hit one, but he couldn't be sure. *Don't waste your ammo*, he told himself. Outside, he heard whispered voices, but he couldn't make out what they were saying. It was silent for a moment. He heard the cat, hidden off in a corner, meow once.

Then they came again.

There was a dull thudding noise against the front door, followed by a splintering sound, as if someone was swinging an ax against it. This continued for a while before the wood began to give way, and the door was finally shattered and separated from its hinges, its pieces falling inward. Two more men rushed into the cabin, one after another. The blast from the fowling piece caught the first squarely in the chest and spun him around and he fell across the body of one of those already dead. Then Cain took up his handgun and fired at the second man. He was huge, six five and broad shouldered, thick bellied, carrying a Jennings repeating rifle in his hands. The buckshot from the revolver hit him straight on, but its impact was considerably less than that of the fowling piece. It seemed to anger him more than slow him down. He kept plodding forward, cursing Cain, his mother, cocking the lever of his Jennings rifle and firing as he came on. Cain hit him with three more shots before he gave up and fell to the floor. And when he was down, though he didn't move, Cain shot him again for what he'd said about his mother. He had one shot left, and he fully expected them to charge again, finish him off before he had a chance to reload. Inexplicably, they waited for a while, which gave him time, at least, to reload his Colt.

By now it was almost fully light out. He made out five bodies lying in various poses on the floor of the small cabin. The place smelled like a slaughterhouse, of blood and urine and shit. This time, before they charged, one man took up a position at the front window and with a pair of revolvers laid down some fearsome covering fire at

Cain. Having to keep his head low, the best he could do was to fire blindly over the table. He killed the first man just as he reached him, but the second was able to grab hold of one of the table's legs and pull it away, exposing Cain. The man had brought with him only a small-caliber pepperbox, and he squeezed off several shots at point-blank range, but he shot wildly, jerking the trigger, and only one hit the mark. It tore into Cain's right thigh. For his part, Cain calmly turned his Colt on the man and with a single shot blew off most of his face. A third man had changed his mind and turned tail for the door. Cain shot him in the back, and he staggered and fell forward. He started crawling for the door when Cain shot him again in the ass.

"You goddamned son of a bitch," the man cried. Cain cocked his gun and squeezed the trigger again, but there was only a hollow click followed by the most sickening silence he had ever heard.

At this point, Preacher rushed into the cabin. He was still wearing his derby, but instead of the North pistol, in each hand he clutched a revolver. He stood there for a moment, laughing, a kind of wild, high-pitched braying sound, like a mule gone mad on jimsonweed. "I told you, dint I?" he said. "That I'd kill you." Then he moved toward Cain, firing as he went. Cain took cover behind the table, the lead splintering the wood as it tore into the top. When he reached Cain, Preacher grabbed the table and flung it aside. Smiling the demented grin of the mad, he stared down at Cain, his dark snake eyes cold and glossy, the birthmark on his neck blazing.

"You oughtn'ta messed with me, Cain," Preacher proclaimed.

"You're a gutless fool," Cain taunted.

"Gutless?"

"That's right. A gutless fool."

Preacher let out a laugh. Instead of shooting him outright, though, he holstered his guns and removed his bowie knife from the sheath on his leg. "Now we'll see who's got guts, Cain," he said, licking his thumb and testing the sharpness of the blade.

Cain watched him, waiting.

As he squatted down, Cain pulled the derringer from his pocket and cocked it in one motion. Preacher stared at the thing, dumbfounded for a moment. Then he started to lunge at Cain with the knife, but

Cain fired first, the ball striking Preacher in the face. It entered below his left eye, and the force of it jerked his head back so that he was looking at the ceiling. His arms commenced to flap awkwardly at his sides, as if he were a bird trying to take flight for the first time. Finally, his chin dropped to his chest and he fell backward onto the floor, his legs bent beneath his body like some contortionist.

One of Preacher's guns had fallen out of the holster and lay just a few feet away. Cain tried to slide over and get hold of it, but with his wounded leg, he found the going difficult. Still, he'd almost reached it when he heard a voice say, "Hold it right there, Cain."

He looked up to see Eberly standing in the cabin's doorway. He held a small-caliber pocket revolver and was glancing around the room. At first Cain thought it was in distress at all the bodies littered about, all the men he'd sent to their deaths. But then he realized Eberly was only looking for Rosetta, that the dead didn't matter a jot to him. Eberly picked his way carefully through the bodies and gore, as one wearing a new pair of boots would a cow barn, and came over to Cain and stood looking down at him.

"It didn't have to be like this," Eberly said.

"You're right," Cain replied. "You could've gone home."

The man didn't think it funny. "This wasn't any of your affair."

"You made it my affair. I didn't want to go after her, remember."

"Where is she?"

When Cain shrugged, Eberly kicked him in the face with his boot.

"Do not try my patience. Where is she?" he asked again.

Cain just stared at him with a smug look.

Eberly squatted down beside Cain. "Do you want to live?"

"We both know you're not going to let that happen."

"Tell me where she went and I shall let you go. You have my word."

Cain laughed. "Go to hell."

Eberly stood and cocked the hammer of his gun.

"I shall find her with or without your help."

"You found me, then," a voice interrupted. Cain angled his head to see Rosetta standing in the doorway. She was holding the big Tranter in both hands and aiming it unsteadily at Eberly. Cain doubted she could have hit him from that distance.

"Rosetta," the old man exclaimed. "I have missed you so."

She snorted.

"I have. Please, come back with me."

"You let him go."

Eberly still had his gun pointed at Cain. "Put it down, Rosetta," he said, "and we'll talk."

"No, you let him go first."

"Give me the gun," Eberly said.

Cain spoke up then. "Don't, Rosetta. Don't listen to him."

"I will let you keep the child," Eberly offered, reaching out his hand toward her. "Just come home with me."

Cain thought it funny that he used the word *home*. As the old man took a step toward her, she yelled, "You stay there." When he continued, she turned the gun on herself, placing it against her temple.

"Easy," the old man called to her.

"Rosetta, no," said Cain. "Don't do this on account of me."

"It ain't on account of you."

"Put the gun down, Rosetta," Eberly said, "and I'll let him go. I promise."

"Let him go first."

"All right," Eberly conceded.

"Go, Cain," Rosetta said.

"I'm not going to let you do this."

"You don't have any say in this, Cain. Now go. Go or I'll shoot this here gun."

Cain grabbed hold of the fowling piece and used it as a crutch to stand. When he was upright, he glanced at Eberly, then hobbled toward the door. He stopped before Rosetta. "Don't do this," he said in an undertone.

"Go," she told him, her eyes cold, a metallic gray. He saw in them a deadly resolve.

"Think of your baby," he said to her.

"Just go."

He thought of trying to wrest the gun from her, maybe getting off a shot at Eberly, but then, he might only end up messing up her plan, if she had one. As he limped past her he said, "I love you." She didn't take her eyes off Eberly.

"Go," she said. "Whilst you still have the chance."

Cain had almost reached the horses when he heard the first shot, followed shortly by another. He recognized the first; it was, he knew with dread in his heart, the vicious retort of the Tranter. The second must have been Eberly's gun. "Rosetta!" he'd cried as he hobbled back to the cabin. "Rosetta!" He didn't know what to expect. When he entered, he saw her kneeling beside the old man. Eberly had taken a round in the middle of his chest and it was obvious he was dying. His eyes were hollow shells, his breathing already a death rattle.

Cain got down beside Rosetta. "Are you all right?"

When she looked up at him, he saw that she had tears in her eyes.

Sharpsburg, Maryland
September 16, 1862

Night. He sits by the fire, drinking a cup of strong, bitter chicory and trying to read. He feels as he always does the night before—expectant, his belly filled with a nervous energy. He knows full well what the morning will bring. He will have to lead men into battle, some to their deaths, many hardly more than green recruits just signed up to fight. Two days ago at South Mountain, they'd skirmished with McClellan's Federals and were handily routed, driven back through Crampton's Gap. Recently he has noted the subtle change in the eyes of his men. The early victories in the first year of the war have come at a high price. The sweet taste of success at Sumter and Seven Pines, Cold Harbor and the First Manassas has spoiled them, made them vulnerable to the eventual setbacks that had to follow. Even as late as a few weeks ago, with victories at Second Manassas and Chantilly, there was the bright glow of confidence in his men. Now, though, that optimism and swagger has leached out of their eyes, and the jaunty bounce has left their step. Cain sees a creeping doubt in all things they do, a tentativeness that corrodes the will.

From the beginning, he felt that the Old Man's plan to invade the North was a grave mistake. Now he knows it to be the case. A gambler himself, Cain knows when a man is bluffing, and for all of Lee's bluster about finally bringing this damned fight to the Yankees, this sortie into the North is mere show. An act of desperation. The South's best, in fact, its only hope, was in staying home, fiercely protecting its own soil like a she-bear its den. Now he's certain that it isn't just this campaign, but the entire enterprise that is doomed. Utterly, irrevocably doomed. More than ever since the war commenced, he's reminded of Milton's Satan. Like his fight, the South's is both noble and doomed from the start. Then again, hadn't he known that from the start, when he first decided to return? In fact, wasn't the South's cause lost with the first cottonseed that was shoved into the soil, the first African setting a manacled foot on these shores, the first crack of a whip across a Negro back?

Cain had been living in San Francisco when the news about the war reached him. He had struck his own gold in California, though he never lifted a pick or shovel. He'd been doing well for himself, winning at the card table, parting drunken miners of their hard-earned gold. Well enough that he was living at the fancy Oriental Hotel, dining at the best restaurants, employing the services of a tailor to fashion him a whole new wardrobe. He'd managed to give up the laudanum, and while he still enjoyed his whiskey, he made it a rule not to drink while playing. He'd had no plans on ever returning east.

And yet, as soon as he'd read about the outbreak of war, he knew he had no choice. No matter where he lived, no matter how far away he went, he was and always would be, at heart, a southerner, and he felt it his sacred duty to come to the defense of his home. Despite everything, the South was his birthplace, where his mother was buried, where his roots were. It had nothing whatsoever to do with defending slavery. In fact, he'd come to detest the peculiar institution and everything associated with it. Once, in a card game at the International Hotel, an ill-mannered Texan, on a bad losing streak, asked Cain if he might put up as a wager his Negro valet. When Cain objected, saying that he didn't condone such a thing as betting a man, the Texan started to harangue him, called him a nigger-loving disgrace to his southern heritage. In the past Cain might have beaten the man silly, but instead, he gracefully acquiesced and permitted him to wager the slave. After winnng the hand, Cain promptly gave the slave his freedom. No, it wasn't what the South was fighting for that stirred his heart and his allegiance. It was the simple fact that it was fighting, fighting for its very existence, for its way of life. So he bought passage on a steamer that took him back to Richmond.

Several days earlier they had come up the Potomac under Jackson's command. When they passed within sight of Harpers Ferry, he'd heard a soldier behind him say, "That there's where this whole mess started with that crazy fool Brown." He thought of John Brown, dead now these past three years. Captured by Lee, tried for treason, hanged like a common criminal.

But the man he remembers is not the one most southerners imagine. Not the simple, crazed demon that others have made him out to be. And he was sure as hell no fool. He knew exactly what he was doing. Their conversation stays with him even now. He recalls what Brown had told him, how the country needed a lot of killing, and, indeed, in that respect, he's gotten his wish—in spades. The soldier was right about one thing: if there had ever been doubt of the war's ironclad inevitability, Brown's storming of the arsenal put an end to that once and for all. After that, there would be no turning back, no more compromises or appeasement, no more conciliatory-minded Websters and Clays to work out further delays. Only war. In death now, Brown has, to some at least, become a kind of martyr. For Negroes, he has taken on the divine status of a Moses leading his people to the promised land. Cain also recalls that day in Harpers Ferry, ages ago it seems now, when he sat on the grass with Rosetta and she asked him what he would do on such a fine day.

Cain lays down his copy of Milton. From the breast pocket of his tunic, he removes an envelope and opens it carefully. Inside is a piece of paper, frayed from handling, fragile now as an old woman's skin. He opens it and starts to read. *My Dearest Cain*, it begins. It is a letter from Rosetta.

After they'd made it across the Ohio, they had found a doctor to tend to his leg, and when he'd recovered enough, they set out for the

Gist Settlement. It was her choice to go there instead of heading up to Canada. For one thing, she needn't fear Eberly coming after her anymore. Besides, she told him, she wanted to be with her own kind. She no longer brought up the possibility of coming west with him. It was as if something had changed in her after what had happened in the cabin, as if all that bloodshed and death had brought the realization to her that whatever they'd had was over now, that they belonged to separate worlds, and that it was time for her to return to hers. Before he left the settlement, they hugged one last time. As he mounted up, she said to him, "Take care of yourself, Cain." He looked back over his shoulder once to see her standing there. She looked so beautiful in the morning light he was half tempted to turn around, to say the hell with what the world thought. But he kept on riding.

He had assumed that that would be the last he'd ever hear from her. But as with all things regarding Rosetta, he should have known she was a woman beyond predictions. Two years ago, at the hotel in San Francisco, he had received a letter from her. He wasn't sure how it had found him but it did. In it she told him some about Gist, that the people there turned out to be friendly, had taken her in. She was teaching in a small school they had started. She said she liked that, liked working with children. She also told him that the baby she had carried all those miles, had run away to protect, had died in childbirth. She said maybe it just wasn't meant to be. She said she missed him, would always miss him. When Cain read this part, he'd felt a surprising ache in the unprotected part of his chest just below his sternum. He wouldn't have thought that could happen to him, not all this time later. Then he recalled how Rosetta had said pain sometimes makes a body feel alive. She closed the letter by saying that she hoped Cain had found whatever it was he was looking for. He wasn't sure if he hadn't already found it and like a damn fool had let it go.

Cain carefully folds and puts away the letter. Then he picks up his Milton and begins to read again.

"Captain Cain?" comes a voice.

"What?" he says, turning to see a young private standing there, holding a scorched pot of coffee.

"You be wanting more coffee, sir?"

Of course, it's not really coffee at all. Since the blockade, that has been a forgotten luxury. And yet the chicory's bitter warmth will see him through till morning.

"Much obliged," Cain tells him. He removes his spectacles and looks up from his book. In the woods across the cornfield to the north are the campfires of the Federals. The night is dotted with their glow, like a thousand fireflies. He watches as the private pours him another cup from the pot. He's new, just arrived a few days before. A boy from the western hills, pink faced, can't be much more than sixteen. He doesn't even shave yet, has this fine down along the angle of his jaw. In his eyes Cain sees the familiar fear of the unknown on the eve before a first battle, a fear he tries to cover with a stiffening of his jaw.

"Thank you, private," he says. "It's Joshua, correct?"

"Yes, sir," says the boy.

"Do you have a family, Joshua?"

"My mam and sisters. An older brother died at the First Manassas."

"I'm sorry to hear that."

"That's why I done signed up. I want to kill me some a them Yanks."

Cain nods.

"Tomorrow, you keep your family in mind, son. Don't try to be a hero."

"Yes, sir," the boy replies, but Cain can tell he's not convinced. He hungers for blood. For Yankee blood.

"Good night, private," Cain says.

"Good night, sir."

To the east, the faintest lightening of the darkness has begun. Still, there is time yet, so he opens his book and begins to read.

ACKNOWLEDGMENTS
AND SOURCES

I am indebted to many in the writing of this book. First of all, the
following nonfiction books proved extremely helpful: *The Book of
Boston: The Victorian Period* by Marjorie Drake Ross; *Incidents in the
Life of a Slave Girl* by Harriet Jacobs; *Fugitive Slaves (1619–1865)*
by Marion Gleason McDougall; *The Slave Catchers* by Stanley W.
Campbell; *Beyond the River* by Ann Hagedorn; *Shadrach Minkins* by
Gary Collison; *The Trials of Anthony Burns* by Albert J. von Frank;
Articles on American Slavery: Fugitive Slaves, edited by Paul Finkelman;
Runaway Slaves by John Hope Franklin and Loren Schweninger; *The
Black Hearts of Men* by John Stauffer; *Slave Testimony*, edited by John
W. Blassingame; *Narrative of the Life of Frederick Douglass*, edited by
William L. Andrews and William McFeely; *Douglass Autobiographies*
by Frederick Douglass; *American City, Southern Place* by Gregg D.
Kimball; *The Beleaguered City* by Alfred Hoyt Bill; *The Complete
Book of Gun Collecting* by Charles Edward Chapel; *Colt: The Making
of an American Legend* by William Hosley. Also the online versions
of several books: *American Slavery As It Is* and *19th Century Slang
Dictionary* by Craig Hadley. I also owe a debt to the following novels:
Paradise Alley by Kevin Baker, *Cloudsplitter* by Russell Banks, *The Price
of a Child* by Lorene Cary, *Walk Through Darkness* by David Anthony
Durham, and *The Cattle Killing* by John Edgar Wideman.

On a personal level, I want to thank a number of people and

organizations: to Fairfield University, especially my friend Linda Miller as well as all the helpful people at the library there; to Sarah Sexton, a wonderful aid who read through several drafts and made changes and corrections on all equine matters; to Dr. David Page for advice on nineteenth-century surgical procedures; to *The Leaflet* where part of chapter 3 originally appeared; to Rick Russo for his close reading and many thoughtful and kind suggestions that helped to improve the book; as always, to Nat Sobel and Judith Weber, not only for their insightful comments about the work itself but even more for their unfailing loyalty and unswerving support throughout the many years of our association and friendship; to David Highfill, the writer's ideal editor, one who is both supportive and discriminating, congenial and wise beyond his years, the sort of editor that a writer hopes for all his days; and last, to Diane Les Becquets for helping to shape the novel from its very inception on a ridge in the Colorado Rockies to its final word, as well as for helping to shape the writer. My thanks to all.